PROMISING *today*

A. M. KUSI

Published by A. M. Kusi 2024

amkusinovels@gmail.com

Visit our website at www.amkusi.com

Editor: Lauren Clarke of CREATING ink

Sensitivity Edit: Renita McKinney of A Book A Day

Proofreader: Judy's Proofreading

Cover Design: Regina Wamba of ReginaWamba.com

OTHER BOOKS BY A. M. KUSI

Stepping Into Tomorrow

(Book 1 in The Emerson Family of Shattered Cove)

Risking Forever

(Book 2 in The Emerson Family of Shattered Cove)

Wishing for Yesterday

(Book 3 in The Emerson Family of Shattered Cove)

A Fallen Star (eBook FREE on all retailers)

(Book 1 in The Shattered Cove Series)

Glass Secrets

(Book 2 in The Shattered Cove Series)

Defying Gravity

(Book 3 in The Shattered Cove Series)

The Lighthouse Inn

(Book 4 in The Shattered Cove series)

His True North

(Book 5 in The Shattered Cove series)

In The Grey

(Book 6 in The Shattered Cove series)

Brave Love

(Book 7 in The Shattered Cove series)

Hope Between Us

(Book 8 in The Shattered Cove series)

Beautiful Collision

(A Shattered Cove Novel)

One Holiday Kiss (eBook FREE on all retailers)

(A Shattered Cove Short Story)

Under My Skin (eBook FREE on all retailers)

(A Shattered Cove Short Story)

The Orchard Inn Series

(Our first complete steamy romance series.)

For a complete list of all our books, visit:

WWW.AMKUSI.COM/BOOKS

This book is dedicated to all you other humans out there who can't remember if you ate lunch but can name 948 facts about something you're passionate about . . . while you bend over Daddy's lap and take your punishment like a good girl.

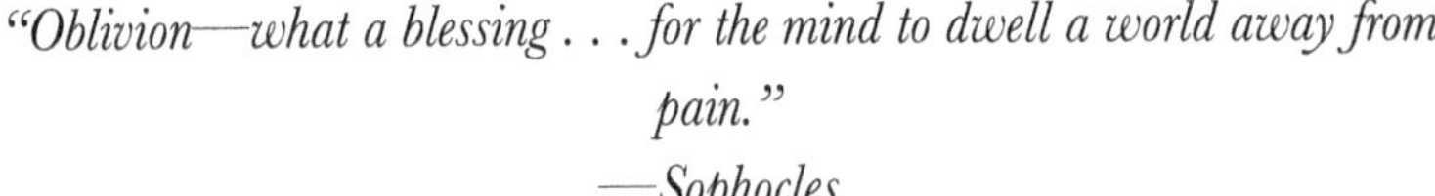
"Oblivion—what a blessing . . . for the mind to dwell a world away from
pain."
—Sophocles

"You haven't even met the best version of yourself—not yet. The most healed. The most fulfilled. The most content. And meeting that 'you' is worth fighting for. So keep learning and growing."
—Topher Kearby

TABLE OF CONTENTS

GET A FREE SHORT NOVEL

Join our newsletter to get a FREE short novel that's not available on any retailer. Plus updates about new releases, giveaways, pre-orders, sneak peeks, and more.

Visit the website below to join now.

WWW.AMKUSI.COM/NEWSLETTER

TRIGGER WARNING

This book contains material that may be triggering for some readers. The warnings for this include: talk of past sexual assault as a young teen, BDSM (Bondage, discipline/Dominance, submission/sadism, masochism), primal play, CNC (consensual-non-consensual play), murder, abduction, war, mild torture, serial killer, AIDs, death of a parent, addiction, and cannabis use.

PLAYLIST

"Drop Dead" by grandson, featuring Kesha and Travis Barker
"Healing" by FLETCHER
"Keep your demons" by TAELA
"Welcome to Paradise" by grandson
"When You Say My Name" by Chandler Leighton
"Daddy Issues" by The Neighborhood
"Feel" by FLETCHER
"Do It Like A Girl" by Morgan St. Jean
"Smile For The Camera" by UPSAHL
"Take Me Away" by New Medicine
"Sweet Dream" by Bohnes featuring Underoath
"SUPERHERO" by Aim Vision
"My Name Is Baybe" by Baybe
"Nails" by Call Me Karizma
"Till Our Last Day" by Bryce Savage
"I Want To" by Rosenfeld
"Skin" by Rihanna
"Set Me On Fire" by Estelle
"Own Me" by bülow

"Sweet Little Lies" by bülow
"i wanna die" by Nessa Barrett
"Daddy" by Ramsey
"Dark Side" by Ramsey
"PLEASE" by Omido & Ex Habit
"Make Me Fade" by K. Flay
"you broke me first" by Tate McRae
"Something's Gotta Give" by Camila Cabello
"Sad Together" by Olivia O'Brien
"i can't get high" by Royal & the Serpent
"Love Abuser (Save Me)" by Royal & the Serpent
"So Pissed" by Bohnes
"While You're At It" by Jessie Murph
"@ my worst" by blackbear
"Help" by Papa Roach
"Save Me Now" by Mike Perry
"Kiss Me" by Dermot Kennedy
"Fuck It" by New Medicine
"Lifetime" by Three Days Grace
"Who Do You Want" by Ex Habit
"If You Don't Like Me" by Chloe Adams
"A Letter To Everyone Who's Hurt Me" by Chandler
Leighton
"Curiosity" by Bryce Savage
"Control" by Bryce Savage

1

NOVA

"Where the hell am I?" Nova Emerson turned down the radio as her truck bounced over a pothole in the quickly fading daylight. The headlights glinted off puddles on the dirt path ahead of her. Tall dark trees lined both sides of the road, only clearing when there was a pull-off littered with abandoned rusted vehicles and old buildings.

This is certainly the scenic route home.

As soon as she'd seen Chad wave in her periphery in town, she'd been in flight mode. The man couldn't take a hint. You'd think not calling and totally ghosting after a one-night stand would have been enough of a message. But Chad was determined. If only he'd been half as determined to find her clit, then maybe they could have had another round.

When he'd waved to her at the crossroads in town, she'd averted her gaze so he'd think she didn't see him. But when he'd turned to head the same way she was driving—the opposite of which his blinker signaled—she'd gone into flee mode.

She'd sped up and taken turns to lose him. She'd forgotten how clingy he was.

"If I remembered, I wouldn't be lost so close to my own goddamn hometown," she grumbled under her breath. *Where am I?* Nothing had looked familiar for miles. *I'll probably recognize whatever's around this corner.*

That was what she'd thought about the last three though . . .

Her shocks creaked as she drove slowly over the deep divots with a wince. She'd driven off fast and taken so many turns, she was pretty sure she'd crossed the boundary into Dark Cove. It had been twenty minutes since she'd seen another set of headlights coming either direction.

"This is the worst time to have a terrible sense of direction," she mumbled to herself.

She guessed it was time to use her GPS. Nova picked up her phone, but it rang with the wedding march. She tensed. Only one person had that ringtone. *If I don't answer, she'll just keep calling.* And the last thing Nova wanted to do was worry her mother—the woman who had quite literally saved her life.

She shut the music off and clicked answer. "Hello?"

"Hey, baby girl. I just wanted to check in and see if you had everything ready for the consult tomorrow and the wedding this weekend?"

"Yes, Mom. It's all taken care of."

"Great."

A beat of silence passed before Nova said, "Well, if that's all, I guess I'll—"

"I noticed your car wasn't in your driveway. Are you on a date tonight?"

Nova rolled her eyes. "No. You know the guy I've been seeing lives out of state. I made some deliveries to the nursing home and stopped to get some dinner at the diner and a drink —by myself—at The Shipwreck. I'm headed home now."

As soon as I can find my way out of this place. A large industrial-sized abandoned building appeared in front of her. Her headlights glinted off broken glass in the windows. It had an eerie feel to it. She shivered.

"Nova? Are you even listening to me?" her mother asked, clearly frustrated. Nova had zoned out again.

"Yes, of course," she lied.

"When am I going to get to meet this mysterious boyfriend? You're still seeing him, aren't you?"

Nova sighed. The last thing she wanted to do was hurt the woman who'd chosen to be her mother. "I know you want me married like the rest of your children and popping out grand-babies like it's nineteen fifty. But you know I like to take things slow." *Slow as in never gonna happen.* Why would she let a man get that close again just to stomp what was left of her heart to bits? No fucking thank you.

"I know. But there is such a thing as too slow. You know . . . ca— . . . al— . . ."

"I think I'm losing service. You cut out. Can you hear me? . . . Hello?"

She pulled the phone away to look at the screen. *Call dropped.* "Thank you, universe."

A loud pop sounded. The car jerked to the side. She gripped the steering wheel for dear life, trying to right it. The phone went flying. A metallic grinding noise whined as she pulled to a stop.

"Fuck!" Nova looked around the surroundings of the vehicle. Just abandoned buildings and overgrown woods, lit only by the dim glow of her truck's headlights.

She exhaled and reached to the floor for her phone.

No signal.

She sighed and took one last glance at her surroundings before climbing out of the truck. She turned on the flashlight on her phone and inspected the rubber tread, pausing on the back driver's side tire . . . or what was left of one. It was blown to bits with jagged rubber bits sticking out of the shredded tread. She hadn't even been going that fast. What could—

"Shit." She grabbed the four-by-four with long sixteen-penny nails sticking out of it. She tugged, but it was embedded too deep in the mangled tire.

"So much for the universe being on my side," she grumbled as she let the board hang from the rubber.

A twig snapped behind her. She whirled around, tense and alert. Four men stared at her from fifteen yards away, their faces lit by the orange glow of the barrel fire they surrounded in front of a decrepit apartment building.

I certainly picked the worst place to get lost. Wait—that doesn't make sense. Who chooses to get lost? And if they decide where, are they really lost?

A shout pulled her back to her present predicament. One man shoved another before they laughed.

The hair on her skin stood on end. Her heart thudded. All her senses were on alert. Crickets chirped as a bead of sweat dripped down her forehead. The sun might have set ten minutes ago, but it was still summer, and today was a humid one. She spun around, her back to the men around the barrel, taking in her surroundings. A large industrial building sat to the right of her truck with boarded-up windows. Maybe an old factory? A few flickers of light bled from behind the rotting boards somewhere inside. The bottom-floor windows had fared even worse, with boards ripped out in some places and broken glass littering the ground.

I need to get out of here.

Nova grabbed the tire iron and jack from behind her seat.

She set the phone light on the back of the truck for light and got to work cranking the jack until what was left of the tire was off the ground.

"What do we have here?"

Nova pulled the knife from her boot, keeping it in one hand and the tire iron in the other. She whipped around.

Two men approached her. The missing posters of her friends flashed in her mind. What if these were the killers? What if they abducted her? What if—

"Did you get lost, girly?" the one with the missing tooth asked.

"I don't want any trouble." She was proud of how firm her voice sounded, despite the terror gripping her chest in a vise.

"Looks to me like you've already found yourself some." The other nodded towards her tire.

"Nothing I can't handle."

"You got a few dollars to spare?" the first one asked as they crowded her, one going to her left and the other to her right. She swallowed. She might be able to take one on, but two at the same time?

Why did I turn down this road? I should have just faced Chad and told him I'm not interested.

Fuck, I didn't even tell Mom where I am.

What if these two kill me and that was the last conversation we had? No.

Nova was not going down without a fight. She straightened her shoulders and tipped her chin up.

"I don't carry cash. Now, if you two gentlemen would be on your way, I'll return to my business and get out of here."

"No need to hurry, girly. Bruce and I here are just looking for a little fun," the second one took another step forward.

"Back up!" she yelled, raising the tire iron.

Both men looked at each other and laughed.

"No need to get your panties in a bunch," Bruce said, his eyes dropping to her crotch lasciviously.

"Look, buddy, you'd better back the fuck off or I will break the teeth you have left."

Bruce's eyes widened before he scowled at her.

Nova had been told a time or a hundred that her mouth would catch up to her one day. Didn't stop her though. She'd never been good about keeping quiet. Besides, she'd tried to be nice, even called them gentlemen. Everything that happened next was on them.

"Bitch thinks she's so much better than us—"

"I think she made herself clear. Beat it," a deep voice said.

The other two men glanced towards the front of Nova's truck. Nova didn't dare take her eyes off the two threats in front of her.

Oh, Goddess. What if it's going to be three against one?

This isn't happening.

"Come on, we're just having a little fun," Bruce said.

Heavy footsteps sounded closer as the third man rounded the truck. Everything screamed at Nova to run, but she was trapped. She had a weapon in each hand, and some self-defense skills her brother had taught her. Even if this guy scared the other two off, she'd still have to deal with him. Nova pressed her back against the truck.

The third man stepped closer, the reflection of her phone light highlighting coal-black eyes. His face was all sharp angles and severe expression. The slope of his nose was a little off-center, like he'd broken it in the past. A five o'clock shadow peppered his jaw. He was *hot*. But Ted Bundy had been an attractive man too. Nova wasn't gonna fall for that.

His deep voice lowered an octave as he faced the two men down. "Get the fuck out of here."

"Or what, pretty boy?" Bruce snarled.

The newcomer tilted his neck to the side and cracked it before staring back at the men, menace lacing his voice. "You lay a hand on her and it will be the last thing you do."

Holy fuck. That was hot. Like the heroes right out of her romance novels. Which meant it was too good to be true. Hottie with the deep voice probably wanted to murder her all by himself. She swallowed, the idea terrifying. So why were butterflies swirling in her belly?

"Mouthy bitch isn't worth it anyways," Bruce said, scowling before he turned and walked away, his partner spitting on the ground by the newcomer's feet before taking off towards the abandoned factory building behind Nova's truck.

Nova stared at the new man, her heart racing a million times a minute. Was he going to attack her?

"I'm not going to hurt you," he said, as if reading her mind.

"That's probably what all serial killers say." She gripped the tire iron tighter.

The corner of his mouth tipped up before his full lips flattened into a straight line once again. "Get in the car and lock the doors. You can hand me the tire iron and I'll put the donut on."

"And give you my only weapon?" she scoffed.

"You can always stab me with the knife you've got hidden in that other hand if I step out of line."

She sucked in a breath.

"Get in the car," he ordered.

She bristled. She'd never been good when people told her what to do. It only made her want to do the opposite. "I don't need your help."

He sighed and shook his head. "Stubborn, aren't you?"

She tipped her chin up, which still didn't help. She barely

stood five foot four and he was taller than her brothers—at least six foot nine. If he really wanted to do her harm, he probably could. *Not that I wouldn't get one good stab in.*

"Listen, it's been a long day, and hot as fuck. The mosquitos are biting me and I don't have time for games. Get in the truck. Lock the doors. And give me the tire iron so I can fix your tire and you can get the fuck out of here and back to where you belong."

"I—I don't even know you."

He leaned his head back, hands on his hips like he was counting to ten. This was not abnormal. Nova tended to push people's buttons and got these reactions a lot.

He looked straight at her and held out his hand, palm up. "I'm Jude."

She shifted on her feet, weighing her options as he waited patiently. His heavy gaze didn't leave her for a moment. Her gut told her this guy was not going to kill her or rape her, but her gut had been wrong about men before.

"Fine." She backed up, not letting him out of her sight as she climbed into the driver's seat backwards and shut the door. She rolled down the window a few inches and handed the tire iron out. He took it and got to work. The car jostled as he finished unscrewing the bolts from her tire and tossed it into her truck bed.

Nova glanced around them. No one else was in sight around the dark abandoned buildings from what she could see. Though that wasn't saying much. Those two other men hadn't exactly just melted into the shadows. Were there more watching and waiting? The men around the fire to the far left didn't try to approach, but their wary watchful gazes slicked across her skin like ice.

What if they join forces with the other men who Jude scared off? Will this Jude guy stick around? And if he does, we will still be outnum-

bered. I need to find a better weapon. Nova searched the front seat of her truck. *I just need—*

A knock sounded against her window.

Nova screamed and jumped in her seat, whirling around.

Jude stood at her window, one eyebrow quirked up. With her cab lights on, she could see him a little more clearly. If she'd thought he was hot before, that was nothing compared to how he looked in the dim light of her interior. *I really need to get a grip.*

Heat bloomed in her core, making her panties wet. *I'm so fucked up.*

He handed her phone to her through the window, his hands covered in black grease and dirt.

"That was fast," she said.

He was good with his hands. *I bet he knows how to find a clit.*

"Get someone to put a new tire on tomorrow. You shouldn't go far with the donut. And stick to the main roads. I don't want to see you down this way again." His tone left no room for argument. "You don't belong here."

With that parting shot, Jude spun around and walked around the front of her truck, his ass a spectacular sight in his camouflage pants.

She wasn't sure whether or not she wanted to thank him or argue with him for bossing her around like that. By the time she shouted a "thank you" it was too late—he was already far ahead by the edge of the factory.

She slipped the truck into gear and drove forward slowly. The ride was much bouncier with the smaller tire. Jude walked ahead off to the side of the road, veering to the right at the edge of the big factory building. She passed as he stopped at the rear of a truck with Michigan plates and climbed in the front without one more glance in her direction.

Did he live there? Was he homeless? She kept driving. Her hands trembled, the adrenaline wearing off.

"What the hell just happened?"

She'd almost been in big trouble—that was what.

Her brothers most definitely didn't need to know about this. It would be bad enough when she got home and they realized she'd been gone this late without one of them hounding her.

Nova blew out a breath.

She really did need to be more careful. The last thing she'd want to do was cause more hurt for her family. They'd suffered enough loss.

But the truth was there was a killer out there who was taking people from Nova's past. She was obviously going to be on that list. That was why she'd be ready for that asshole when he came.

She tucked her lucky knife back in her boot—a gift from her brother Ricky.

"You want me, motherfucker?" Nova pressed on the gas and turned onto a paved road. "Come and get me."

2

JUDE

*J*ude King *stood in the darkest shadows, his attention glued to the tiny woman hunched over the steering wheel. Blood trickled from a gash on her forehead as she blinked her eyes open. Those light brown spheres, hazy with confusion, were aimed at him. Her small pink tongue darted out of the side of her full lips as she concentrated, her focus darting around. Steam rose from the front of her truck with a hiss.*

"Jude?" His name fell from Nova's mouth. "What happened?"

He stepped forward, reaching out to help her from the car, but he froze. The cold steel of the tire iron was heavy in his hand.

"Oh my god!" Nova panicked, clawing at her seat belt, scrambling for an escape. Her seat belt clicked. He snapped into action.

She crawled farther into the cab, but he wrapped his hand around her arm and pulled her out.

"Stop! Please!" she cried as he yanked her out of the truck and pushed her against it, gripping her throat and pinning her to the wreckage.

"Where is she?" he demanded. God, this isn't like me. *He could smell her fear. The metallic scent from her wound permeated the air. It only got thicker.*

There was so much red.

It dripped down his hands, covering them in crimson. He shook his head, dropping the tire iron. It splashed into a puddle of blood. Even the ground was red. He backed up. The woman in the truck was no longer alone. Body after body littered the ground, camouflage uniforms stained with blood. He was no longer in Shattered Cove but back in the Middle East. The dead were his brothers—the men who'd depended on him to keep them alive.

But they were all gone.

All except Nova Emerson.

She looked different than she had in the pictures he'd obtained. She was staring at him with so much fear he could taste it.

"You did this," she accused.

"No." He shook his head.

"You killed them all."

"Shut the fuck up!" he screamed, pulling at his hair.

"What are you going to do with me?" She tipped her head to the side. "You'll never find your answers if you kill me too."

Jude gasped out of the nightmare, jolting upwards. His head knocked the top of the bunk bed above him. Pain lanced through his skull.

"Fuck!" he growled, holding the wounded spot.

His chest heaved as he blinked his eyes open. The dimly lit room looked the same as it had for the last month. All his earthly belongings were tucked away into a rucksack and a pack under the bed. His minimalist belongings had made moving from Michigan to New Hampshire much easier.

His skull pounded as he climbed out of bed and stumbled towards the window in the room. Tipping his head against the cool glass, Jude stared at the twilight sky peeking through the clouds. He forced deep breaths in, one hand to his throbbing forehead and the other to his racing heart.

He just wanted the nightmares to stop. Every time it was

the same: dead bodies of his fallen brethren. Ghosts reminding him of his failures. But the accident was new, and so was Nova Emerson with terror in her eyes.

Jude switched into his running shoes, keeping on his basketball shorts and the thin T-shirt he'd slept in. He locked up his room and slid the key into his pocket.

"Heading to the gym?" a gruff voice behind him asked.

Jude whipped around. His friend Reaper stood in the hall, holding a cup of black coffee.

"Christ, you scared me."

Reaper scoffed—the closest Jude ever got to hearing the man laugh. Their relationship had been born out of necessity and threat. Reaper was a man who lived up to his namesake. It was better to befriend death than be its enemy. And that was how their friendship had been born.

"Casanova has the music blasting in the gym, so just bring your earplugs unless you want to hear the shit he listens to." Reaper took a quiet sip of his coffee. Dark tattooed hands engulfing the whole mug.

"I'm gonna go for a run," Jude said.

Reaper gave a nod. "Piper and Blade are bringing breakfast. Then we'll all sit down and go through the plan. See what we're missing. You ready to do your part?"

Jude stiffened. It felt as if his friend was looking right through Jude. "I'll do whatever it takes to get this bastard."

"Good." Reaper took another sip.

"I still think I'd be better off with your motorcycle club friends. I can travel and—"

"Nova Emerson knows the Pirates. She knows what we do and who we are—at least what the rumors say. You want honest answers, we need you on recon. We need someone she doesn't know, someone who can slip into that family and find out if Nash or Nova have anything we can use," Reaper reiterated the same conclusion most of his club had come to.

Only Piper, the president's wife, had suggested they ask Nova. But what if Nova had something to do with all of this? Or was protecting one of her brothers and tipped them off? It couldn't be coincidence she'd had a connection to all of this. And Jude needed answers. There was too much on the line to risk it.

Jude nodded. "Right. I'll find a way in."

Reaper walked forward, the LED purple lighting casting him in warm violet shadow. "You got this. We'll do our part. I've got Axel digging up all he can. Reaching out to his contacts on the dark web. If there's something, he'll find it."

"I appreciate your help—and theirs. It was really amazing of you to get me a place to stay long term on short notice. And for all your help with my fuckups."

"You can thank Blade for the room; it's his and Piper's club."

"I'll do that," Jude said.

"Be back by ten. We'll go over everything and solidify the plan." Reaper spun around and walked down the hall, disappearing into the shadows.

Jude turned to the opposite side, passing multiple doors with gold-plated numbers marking each one. Erotic moans escaped a few as Jude made his way through the hallway and down the large staircase into the main room of Club Dynamic. There weren't many people here at this hour—just those who lived there or had rented rooms for the night. The cleaning crew was busy at work. One person sprayed down a Saint Andrew's cross while another wiped the paddles and other impact instruments hanging on the wall for the members' use. The usual red lighting was switched to white.

Jude continued to the exit. No matter how many times he

came and went from this place, the sheer size and deviant luxury of it still impressed him, though he couldn't bring himself to utilize any of it but the room he slept in. How could he enjoy a few hours of escape while he carried so much guilt? When *she* needed him?

Jude shook his head and jogged past the reception desk and out the front door. He took off towards town. Ten miles was more than enough time to burn off the frantic energy of his nightmare.

He'd chosen a route through no-man's-land on purpose, headed for Shattered Cove. He'd get a feel for the town and gather information. That was his job—recon. According to Reaper, this was where Jude would find answers.

His steady footfalls lulled him into focus as Jude jogged down the paved road and took a right. Eventually, the pavement ended and a dirt road began. Dogs barked behind chain-link fences sectioning off dilapidated trailers and old campers. A few people milled about smoking and staring at him. He bypassed an old man pushing a cart full of empty bottles and the few items the man probably owned. He'd overheard a few others refer to him as Socrates. That was why he'd been by the abandoned factories last night—looking for answers. And then Nova had all but fallen in his lap.

"Don't run so fast you miss out on the meaning of life!" the old man said to him. Jude pulled out a twenty-dollar bill and handed it over.

"Bless the man that gives, so shall he be given to," Socrates said.

"Have a good day." Jude continued on.

Soon, the stench of garbage and unwashed bodies faded, giving way to the greenery around him. Big trees lined the road on either side, blocking most of the sunlight, which was a welcome respite on this hot August day. Jude focused on his breath, pushing his muscles as he sped up. A cool breeze carried the scent of flowers as he neared the main township of Shattered Cove. Suburban homes with three-car garages and fenced-in properties popped up. The sound of a saw whined from an open garage to his left. Soon the neighborhood would be alive with kids' laughter and bouncing basketballs on paved driveways. Jude pushed himself into a sprint the last half mile.

By the time he headed into the Stardust Café, the sun was higher and he was calmer.

He walked in, wiping the sweat from his brow as the scent of cinnamon and apple made his mouth water.

A woman smiled from behind the counter. "Good morning. Can I interest you in an apple muffin, fresh out of the oven?"

"Just a black coffee, please." He pulled out his wallet, removed a few dollars cash, and placed them on the counter.

"Coming right up." She grabbed a cardboard cup, filled it with fresh coffee, slipped a lid over it, and handed it to him.

"Thanks." He turned, sipping the drink as he headed back out into the fresh summer air. Not many other people were out and about this early. He loved it. The early hours were always more peaceful. He strolled over to the bulletin board against the brick wall. Papers flitted in the warm wind. A lost cat poster had contact information for the owners. A few signs sharing babysitting information were spread throughout. And a couple apartments were for rent. There was one weathered and partially ripped paper in the background. He pulled it out.

Help needed: farmhand.

The Emerson Family Farm is looking for a responsible and hard-working laborer. Experience preferred. Contact Renita or James Emerson.

All the tags with the number on them had been torn off. His pulse picked up. It might have been too late. But if there was a chance . . . Jude smiled. He'd come all this way looking for Nova Emerson. He'd about swallowed his tongue when she'd about fallen into his lap last night. Instead of doing what he came for, he'd helped her and let her go. *But that might work in my favor.*

Jude could have blamed it on the shock of seeing Nova in real life for the first time. Those long-distance shots and the few photos she shared on social media didn't do her justice though. Not when compared to the sight of her wielding that tire iron and knife while standing up to two men much bigger than her. The image sent a fresh burst of whatever'd had his chest tightening last night through him. He couldn't name the feeling because for so long all he'd felt was anger and guilt. But that was why he was here in Shattered Cove, using all his resources to locate the one and possibly only person who could give him the chance for redemption—and revenge.

He took another sip of his coffee and pulled off the whole poster. This was his way in.

Nova Emerson was going to give him answers—whether she wanted to or not.

Jude had a plan; he just had to stick to it. And he'd have to do it fast, too.

Time was running out.

3

NOVA

Nova licked her spoon, savoring the last of the ice cream as her front door opened.

"Tell me that isn't your breakfast," her mother chastised.

"This isn't my breakfast." Nova tossed the empty container in the trash and added the spoon to the growing pile of dishes in the sink.

Her mother shook her head. Her disappointment was palpable.

Nova shrugged. "You told me I should eat breakfast. Now you're complaining that I did."

"Ice cream is not—you know what, I don't have time to get into this." Her mom sighed and took a barstool at the island. "Why was your front door not locked?"

Nova turned her back before rolling her eyes. Suddenly the idea of doing the dishes didn't seem so daunting. Anything was better than another lecture from her mom on what she should be doing or how she should be living her life.

She turned the water on, rinsing the pasta sauce from a

bowl she'd used the night before . . . or was it two days ago? "Because my brothers have locked this place down like Fort Knox. A bunny can't even hop around our land anymore without setting off some light or camera sensor."

"I don't like the idea of you living alone here. Not while there's a murderer on the loose."

And not in general, either, since you won't stop trying to set me up. But Nova wouldn't say that out loud. Her mother may have been too much in her business, and it may have been driving her crazy, but Renita only did so out of love. And Nova was lucky to have her after her own biological mother had died, leaving her in foster care for a short stint before the state had located her mother's half sister, Renita Emerson. Renita had shown up at her group home and adopted her as soon as the papers could be filed. She'd taken Nova in and given her a family and love. The least Nova could do was not disappoint her.

"Nova, are you even listening to me?" her mom asked.

Nova shut the water off. She sighed. She really needed to stop zoning out on people. "It's not my fault. My brother stole my last roommates."

Her mom let out a frustrated sigh, eyeing a messy pile of mail sticking out of the fruit basket.

Oh, I wondered where I put those.

"Have you thought of hiring a bookkeeper?" Her mom sat at the bar in front of Nova's laptop and the piles of receipts.

"No. I can do it. I just need time . . . and motivation. I've had a lot going on with the seedlings and managing every-thing else with the weddings."

"You need more help. If your dad and I get any bites on the ad we placed, they can assist you with your harvest," her mom offered.

"That would be nice." However, Nova was very particular

about how she liked things done in her grow houses. "But I think I've got things handled. I'll catch up this weekend."

Her mother's lips pursed as if she'd heard that excuse before—and she had. But Nova meant it this time . . . really.

"I'm worried about you," her mom said, taking her hand.

Nova turned to her. "I'm fine. My cannabis is growing beautifully. I've got another dispensary in Maine that wants to order some of my infused cookies and cannabis flower. Things are great."

"And you've got a man you're seeing," her mother added.

"Right." Nova's voice came out a bit higher as she picked at her nails. Her made-up long-distance boyfriend was the best. He didn't bother her. It wasn't hard to meet his needs. The only downside was the sex that didn't exist. But Nova had a great imagination and toys. And when that wasn't enough, she'd venture into town and find someone to spend the night with. Men, women—she didn't discriminate.

Renita gently placed her hand over Nova's, stilling it. "I just wonder if you purposely keep choosing men who're far away so you don't have to risk getting so close to them because of losing Brooks."

Nova cringed. Talking about the death of the man she'd almost married still stung—but not for the reasons her mother thought. She'd stuffed all things Brooks down deep in a bottle and buried that sucker under cement.

Nova had never told anyone what she'd found out after Brooks had died—not even her mother.

She'd never let anyone get that close to her again.

"Listen, my boyfriend is truly great. We're close enough. He just happens to live out of state. There's nothing else to read into it." She turned her face away from her mother. Lying was not Nova's strong suit, but she really didn't want to talk about this anymore.

"Is this Peter?" her mom asked.

"Who's Peter?"

"Your long-distance boyfriend." Renita crossed her arms over her chest and narrowed her eyes.

Oh, shit.

"No, Peter and I broke up like four months ago. I've been seeing someone else."

"And what's this one's name?"

Fuck. Fuck. Fuck. Nova needed another name, and she'd already cycled through The Beatles except for Ringo, because who the fuck named their kid Ringo? That was a bit too obvious.

"I told you his name, haven't I?"

"No. You've told me you've gone to visit him a couple times. Valentine's you were gone overnight. He can't live that far. Why hasn't he visited you?"

"Um, well, he's very busy. But we're planning a trip soon."

"What's his name?" her mom repeated.

"It's . . ." *Fuck. Fuck. Fuck.* Dark eyes flashed in her mind. "Jude. His name is Jude."

"Well, I want to meet this Jude. Make sure he's deserving of my daughter," her mom said.

"I'll get right on that." Nova forced a smile. "But first, I need to get my truck to Link's garage so he can put a new tire on."

"What happened to your truck?"

Nova waved her hand dismissively. "Just a flat. Link said he could squeeze me in this morning."

"You have an appointment with the couple from New York looking to get married at the farm in two hours."

"Oh, right. I'll be here." Nova grabbed her wallet off the counter along with her keys and darted for the door doing her ritual mental checklist in her head. *Phone. Keys. Wallet. Shoes.*

"Don't be late like last time!" her mom warned as the screen door slammed behind Nova.

"No one told me it was daylight savings time!" Nova hollered back before climbing into her truck.

She drove slowly towards town, music blaring with the windows down.

"Today will be a good day." She'd manifest the shit out of that because Nova really needed a break for once.

4

NOVA

Nova's skin prickled like someone was watching her. She rubbed the back of her neck and looked around Main Street. A few people rushed by, no doubt on their way to work. Nova smiled at a little girl with her mom, holding hands as they crossed the road. The smell of freshly roasted coffee filtered out into the street, melding with the scent of the flowers. Birds sang, and the warm summer breeze was a nice reprieve from the humidity of August. Still, she couldn't shake the feeling that someone was watching her.

Nova took a deep breath in and forced it out through her mouth. It was probably just her anxiety again.

She continued down the sidewalk, looking both ways before she crossed the road. After jogging up to the door of the hardware store, she laid her hand on the knob, but movement from the corner of her eye caught her attention. She turned. A grey squirrel scampered into the busy street as a car headed straight for it. *Run, little guy!*

Oof! Nova tripped backwards under the force of the

wooden door colliding with her elbow. Pain streaked through her arm as she stumbled behind the door.

She sucked in a breath through her teeth, spinning around to face the careless idiot who'd hurt her. The door swung shut as a giant of a man headed away from her.

"Watch where you're going next time, asshole!"

The man spun around, his eyes widening and then narrowing on her. "I saved your ass and you show gratitude by insulting me?"

It's the guy from last night—Jude! I guess his chivalry ends with changing tires and scaring off men with dubious intentions.

"I wouldn't have had to if you'd stopped and looked before you just plowed through the door," she snapped, holding her injured elbow. *Fuck.* That was gonna leave a nasty bruise.

A woman on the bench waiting for the bus a few yards away narrowed her eyes at them. Nova smiled and waved before taking a few steps closer to Jude.

"You hurt?" Jude asked.

Nova straightened as some of her anger faded along with the throbbing pain. She had a tendency to get angry when she was hurt. And he definitely should have been watching where he was going, but he had helped her last night and he deserved some kindness.

"It'll be fine. And you're right—I do owe you a thank-you for helping me."

"It wasn't a big deal." He wiped his hand over the back of his neck.

"It was to me. You probably saved my life, honestly." She shivered just thinking about it. She had to repay him some-how. "Maybe I can help you in return?"

He hesitated, then eyed her suspiciously. Damn, this man was intense. His eyes were more hazel in the morning light with flecks of gold and green in the light brown. The tight lines at the corners didn't detract from his looks—only added a severeness to his features. The angled slope of his nose with a small notch in it was just a little off-center, adding character. And his lips were full and pillow-like, and surrounded by a day's worth of dark stubble. *I just bet he knows how to use that mouth—*

Jude snapped his fingers in front of her face. "Are you just going to stare at me all morning or what?"

"Uh, no. Sorry, I was in my head." Nova opened her wallet, grabbing the cash she had inside. "It's not much, but—"

"I don't want your money," he grumbled and walked away, turning the corner at the next street and disappearing from sight.

Nova huffed and caught up with him while pulling out a couple twenties from her pocket. "Come on—don't be a stubborn man. Just take the cash, Jude." Her shoe caught on the uneven sidewalk and she tripped, slamming into his back.

His shoulders rose to his ears before he whipped around, anger shining in his expression. "I don't need your fucking money."

Nova rolled her eyes and turned to Jude, but he was walking away again. This time, Nova didn't pursue him. Was it pity? He had seemed to be homeless. She'd just wanted to pay him back for his help. *Would I have offered another man cash for their assistance? Probably not. So maybe it was because I saw him climbing in his truck like he was sleeping there.*

She sighed and checked her watch. She had just enough time to run to the hardware store before picking up the truck from Link's and making it back for her meeting—probably.

Nova took one last lingering look at Jude's ass—she was human after all. And that man's ass would give Captain

America a run for his money. It was too bad her lady parts seemed to wake up for one type of man only—assholes. She should avoid this man like the plague. He'd probably pass through town soon enough anyways.

"Forget him, Nova," she muttered to herself as she walked back towards the hardware store. "The last thing you need is trouble, and that man has it tattooed all over him."

* * *

Nova made it just in time for the meeting with their clients for a barn wedding. She walked them through the facilities and showed them the guest cottage that came with the rental for the bridal party to get ready in, and that doubled as a honeymoon suite for the bride and groom. She answered their questions and took notes of everything she'd need to do to accommodate their wedding requests. After an hour and a half, she waved goodbye.

"Another happy customer, I see," her dad said as he walked down the empty gravel parking lot.

"Yup. We're all set for a December wedding for them. They took the last slot for this year. We're fully booked as soon as I get this information to Mom." Nova held up the clipboard.

Her dad smiled, his brown eyes lighting up as he opened his arms to hug her. "I'm proud of you."

Nova's stomach flipped as she hugged him tight and then waved her hand between them. "I didn't really do much. Just gave them a tour and answered questions."

"This was your idea, wasn't it? You've turned this into a great source of income for the farm."

"Well, with as many ideas as I have, a couple were meant

to stick." She shrugged off the compliment. "I'd better go get this info to Mom before I forget."

"Alright. Sounds good. Let her know I'll be in the back pasture fixing the tractor."

"Will do." She waved and made her way through the parking lot, up the green hill towards her parents' house.

The afternoon sun beat down on her. Looked like today would be a hot one despite the occasional nice breeze. Maybe she'd see if Elise and Isabella wanted to take a trip to the beach with the kids and give her an excuse to play hooky.

She made a mental list of what to pack for the beach as she climbed the steps to her parents' porch and let herself into the house. Nova pulled out her phone and shot off a text to her sisters-in-law. She twisted the handle of her mom's office door, walked in as she pocketed her phone, and froze. Her mouth dropped open as she blinked. Surely she was seeing things.

Two sets of eyes looked up at her entrance, but Nova's were locked on the hazel ones. *What is he doing here?*

Her mom smiled like the cat that ate the canary. "There she is. Jude here is applying for a job. Isn't that a unique name, darling?"

"I-it is." Nova gulped.

"This wouldn't happen to be your Jude, would it?"

Oh shit. Fuck! This isn't happening.

How the fuck was Nova going to get herself out of this mess?

Maybe you should just tell her the truth.

And risk her being disappointed in me? No, thank you.

If Nova had learned anything in life, it was to roll with the punches.

"Hey, Mom. Got the paperwork from the wedding clients for you." Nova set the clipboard on the desk.

She turned to Jude, pleading with her eyes and hoping to Mother Goddess that he still had some of that chivalry left and that their run-in this morning hadn't ruined her last chance of coming out of this unscathed.

Fuck, I'm not high enough for this shit.

5

JUDE

Blood drained from Nova's face, highlighting the freckles across her cheeks. Jude relaxed in his chair, studying the exchange between mother and daughter.

"Could I speak with you for a moment?" Nova asked him, her gaze flicking to her mother before she leaned in and gritted out, "Privately?"

Jude turned to Renita Emerson. She smiled, eyes alight with something he couldn't decipher, which was unsettling. Usually Jude could read everyone.

"Now?" Nova pressed as she shifted on her feet, clearly uncomfortable.

Jude had no idea what was going on. He didn't like the unknown.

"I wouldn't want to be rude to your mother, Nova."

She blinked at him.

"Oh, that's fine. You kids go ahead. We can finish this after you're done," Renita insisted.

Jude stood, putting his baseball cap back on. Nova fled

from the room like her ass was on fire. It didn't take much for Jude to keep up with her as she made her way down the stairs and outside. She ran down the front steps towards a circle of sunflowers on the front lawn. Tall green stalks towered over Nova's small frame with bright yellow blooms hanging overhead, casting half of her in shadow, but she didn't stop moving.

"Where are you going?"

She whirled around. "Away from the house so she can't hear."

"She's all the way in the office."

"Trust me, she has the hearing of a bat, or whatever the fuck has superpower hearing." Nova huffed, swatting a few loose curls from her face. She chewed on her plump bottom lip nervously as she eyed the house. She was cute when she was flustered. He grimaced. He shouldn't be noticing that.

"What's all this about? You don't want me working for your family's farm?" he asked.

"No, that's not it." One tattooed arm came up to wipe her brow. Colorful inked flowers swirled up her arm, intersecting with geometric shapes.

"You don't want your mom to know I helped you out the other night?" He tried to put the pieces together.

She held up her palms, eyes wide and panicked. "Oh, no! She can't know about the other night."

"Why not?" He stepped closer, closing the gap between them.

Nova pulled a vape pen from her pocket and pressed the button frantically. "My life is falling apart—that's why." She slipped the end in her mouth and breathed in, closing her eyes and exhaling a puff of smoke. She did it once more and then turned to him, seeming calmer. "Okay, here's the deal. You saved me last night, and I'm so grateful for that."

Jude shifted on his feet. Her praise made him uncomfortable. "I'm no hero." *I'm the villain.*

"Well, me being not raped and killed last night proves otherwise. But that doesn't matter. What matters is I need a huge favor, and you're gonna think I'm absolutely crazy. But if you help me out, I will owe you, like, big-time. I can give you money or a kidney—literally anything at this point."

"What the fuck is going on?" *Is she mentally unstable?*

"So, my mom can be really intense. And she's done a lot for me, and the only thing she wants is for all her children to be in happy relationships. Only, all my brothers already are and she's relentless when it comes to me." Nova took a breath before continuing her rambling. "I made up a boyfriend who lived long distance from me and this morning when she pressured me for his name, I blurted out yours."

"So your mom thinks I'm your long-distance boyfriend?"

"Maybe?" Nova smiled as her answer sounded more like a question.

"So tell her it's not me."

Her brown doe eyes widened. Something tightened in his chest.

"She'd probably assume I made the whole thing up if I told her it wasn't you after that display in there. Especially since I went from naming The Beatles for my fake boyfriends to Jude . . . which had nothing to do with you. I just like the song 'Hey Jude.'" She winced. It definitely had to do with him.

"But you did make it up."

"But she can't know that! It would destroy her," Nova whisper-yelled, eyeing the house.

"What do you want me to do about it? Pretend I'm your long-distance boyfriend coming to apply for a job at your parents' farm?" He laughed. This woman was certifiable.

Nova blinked and then her eyes moved from side to side, her lips turning up into a smile. "That's a perfect idea!"

"What? No. I wasn't serious."

"But why not? It's brilliant. You play along for a little while until they get off my back. We can have an amicable breakup and you can keep the job if you want."

"You want me, a perfect stranger, to pretend to be your boyfriend?" he asked, bewildered. Did this woman have any sense of self-preservation?

"I know you're not a serial killer."

His blood turned to ice. "How?"

"You had your chance last night and you saved me, remember? It's not like I'd be taking a risk." She waved her hand as if she'd just said the most logical thing in the world.

He stared at her. Could it really be this easy? This hadn't been a part of the plan, but this would be a much more efficient way into her life.

Nova shook her head, wrapping her arms around herself as if she were trying to protect herself somehow. "I'm sorry. Forget I asked. It was stupid. I'll just . . . tell her the truth." Nova looked as if she'd sucked on a lemon.

He waited as she walked back towards the house, scratching underneath the survival bracelet around his wrist. He didn't have time to waste. He'd been meticulous with his plans, but this was a one-in-a-million chance. So he'd do what he'd done his whole life—he'd adapt. Nova was the one with the key to his revenge.

"What's in it for me?" Jude called after her.

Her steps faltered on the porch. She spun around, hope lighting her brown eyes. She walked back towards him, her curls bouncing. Her thick, inked thighs rubbed together, making her hips sway with each step. His mouth watered. She was gorgeous. But that wasn't what he was here for.

"What do you want?" she asked skeptically, licking her lips, hands crossed over her chest.

"I need a place to stay," he lied.

Nova's nose scrunched up. "I mean, as soon as my mom finds out you're living out of your car, she'll put you in one of the spare rooms whether you're my boyfriend or not."

It took a lot to surprise Jude. He'd prided himself on his ability to read people. But the Emersons were throwing one shock after another his way. Who invited perfect strangers to live in their home? Or begged them to pretend to be their boyfriend? And why had Nova assumed he was homeless? That could work in his favor though.

"But as your boyfriend, I'll be expected to move in with you," he pointed out.

"You want to move in with me?" she asked, taking a step back.

He shrugged. "If I'm your boyfriend moving from out of state, I would think things were kind of serious between us."

She cleared her throat. "Right. That makes sense . . . You can move in with me, but not take my money?"

"Moving in with you isn't pity. It's quid pro quo. An exchange of favors so we're almost even. It's part of our cover."

"Oh, good idea! We need a cover story." Nova clapped her hands excitedly. It was admittedly adorable how excited she got about duping her family. Just one more reason he needed to keep his guard up around her. She was willing to deceive the people she was closest to.

"What does this arrangement entail exactly?" he asked.

"When people, mostly my family, are around, you can stand close to me, hold my hand, and, uh, I don't know, do what a boyfriend does."

"How long have we been dating?" he asked.

"We've been dating for four months, but I've been in fake relationships for a year, so I'm basically a professional."

"Christ, you've been keeping this ruse for a year?"

She shrugged. "Give or take a few months. Look, you don't get to judge me. You don't know my mom."

No, he didn't know Renita—or Mama E, as she'd said to call her. But he did know how mothers could be selfish, manipulative users like his own.

"How long do we keep this up?"

"Um, well, how long do you plan on staying in Shattered Cove?" she asked.

He frowned. "Not long. A month or two, max—just long enough to finish the job with your parents."

"Great! Until you leave, then. You get to live with me for free. I'll make sure you get the job on the farm. And I'll owe you, big-time."

"So we're really doing this?" he clarified. How had he gotten himself into a fake relationship with the woman he was hunting?

She held out her hand to shake his. "We're definitely doing this."

He shook her hand, sealing the deal. Energy zapped up his arm. His teeth clenched. *Static electricity.*

Her smile grew, joy shining in her dark brown eyes.

"And a favor to be called in later," he added, forcing his mind away from the dangerous beauty in front of him and back to the task at hand.

"Yes."

Jude had her right where he wanted her—at his mercy.

6

NOVA

Nova chewed on her nail as she climbed the steps to her mother's office. The footsteps behind her were not as loud as she'd expect from Jude's heavy boots. She took a deep breath, turning towards him before opening the door.

"Last chance to bolt." She smiled, but her heart raced. She'd be in so much shit if he didn't follow through with this.

The corner of Jude's mouth curved up in a flicker of a smirk as he pulled off his hat. Jude leaned close to her ear and whispered, "You're stuck with me now."

Shivers crawled up her spine. Uh-oh. She might have bitten off more than she could chew this time. *Maybe I should call this whole thing off—*

Jude's warm calloused hand eclipsed hers on the knob, opening the door to her mother's keen gaze, stealing the choice from her.

Too late now.

"So? Is this your Jude?" Mom asked.

"Y-yes. This is him." Nova glanced at Jude.

His stoic expression didn't change, but he politely removed his ball cap, holding it behind his back, his feet planted apart like a soldier at ease.

He reached out his hand to shake her mom's. "Sorry I didn't lead with that, ma'am. I wanted to get the job on my own merit."

Her mother's cautious smile widened as she shook his hand. "I can respect that. So you're moving here from . . .?" She picked up his application.

"Michigan, ma'am."

"You don't have an address listed on the application." She pursed her lips, searching the page.

The corners of Jude's mouth turned down as he shifted on his feet.

"Actually, Mom, Jude's living with me." She looped her arm with Jude's and gave it a squeeze. Jude stiffened. A zap of energy crackled at his touch and shot up her arm. *Weird.* "We're moving in together, right, baby?" Nova laid it on thick, hoping to the Goddess that her mother would believe them.

Jude tilted his head to look down at her. Man, he was a lot taller this close. And he smelled . . . good. Like the deep woods, strong and resilient with a masculine undertone. And his eyes, they were beautiful this close. There was a ring at the edges of his iris so dark it was almost black, but the flecks of gold and green amidst the lighter brown gave his eyes a lighter quality. Like he was both light and dark and everything in between. You could tell a lot about a person from their eyes.

Mom cleared her throat. Nova blinked, breaking the spell she'd been locked in.

Jude's bicep flexed in her hand as any emotion she'd caught a hint of in his expression vanished.

A tight smile curved Jude's lips up almost forcefully. "Sure thing, Freckles."

Nova's mouth dropped open in outrage as heat bloomed in her cheeks. *Freckles?*

Renita laughed. "And this is the man you've been seeing for the last four months?"

Nova tamped down her anger to look at her mother with a bright smile. Hopefully she didn't look manic. "Absolutely. We just couldn't bear the distance anymore."

"Must be serious if you're moving in together." Her mother's eyes lit up like she was already figuring out how soon she'd have to plan another wedding.

"We're taking it slow. We thought we'd give it a real chance without the distance. But we're still getting to know one another." Nova didn't want her mother getting any grandiose ideas. She just needed enough convincing to keep her off her back for as long as Jude stayed in town. Then she'd take months, perhaps a year to nurse her pretend "broken" heart before she had to figure out something else.

"And how come this is his first visit to see you?" her mom pushed.

Nova opened her mouth to reply but Jude beat her to it.

"I was deployed, ma'am."

Her mother's gaze lit up as Nova whipped around to look at the man beside her with new eyes. Her stomach dropped. Was this part of their ruse? Or was he serious? Why was he living in his car then? Fuck. She'd promised herself never to get involved with a soldier again. Not that this was real.

"What branch of the military?"

"Navy, ma'am."

Her mom nodded approvingly. "Thank you for your service."

Jude gave a nod.

"Are you still in the military?" her mom asked.

"No. I finished my contract last month. Had to get some things in order before I moved out here."

Mom nodded as her attention darted back to Nova. "I see why you've kept this so quiet now."

Nova stiffened. Brooks's face flashed in her mind. "Well, I think that's enough of this interrogation for now. Does he have the job?"

"His résumé looks great. Why didn't you add your military experience on it?" Renita asked.

"Didn't seem applicable to the work here," Jude answered.

"Don't discount your service, son. Nova can get you settled and then show you the ropes. You two will have to come to dinner tonight and you can meet her dad."

"Oh, no. I think Jude's probably tired after his long journey—"

"I'd love to." Jude held out his hand to shake Renita's.

Her mom smiled. "Great. I'll see you both at five."

Jude walked out of the room, putting his hat back on. Nova trailed behind him. The moment they were out of sight of the office, he dropped her hand and bolted out of the house towards his truck. She rushed to keep up, but the view from the back was just as good as it had been this morning, so she wasn't complaining.

I'm in so much trouble.

But there was no turning back now. She and Jude just had to keep things simple.

Right. So, then why did this feel like the least simplest thing she'd ever done?

7

JUDE

Jude lowered his bag to Nova's porch and knocked. Alternative rock bled through the house. Would Nova even hear him over that noise? He'd thought for sure he might have fucked things up in town that morning with her. But he wasn't going to look a gift horse in the mouth. Reaper and his friends had been as surprised as Jude was with the change of events when he'd returned to get his bag. But this was perfect for their plan.

Jude knocked again, pounding his fist on the door.

The music cut off before the door whirled open. Nova stood before him, face flushed as she craned her neck up at him. "Hey. You actually came back."

"Did you think I wouldn't?" Jude picked his duffel bag off the porch.

Nova shook her head and laughed. "Honestly, I thought you ran for the hills."

"Just had some business to attend to." He held up the bags in his hands.

"Right. Come on in and I'll give you the grand tour." Nova waved for him to follow.

Jude entered after Nova into her home, closing the front door and lock with the turn of a handle. No security system except for the cameras outside her porch. He'd spotted several around the property with just a quick scan as he'd passed. But she didn't even have a deadbolt? This woman had no sense of self-preservation. *Or maybe she's the dangerous one.* He'd learned from his time in the SEALs that it was the ones you underestimated that could be the most lethal.

"Welcome to my home." She waved her hand around the spacious living room. A big TV was perched on the wall to the left. A grey C-shaped couch was covered in countless colorful pillows of all shapes and sizes. A few fuzzy blankets were draped over the back of the sofa. She had candles all around, even on some triangular shelves. A built-in bookshelf took up the whole wall to the right with rocks of different colors adorning the shelves. He scanned the titles. One section was devoted entirely to botany, but most of the rows were filled with romance with diverse author names and titles. Several books on different cultures around the world took up one shelf. The top rows had thrillers including murder mysteries and true crime. *Interesting.*

"So this is the living room, and through here is the kitchen-slash-dining area." Nova walked farther inside.

Her kitchen was neat except for the few dishes in the sink and the stack of papers on the counter next to her laptop, covered in stickers. And was that mail sticking out from the fruit basket?

She pointed towards a sliding glass door that led to the backyard. "There's a nice hot tub out there—feel free to use it and make yourself at home. Help yourself to anything in the kitchen. Do you cook? I like to cook sometimes, but I order out a lot too."

"I can make a few things."

"Awesome. Maybe we can take turns." She stared at him in silence like she was waiting for something. Her throat cleared. "Right, well, let me show you the rest of the house."

She moved through the space, pointing out bathrooms and a pantry. The basement was filled with storage and her washer and dryer. That might be a good place for him to start searching for the information he needed. He followed her upstairs.

"This room is mine." She motioned with her thumb to the door to the left of the stairs. "But through here is a bathroom you can use, and you can have your pick of the guest bedrooms."

Jude peeked in the first one with white shiplap walls. Gold geometric-shaped art and watercolor prints with inspiring quotes adorned the walls. A dreamcatcher with white and grey feathers hung above the queen bed, which was covered in at least ten light jewel-toned pillows. Jude cringed. *Why would anyone need so many pillows?*

He turned around, walking to the room farthest down the hall with dark walls and a nautical-themed decor. This was more his style, but he'd be too far away to hear her if she went out in the middle of the night. Much to his dismay, he returned to the first bedroom, dropping his big bag on the bed.

"Can you just keep this door closed, so if my nephew or nieces stop by, they won't tell the rest of the family we're not sharing a room?" Nova asked, wringing her hands together in the doorway.

"Do they come here often?"

She nodded. "Bailey also hangs out here a lot. She's my

brother Ricky's foster placement, but I know they have plans to officially adopt her once she gets a little more settled, and when they're sure she wants it. We're a close-knit family. Hence the weekly family dinners. But tonight it should just be my parents, which will be enough pressure as it is."

He scoffed. "Not close enough to tell the truth about your imaginary boyfriend to though?"

Her eyes dropped to the floor as hurt streaked across her expression, piercing his gut. But why should he care? She was just a mark—a target he needed to extract information from.

"If you . . . I'm sorry." She exhaled, closing her eyes.

Now he really felt like an asshole. Why was she apologizing to him? Was this part of an act?

She blinked her eyes open, resignation lit in her expression. "You know what? I can just tell them I made the whole thing up and made you go along with it. You don't need my issues."

"No." Panic charged through him, his body tense as his heart raced.

Her full lips parted while she studied him. "No what?"

"You'll make me look like a liar too. I need this job."

"Right. I'm sorry I got you tangled in my mess. I'll make it up to you somehow."

He gave another stiff nod and breathed a sigh of relief. He'd almost fucked everything up. He needed to tamp down his emotions and take control of himself.

She glanced to his bag and back to him. "Do you need help bringing anything else in?"

"Nope. This is it."

Her eyes flared wide. "That's all you have?"

Didn't make sense to hold on to things when you moved from place to place like a nomad. "Yup."

She blinked and chewed on her bottom lip.

"You ashamed of me?"

Her nose wrinkled. "Why would I be ashamed of you? I barely know you."

"Because all your fake boyfriend's earthly belongings fit inside this bag."

She shrugged like it really didn't matter to her. "Can't imagine anyone would choose to become homeless. Usually our homes are taken from us in one way or another."

Right, she also thinks I'm homeless. "Our?"

She smirked. "Don't forget you don't know me either, sailor."

Fuck, he really liked her attitude. Made him want to bend her over his knee and spank the sass right out of her until she begged him for mercy. She would find none.

"Actually, I was a SEAL."

She laughed and shook her head. "Of course you were."

What was that supposed to mean? He'd never had someone laugh when he told them that. Usually they dropped their panties. Was that what he wanted Nova to do?

Images of her curvy, tattooed body laid out on this watercolor comforter flashed through his mind. They could have a lot of fun together once he tossed the god-awful pillows on the ground.

No. He shut down the fantasies with angry force. He couldn't afford to get distracted. He was there on a mission. Failure was not an option.

"So we have to be at your parents' at five?"

Her smile faded, and he wanted to kick himself. But it was for the best.

"Yeah. If you want to shower, there are fresh towels in the closet of the bathroom."

"Should I take that as a hint?"

Panic flickered through her wide eyes. "No! Of course

not." A dark hue painted her brown cheeks. "You smell great." She blinked. "Not that I—I mean—you look good." She clapped her hand over her mouth and shook her head before exhaling.

He liked seeing her so flustered. It was entertaining, like he was a cat playing with a mouse.

"Fuck a duck." She wiped a hand over her face.

Her dirty little mouth made his cock hard, and that was a complication he didn't need.

She stared at his chest. "Look, there are extra razors and toiletries in the drawers and cupboards. Help yourself."

"I don't need your pity."

Her lips thinned. "It's not pity. It's hospitality. Promise." She dragged her finger over her chest, marking an X. "I'll, uh, leave you to it. We can head over at like five minutes 'til five. I'll meet you downstairs." She turned and left, closing the door behind her.

Jude opened his duffel bag and pulled out a fresh pair of clothes for dinner and laid them neatly on the mattress. He took out his toiletry bag next and closed his luggage before stuffing it under the bed. He'd learned long ago there was no use in unpacking—a habit he'd taken from his nomadic childhood and carried with him into the military.

It made it easier to leave when things got messy. And living with Nova Emerson was bound to get complicated.

But he was in. It was time for phase two of the plan.

8

JUDE

J ude followed Nova down her porch steps at ten minutes past five. Her flip-flops flapped along the way. He walked beside her, keeping her in his periphery as he took in their surroundings.

She pointed off to the left. "My grow house is over there in the back field. I have a few different ones out back. That's where my babies are. Have you ever grown cannabis before?"

He surveyed the lay of the land, noting the cameras again. "No."

"Not even in high school or college?"

He turned to face her. "Is that a problem?"

She laughed, a sweet sound that danced from her and wrapped around his whole body, making his chest tight. *What the fuck is that?* Trouble, that was what she was.

"So you were either the rich kid that didn't have to grow his own, a Goody-Two-shoes, a jock that didn't want to risk a piss test and lose a chance at a scholarship, or a—"

"Why do you care so much?"

She cocked her hip to the side and crossed her arms over her chest. "Maybe because you're living with me for the foreseeable future and I'm entrusting my physical safety in your hands, as well as the safety of my family."

He stared back at her determined brown eyes that glinted with promise of retribution for anyone who crossed her or someone she loved. If only Jude had some of that fire, he wouldn't have been in this mess.

"And somehow figuring out how or why I haven't grown weed gives you that information?"

"Interesting how you avoid the question and get all defensive."

He opened his mouth to argue with her and then slammed it shut with as much self-control as he could muster. She was trying to read him. And he sure as hell wasn't gonna make it easy.

"None of the above."

A beat of silence passed as they stared at each other. If she thought he was going to volunteer information, she was dead wrong.

She sighed. "Look, my gut tells me that underneath all that scowl and grumble, there's a guy with a good heart."

The beating in his chest stuttered. She thought there was good in him? Oh, how wrong her instincts were.

Her eyes sparked with something he recognized. Something that told him he might have just met his match. "However, if you try and hurt me or my family, things won't end well for you."

With that parting comment, she spun on one flip-flop and headed down the grassy hill towards her parents' home.

Hot damn, if it wasn't the sexiest move. But Jude would be in deep shit if he couldn't stop lusting after his target.

"Come on. We're gonna be late," she called back to him.

It didn't take much for him to catch up. She was like a curvier version of Tinker Bell, tiny in stature yet voluptuous. Her ripped shorts showed off toned, thick legs with a tattooed snake slithering in a skull with dark red roses on her right thigh. Her toenails were painted black like her half-chewed fingernails. She wore a crop top with a unicorn puffing on a joint blowing rainbow smoke, showing off a sliver of Nova's round belly. Two small circles stuck out on the side of each nipple imprint on her shirt. *Is she pierced?* Dark curls bounced on her head with each step, wild and free like the woman beside him. And those damn rusty freckles sprinkled over her nose and cheeks were like stars in the sky. He wanted to trace his finger over each one and map them.

Jude shook his head. Was this woman a witch? He never obsessed over a woman like this, especially not when so much was on the line.

He angled his body so he could put some distance between them.

"The barn over there has sheep, pigs, and a couple beef cows. Oh, and a couple dozen chickens are in the coop next to it with the fenced-in run. That's one of the chores you'll probably be helping with. As well as the grow houses, and maybe even the fields and orchard. It's a kind of co-op effort—everyone helps where there's a need when we have spare time from our own projects."

They climbed the worn path up a hill as her parents' home got closer.

"Shit." She stopped abruptly.

"What is it?" Jude scanned their surroundings, his body on alert for a threat.

"My brothers are here too."

Jude eyed the trucks in the driveway. "Is this where I act like I'm scared they'll beat me up?"

She scoffed. "No. They prey on weakness. You have to give it to them back just as hard."

Just when he'd thought she couldn't impress him more. "Is that why you have such a hard time finding a real boyfriend to bring home?"

Pain swirled in her gaze, dimming some of her shine. The urge to take it away rose, but he quickly tamped it down.

"Yes and no." She exhaled. "They can be a tad overprotective, but they mean well. And they're all blissfully in love, so their partners and their kids will be here too and probably have lots of questions for us."

Jude didn't like crowds, and it must have shown in his body language, because Nova looked at him, frowning.

She gave him a half-smile, her eyes lit with sympathy. "We can be quick. In and out. Dinner and then I'll make an excuse. If you want to leave earlier, we need a code word."

He searched her expression for any humor but only found genuine concern. That big heart was going to get her in trouble someday. Made her trust too easily—and he was the perfect example of a reason she shouldn't be quick to do so.

"So this is a serious mission?"

Her mouth dropped open and her whole face lit up. "Did you just make a joke?"

He grumbled and looked towards her parents' home. Movement at the window drew his attention. A few faces poked through the curtains, staring at them.

More of that addictive laughter tumbled out of her like a ray of fucking sunshine. "It's okay. We can pretend you're a big, tough Navy SEAL without humor if you want."

"Let's go. We're already late and we're gathering quite the audience." He nodded towards the house.

Nova spun on her heel. "Fuck. Okay, code word for emergency evacuation is red."

"Red?"

She gave him a saucy wink. "It's your safe word."

Hot arousal thrummed through his veins. Jude leaned forward, pinching her chin firmly in his hands, forcing her to look up at him. He shouldn't be doing this, but he couldn't help it—just one little touch. Her hot breath coasted over his lips before he stopped. Her pupils dilated as he searched their depths for the answers he so desperately needed. But what he found was so much worse.

"The only one between us that needs a safe word would be you. And I have no doubt it would be *mercy*. Because by the time I'm finished with you, you'll be begging me for it." He licked his lips as her throat bobbed, her eyes almost completely black now. She wasn't unaffected either, and that made him feel a little better about his predicament. "Now turn around, march that ass inside your parents' home, and play your part like a good girl."

He backed up, letting his arms fall to his sides. He flexed his hand, trying to get rid of the electric pulsing that happened whenever he touched her.

She stood dazed and unmoving, staring at him like she wanted him to make good on his promises.

"Nova." His voice came out harsh.

She startled and blinked as if she'd been lost in her own fantasies. It seemed he'd found a way to make her speechless after all. He needed to keep his distance from her. She was dangerous in more ways than one, and he had to remember that.

"O-okay. So, we're going in." She straightened her shoulders and took his hand.

Her warm fingers interlaced with his own. Electricity

hammered through him at the contact again. He yanked his palm away.

Hurt flashed in her expression before her attention flicked to the window a few family members peeked out from.

"It's just for a few minutes and then I'll keep my distance." She wouldn't look at him.

He forced a deep breath into his lungs, bracing himself for the contact before he grabbed her hand and interlocked his fingers with hers once again.

They walked to the porch and up the steps. He had no idea what to expect from this encounter. Jude didn't have much experience with family dynamics. And what he had experienced was anything but positive. Renita had seemed nice enough, but Jude's mom knew how to put on a show too. Maybe after spending a little more time with her, he could get an accurate read. Anyone could pretend—Jude would know. He'd been doing it his whole life. Entering the Emersons' home would be like walking into a minefield. And the only person that kept him tethered here was the one person he couldn't afford to get close to.

Nova reached for the door as it swung open. Renita stood there with a big smile and a man by her side.

"Welcome to our home, Jude. This is my husband, James," Renita introduced them.

James reached out his hand to shake Jude's.

"Nice to meet you, sir," Jude said.

"Same to you, son. Come on in and make yourself comfortable. Dinner's been ready since five." Both her parents looked at Nova.

"It's only quarter after. And I didn't realize you were inviting everyone. I thought it was just going to be us," Nova argued.

"We all wanted to meet your mystery man, so get in here

already!" another deep voice called from inside the home—no doubt one of Nova's brothers.

Nova turned to Jude as her parents stepped to the side, making room for them. "Ready or not, here we go."

He was most definitely not ready.

9

NOVA

Nova sat beside Jude at her parents' long table. Ricky narrowed his eyes at her. Only he and Everett knew the truth—that her long-distance boyfriends this past year had been completely made up. She needed to get them alone and shut them up before they ruined this whole thing.

"My wife said you're in the Navy?" her dad asked as Jude swallowed a bite of his dinner.

"Yes, sir. My retirement went through last month."

"I was in the Army myself. But I suppose if my daughter thinks you're worthy of her, a sailor will be welcome in our home," her dad teased.

Jude gave him a nod of acknowledgement and then took another bite of her mom's pulled pork.

"Wait, you're military and she still gave you a chance? Damn, man. You must be the one," Roman added.

Nova's stomach coiled and knotted with anxiety. Could she ever escape her past?

Jude gave her a questioning look.

"How'd you two meet?" Ricky asked, wrapping his arm around his fiancé, Everett.

Jude wiped his mouth with a napkin and relaxed back in his chair like he was at ease, but Nova could feel the way his thigh tensed against hers.

"Oh, well, we um. We met . . . at a bar after I broke up with Paul." She looked at Jude for help.

"You mean Peter?" Renita asked.

"Right, Peter. Must have just blocked the man from my memory. He was so . . . boring," she squeaked.

"Don't be shy, Freckles." His arm draped over the back of her chair, his fingers coasting up and down her shoulder. That small contact made her skin break out in goose bumps.

"We met at a bar. I went to order my buddy another round and she bumped into me, spilling her drink all over my shirt."

Roman chuckled. "That sounds like Nova."

She kicked her brother under the table.

"Ow!"

Nova smirked. Jude's chest moved like he'd chuckled but no sound came out.

"What happened next?" Elise, Roman's wife, asked, leaning in.

"She offered to buy me more drinks and another shirt. But I asked for her number instead. I was only in town for the weekend, but I just couldn't stay away."

"Awww." Isabella, Nova's other sister-in-law, pressed her hand to her chest. "That's so romantic."

"So you had a weekend fling with my sister?" Nash glared at Jude.

Nova turned to her brother. "Like you're one to talk. You knocked Isabella up after knowing her less than a couple hours and then were an asshole to her when she came back and told you she was pregnant with Alba."

Nash pulled Isabella closer to him and kissed her cheek, seemingly chastised.

"Leave your sister and her boyfriend alone," her mother added.

None of the Emerson siblings would dare defy their mother. Nova gave her mom a smile. Renita winked at her.

"So you guys kept in touch?" Isabella asked.

Nova grabbed Jude's face and squished his cheeks together, taking her chance. *Payback time.* There was no way he'd let her get this close without an audience, and the glare aimed at her proved it.

"I couldn't resist this sad puppy-dog face. He's quite the charmer when he wants to be."

Jude pulled her hands off him, wrapping his big bear hands over hers and pulling them into her lap, pinning them to her thigh.

He smiled, but it didn't reach his eyes. Simply a mask. But it was the first time she'd seen those lips curl up, and the dimples show on his cheeks. Damn, he was breathtaking. "We kept in touch while I finished up my contract. Met up when we could. And then after my retirement finished going through, I knew there was nowhere else I'd want to be."

Nova's lungs stuttered as the full weight of his smile landed on her. He almost had her believing him. He was good. Something churned in her stomach—a warning. He might have been saving her ass, but he was a smooth liar. She needed to remember that.

"What about your family? Are they in Michigan?" her mom asked.

Jude's body went rigid. "My parents are dead."

"I'm so sorry," her mom said.

Nova's heart broke for the man next to her. She was learning all of this along with her family. She knew what it was like to lose both your parents. She'd been lucky when the Emersons had welcomed her into their home as their own. Maybe she and Jude had more in common than she'd realized.

"When do you want to start work?" her dad asked.

"Leave him alone, Dad. Jude isn't even settled in the house yet, and—"

"Settled? In your house?" Ricky asked.

"Yes," she gritted out. "We're moving in together."

"Shit. I didn't realize it was this serious." Roman looked between the two of them.

"Is it that hard to believe I found someone who likes me enough to live with me?" She couldn't hide the hurt that bled from her voice.

"That's not what I meant," Roman said.

"Look, you all didn't want me living alone with everything going on. I don't see why you're making this a bigger deal than it is," she snapped, angrily digging her fork into her mom's mac and cheese.

The room fell silent. Even baby Alba looked up.

Oh, shit. If Jude asked what they were talking about, it would look like her relationship was flimsy with him—too flimsy for them to be cohabitating.

She wrapped her arm around Jude's waist and leaned in. Christ, the man's body was pure granite.

"Actually, that's why Jude is moving in with me. He was also worried about my safety and that's one reason he wanted to get here so quickly." Surely her overprotective brothers would buy that hook, line, and sinker.

Roman and Nash looked at Jude seemingly with new eyes. But Ricky stared straight at her.

"Nova Akua Emerson," Ricky warned.

"Ricardo Andrew Emerson," she deadpanned, crossing her arms over her chest.

"Why don't you help me get dessert for everyone?" He stood and left the table, not giving her a chance to refuse.

She turned to Jude. "I'll be right back."

"Sure thing, Freckles," Jude answered as if he didn't have a care in the world, but the hard set of his shoulders told a different story. And why was he using that goddamned nickname?

"Nova!" Ricky yelled from the kitchen.

"I'm coming. Hold on to your panties."

"Uncle Ricky wears panties?" her niece Ariel asked.

"He sure does," Nash answered.

Nova laughed as she headed into the kitchen.

Ricky's scowl was unmatched as he grabbed her arm and pulled her up the stairs, out of hearing range of their family.

"Geeze, you don't have to be so dramatic."

"I'm the one that's dramatic? That's rich, coming from someone fake dating men for a year and then showing up with a complete stranger for dinner and announcing he's moving in with you!" Ricky whisper-yelled.

He had a point. But she wasn't going to admit that. She crossed her arms and huffed. "So we've been seeing each other less than everyone thinks. Doesn't change much."

"How long have you known him?"

"A while."

Ricky grimaced. "Tell me he isn't a complete stranger."

"He's not."

Ricky studied her and shook his head. "There's a killer on the loose, and you could be his next target. Don't you think you should be more careful?"

"I am being careful!"

They both looked at the door. Had anyone heard her outburst?

"Jude is a good guy," her voice softened.

"How do you know?"

"He saved me. Okay? I got into some trouble, and he had an opportunity to hurt me, and no one would have known. But he didn't. He helped me and the truth is . . ." She took a deep breath. Ricky needed to believe she was safe or he'd blow her whole cover. "I fell for him. And he reminds me of you, actually, with a hard outer shell but is a complete softie inside."

"Nova, I swear, if you're fucking with me—"

"I'm not. Besides, you owe me. I helped you and Everett out after your dumb ass nearly got you both killed."

"So you're blackmailing me?" he snapped.

"No, I'm holding you to our end of a deal. Jude is a good man—I've seen it."

"He's lying to them, letting them all believe you've dated for months."

"And you lied to yourself for decades, and all of us, about you and Everett. How is that any different?" She pushed.

Ricky sighed, tipping his head back as he ran a hand over his face. Pure frustration pulsed from him. "You promise me you trust this guy?"

"Yes."

"And you'll let me know if that changes? If he does anything that doesn't feel right?"

"Yes. Now can we get back down there before Mom scares him away with talk of weddings and babies?"

Ricky snorted and put his arm around her, pulling her in for a hug. "Fine. But after this we're more than even and you never bring up a favor I owe you or the exploding shed again. In fact, you need to destroy the evidence now."

She chuckled. "I haven't had the evidence for years."

His eyes widened as he pulled away. "But you said—"

"I lied. I needed something, being the only girl with three big brothers, to keep you in line."

"You sneaky little brat."

She shrugged and left the office. "But I do have pictures of you lying in Mom's torn-up flower garden from a few years ago." Nova took off down the stairs as Ricky cursed behind her in pursuit.

She needed to get back to Jude and get them both out of her parents' house before her family discovered the truth.

If they found out what was really going on, her parents would get hurt in the aftermath. Maybe she should have thought about that before. But it was too late now. She'd committed to this. Hopefully it wouldn't come back to bite her in the ass . . .

The image of Jude's teeth sinking into her flesh flashed through her mind.

Maybe a little ass biting wouldn't be that bad after all.

10

———————

JUDE

J ude waited while Nova closed the door to her house, though she didn't bother locking it. This woman was reckless.

Now's my chance.

"What the hell was that?"

She sighed and headed for the kitchen. "That was the Emersons. I told you they can be overbearing."

Jude trailed after her, leaning against the wall separating the living space and kitchen. "Don't play dumb with me."

Nova opened the fridge, despite just finishing dinner at her family's. She stared into the appliance like it had all the answers in the world and then shut it. "Living with a room-mate one-oh-one: communication is key. Please enlighten me as to what the hell you're specifically talking about." She pulled a joint from the cigarette case from her back pocket, left the case on the counter and headed outside.

He followed her out to the back porch as she lit up, wrapping her plump lips around the small end of the joint, her breasts rising with her inhale.

A puff of smoke curled from her luscious mouth, rising into the summer night. The golden setting sun gave way to a rainbow of pinks and purples on the horizon. Yet somehow his attention was drawn back to the tiny little minx relaxing like a pinup on the outdoor couch.

"I'm talking about the comment about you being in danger."

She flinched. "Oh."

He scoffed and took the seat next to her. The herbal aroma of weed drifted over him as she took another puff.

"It's nothing, really." She offered him the joint and he shook his head.

"Didn't sound like nothing," he argued. This was his opportunity to see what she knew. This was his in.

She blew out a breath, tipping her head back, and she closed her eyes. "This is really going to ruin my buzz."

"If I'm going to pretend to be your boyfriend, I deserve to know. Don't you think?"

She took another hit but sat up. "Fine."

"Did you put me in danger with this arrangement, Freckles?" he asked.

She scowled at him. "No. I never would have suggested this if I'd thought it would put someone else at risk. But you're a SEAL; isn't danger like what you live for?"

"You're deflecting again."

Her big brown eyes flared. *Caught.* She sighed, pinched the end of her joint, and set it on the table. She wiggled out of her flip-flops and folded her legs underneath her on the couch.

"You're right—you have the right to know. And to make us seem more believable, you need to have this information, I guess. I just . . ." She shook her head, but there was a tightness in her shoulders that hadn't been there before.

She clearly didn't like opening up. That made two of them.

"I guess I should start at the beginning." She took a deep breath and then let it out. "Years ago, my brother Nash was engaged to a woman who went missing. For years we didn't know what had happened to her. She just vanished overnight. They'd gotten into a fight. I always suspected she cheated on him but never had proof."

That's something I didn't know. Trouble in paradise is a great motivation for murder.

"He left with me to go to a convention in California, and when we returned, his fiancée was gone." She blinked, a beat of silence passing before she continued. "Things were bad for a long time. But then he met Isabella and found his happiness." She smiled and then shook her head. "Sorry, I'm getting sidetracked. Two years ago he got a note from Anastasia's killer—directions on where to find her body." Nova rubbed her arms as if she were cold despite the humid summer night.

"So she was killed?"

Nova turned to look over her shoulder into the ever-darkening woods. "Whoever it was buried her on the hill on our property."

"That's fucked up, but I don't see how that puts you directly in danger," Jude said.

She looked at him, studying him in the setting sun, like if she tried hard enough, she'd be able to see through him. *Good fucking luck, Freckles.*

"There have been others."

He stared at her in silence. In his experience, words weren't always needed to convince someone to spill secrets.

"There have been more women who went missing and then showed up dead. The FBI got involved because the deaths were linked, and it crossed state lines into Massachusetts."

"I still don't see how this connects with you."

She closed her eyes, taking a moment, as if she were steeling herself. As much as she tried to seem unaffected by this circumstance, it was obviously taking a toll on her. Denial and avoidance wouldn't get her far—he would know.

Nova stared back at him. "I knew all of the women, including the one who just went missing a few weeks ago."

Ice slid through Jude's veins. "When did you last see her?"

"I haven't. Not since we were teens."

"How did you know she went missing?"

"The sheriff found out and told me."

"Why would someone be coming after you all?"

"I don't know! Okay? I don't fucking know." Her glazed eyed welled with tears. "If I knew, then I could help end this. But I can't. I'm fucking useless, sitting here day after day, just waiting."

"How did you all know each other?" he asked evenly.

She winced, her watery eyes filling with untold pain. She blinked a few times and wiped her eyes.

Compassion wasn't something Jude was capable of, not since the only woman he loved had pushed him away. Still, a weight descended on his chest, wrapping around his torso and squeezing tight at the sight of Nova's distress.

She sniffed. "We were in the same foster home for a little while."

"Who was?"

"The three women who've been murdered, the one that's missing, and myself."

"And your foster parents. Anyone else?"

She shifted, her eyes falling to her hands as she picked her skin at the nail beds. Nervous habit?

"Their niece and one other girl. Any of us could be next, in theory. That's what my family is worried about."

Jude leaned in, tipping her chin so she would look at him again. He'd read the court documents, but he wanted her version—desperate to know every detail. Information was power. He just needed a break and a few more pieces of the puzzle so he could get his redemption. "What happened in that house?"

The blood drained from Nova's face. It was as if an invisible door had slammed shut between them. Nova scrambled to her feet. "I've only ever trusted one person with that information and he used it against me. Since you're just my fake boyfriend, I won't be going back down Memory Lane."

Something a lot like regret speared through him. He'd pushed her too far too fast.

He nodded. "Thank you for sharing what you did."

Her eyes widened as if she hadn't expected his gratitude. Shit, he hadn't expected to give it either. This woman made Jude react in responses that were not natural for him. She was dangerous in all the ways he couldn't afford.

Nova walked towards the sliding door. "Goodnight."

"Night." His voice scraped from him. He turned towards the woods just as the last of the pink sky faded into indigo twilight.

"Jude?"

"Yeah?" His attention darted back to her, standing in the doorway.

"Breakfast is at eight and then I'll be heading to work on the farm if you want to tag along."

"Will do."

She nodded and closed the door behind her. He waited on the back porch a good half hour before he went inside. He played the new information she'd given him over and over in his mind, lining it up with what he already knew. His skin itched with the need to do more. Waiting there was killing him. Each day that passed made him feel more and more hopeless.

Jude pulled out his phone and texted the only man in the world he could trust.

> Jude: Any news?

> Reaper: The addresses were a dead end. I've got Ax working on the financials to see where they lead. I'll update you as soon as I know something.

> Jude: I should come help you.

> Reaper: You're exactly where you should be. We talked about this. She would recognize me. You're the only one who can get the inside recon.

Jude sighed and ran a hand through his hair.

> Jude: We had a conversation about her time in the foster home but she's hiding something.

> Reaper: You know what to do to get answers. Keep me in the know.

> Jude: You let me know the second you find out anything on your end.

> Reaper: You have my word. We'll get him.

Jude locked the door behind him, doing the same with all the windows, and the front entrance before shutting off all the lights and made his way to his room.

The light bled from underneath Nova's closed door. Something pulled him towards it. His hand reached out, itching to knock. But what would he say? He didn't like that he'd brought things up that caused her pain. He knew better than most what being triggered did to someone. But there was so much more on the line.

He couldn't afford weakness. He owed Sal a debt he could never repay, but vengeance was a start. And Nova was the only one with answers. He'd do everything he could not to hurt her, but one thing that he'd learned from his time as a SEAL was that there had to be sacrifice for the greater good, even if that meant casualties.

Jude stepped away from the door, his hand fisting at his side as he locked himself in his own room, not even bothering to turn the light on.

Darkness was all he'd known. And someday soon, it would come back for him. He just needed to make sure he'd done right by Sal before it did. He owed her that much. He owed her everything because he'd failed her.

But he'd make it right, no matter the cost.

11

NOVA

Nova stood on tiptoes on an old ladder holding up the new string lights. She could almost reach the nail on the beam. She just needed a little more—

"What the fuck are you doing?" Jude's deep voice slashed across the open space of the event barn like a whip.

Nova gasped, losing her footing. Gravity pulled her down, her eyes widening as she braced for impact.

Oof!

She thudded into a hard chest, but it wasn't much more forgiving than the wooden floor would have been.

She looked up at him, his sweaty, muscular body molding to hers like nothing she'd ever felt.

Longing and arousal spun from the connection as she stared into his hazel eyes. There was something familiar in them.

"Are you trying to get yourself killed?" he snapped, stepping away so fast she wobbled on her feet.

Anger and embarrassment quickly replaced any attraction her traitorous body had had. "I wouldn't have fallen if you hadn't come in here yelling at me." She crossed her arms over her chest and huffed.

Jude's gaze dropped to her breasts before his jaw hardened. "I wouldn't have yelled if you hadn't been risking your life like that."

"My life?" She laughed. "Hardly. I do this all the time."

"And that was your last." He shoved a water bottle at her.

She took it, raising an eyebrow in question.

"Drink."

Nova rolled her eyes. "Bossy much?"

His gaze narrowed on her. "You've got quite the mouth on you."

"Thank you." She twisted the cap off and took a sip of water.

He shook his head and picked up the fallen ladder before climbing up and hooking the string lights on the nail with ease.

"Show-off," Nova teased under her breath.

Jude climbed back down. He tugged the bottom of his T-shirt up to wipe the sweat off his brow.

Holy shit. The man had more abs than should be legal, and they were shiny with sweat slicked from a hard day's work. Her mouth watered with the urge to lick his stomach. She'd start at the top, lapping her tongue over the deep grooves of each ab, swirling around the tattoo on his hip, then down the V. Her knees wobbled and her heart raced. He'd been hot with a shirt on when he got back from his morning run, but fuck. Jude was the very definition of perfection bare-chested. *I bet he looks like a work of art naked.*

"You okay?" Jude asked, his shirt falling back into place.

"Hmm? Yeah. Of course." She took another drink of water for her parched throat before setting the bottle down.

"Your cheeks are flushed. Maybe you should sit down in the AC for a bit."

She waved him off. "I'm fine. Did you need something?"

He looked around the barn where they held the weddings, his attention flicking to each one of her open bins scattered around the space and the few miscellaneous piles.

"What the hell happened in here?" he asked.

"I'm just cleaning up. We have wedding events almost every Saturday this summer. Mom likes to keep Sundays open for family days, so cleanup happens Mondays."

"Were you cleaning out storage?" He motioned to the bins.

"Oh, no. I was going to sweep and mop, but then I saw the dust on the shelves where we hold the candles on the wall. I figured I should dust first or it would just make the floor dirty again. I got to dusting and saw the beams needed it too. So I got the ladder out and found the extra string lights. I remembered I needed to change one, and then I couldn't find the right bin, and . . ." She motioned to the giant mess she'd created in the process. "This happened."

"Well, I'm done cleaning out the animal pens. I'll help you get this sorted."

Oh. Wow. He was offering to help? Maybe Mr. Grumbly Hotness had more to offer than a great set of abs after all.

"Thanks. The bins can go back in the room over there with the rest of storage." She pointed to an open door off to the side by the bathrooms.

He got to work, packing up the boxes and bins. Somehow she always bit off more than she could chew. A seemingly simple task turned into much more. Before she knew it, one project had turned into five and she had no energy or motivation to finish any of them. She understood how that could get annoying to other people—it drove her nuts too. But she couldn't exactly control it.

"You gonna watch me all day or help?" Jude asked without looking up. He stacked three bins in his hands and carried them to the storage room.

Nova snapped out of her fog. "Right." She grabbed the broom and started in the far corner while he cleared the space. It was always easier when she had someone working alongside her. "So, I was thinking . . ."

Jude closed the door and wiped his hands on his cargo pants. "Yeah?"

"We should probably talk some more and get to know each other. I've told you a lot about me, but I don't know anything about you. My family will ask, and I don't want to have to come up with something."

A dry sound left his lips like the start of a chuckle. "You mean you don't want to come up with any more lies?"

"No, I don't."

He picked up the Swiffer and started mopping up behind her where she'd already swept. Was he just going to ignore her now?

"What do you want to know?" he asked.

"Tell me about you. Who are you, Jude King?"

"Not much to tell. Dropped out of high school and got my GED, joined the Navy, and worked my way up to SEAL. Got out a couple months ago."

"You dropped out of high school?"

"Maybe omit that tidbit if you're trying to impress your family."

He was ashamed of his past—that much was clear. But Nova understood that kids didn't just stop going to school and join the military unless they had good reason.

"Why did you join the Navy?" she asked.

His expression hardened. "It was a way out."

Had he been in a bad situation at home? Or did he have a learning disability that he hadn't received help for? Roman was dyslexic, and without the accommodations her mom fought for, he would have had much more difficulty finishing high school, much less getting a degree. "Sounds like you knew what you wanted and didn't want to waste time getting your diploma."

Jude froze, turning to her and studying her intently like he was trying to decipher some kind of puzzle. He turned away.

She cleared her throat. "Any siblings or family I should know about?"

Pain flashed so potent and powerful in his eyes before bleeding out into his expression, in the lines at the corner of his eyes and the grimace of his mouth. Just as quickly as it had come, it disappeared behind his stoic mask.

What's that about?

"There's no one." His voice came out rough.

Her heart hurt for him. "I'm sorry."

"I don't need your pity," he grumbled.

"It's not pity. It's sympathy. I know what it's like to not have anyone. It's a feeling I wouldn't wish on anyone."

Jude didn't say anything. His attention stayed on the swish of her broom as she finished sweeping the room. He put the ladder away and continued to mop behind her, the scent of the cleaner melding with the summer breeze and flowers that floated from outside the open barn door.

Nova put the broom and dustpan away and then picked up the bottle of water, taking a long drink.

"Thanks for your help. I need to go check my plants and I can give you a tour of the grow house if you want? I'm about three weeks to a month away from harvesting this crop."

Jude tucked the mop back into the closet and shut it before joining her.

"Why cannabis?" he asked, stepping outside.

She followed, the heat of the August sunlight sinking through her tank top and cutoffs, making her sweat. God, she must look disgusting. Nova pulled her short curls off her shoulders and placed the cool water bottle on the back of her neck.

"How much time do you have?" She laughed.

"Not like I have anywhere else to be."

"Right. Well, my family has this beautiful farm. Nash started a fishing business, my other brothers are beekeepers and run Emerson Apiaries, and there I was, a Jill-of-all-trades and master of none, as my friend Bea would say. I wanted to find some way to contribute, but I'm not so great with book-work and things don't tend to keep my attention if I have to do them over and over. I like variety."

"Why is it so important to stay on the farm rather than starting your own thing somewhere else? Seems like you're under a lot of pressure here if you're having to make up a fake boyfriend to keep your family happy. Why put in all that effort?"

She sighed and headed up the path to her house. "I owe my parents a lot. They adopted me when I had no one, no questions asked. They've always treated me like their own. And I just want to make them happy."

"What about your happiness?" he asked, appearing beside her.

"I'm happy."

A beat of silence passed.

"You don't believe me?" she asked.

"I don't know you, Nova."

"Right. Well, I am. Happy, I mean. I like my life the way it is—how did we get on this topic? Oh, you wanted to know why I started farming cannabis."

"Right."

"Well, I started smoking weed in high school, and I found that it helped with my social anxiety, and different strains helped me focus or sleep when my ADHD meds didn't cut it. I realized I could help other people find relief with the medical benefits of weed and do my part to fight the stigma. Some people relax with a glass of wine at the end of the night; I reach for a joint or an edible. Why not grow something that helps me and others? That's how my business, Stoner Girl, was born."

Nova paused just long enough to take a breath. "Did you know that one in five cancer-related deaths is because of malnutrition? Twenty percent of cancer patients that pass away do so because they are not getting enough nutrients and food into their bodies. Cannabis can literally save lives." She turned to him, catching his stare. "Why are you looking at me like you're impressed?"

The corner of his mouth quirked up before he shook his head. "I've never met anyone quite like you."

"Is that good or bad?"

"I'm not sure, Freckles. I'm not entirely sure."

"Okay, hold up." She pressed her hand into his chest to stop him feet away from her front steps.

He looked down at the connection and then back to her.

She may have let her palm linger, taking advantage of feeling so much muscle. *Shit.* She yanked her hand away. The last thing she needed was to start groping her fake boyfriend. She really needed to get laid, preferably soon and not with her new roommate. *Nope.* That would be a bad idea.

"What's going on in that very active little head of yours?" He tapped her temple.

"I—why do you keep calling me Freckles?"

One of his eyebrows quirked up as his calloused fingertip connected one spot on her cheek to another—no doubt he was tracing her actual freckles.

Fuck, why did that make her panties wet? She shivered. *No. Bad girl. Calm the fuck down. We can't fuck where we sleep. That would be a terrible idea.*

"You don't like it?" he asked.

"No." Shit, why had her voice come out breathy?

"Liar."

She smacked his hand away. "Am not."

He actually chuckled this time. His eyes sparked with humor and a layer of mischief. "I thought couples used those nauseating endearments all the time. You were laying them on thick yesterday, *baby*. At least mine is original."

"Not that one. Literally anything else—well, I mean within reason."

"Nope. You're Freckles to me."

Of course he'd home in on one of her biggest insecurities. But Nova wasn't ever one to take something lying down. She could acknowledge she was a petty bitch sometimes.

"Fine. I'll just have to come up with something equally annoying, then."

He shrugged like he couldn't care less. "Good luck."

Challenge accepted.

"I'll do it," she threatened.

"I'm sure you will. Have you eaten lunch?" he asked.

"Not yet. I want to check my plants first." She veered off towards her truck.

He grabbed her wrist and firmly tugged her towards the house. "You need lunch first."

"Excuse me? Who the hell are you to tell a grown-ass woman what she needs?"

"Obviously you need it."

"I'm not hungry." Nova's stomach grumbled, betraying her.

That damn knowing eyebrow quirked again as he gave her a skeptical look. "Why do you have to fight me on everything?"

"Why do you have to be so bossy?"

"You'd better be careful with that sass. I'm only human."

"What does that mean?" she pushed.

He tugged her against his chest, framing her chin in his grip and forcing her to look up at him. "It means, Freckles, that you are toeing a very thin line. If you don't march that sexy little ass of yours into that house right now and eat something, I may have to bend you over my lap and spank it."

Her mouth dropped open. Surely she was hallucinating. The sun had gotten to her. That was the only explanation for the sudden flush that seared her body. The wetness soaking her panties. The fact that this sexy, bossy-as-fuck man was issuing orders and threats of punishment if she didn't take care of herself . . . God, it only made her want to rebel more. It woke up a part of her she'd long thought buried. And that scared the shit out of her. *Because I still crave it.*

"Fine. I'll eat."

"Good girl." He released her and stepped away so fast Nova faltered, swaying on her feet, but his hand was there to steady her.

She pulled away from him this time, stomping up the steps to her front door. She stopped and whirled around with the biggest smile on her face. "Whatever you say, *Daddy.*"

The heat in his gaze could have burned the house to ash. *Bingo.* She'd found the perfect name to push his buttons and taunt him.

Let the games begin.

12

NOVA

Sunday morning, Nova tiptoed down the stairs. She'd actually gotten up on time despite the late night thanks to her three alarms. She had a lot to do today, including some wedding cleanup. After yoga with her sisters-in-law and Everett, she had to get to the mountain of paperwork waiting to be filed or come next April she'd be completely overwhelmed. Dread filled her belly. If she was lucky, someone would have a crisis at yoga and she could have an excuse to do something else today.

Nova slipped on the second to last step, her stomach jumping to her throat as gravity—her nemesis—pulled her down.

She gasped, reaching out for the railing as her tailbone hit the floor.

"Ouch!" She rolled to her feet, checking over her shoulder. She didn't want to wake Jude. He'd been pulling long days all week, despite her telling him it wasn't necessary. The man didn't sit still for long at all, going out for runs every morning and sometimes later in the evening too. It was like he always had to be doing something. *Or has he been trying to avoid me since our run-in on Monday? Maybe I took things too far, calling him Daddy? Stupid.* Anxiety curled in her stomach as the interaction played through her mind, over and over. *He threatened to spank me. If anyone crossed a line, it was him.* She nodded as the twist in her stomach eased.

Nova opened the fridge. Eggs, leftovers, or chocolate pudding? She really needed to get groceries, especially with a whole-ass man living with her now. She grabbed a pudding and shut the door. Nova got a spoon from the dish drainer and made her way to the counter where her laptop lay. She dug into her sugary breakfast and signed in.

"What's this?" She eyed the open document. She'd never installed this software. She eyed the stack of endless paperwork to her side, but it wasn't exactly how she'd left it in a haphazard pile. It was organized and separated with paperclips into categories.

"Who would . . .?" *No . . . would he?* Had Jude done this?

Jesus, did the man ever sleep?

She downed the rest of her pudding, scanning through the document. Everything was in there, organized better than she could have ever dreamed of doing herself.

"See? I am an excellent judge of character." She smiled and slid off the stool, tossing her garbage away and leaving the spoon in the formerly empty sink.

The man even did dishes. *I might just need to keep him.*

Whoa. She needed to slow down.

I'm not keeping any man. Ever.

Nova checked her watch. She needed to leave now to make it to the yoga studio in time.

She pulled out her phone and texted Everett, making sure he was still coming, and slid it back into her pocket. She walked to the door and slid on her Doc Martens, leaving them untied, doing her mental checklist. She took the knife her brother had gifted her and slid it inside the boot before she opened the door and stepped outside.

Warm sunshine greeted her with a tease of dew still clinging to the air. She inhaled the fresh scent, tipping her face towards the heavens. The floral scent of flowers wrapped around her with a hint of . . . coffee? Her eyes snapped open and she turned. Jude was stretched out in her Adirondack chair, eyes focused on a pad of paper, with a pencil in his hand and a cup of coffee on the armrest.

"You're awake."

"What gave it away?" he answered sarcastically, not even looking up from the page.

"Even grumpier in the morning, I see." She walked up to him.

His arm tensed, the pencil stopping on the page.

"Can I see?" she asked.

He flipped the book over. "It's private."

"Sorry, of course." Her toe dragged along the wooden slats of the porch. "Well, um, tonight my family is having their weekly get-together. It's an outdoor movie night by the barn. Do you want to come? It's something the kids can watch, so it's probably that new Marvel movie that just came out."

A beat of silence passed, and he still didn't look at her.

"You don't have to."

"Would your real boyfriend go?" He scratched under the braided cordage bracelet on his wrist.

She snorted. "My ex hardly ever showed up for family functions . . . I can say we have other plans if you want a night off."

"No. Let's do it. What time?"

"Starts at sundown. We can take my truck down to the barn. Are you sure? You don't have t—"

"I'll be there. That was our deal, right?"

"Right." She wasn't sure why his response disappointed her, and she sure as hell wasn't going to examine it further. "Did you organize all that paperwork on the counter?"

"You need to hire a bookkeeper when I leave."

"That's what they keep telling me," she said under her breath. "So you did all that? And that program? How'd you do that without my password?"

A puff of air left his nose like a quiet snort. "You should have picked something harder than *stoner* as your password if you didn't want people getting access."

She narrowed her eyes. "Most people respect personal privacy."

"Well, it needed to be done. The program I downloaded is easy to use, and if you ever run into trouble, the help desk is open twenty-four seven."

"I was seriously dreading that task. You really didn't have to do it, but thank you."

He shrugged. "I am an employee of the farm. I saw a task that needed to be completed, and I did it."

His words pierced her bubble of joy, creating another degree of separation between them.

"Right. Be sure to add those hours on your time sheet." She eyed her truck. "I'm gonna be gone for a couple hours. I'm meeting my sisters-in-law and Everett at the yoga studio in town before I run some errands. I noticed we're low on groceries. Text me a list of what you want to eat and I'll pick it up."

"I don't have your number."

"Oh, right." She handed him her phone. "Just add yours in here and text yourself so you'll have my number too."

He tapped the screen, entering his information, and handed it back to her. Her hand slid against his, that same tingle of energy dancing up her fingers. Jude pulled his palm away, and grabbed his cup of coffee.

"Right, well, I'll see you later." She turned and walked to her truck, peeking in her rearview mirror one last time.

She expected Jude's head to be focused on his book, but his eyes met hers in the reflection. Maybe he wasn't as unaffected by her as he liked to portray.

She shifted the truck into drive and headed towards town.

* * *

Nova walked into the yoga studio. Sage-green walls made the space seem earthy and welcoming. She walked up to the reception desk at the front and greeted her smiling cousin. "Hey, Mia."

"Hi." Mia smiled as a cute little girl poked her head out from behind the desk.

"Auntie Nova!"

"Hello, munchkin, are you Mama's big helper today?" Nova bent closer to the little girl and gave her a hug.

"Yes!"

Mia laughed, smiling at her daughter. "She is until Papi comes. He's just stopping by the café to pick me up a lavender scone and coffee with Matteo. Then we're going to head out for a fun family day at the beach."

"Oh, that sounds fun. Collect some shells for me."

"I will," her niece said.

"Are they back there?" Nova asked Mia.

"Yeah, class started like ten minutes ago. You got your mat?"

"Shoot. I forgot in my hurry out the door." Nova slapped her forehead.

"I got you covered." Mia pulled out a rolled yoga mat from behind the desk and handed it over.

"Thank you. You're a lifesaver."

"You're welcome."

Nova skirted around them, finding her way to the large classroom with the giant sea-glass-stained window. The colors danced across the wood floor with the sunlight shining through in a rainbow of gorgeous reflections.

She found her friends and laid her mat between Elise and Everett. Isabella peeked up from the other side of Elise and gave her a welcoming smile. A few other students stood half bent on mats around the room. The instructor was leading them through a forward fold.

Nova quickly got into pose.

"I wasn't sure you were gonna show up," Everett whispered.

"Sorry. I got held up."

"I hope that's code for you got laid this morning. It's about time you got a happy ending." Elise snickered.

The yoga instructor paused her directions.

Nova looked up in time to see her give her a warning look. Nova mouthed, *"Sorry."*

"Save the good stuff for after class. I can't hear you from so far away and I want the juicy details," Isabella whisper-yelled, earning herself a pointed look from the instructor.

"Now let's move to a sitting position. Cross your legs like this," the teacher instructed, modeling their next pose.

Nova moved to sitting, but her phone cut into her ass cheek. She pulled it out and set it on the mat beside her.

She breathed and followed the class for a few minutes before Everett leaned over and whispered, "Will you be my best maid of honor for the wedding?"

Nova turned to him, a huge smile on her face. "Yes!"

A throat cleared. *Shit.* The instructor was glaring at her now.

"Yes, I will. That's such an honor."

"We can talk more after class." He winked.

A few minutes later, she was in warrior pose when her phone dinged.

"All phones should be on silent for the duration of the class," the teacher announced.

Nova rolled her eyes and shifted to grab her phone but Everett held it. "It's your dad."

Why would her dad text her? He never texted. The man called or talked to her in person only, no matter how hard she'd tried to convert him to messages.

She took the phone back, switching it to vibration.

> Daddy: Stuff for salad. Milk. Cheese. Bread.
> Steak. Burger. Potatoes. Pasta.

The list went on.

Wait a minute. Her face flushed. This was not her father. This was Jude! He'd put himself in her phone as Daddy? She smiled and shook her head. Point one for the sailor. He wanted to pretend he could handle any nickname she came at him with. Ha! This was going to be fun.

"What is it?" Elise asked.

Nova closed her phone and put it screen facing down on the floor.

"Nothing."

"Then why do you have that mischievous look in your eye like you're about to do something you might regret?"

"I don't."

Isabella leaned forward. "You kinda do."

Nova sighed and turned to Everett.

"Don't look at me for support. You and I still need to have

a conversation about your new *boyfriend*." He narrowed his eyes.

"So much for a bestie having my back," she grumbled.

She focused on the instructor, moving through the poses and stretching her body. Yoga was one of her favorite ways to exercise. It built her core strength, helped her improve her balance, and made her more flexible, which came in handy for fun sexy times.

"Thanks so much for joining my class today. Namaste," the teacher said with a smile as they finished.

"Well?" Elise asked, reaching for her water bottle on the floor by her mat.

"Well what?" Nova asked.

"Why did you look like you were up to no good?"

"I'm just thinking of what kind of shenanigans we can get up to for Everett's bachelor party. Since I'm the best maid of honor, I get to plan it, right?" Nova asked.

She didn't like stretching the truth with her family or friends. But she'd dug herself into a hole. Not to mention she'd dragged Jude into this. If her family found out and got mad at him, Jude would be back to living in his car without a job. She didn't want that—not when she could help him. SEALs made good money, so the fact that he was homeless now meant something bigger was going on. He'd saved her ass in more ways than one. She owed him. This had also gotten her mom off her case and stopped Renita from trying to set Nova up at every turn.

But I certainly hadn't counted on this getting so complicated.

"There won't be anything crazy. The last thing I need is for shit to go down before the wedding. We've been through enough drama," Everett ran a hand through his hair.

"Aww, don't worry. It won't be anything too crazy. Just fun," Nova assured him.

"Don't trust her," Elise added. "She invited strippers to mine and my mother was there."

"Your mom had a blast. She asked me to run out and get her more dollar bills," Nova argued back.

"Do you know how mortifying that was?" Elise's pale skin flushed pink.

"At least she didn't convince you to hire a male stripper to show up at your future husband's bachelor party," Isabella said.

"Hearing about it later was priceless," Nova said.

Isabella smiled. "It was pretty funny. And now we know why Ricky freaked out." She looked at Everett.

Everett chuckled. "I think we might just do a joint bachelor party at the Queen in Concord. It has a lot of meaning for us. And our friends live nearby."

"Oh, the gay club? That has potential." Nova tapped her lip, letting her ideas run wild. Glitter and shots and drag queens—oh, the fun they could have!

"Don't even think about it." Everett pointed his finger at her. "You stick to wedding planning only."

"Geesh! You're no fun." Nova pouted.

"How's things going with Bailey?" Elise asked Everett, but Nova's attention caught on the gorgeous stained-glass window again. The sun glinted through the sea glass, shifting the colors onto the floor. It was so pretty. *I wonder if Jude likes yoga?* He seemed to be more of the gym type, like Ricky. Maybe he and Ricky could go together sometime. Jude seemed like he could use a friend.

Wait, what? I'm not supposed to be helping him get more attached here. So instead, she focused on how she could get Jude riled up again. Because that man might like to seem like he was calm, cool, and collected, devoid of emotion, but she'd pushed his buttons Monday. It was like a high, getting Mr. Stoic to respond. The little devil on her shoulder wanted to see just how far she could push him before he snapped. What would Jude look like if she pushed him to the edge? What would Jude look like when he really let go?

Fuck. The idea of him naked, coming above her—

Maybe a little fun with her fake boyfriend was just what they both needed. He'd move on, and they'd both be on the same page. No hearts would get broken. Just some good sex between roommates. He didn't seem like the kind of person who got attached. And that was perfect, as far as she was concerned.

Time to kick this up a notch.

13

JUDE

Later that night, Jude glanced at the orange glow highlighting the dark blue mountains in the distance, soaking in the last rays of the sun that had set minutes ago. This place was really beautiful. He'd had the privilege of traveling around the world. And each place had its own form of beauty, whether it was in the desert, the mountains, the jungle, or even small country towns. But there was something different about Shattered Cove. It felt welcoming, almost like home—not that he'd ever known one. Jude imagined this is what it would feel like.

What the fuck am I saying? He was there for one reason and then he was leaving.

Nova stumbled over nothing before righting herself. The woman seemed to trip on air.

"I could have carried that blanket too," he offered as they continued down the hill towards the event barn.

"Psh! I got it. Your hands are full with the basket."

"I have two hands."

"So you do. Congratulations," Nova said sarcastically.

"One's free to smack your behind for being a smart-ass," he clipped.

Her cheeks flushed. Fuck, he loved getting a reaction out of her. Especially when her eyes blazed with challenge like they did now, promising she wouldn't give in easily. Why was it so hard to stay focused on his objective with Nova around? He'd completed missions that required ultimate discipline and self-control. *But for some reason, I can't stop myself from flirting with this woman.*

"When you look at me like that, Freckles, it gives me all kinds of ideas."

Her gaze widened and then darted to the grass in front of her as they made their way towards the family's barn.

"You know what I think?" She stopped, turning to him with her family only yards away, just out of hearing distance as she leaned in.

"What's that?"

"I think you're all talk." She winked and sauntered away towards the back of her truck already parked in line with her brothers'.

He shook his head and smirked. She was playing with fire and it was only a matter of *when*, not *if*, she'd get burned.

Jude carried the basket over to her truck and set it on the tailgate. She bent over, giving him a wonderful view of her heart-shaped ass. Nova spread the blanket over a foam mattress pad that covered the whole space with a few colorful fluffy pillows already in place. A string of battery-powered lights twisted around the truck bed, giving enough light to see the chairs spread out facing the barn wall. A young teen boy, Eli, from what Jude remembered, sat in a chair beside a little girl huddled over a book with a flashlight. A toddler walked unbalanced, picking blades of grass and attempting to put them in her mouth, but her father, Nash, was right behind her, taking them and shaking his head, making funny faces so she'd laugh. His wife, Isabella, sat on the tailgate, watching them with an amused smile. Renita and James sat in a solid pair of Adirondack chairs like the ones on Nova's porch, having a drink and sharing a bowl of popcorn.

"Okay, who's ready for the movie?" Everett asked clapping his hands together.

"ME!" Eli and Ariel yelled together.

"Play it, Ricky," Elise added.

"Alright. Here we go," Ricky said from behind the projector.

"You afraid I'll bite?" Nova asked, drawing his attention back to her.

She was under the blanket, leaning her back against the cab of the truck bed.

He pushed the basket closer to her as he climbed in to join her. "Not in the slightest. Just make sure when you do, you leave marks, because I sure will." He flashed her his teeth as he sat next to her.

She smiled and shook her head. "Promises, promises."

Boy, she was lucky he had so much self-control. If she was his submissive, he'd whisper a threat in her ear he'd promise to make good on and tease her under the blanket with her whole family around. But that would lead to complications he couldn't afford.

"Keep pushing, Freckles."

She opened her mouth as if she were about to say something but the projection lit up against the white screen on the side of the barn and the movie started playing.

"Can I sit with you?" Bailey, the teen girl Ricky and his fiancé, Everett, were fostering, asked.

"Of course you can." Nova patted the opposite side of the truck bed to the one Jude was on.

Bailey cast him a quick glance and climbed in as the opening credits rolled. "Thanks. I think Everett and Ricky need some time alone."

"Are they insufferable as always with their inability to keep their hands off each other?" Nova laughed.

Bailey giggled. "Yeah. And you have the best snacks."

"I sure do. Jude, pass me the basket, please, sweetie-pie?" She gave him a shit-eating grin.

She was going to be in so much trouble for that.

He handed her the basket.

She opened it and pulled out drinks and every kind of snack imaginable, offering Jude his pick. But he shook his head.

She shrugged and dove into a bag of Cheetos.

"Anyone here need popcorn?" Elise asked.

"Yes, please," Bailey said.

Elise handed a big bowl to Jude. He passed it to the women next to him.

"Here. You might need this to make it through your first Emerson movie night." Roman handed him a beer.

"Thanks."

Roman nodded and slipped his arm around Elise as they made their way back to their seats.

The sky was completely dark. The only light came from the string LEDs and the movie. Subtitles lined the bottom of the screen. Crickets chirped in the background, melding with the sounds of explosions from the superhero movie. The scent of buttery popcorn and good beer wafted up around him.

They'd been the last to arrive; everyone had already been set up. Had Nova done that on purpose to cut down on conversation time? Or was she just late to everything? The woman seemed to have limited sense of time.

Nova pulled out her vape pen, taking a few hits before offering him one. He shook his head and she tucked it away.

Bailey and she shared the popcorn, stuffing themselves with that and candy, the Cheetos forgotten.

The movie droned on in the background. Jude hardly paid attention. Instead, he studied the people around him. They laughed together and talked intermittently through the movie. Eli flapped his hands when he got excited and spoke in a monotone voice, interrupting the movie every now and then. No one batted an eye or yelled at him to stop. This whole family just seemed . . . accepting. Welcoming. Was this what a real home felt like? There was that word again.

Nova shifted, pushing her snacks aside, rubbing her arms. The temp had dropped and a cool breeze blew in. Bailey pulled on a hoodie that had been tied around her waist and snuggled into Nova. Jude slid under the blanket so he could pull it up enough to cover her arms.

She still rubbed her arms and shivered. He shucked off his own hoodie and slid it over her head.

"What the—"

"I believe 'thank you' is what you're looking for," he whispered.

She slipped her short arms through the holes and her head poked out. She was drowning in his clothes but she looked so fucking cute. Like a little angry kitten with blunt claws. Harmless and adorable.

"Won't you be cold?" she asked.

"I'm hot-blooded. But thanks for caring."

Her nose wrinkled in the light of the movie but her mouth curved into a smile. "Thanks. But next time warn me when you cover my head with material. Jesus, I thought I was being kidnapped for a minute."

"In a truck between two people, surrounded by family. You

thought a kidnapper would what? Climb over the front of your car, put a cloth over your head, and drag you out from between us without anyone noticing?"

"I didn't say it was logical," she grumbled, snuggling into his side. It was his turn to be surprised. "Put your arm around me, *boyfriend*." She enunciated the word as if to make it clear this was for show only.

He obliged. The warm softness of her body pressed against his sent a rush of rightness barreling through him. Fuck, this wasn't good.

He looked around them. Renita's attention flicked to Nova every now and then. Her brother Ricky stared daggers at him.

Her brothers were protective of her . . . but would they kill for her?

Nova's warm hand slid over his cheek, turning his attention to her.

"Don't let him worry you. He's just an overprotective asshole sometimes."

He nodded and her hand fell away. He missed the contact instantly. What the hell was this woman? A witch? Normally, Jude didn't like to be touched by people, even barely by his submissives. And he definitely didn't cuddle. Just one more reason to get what he'd come for and get the hell out of Dodge. Nova was too easy to care about. Her rough, spiky edges only made him want to know more, to find out who had made her put her guard up so high.

But if Jude had learned anything in his thirty-four years of life, it was that caring for someone was dangerous. It made him weak. And he'd failed everyone he'd ever cared about. That was how he'd gotten himself into the whole mess he was in now. That was why he was there, pretending to be his mark's boyfriend. He'd failed the only woman he'd loved on this planet, and all he was left with was the possibility of revenge and the small hope that it wasn't too late.

Nova's eyes blinked slowly and soon they didn't open at all. She'd fallen asleep against his shoulder, tucked into his body like she was his to care for, like she felt safe with him—a monster. A man who'd committed horrible acts in the name of justice and honor.

The credits rolled and Bailey slipped out of the covers and climbed out of the truck, but Jude stayed there, not wanting to move and wake Nova. He wasn't ready for this feeling of being part of something bigger than himself to be over. Not wanting this fleeting moment to end and reality to come crashing back in.

"She never makes it to the end of the movie," James said, placing his arm on the edge of the truck and smiling over at his adopted daughter.

Where was Jude's mind at? He hadn't even heard the man approach. Christ, he needed to get his head into the game.

"Usually I just bundle her up and close the tailgate. She'll sleep here until morning. But I'll leave that to you tonight. I don't think she should be left alone anyhow with everything going on." James leveled his eyes on Jude, a silent warning in them, and a challenge, too, to keep his precious daughter safe.

"I promise to watch over her."

"Good man." James nodded and patted Jude's shoulder before turning and helping everyone pick up the food and supplies from the movie. In about fifteen minutes, the family was done, leaving for their respective homes on the property— except Ricky. He walked over, his jaw tight. Jude braced himself.

Ricky's eyes dropped to his sister and his expression softened. "I know you're her made-up boyfriend."

That was not expected. Jude remained quiet as Ricky

looked him over as if assessing. "My sister can be impulsive, but she usually has good judgment of character. So I'm gonna trust her opinion of you."

"But?" Jude asked. He knew one was coming.

"If you harm a hair on her head, I will tear you apart, SEAL or not."

Jude nodded, his respect for the man racketing up a notch. *If only I'd been that protective before.* "Understood."

Ricky gave one last glance to his sister and then turned away and left in the same direction Everett and Bailey had walked.

Jude exhaled and adjusted to help Nova lie down properly. She moaned in her sleep, turning towards him and curling up in his arms so that her head was on his chest under his chin, clinging to him like a spider monkey.

He chuckled quietly. She'd be mortified if she was awake. Jude stared up at the millions of stars twinkling in the sky. It was so much easier to see them out here in the country. Reminded him of the desert.

No. He didn't want to think of that. He wanted one night of reprieve from the ghosts that haunted him.

Jude rubbed Nova's back in what he hoped were soothing circles and held her close. He inhaled the top of her head. The faint aroma of cannabis clung to her, but it smelled good mixed with her spicy amber scent. His eyes drooped farther closed with each inhale. He'd never held a woman like this— at least not since—no. He didn't want to go there either.

Jude opened his eyes, studying Nova's face under the dim string lights. Freckles splattered across her cheekbones and nose like the constellations in the sky above them. He gently traced each one, connecting them, and played a game of pretend like he'd done so many nights of his life under the stars, wishing for something better than the hellhole he was in.

Her eyelashes fluttered as she let out the cutest little mewl. She appeared so much more innocent when she was asleep. Gone was the spitfire he knew during the day—left behind was this vulnerable curvy woman who called to his body in all the right ways. *If only I was a better man.*

He traced the dots one more time. One freckle was larger with so many tiny ones to the side, just like a shooting star. If he hadn't given up on wishes and become so jaded, he might take it as a sign.

So instead, he closed his eyes and held Nova close, pretending that he'd found that peace and happiness he'd searched for his whole life—the illusive happily ever after he'd only ever read in story books that he'd read aloud to *her*.

Just for tonight, he'd let himself believe he was worthy of it all—worthy of a woman like Nova. Because tomorrow, the sun would rise, and with it the reality that he was in way over his head on his quest for the truth.

14

NOVA

Birds chirped loudly as Nova stirred awake. *Goddamnit they're loud this morning.* She shivered and snuggled deeper into the blankets. *Did I leave a window open?* Her bed was cozy and warm, especially on one side. She inhaled. *Yummy.* Her blankets smelled like—

Nova's eyes shot open. *Holy shit.* She was snuggled up to Jude. She froze, hoping she didn't wake him. She was clinging to him, with one arm over his torso, her thigh brushing against his hard erection.

The impulse to move her knee just the tiniest bit shot through her. She closed her eyes and forced a breath out. *Don't do it. He's sleeping. I'd practically be molesting him.*

They hadn't quite crossed a physical boundary yet . . . well, before the full night of snuggling. But if they were unconscious, did it count?

She opened her eyes once more and took the time to really look at him up close. He had a scar on his upper lip; it stood out along his perpetual five o'clock shadow. His chest rose and fell evenly as she tilted her head carefully to get a better view. He was handsome, no doubt about it. But he was also rough around the edges and had a hardness to him that gave Nova the feeling he'd been through his fair share in life. Maybe it was his military experience? Maybe it was something that had happened before? But that wasn't all there was to Jude. Usually the hardest shells covered the softest center. It was the guys who seemed too good to be true that were.

Jude's Adam's apple bobbed before his mouth parted.

"Done lookin' your fill yet?" His eyes blinked open, and he stared straight at her.

She tensed. He'd been awake this whole time?

Embarrassment soaked through her every cell as she pulled away, sitting up and brushing the mass of curls from her face. They probably were a mess without her silk bonnet.

"Sorry. I just . . . you looked so peaceful." She rubbed her arms, still covered in his hoodie that smelled like him—delicious. She wanted to pull it up to her nose and take another deep inhale, but that would only make this awkward situation even weirder.

She needed to change the subject and get his attention off of her. "I guess we both fell asleep during the movie."

"Your dad mentioned it happens every time."

She chuckled. "Not every time . . ."

He arched an eyebrow at her.

"Okay, fine. Usually, yes. But it looks like I wasn't the only one." She motioned to him. "You fell asleep too—why else would you still be here?"

Had he stayed for her?

Jude's attention flicked to the truck bed. He nodded. "Yeah."

Nova's stomach took that time to rumble like she hadn't eaten in days. But really it was the fact that she'd eaten so close to bedtime. That always made her ravenous in the morning for some reason.

"Looks like it's time for breakfast." She shoved the covers off and climbed out of the truck, looping around the driver's side door.

Jude swung onto the ground, landing on his feet before he rubbed the back of his neck and stared towards the woods.

"You coming?" she asked.

Jude shook his head. "Just to get changed real quick. I promised your dad I'd help with the tractor stuck in the field. And then I got a busy day preparing for the market tomorrow."

"Oh, okay. Well, you need some water and food to take with you."

"Worried about me, Freckles?"

She put both her hands on her hips. "So what if I am?"

He looked straight at her—through her. "I'd tell you not to waste your time."

Jude's words felt like a sledgehammer knocking her chest. Before she could respond, he jogged away towards her home, not even bothering to wait for her.

And here she'd been hoping they could fuck all this sexual tension out of their systems. Despite his flirting last night, it seemed he didn't even want to share breakfast with her, never mind eat her out.

She exhaled and climbed in her truck, starting it up as she stared in her rearview mirror at his back. As soon as her mom saw his empty hands, she'd hand him a gallon of water and a wrapped sandwich to go after forcing whatever breakfast she'd made for Dad down his throat. So Nova shouldn't worry, but his words stuck with her all day as she checked on her plants, watering and trimming where she needed. Bailey came over after school to hang out. They made homemade pizza. She made an extra big one for Jude with lots of bacon. But he never showed. Jude had gone for his usual run, come home and showered, and left without a word. But that was hours ago. Bailey headed home and Nova was once again alone in her empty house.

The sun was just about set. Her dad was no doubt home from his full day on the farm.

Where is Jude?

Jude's words played over and over in her head. She blew out a breath. There was no use in worrying over someone who'd made it clear he didn't want her to. And since when did Nova care about a man other than how long he could keep his dick hard?

She let out a frustrated growl. "Don't let him get to you, Nova. He's probably like all the rest. You know better." *Mama always said when a man told you who he was, believe him.*

It was probably because she was dick starved and he was sex on a stick, sending her libido into overdrive. She needed a few orgasms to get herself under control. Looked like some solo time was in order.

She jogged up the steps to her bedroom. Nova quickly changed into a bikini and slipped a pair of nipple clamps underneath, careful of her piercings. She went to the back porch, uncovered the hot tub, and placed her supplies on the table beside it with a drink.

The scalding water felt good after a long day of work. She lit her joint and inhaled, filling her lungs before letting her breath out. The plume of smoke rose towards the darkening sky. She sighed, relaxing into one of the seats within the hot tub as the water bubbled around her. Something was missing —music!

Nova turned towards the Bluetooth speaker on the side

table, turning it on to something sexy. "When You Say my Name" by Chandler Leighton—perfect.

Nova settled into the hot tub, wiggling her feet back and forth, taking hits while the water swirled and lulled her into a relaxed buzz. Tingles traveled from her forehead down her neck and spine, gathering in her center. The lights were off in the house, so when Jude got back, he'd have to turn one on and alert her to his presence. She hadn't turned any on for the porch either except for the ones in the hot tub, giving it a red glow. The only other light was the remnants of the sunset, turning the sky purple streaked with indigo.

She nodded to the beat of the song, letting her hand wander to her breast and cupped it through her bikini top. She finished her joint and set what was left in the ashtray beside her. She tipped her head back, closing her eyes as her other hand slipped under the water, moving her bottoms aside.

She swirled her finger around her clit and gasped. She was so ready. So needy.

Filthy slut's already dripping for me.

She moaned at the imaginary voice in her head. It was deep and decadent—Jude's voice.

If she couldn't have the real thing, a fantasy would have to suffice.

He'd walk over and demand she spread her legs.

Show me what's mine.

Arousal shot through her. Her legs closed tighter in response. She wouldn't give in so easily. The resistance was half the fun. He'd have to work for her submission. Earn it.

What did I tell you, Freckles? Fuck, even fantasy Jude used that stupid nickname. So why did it turn her on more?

His big, rough hands would pry her knees apart, pinning her down as she tried to wiggle around on the bed. But he'd be stronger than she was. He'd press her face into the mattress and pull down her bottoms.

Nova's hand untied the sides of her bikini and let it float in the water.

Jude would grind his hips into hers, pressing her to the bed. His hard, ready cock would line up with her slick wetness, and he'd tease her.

Her fingers dipped into her folds, circling her clit, making her toes curl and bringing her to the brink of pleasure. Decadent warm tendrils of restrained bliss unfurled, stretching out to her limbs. Sweat dotted her brow as she slid two fingers inside.

Think you can resist me? Stop trying to hide what a sexy whore you are. Keep your legs open for Daddy.

"Oh God!" Nova's eyes flew open as her orgasm crested and screeched to a halt.

She gasped.

Jude stared at her through the open sliding door, his eyes heated in the reflection of the red tub.

"Don't stop on my account." His voice was pure gravel and, if she wasn't mistaken, need.

"W-what?" she asked, despite her fingers still being inside her. Embarrassment burned her cheeks, but she was still so fucking turned on. She'd edged herself and the focus of her fantasy was standing in front of her, watching—demanding she continue. She would have thought her weed had been laced with something causing her to hallucinate if she hadn't grown and rolled it herself.

Jude stepped forward out of the shadows and into the rising moonlight. His aura was dark and intense like the man commanded the very air around him, stealing up all the oxygen.

"I said, keep going."

Oh, fuck. Nova bit her lip, holding back a moan.

"You were watching me?"

"You're out here in the open. Not like I snuck in your room like a Peeping Tom."

"Still—"

"Don't tell me you're embarrassed." He smirked. Damn, that devilish half-smile only made him hotter. "Not with your fingers still inside you."

"I'm not ashamed. Almost everyone does it. It's natural," she huffed.

"It's sexy as fuck."

Wait, what? Her chest heaved. He liked what he saw?

"Come on, Freckles. Finish what you started."

"This wasn't a part of the agreement." Reason tried to move to the forefront. This . . . this was crossing a line. Changing things between them. But who the fuck could resist an opportunity like this?

"Maybe we should amend that."

Her eyes widened in surprise. Could she do this? A no-attachment fling with her fake boyfriend? She'd never had trouble falling too far in the past . . .

A small warning blared in the back of her mind, but it was muddled with the weed and her building desire.

"What do you want?" she asked.

"I want to see you finish what you started. Play with that pussy until you come like a good girl."

If he thought she'd back down—he was wrong. Was he testing her? She swirled her fingers around her clit, reaching behind her neck to untie her bikini.

Her top dropped into the water, revealing the glint of her silver nipple piercings and the chain linking the clamps.

His eyes dragged down her chest, flames of desire reflecting in their depth. She felt so powerful having all his attention like this. Would she call his bluff or did he really want to see her play with herself?

She palmed a breast and slid a third finger inside her. Nova's mouth dropped open as she arched her back. A moan escaped.

"Fuck," Jude cursed, moving even closer. If he reached out, he could touch her. She locked eyes with him, fucking herself with her hand.

He wanted this—looked like he needed it. And she wanted to give it to him.

"That's it. Fuck yourself, but spread your legs and move your top so I can get a better view."

She moaned, holding her legs still despite her instinct to obey. It took all her self-control.

A low rumble came from his chest as he leaned in, gripping her chin and forcing her to look at him.

"Don't be a brat. Be a good little whore and spread your legs."

Her eyes rolled up as her legs opened, and she shoved her top away. How the fuck did he know just what to say?

"Good fucking girl."

Pleasure exploded through her every cell as she preened from his praise. Her back arched in response to the building pleasure. She was a ticking time bomb, riding the edge of her orgasm, waiting for the finale.

"Look at those tits, bouncing as you fuck yourself. So beautiful. I fucking knew you'd be pierced." Jude's words only added fuel to the wildfire raging within her. She was going to come soon, despite wanting to make the moment last.

"Play with them," he ordered.

She tugged at the metal chain. A pinch radiated pain through her nipples. She cried out, slamming her eyes closed at the mix of pain and pleasure. She was *so* close. Her toes curled. Every cell was alive and attuned to Jude's voice and searing gaze, raking over her body. Her head was floaty and relaxed, each sensation enhanced thanks to the weed. His hand slipped down to her neck, applying firm pressure to both sides.

"Open your eyes, baby girl."

She obeyed. Desperation crashed into her. Sparks and shimmers danced across her vision at his show of control. This was the dominance she craved and had gone without for so damn long.

"Now, fuck yourself harder and come for Daddy."

"Ohhhh fuck!" Nova screamed as her orgasm exploded through her, shattered her from the inside out. Ecstasy blasted through every nerve ending, building and building like an avalanche of pleasure until it eventually receded.

She blinked as Jude came back into focus. Aftershocks rippled through her as she removed her fingers and brushed her thumb over her clit. She unclipped her nipple clamps with a hiss.

She wanted to ride him until the sun came up. Wrap her lips around his cock. Let him fuck her until she lost her voice from screaming.

Nova reached for Jude but he backed away, shaking his head.

Her brows drew together in confusion. *Does he not want to get in the hot tub?*

She rose to her feet naked, before she stepped out, dripping over the floor.

His eyes seared down her flesh like a hot iron. Did he like what he saw? She wasn't small in any sense of the word besides her height. Nova had a round stomach and thick thighs, dimpled with cellulite. It wasn't everyone's cup of tea, but it was her body and she embraced it.

Jude seemed to be into it . . . but now, with his hesitation, doubts crept into her mind.

He reached towards her. Hope, buoyant and warm, filled her belly. But it popped like a water balloon when he picked up the towel beside the table and handed it to her.

"What's this for?" she asked.

"Towels are usually used to dry off with and maybe cover up."

Cover up!

Nova ground her teeth, humiliation burning her skin. She yanked the towel from his grip and threw it at his head. It hit her target but her victory was overshadowed by the reality that he could have stopped it if he'd wanted to. Which meant he'd let her hit him. He wouldn't look her in the eyes, instead staring at the puddle she was making on the floor. Was this a game to him? Was this just him teasing her to one-up her?

"You're an asshole." She stormed off naked into the house, leaving a trail of water behind her. Tears burned her eyes, but she wouldn't let him see that he'd gotten to her.

Besides, what did she have to cry about really? She'd gotten the best orgasm of her life. So she was the real winner here.

Nova nodded and slammed her door shut. Now, the game was on. Jude King would pay dearly for humiliating her. She was going to make him regret it.

15

JUDE

I'm such a fucking idiot. Jude beat himself up for the thousandth time since the night before. Things between him and Nova were not supposed to get this . . . complex. He needed information and that required a degree of perceived closeness, but last night he'd almost crossed a line he could never uncross. Fuck, it had taken everything in him not to reach into that hot tub and feel what it was like when she came on his fingers. His jaw was sore from how hard he'd bitten down, forcing himself to hold back. Like an idiot, he'd hurt her, handing her that towel. He'd used every last bit of self-control he could muster to do it. But the glare she'd leveled at him was proof enough Nova hadn't taken it the way he'd intended. *I was only trying to protect both of us.*

Jude carried a crate of fresh-grown veggies he'd picked from the farm gardens that morning and set them on the table the Emersons had at the Dark Cove farmer's market. Nova moved to the opposite side of the table under their pop-up gazebo that shaded them from the sun. She straightened signs and smiled at a potential customer who waved as they walked by.

It was early in the day. A lot of vendors were still in the process of setting up, but a few people were already milling about in the park with light chatter and birdsong accompanying them. A light breeze blew through, offering respite from the early morning sun on the beautiful summer day along with the shade of the trees lining the walkway to a water fountain at the center of the park.

A few minutes later, vegetables were exchanged for cash and she was back to avoiding looking at him and keeping herself busy anywhere he wasn't.

Something dug under his skin at the knowledge that he'd hurt her. He hadn't meant to. But she'd been so tempting with her head thrown back, cheeks and chest flushed from her impending orgasm. And the way she'd responded to his commands—fuck, she'd been a dream.

I'm not here to start something with this woman—I'm here to find answers. But his slip last night could have cost him. She was never going to open up to him now. That was probably why he was so unsteady today. It had to be. Jude just needed to stick to the plan. The problem was, the more time he spent with Nova, the more it seemed his initial judgments had been wrong about her—and her family. Maybe he should just leave and join Reaper and his team. But then all this would have been a waste. Guilt crashed over him. *Hang on, Sal. I'm coming for you.* And the quickest way was through Nova.

"I'm gonna go grab some breakfast from the bakery stand. Do you want anything particular?" Jude asked, hoping a white flag of cinnamon buns could dig him out of this mess and earn him a place back in her good graces.

Nova tipped her chin, glaring at him before giving Jude her back.

"Just gonna give me the silent treatment now, Freckles?"

She whirled around. "Don't—" She looked at the few heads that had turned after her outburst. She seemed to force a smile and then stepped closer to him, jabbing her finger at his chest as she whisper-yelled, "Don't fucking call me that!"

There was that fire he loved so much.

Wait. Love was a strong word choice. It was one of the things that he *liked* about Nova. She didn't back down from a challenge, just like him. She made a worthy adversary.

He smirked, capturing her finger in his. He pulled it down, tracing her palm with his other hand.

She tugged her arm but he held fast.

"I enjoyed the show last night." The only way to get past her fire was through it. He had to respect her for the fact that she didn't just brush things off. He liked her fight.

"You have some nerve," she said through gritted teeth.

He took a deep breath. What could he say to that except agree? "I'm sorry." His voice came out full of gravel over the phrase that so rarely left his mouth.

Nova's eyes flared like she hadn't expected an apology either before her gaze narrowed, causing the little wrinkles in her nose to appear. "You didn't have to make fun of me."

Surprise shot through him and then confusion. "What do you mean?"

She exhaled and pulled her hand back, and he let her this time. She tucked a curl behind her ear, straightening a few honey jars that didn't need it.

"Nova?" he pressed.

"Just drop it, okay? We can pretend it never happened."

He stepped up behind her, wrapping his hand around the back of her neck and gently turning her to face him. She fought it for a minute and then looked up, resolve in her expression.

"Why did you think I was making fun of you?"

She rolled her eyes. His cock twitched. He was only human, and this little curvy woman played his body like a goddamned fiddle and she didn't even know it—lucky for him.

"You said we needed to amend our arrangement. And then . . ." Her cheeks took on a pink shade. "You know. And then you rejected me while I was standing there naked, offering to return the favor."

Something unbidden lashed inside of him at the thought that all they would share between them was an exchange of favors. He was far too preoccupied to ask himself why. He shoved that uncomfortable feeling away as understanding sunk in. She'd felt rejected by him—thought he didn't want her.

"It's not a big deal. You're not into me like that. Good to know. It will make the rest of our time together easier with that out of the way." She brushed him off.

Jude froze. He was angry at himself for making her feel like less. Confused as to why he cared so much how she felt when he hadn't with any other woman before. He wasn't a complete asshole—he usually let them know what he was there for and what he wasn't. Jude was supposed to be finding answers and instead he was getting wrapped up in Nova. He didn't have time for that.

"Hey, Nova," a beefy man with a slick smile and a collared red shirt called from across the folding table of farm goods.

Jude glanced at Nova on instinct. Her eyes widened with a flash of panic before she gave him a smile that didn't reach her eyes. Was she afraid of this guy?

"Hey, Chad."

Chad gave Jude a once-over before seeming to dismiss Jude with a sniff. He picked up a zucchini like he was there to buy vegetables, but it was Nova who he eyed like a piece of meat.

"I saw you the other week at the crossroads in town. I tried to get your attention, but you floored it," Chad said.

"Yeah, I was late for something." Nova's voice rose, a confirmed tell she was lying.

Jude studied the man from his rich-boy haircut slicked neatly with gel to his too tight button-up, down to his leather Sperrys. The few diamonds on Chad's gold watch glinted in the sunlight as he tossed the vegetable from one hand to the other. There was something about the guy that set Jude's teeth on edge and sent his instincts to instant dislike and suspicion. The feeling wasn't exactly tangible or explainable—more like a reading of energy. Jude wasn't into that woo-woo shit, but when you'd grown up around enough dangerous people, you learned to recognize threats, and trust your instincts. And this fucker was giving off slimy and dangerous vibes. The way he looked at Nova like she was a toy he wanted, and not in the fun consensual way . . . this man thought he had some form of claim over her.

Jude's hand wrapped around Nova's shoulders, and he tucked her closer against him. Despite being mid-argument before Chad's appearance, Nova went willingly, telling Jude his asshole radar was on point. Jude ignored the rush of contentment that spiked with her arm sliding around his waist in return.

That got Chad's attention. The cocky man focused back on Jude as if finally seeing him as a threat.

"Well, anyhow, I thought I'd find you here. I was out on the yacht for the market in Shattered Cove on Sunday." Chad droned on about his time at sea while Nova kept a smile plastered on. It was probably his daddy's boat. Jude knew the type of guy and Chad screamed *overcompensating*. Where was her attitude with this guy? Why wasn't she telling him to shut the fuck up? At the very least she should roll her eyes. *Does she like him?*

Something sour burned in his gut. Was Chad Nova's type? Jude was nothing like the overgrown frat boy in front of him.

Or maybe she doesn't give him attitude because she doesn't feel safe with him.

The realization was like a punch to his stomach.

"You should come next ti—"

"How did you know she would be here?" Jude interrupted Chad.

The man's smug smile faded just a little. A pulse of victory thrummed through Jude's body.

"Because we have a . . . history." Chad smirked. "Who are you?"

"I'm the boyfriend."

Chad's pale skin tinged red as his attention snapped to Nova, anger flashing in his blue eyes.

"Chad, this is Jude. Jude this is a . . . friend from high school," Nova introduced them.

Chad's jaw pulsed, anger lighting up his gaze. "How long have you two been dating?"

"Did you see the tomatoes? They're super ripe and great for sandwiches." Nova picked up a fat red tomato and held it out to Chad.

Chad shook his head and put the zucchini down. "Nah, I'm good."

"Then maybe you should move on if you're not buying anything," Jude suggested.

Chad glared at him.

Nova dug her nails into his side.

Jude let his hand wander up Nova's arm as he bent down to kiss the top of her head before he pulled her closer into him. "We were just about to get breakfast, weren't we, baby girl?"

"Uh, yeah," Nova squeaked. "But if Chad wants to buy something—"

"You know I love your honey." Chad's smug grin was back, but he looked at Jude when he said it, the double meaning waving in the air like a red flag in front of a bull.

"It's actually her brother's honey," Jude said. For some reason there was a lot more bass in his voice than usual.

Chad scowled. "I think I'll come back some other time when you're not so busy, Nov."

Jude's teeth ground at the casual use of a nickname. Like Chad knew her as far more than a *friend*.

It shouldn't matter. She's not mine. Despite the reminder, everything in Jude's body tensed as he stared Chad down.

Chad waved to Nova with a wink and walked away.

"What was that about? You just lost us a customer." Nova shook her head as she moved further from him once more.

"Does he show up where you are often?" Jude asked.

"What? Why?"

"Answer the question."

"You can't just scare away our customers and then demand things from me. I'm the boss here," she huffed.

"Does he *coincidently* show up often, Nova? Answer the damn question."

She stomped her foot and crossed her arms over her chest. "What do you care?"

"You have a killer after you. What if it's him?"

Her eyes widened and then her brows drew down. "Chad? No. He might be a dick, but he's not smart enough to pull something like that off. And he didn't know any of the women. He might have met Anastasia, because she lived in Shattered Cove, but no one else."

The man still didn't sit right with Jude.

"Look, never in my 'please pretend to be my boyfriend' agreement did I say you needed to act like the jealous partner." She pulled out the lettuce from a crate as more people walked by. A small line of people filtered from one vendor to another. Acoustic guitar music started from the gazebo in the not too far distance.

"I wasn't acting jealous."

She laughed. "Then why were you touching me so much and giving him the 'back the fuck off' energy? You think with three brothers I don't know a pissing contest when I see one?"

Jude stepped into her space, unable to hold back any longer. His voice came out as a growl. "As far as anyone knows, you're *my* girlfriend for all intents and purposes for however long this arrangement lasts. I don't take kindly to other men making a move or flirting with what's mine in front of me or otherwise. And I especially don't like rich boys overcompensating for tiny dicks insinuating they know a whole lot more about my girlfriend than her favorite subject in high school."

Nova stared up at him as if in pure confusion that morphed to shock. He was so close to her face he could smell her breath laced with the fruity scent of gummy bears from what she passed off as "breakfast."

She searched his eyes, suspicion in those light brown spheres. "Why are you still acting jealous, then? No one's around for you to fool."

"I'm only fooling myself." Jude's control snapped. The idea of another man having a shot with Nova before he'd even gotten a taste was too much to handle. He didn't wait for her to come up on tiptoes. He gripped the back of her head, sliding his hands through her curls, and pulled her forward.

Jude bent low enough to capture her mouth with his, and

he wasn't gentle. He cupped her ass as he lifted her against his hips, leaving no room for doubt that at least in this moment she was his. Her legs wrapped around him as she gasped. He took advantage of her open mouth, sliding his tongue inside, stealing her taste. God, she could kiss. Pillow-soft lips melded with his with none of the hesitancy he'd expected. Nova kissed like she lived—reckless, free, and so damn playful. He matched her intensity as longing slammed through him. She nipped at his bottom lip, biting him hard enough to leave a mark. Lust exploded inside him. His cock turned to steel in his jeans, wedged against her tiny shorts. This kiss was pure black magic. His little witch must have put a spell on him because everything fell away except the beat of her heart against his. The taste of her on his tongue. The little sounds she made as he ground his cock against her. *Mine.*

"Yo, there are kids present!" someone yelled, finally snapping Jude out of the kiss. He pulled back, staring at Nova. Her brown skin was flushed with what he hoped was the same arousal that was thrumming through his veins. The skin around her puffy lips was reddened, no doubt by his scratchy beard. Her glazed amber eyes blinked hazily before she shook her head. She looked over his shoulder as if remembering where they were, like she too had forgotten. Nova slid down to her feet and cleared her throat.

His lip still stung where she'd bitten him. Jude gave a genuine smile for the first time in a long time. He'd have that little reminder with him for the rest of the day.

Christ. What am I doing? He was losing sight of his whole mission. He couldn't afford that. But Nova was so tempting in a way he'd never encountered before.

Jude ran a hand over his face and blew out a breath. This had just gotten way more complicated.

I'm so fucked.

16

NOVA

He kissed me. He picked my ass up and manhandled me and —that kiss. Holy shit. Her panties were damp just thinking about it as she sliced spicy Italian sausage at her kitchen counter. All she'd done since yesterday morning was replay that kiss in her head like a record stuck on repeat. Jude King had kissed her and then . . . avoided her the rest of the day. She wouldn't have thought that was possible, working the farmer's market together, but she'd underestimated his drive apparently. He'd stuck to one-word replies and gone to his room as soon as they'd returned home. Then this morning, he'd left before she woke. She'd spotted him coming out of the barn this afternoon, but he'd headed towards the fields away from her.

Was she that bad of a kisser? Their chemistry was off the charts. There was no way he hadn't felt that. His cock had been hard as steel against her shorts. *You can't fake that.* Or the fear she'd caught a glimpse of after he'd released her.

What was holding him back? She'd made it clear she was a willing participant. So why all this hot and cold? What was he scared of? Nova tossed the sausages into the cast-iron skillet. They sizzled in the oil.

Maybe he liked toying with her emotions? No. He didn't seem the type. But what did she really know about Jude? He was alone with no family. He was homeless, living in his car despite being just out of the Navy. No one was homeless by choice. Had he gambled away his money? Did he have mental health problems?

She pulled out her phone and searched reasons why a veteran would be homeless. She blinked at the statistic on the page.

"There were thirty-three thousand homeless veterans in America last year." Reading it aloud didn't make it any easier to believe. Thirty-three thousand people who'd risked their lives fighting for the United States were without a home. That meant these people were going hungry and cold, left out to face the elements and all sorts of abuse on the streets.

She scanned the page once more. "Twenty veterans commit suicide every day in America."

She tucked the phone in her pocket as she blew out a breath. Nova stirred the sausages. Maybe Jude was dealing with his own struggles and didn't want to let anyone close enough to see. Nova could understand that. She'd thrown him into this stressful game of make-believe, and they barely knew each other. She hadn't once taken into account his situation.

"Sometimes you can be really selfish, Nova," she chastised herself and dropped some salt into a pot of water for pasta.

The front door opened and closed. She turned around as Jude walked in with socked feet. He must have left his boots outside so as not to track in stuff from the farm. *That was thoughtful.* He veered straight for the stairs.

"Hey, dinner's almost ready."

Jude hesitated on the first step, his dirt-streaked hand resting on the banister. "I need a shower."

"I'll—"

Jude raced up the stairs.

"Wait for you, then," Nova finished in the silence of the kitchen and shook her head.

A timer went off. She grabbed the oven mitts and slipped them on before opening the oven and pulling out the cookies.

She inhaled the sweet scent of melted chocolate and delicious brown sugar cookie base. Was there anything better than that scent? Her mouth watered.

Jude smells pretty good too.

She laughed at herself and shook her head, placing the cookies on the cooling rack. Those were for her customers, but she couldn't help but make an extra few for later. What was better than pot brownies? Weed cookies with her own infused butter.

Something on the stove hissed. She turned, having forgotten for a moment she was cooking. The water for the pasta bubbled over the edge of the pot. She turned down the gas stove, removing a little of the water before she added the dried pasta and then set another timer.

She finished making dinner, yet there was no sign of Jude. The water wasn't flowing through the pipes, but he still wasn't down. She poured herself a glass of iced tea and took a sip. Should she plate their food? It might get cold before he came down. She was going to wait. She didn't like this awkwardness between them. She wasn't one for confrontation, but Nova also wanted to make sure she wasn't taking advantage of him. After what she'd read, it made her want to give him the benefit of the doubt. Maybe he was suffering from trauma of some kind.

Nova tapped her fingers on the table for a full minute

before reaching for her phone. *I should check in with Amanda and Carrie. Make sure they're still alive.* Nova shook her head as if it would erase the dark humor. *I'm such an asshole.*

She clicked the message thread with Carrie first and reread the last few messages. Since the other girls had started disappearing, Nova had begun checking in with the girls that she used to live with. She'd found the other women and let them know what was happening.

> Nova: Hey! Just checking in. Any updates?

> Carrie: No.

> Nova: How do I know this is really Carrie? Blink twice if you need help.

Carrie sent a picture of a hand giving the middle finger with blue chipped nail polish.

Nova chuckled again. Would the other women hate her for what she'd done? Would they blame her for this psycho? Dread settled into her shoulders, dragging them down.

> Carrie: Still alive, sorry to disappoint. Any updates?

> Nova: No. Sorry.

Nova swallowed. *Sorry for fucking up everything.* But she wouldn't send that.

Carrie gave her message a thumbs-up. She kept their convos short and to the point. Not one for chitchat. Amanda on the other hand . . .

Nova glanced at the stairs. Still no sign of Jude. She clicked Amanda's messages and ran over the last one her friend had sent.

> Amanda: So, anything new with you? Maybe we should catch up sometime? I'd love to get together and talk. We might help each other remember something that could help the investigation.

"Shit." Nova clicked to reply. She'd sworn she had, but apparently she'd forgotten . . . again.

> Nova: I'm really sorry. I thought I replied but never did! Just wanted to check in and see if you were doing okay? Or if you had any updates?

Nova set her phone down and glanced at the stairs once again, tapping her fingers on the table impatiently.

Ding!

Nova clicked on the new message.

> Amanda: I'm okay. A little lonely without my boyfriend here. Staying busy at work. Any chance you want to have coffee sometime?

Nova clicked to reply but hesitated. Maybe they should meet in real life. Everything in Nova's body tensed at the thought, her stomach doing summersaults. Was she really ready to face the women from her past? *What if they blame me? But what if something happens? Would I forgive myself for not meeting up with them?*

> Nova: I'll let you know when I'm free!

That should buy her a little time. She switched to her reading app and pulled up the dark romance she was halfway through. Nova took one more lingering glance at the stairs and then focused on her book.

* * *

An hour later, Jude came down the stairs. His cheek pulsed as his gaze landed on her and then his attention shifted to the empty plate in front of her and the one in front of an empty seat. "You waited for me?"

"Should I not have?"

"We're not really dating, Nova." His voice had an edge to it.

She nodded, smiling despite the hurt his words caused.

"I haven't forgotten. But you're technically a guest and it's polite to wait for your guests before you eat." She stood, grabbing the two empty plates off the table.

She handed one to him and went to the stove, piling pasta Alfredo on her plate and spicy Italian sausages with shiitake mushrooms and broccoli before sliding it into the microwave to reheat.

"Don't wait up next time. And you don't have to cook for me."

She shrugged. He was obviously trying to push her away, and she could relate to that. *I'm not going to take it personal.*

"You cook for me too, so I thought it only fair. I was home and you were still working, so it made sense. You can cook tomorrow if it helps your pride."

She pulled her food out with still a few seconds to go and grabbed a fork, setting herself up at the table.

"It has nothing to do with my pride." He set his food in and punched the numbers into the microwave harder than he needed.

"Then quit acting like a pouting toddler." She stuffed the first bite of food in her mouth. Fuck, it was hot. She took a sip of her drink to cool her mouth off.

"Watch it," he snapped, setting his plate down across from her, his big hand engulfing the fork.

Despite his grumpy demeanor, his eyes sparked when she argued with him and pushed his buttons. She smirked. This is what he needed to distract him from whatever had crawled up his ass.

"Or what? Will you ignore me some more? Huh? Oooh, scary. I'm shaking in my boots over here."

He shook his head, his fork scraping over the plate as he dug in.

She covered her ears and winced. "Ugh! Don't make that noise."

The corner of his mouth briefly curved up as he chewed and swallowed. "Does it bother you?" The bastard did it again.

She narrowed her eyes at him and pointed her fork. "I'm warning you, buddy. Do it one more time and you *will* regret it. Just ask Ricky what happens when someone fucks with me."

A short-lived chuckle rumbled from his chest as he shook his head. His eyes flared and lines appeared in the center of his forehead, like he was as surprised as she was that he'd laughed.

"Wouldn't want to risk it." He took another bite.

"Smart man."

"They don't let idiots into the SEALs," he retorted.

She smiled. "There he is."

His eyebrows rose in question.

"It's nice to have you back after you went radio silent yesterday."

His expression grew somber as he focused on his food again.

Nova reached out, pressing her hand over his across the

small table. He didn't move—he just stared at their connection.

"I won't get all clingy and attached if that's what you're worried about. And I hope you know there is no pressure to do anything at all. You can stay as long as you want and work as long as you care to for my family's farm. It would be nice to find a common ground so we don't have to tiptoe around one another."

A beat of silence passed.

She sighed and pulled her hand back, then picked up her fork and dug in for another bite.

They ate in the quiet for a few minutes.

Jude cleared his throat and looked straight at her, his voice low, so full of hesitancy and vulnerability. "I'll try to not be so much of an asshole."

She couldn't hold back the beaming smile that no doubt lit her face. "Good. So, truce? We're friends?"

A puff of air left his nose, and another half-chuckle. "You don't want to be friends with me, Freckles."

"Why?"

"Because my friends tend to . . ." He stopped, his mouth slamming shut. "Never mind."

She didn't push despite the urge to ask. How could you leave someone hanging like that? She pretended like his vague comment wasn't wreaking havoc with her curiosity. She'd went to bed wanting revenge, but a little sleep had helped her gain some perspective. She didn't really know Jude. He was doing her a big favor. Maybe she just needed to forget anything sexual and focus on befriending him. Tonight was progress and they needed that. *Look at me, acting all grown up.*

"Well, I'll be your fake friend while we're fake dating. How about that?" she teased.

He shook his head, with a sly tilt of his mouth. The urge

to crawl into his lap and kiss it rose. She knew what he tasted like. What that scratchy beard felt like across her skin. Fuck, it would feel even better on her thighs. Her body flushed hot with arousal.

She stuffed one more bite of food in her mouth and got up abruptly before she ruined their fragile truce by doing something impulsive.

Two wins for me today in a row. She was on a roll.

Nova excused herself and headed upstairs. There was only so much a girl could do before a sausage joke made it out of her mouth. With the way he'd reacted after the kiss, asking him to suck his dick probably wasn't going to help their situation.

She needed a little solo time in the shower.

"Goodnight." She waved, running up the stairs like her ass was on fire when in truth it was so much worse—it was her whole goddamned body. She burned for this man.

Hopefully, when all was said and done, she wouldn't end up as a pile of ash.

17

JUDE

J ude rinsed his plate and Nova's before slipping them in the dishwasher. He closed it and leaned against the counter, crossing his arms over his chest as he stared at her kitchen. Snarky quotes on fridge magnets had made him shake his head when he'd first seen them. She had a few knickknacks spread on shelves. Colorful rocks graced every window and shelf, some dustier than others. A bundle of some sort of herbs, half-burned, rested on a colorful shell. Jude moved across the kitchen, not able to resist the cookies cooling on the rack and helped himself to two.

They melted in his mouth, gooey and delicious. Fuck, she could bake. He groaned aloud. Damn it. Guilt pressed on his shoulders. He'd been a dumbass for avoiding her. As if hiding would help him not have to face his real problems. Jude was losing hope by the day. He'd always been good at following his commander's orders. The expectations were clear. But now, with so much on the line, he was lost and unmoored. He couldn't find stable ground. It was like he was free-falling down a dark pit. Nova's face flashed in his mind's eye as he swallowed down the second cookie. Kissing her had been the one moment he'd felt like he was exactly where he should be. And that was dangerous. He couldn't afford to get sidetracked. He'd been a mess all day, searching every inch of the farm that he hadn't gotten to in the last week. His answers were not out there. Not up on the hill where they'd discovered Anastasia's body. Not in Nova's basement, where he'd thought he might find a scrap of something resembling a clue.

He grabbed another cookie, taking a bite as he walked into the living room. He stopped by her bookshelf, scanning the titles once more. Murder mystery, horror, botany, romance, psychology, and true crime. She had a little of everything. That made sense. She seemed like the kind to get bored easily with the same thing.

Nova had somehow pulled him out of his funk today. It was clear his actions had hurt her, but rather than lashing out, she'd done the opposite. She'd cooked for him. She'd baked. And then what she'd said at dinner—she was too good for him. Too innocent for the darkness he'd brought.

But she's my only hope for redemption.

He was using her and he hated it. Now that he'd gotten a peek of who she really was, he questioned everything. Jude shook his head and walked up the stairs.

Light spilled out into the hallway from Nova's cracked door. The sound of the shower running came from the en suite bathroom inside.

He turned to go back to his room, but she made a noise. It sounded like a grunt. His ears perked up as he turned to her bedroom.

"Nova?" he asked, pushing her door open a little more so he could peer in.

Her scent assaulted him. Amber and honey. Sweet and musky. He was drowning in it. His cock surged with blood. His pants grew tighter. Clothes were strewn over the floor. A basket of unfolded laundry sat in a chair beside her unmade bed. The drawer beside her mattress was cracked open.

He shouldn't be in here. But that didn't stop him. Jude didn't need to walk over to see what was inside—he'd already done a full recon of the entire place. That was where she kept her sex toys, condoms, lube, and other fun things. Which meant—

A moan came from the shower.

Fuck me.

Against his better judgement, his feet carried him towards her open bathroom door as steam spilled through it. Now he could hear the low buzz of whatever toy she'd brought in with her.

"Fuck, yes, Daddy. Give it to me harder." Her voice came out breathy and soaked in need.

Jude pressed a hand over his cock, trying to get himself under control. He'd never reacted like this—at least not since he was a horny teenager. His touch only made it worse.

Scorching desire lit his veins on fire. He slid his hand down his sweatpants, palming his cock.

A soft moan filtered to him along with a repetitive squelching wet sound.

Jude closed his eyes, grinding his teeth as hard as he could. Was she using the sparkly blue dildo with her vibrating toy? The image of her bent down in the shower, fucking herself on the dildo suctioned to the wall while she held another toy to her clit was painted in vivid colors in his mind. His skin tingled from his skull down his spine. Everything started growing fuzzy. He squeezed his dick hard, hoping the pain would calm his raging hard-on. But it only made it worse.

"Just like that. Deeper. You feel so fucking good."

Fuck, her mouth was dirty.

Would she keep going if he walked in? She had last time. Would she open that sassy mouth so he could fill it while she fucked herself on the toy?

Jude bit back his groan, drawing blood from his cheek. He swallowed down the iron tang as he lost the battle with self-control. His hand defied him and tugged on his dick.

His eyes rolled up, sparks and shimmers appearing in his vision.

"Oh—oh—" Nova gasped.

Jude jacked himself off quicker, thrusting into his hand, unable to stop himself as he pictured her taking his cock, crying out for him. That pretty brown skin tinged with copper. Her damp curls, stuck to her face as he fucked her.

He grunted as hot cum exploded out of his cock. He gasped and fumbled back two steps before he got his balance, grasping the edge of the doorframe. Jude panted, the fog of lust clearing some. The shower shut off and he did an abrupt about-face, darting to his bedroom and shutting the door. He winced with the noise. He looked down at the wet spot in his pants.

"What the fuck has she done to me?"

He didn't come in his pants—ever.

Jude changed, yanking them off and rolling them into a ball, then placing them in his dirty laundry bag. He wiped off with a towel and slipped a fresh pair of pants on.

His heart fluttered in his chest as a bang came from Nova's room. He jumped. Something . . . wasn't right. His skin tingled hot and cold. He pulled his shirt off and tossed it on the bed.

His heart fluttered in his chest. What was going on? Anxiety rose, his pulse pumping faster and faster the stranger he felt. A wave of something heavy hit him. He lay down, like he couldn't fight it. His head swam. The room was spinning. *Something isn't right.*

He clutched his chest, the anxiety only making it worse. *Am I having a heart attack?*

He couldn't die. Not without finding answers. Not without redeeming himself.

Jude gasped in a breath, but it didn't feel like enough. Was there air in the room? He searched frantically around. He rolled out of bed, groaning as he fell on the floor. Why weren't his legs working? Why were his limbs slower than usual and tingling? He managed to open the window with fumbling hands and sucked in a lungful of the night air. The breeze felt good on his skin, caressing him, snaking up his flesh. But his mind and body were sluggish.

True fear reared his head as panic constricted Jude like a snake twisting him from the inside out. He'd been drugged somehow. How could someone have poisoned him? *Dinner. Nova.*

It seemed his instincts had been wrong all along. Nova was far more dangerous than he'd realized.

He'd fallen for her act like a total sucker. And now more than one person might die because of his weakness.

Jude reached for the bed and crawled back to it. He wouldn't go down without a fight. He—his mouth was dry as sandpaper. And his limbs felt as if he were moving through deep sand.

"The fuck did you do to me!" he yelled and rested his head on the bed, half on and half off.

The room spun, and his eyes felt so heavy.

But he wasn't going down like this. He couldn't.

Sal was counting on him.

18

NOVA

"The fuck did you do to me!"

The shout from down the hall drew Nova's attention. She quickly pulled a T-shirt from the basket of clean clothes by her bed over her head. She dashed out of the room, listening down the stairs. Had one of her brothers come over to start shit with Jude? Had someone broken in? She craned to hear more as a thump and a groan came from Jude's room. She walked over to his door and knocked.

He mumbled something that she couldn't make out.

"Jude? Are you okay?"

No response. She didn't want to barge in—that was his private space. But what if something was wrong?

And somehow my five-foot-nothing ass can handle it when a fucking SEAL can't? She shook her head and knocked again.

"Jude? Is everything okay?" she asked.

"Nothing is fucking okay," he grumbled. "My chest . . . I think I'm dying."

"I'm coming in." She opened the door. Jude was sprawled

out on the floor, his hand clutching his heart. His shirtless chest was on perfect display. She'd thought he was built before, but wow. Her mouth went dry. But something was off. His rib cage heaved far too quickly. Her attention darted to his half-closed eyes, his face strained. She rushed over to his side.

His panicked, glassy eyes met hers. "Whoa, you're faster than I'd thought."

That was an odd comment. "What's wrong with your chest?"

"I think I'm having a heart attack."

She scanned him as his chest heaved, reaching for her phone to dial the ambulance. Her gaze snagged on the crumbs on his beard.

Wait.

"I can't breathe."

Shit. The cookies! I forgot to tell him not to eat the cookies.

She smacked herself in the head. "Jude, does it hurt? Your heart, I mean?"

"No, but it's beating a fucking million miles a minute. And there's like a fluttering."

"Did you perchance eat any of the cookies I made downstairs?"

"Cookies . . . so good."

She breathed a sigh of relief. This was not a medical emergency. "How many cookies did you eat?"

His chest rose and fell as he rubbed it.

"Jude?" She touched the side of his face, pulling his attention to her. His bloodshot eyes hazily focused on her. "How many cookies did you eat?"

"Three."

"Shit."

"Did you poison me?" he asked.

She couldn't hold back the laugh. "Of course not. I would

never waste perfectly good chocolate chips by mixing it with poison—that's sacrilege."

"Something's wrong," he insisted. "I can't feel my arms or legs."

She moved closer, picking up his arm and wrapping it around herself. "You feel me touch you?"

"Yeah. It feels nice."

She rubbed his chest in soothing circles. "See? You can feel your body. You're okay. You're just really high right now. And it's literally impossible to die from too much weed. You might feel like you will, but it's not real."

"It's not?" he asked, and he sounded so vulnerable.

She snuggled into him, continuing her gentle and hopefully grounding caresses. "Not at all. Breathe with me."

She tilted her face towards his and inhaled through her nose, exhaling through her mouth.

He followed her, a bit delayed.

"That's it. Perfect. Now keep doing that."

"You smell really good."

She smiled. She'd felt really good too. Despite the release she'd found for herself in the shower, there was still an undercurrent of lust whenever she was near him. Touching him only stoked the fire. But this wasn't a time to dwell on that. Jude needed her comfort, and that was what he would get.

"You smell good too."

"What do I smell like?" he asked, settling against the side of the mattress.

"Like the deep woods and man."

"What does man smell like? Like body odor?"

She giggled. "No. Just . . . yummy. It's hard to explain."

"I feel heavy like I can't move, but light at the same time."

"That's normal with indica—at least, when you have a lot. Do you want to lie on the comfy bed?"

"Yeah."

She got up, extending a hand to him when he didn't budge.

"I don't think I can move."

"I'll help you." She slid her hand into his and pulled. Jude grunted with the effort and made it to his feet before collapsing in the bed, narrowly missing the side table.

"Careful." She turned off the light.

"The room is spinning."

"Oh, that's no fun. Just lie still." She climbed in next to him, returning to his side, curling up in his arm and rubbing his bare chest. He needed connection to help ground him and this was the best way. That was the only reason she was snuggled so close. Even if she happened to enjoy it, this was purely for his benefit . . . That was what she kept telling herself as she relaxed into his arms.

Minutes passed without him saying a word. His eyes drooped closed.

His breathing evened out, and she sighed in relief. Bad trips weren't any fun. She kicked herself for not warning him about the edibles. She'd meant to and then gotten distracted by her slick pussy and the aching need that he'd stirred up in her.

"I'm sorry I forgot to tell you about the cookies."

"Mmmm. Can I have another one?"

She chuckled. "Not tonight. You hungry?"

"For so many things."

"Let's wait a bit and make sure you're not gonna throw up before we get you snacks."

"You're no fun."

She smiled. "Someone has to be the one in charge since you're taking the night off."

"You shouldn't be sorry. I'm the one that has so much to atone for," he said quietly.

"Why?"

His eyes widened. "Can you read my mind now?"

She traced her finger down his forehead to the tip of his strong nose and tapped it. "No. You said that out loud, silly."

He blinked. "Oh."

He remained silent.

"Do you mean when you were in the military? Do you feel guilty about what you had to do?" she asked.

"I failed so many people. My brothers in arms. My—" His voice caught as he looked towards the blowing curtains.

"It's okay, Jude. You don't have to talk about it. But if you do ever want to, I can listen."

A light, cool breeze blew in from the window. She snuggled deeper into his warmth, laying her head on his chest.

"I've done some horrible things."

She didn't say anything, just gave him space to talk as she continued rubbing his chest, switching to his shoulder every now and then.

"I've killed a lot of people."

His confession sent a pit in her stomach. The violence he must have witnessed in the military—that he'd had to partake in. She closed her eyes, breathing in to calm her own anxiety. She hated that for him. That he had to live with that guilt.

"I failed everyone who counted on me."

"You haven't failed me." She tilted her face to look at him. She wanted desperately to give him something good to hold on to.

"Our past doesn't have to dictate our future. We can choose a different path here and now. You just ended your career in the military. Now you can start over. Begin a new life." *Like I did when I got to the Emersons.*

He pulled a wet curl, matted to the side of her face, and tucked it behind her ear. Nova couldn't hold back the shiver his touch elicited. She'd been fantasizing about the man only half an hour ago in the shower. And here he was, suffering because of her forgetfulness.

"You're so soft." His breath coasted over her lips.

"It's all the extra pudge. Makes for a good cushion," she joked.

"You're perfect."

Surprise flared within her.

"I'm far from perfect, believe me." The darkness of her past weighed on her, overshadowing her happiness at his compliment.

"Don't know about that."

"It's the weed talking, trust me." She smiled despite the pit in her stomach.

"You're the first woman I've let touch me like this since . . . since I can remember."

"What?" She froze. "You . . . you don't like to be touched?"

"Not usually more than necessary."

"That . . . must be really lonely."

When he didn't say anything to disagree with her, she asked, "What about . . . I mean, surely you haven't been celibate all this time?"

"No," he answered.

A bite of jealousy lashed out inside her, but she quickly stuffed it down. She had no right to feel that way. She'd had her fair share of partners too.

"So how does that work?"

"I don't sleep with anyone."

She rolled her eyes. "Sex requires some level of touch."

"You can have sex with a partner and not let them touch you. That way I'm in control."

"Ahhh." She smiled. "You like control. Could have fooled me."

"You're teasing."

"Yes."

"Stop it," he said, but his usual seriousness was gone.

"Why?"

"Because I like it too much."

Her grin widened. "Well, now I'm really not going to stop."

"You should."

"What fun would that be?"

"It's not about fun. It's about . . ."

"Jude?"

"You deserve better than me, Nova."

"If you think that, then you really don't know me at all," she admitted.

He gently pinched her chin between his fingers and turned her to look at him again. "I'll only hurt you."

"Maybe I like the hurt," she said, searching his eyes for his reaction. "Maybe I need the punishment."

He shook his head slightly, his eyes dipping to her mouth.

She had to convince him he was wrong. "I—"

"Stop," he said, his lips teasing hers as he spoke. They were so close.

"Why?"

"Because—"

"Jude—"

His hand slid to her throat, pressing against the sides of it as he rolled over on top of her, pinning her to the bed. His eyes flashed with something dark and unhinged. Icy tendrils of fear snaked inside her, dipping low into her belly and turning into arousal.

"Because I fucking want that too, Freckles. I want to push you until you snap and then strip you down until you're nothing but *mine.*"

She gasped as he continued, unrelenting.

"Until you bend for me—breathe for only me. Until you're a writhing, beautiful mess, begging me for relief. Begging me for mercy. And then, only when I've truly gotten to the very marrow of who you are and set you free, would I take my time and mold you back together. Only after I've made you cry. After I've bruised and marked your lush body. After I've truly taken everything you have to give will I revel in the mess I've made."

She squeezed her thighs together, attempting to quell the new ache that bloomed within her.

"Only then, after you've shown me every piece of you that you keep hidden from everyone else, when I've exposed those truths to light, will I be satisfied."

She inhaled a shaky breath. It was like he was inside her head. Like he knew exactly what she wanted—what she needed.

Nova confessed her long-held secret: "I crave it."

He blinked slowly at her.

She continued, "Someone I can trust enough to strip me of all my control, make me submit. To give me pain that makes my teeth ache and my body sore in all the best ways. To dominate me and break me apart and then put me back together better than I was before."

But it also scared the living shit out of her because she'd only ever let one person get that close to her, to have that kind of control over her—her ex-fiancé. And when you let someone in that close with the power to destroy you, that was exactly what ended up happening.

"The question is, Jude, will you be there to pick up the pieces when you're done?"

Hesitation flickered in his dark gaze as he hovered above her.

"I don't know," he confessed, sliding off her and lying back down on his side, facing her. They stayed like that, staring at one another. She wanted to know this man. Find out what the shadows were behind his eyes. Understand the weight he carried on his tired shoulders.

The fact that he made her care enough to want to try? That was what made him the most dangerous.

19

JUDE

Jude slipped from the heavy slumber into a haze, the space between dreaming and waking. He was warm, like he was bathing in sunlight. Jude took a deep breath, holding on to this sliver of peace.

His eyes shot open. Peace? He didn't normally wake up rested. Nightmares stalked him every night, waiting until he'd laid his head down to haunt him. There was never peace to be found.

Jude blinked at the brightness of the yellow walls, his eyes adjusting as his body tensed. A soft little snore came from the weight on his chest. Nova's mass of curls tangled in his fingers, like he'd held on to her all night. Like she'd tethered him, and kept the ghosts of his past at bay.

Despite the fact that she was in his arms, questions swirled in his mind now that he was no longer high. The cookies had been laced with cannabis. She'd slipped something under his nose and made him feel so out of control. Had she planned it? He ran over the events of the night before. His memory was still hazy, but they'd talked. Had she been looking for information? *If she was, could I blame her? Aren't I doing the same thing?*

Despite the conflict going on in his mind, his body was able to gather enough sense to move out from under her, gripping her wrists and sliding on top of her.

Nova's eyes lazily blinked open, a red spot appearing on her cheek from where she'd been lying on his bare chest. Her curls mussed and fanned across the pillow, making him wish he was on top of her for an entirely different reason.

She gave him a small smile and tried to pull her wrist free, but he held on. She frowned. Those wrinkles he'd come to look forward to in her pert little nose appeared. "What—"

"I'm asking the questions," he said, his voice calm and even.

She studied him as if trying to make out if this were a game or not. Her pupils dilated. She liked this.

Someone I can trust enough to strip me of all my control, make me submit.

Her words came back to him. Fuck, he couldn't think of that now. The feel of her softness pinned beneath him with his morning wood didn't help.

"What did you do to me?" The question had a double meaning.

"Oh, you don't remember?" she asked, innocently.

"Tell me again. Did you drug me on purpose?"

She opened her mouth but he let go of one wrist to grasp her chin. "Don't lie to me, Nova. I want the truth."

"I wasn't going to lie. Geesh. You're less of a morning person than I am, huh? Need a cup of coffee before you interact with people?"

"Nova," he warned.

She rolled her eyes as if she didn't fear him at all. He should have been disappointed. People stayed away from him for a reason, and it worked in his favor. But Nova didn't give a shit. She bulldozed over the barbed wire and steel walls.

"I made a batch of cannabis cookies and I forgot to tell you not to eat them. I also didn't think you'd just help yourself to them." She winced. "Sorry. I know you don't like to partake. And you said you ate three, which is a lot, especially for a newbie."

He lingered another moment, searching her eyes for any trace of a lie, a twist of the truth. But he found none. He rolled off her and sat on the edge of the bed, rubbing a hand over his face.

"You stayed." It wasn't a question.

"You thought you were having a heart attack and then I realized what happened and just tried to comfort you. You were scared."

"I wasn't scared!"

A pillow smacked against the back of his head. "Were too."

He turned as Nova crawled over the bed to sit next to him. She pulled his hand into hers. He resisted, but she only tugged harder.

Giving in, Jude sighed. What was with this woman, and what kind of power did she hold over him?

The truth was he'd been terrified last night. And she'd taken care of him. Her touch had grounded him. That was why he didn't partake—the loss of control he'd feared.

He'd opened up and shared pieces of himself he'd never wanted to confess. That made him vulnerable. That gave her even more power. He didn't like the imbalance. It was as if he were free-falling, not knowing which way was up or down. A big part of him wanted to dive into the comfort she offered even for a night. Nova had a way about her—it drew him in like a moth to flame. But fire and fragile wings didn't mix. The romantic notion was more a warning of what would come if you opened up to those feelings—death. Destruction. He'd be left nothing but ash. And he couldn't afford to self-destruct right now. He had someone counting on him—at least he hoped she still was.

"Thank you." The gratitude stumbled out of his mouth, untried as a newborn foal.

"It's the least I could do after my mistake put you in that position. And everything you've done for me. I wouldn't have left you like that."

He closed his eyes. Guilt rushed over him, threatening to consume him. She was too good for the likes of him. She deserved to know the truth.

"I said some things last night . . ." He let her fill in the gaps.

"You have nothing to be embarrassed about. I won't share what you said with anyone. And it's really nothing to be ashamed of—"

"Nothing to be ashamed of? Nova, I told you I get off on hurting people." His focus snapped to hers.

She gave a shrug. "It only makes you a monster if you get off on hurting people who don't want to be hurt. Who don't consent to it."

He stared at her in silence, drinking in her words.

She licked her lips. "Why are you so determined to believe yourself a bad person?"

"Because I am. Make no mistake, Nova, I am not a man who will find himself entry to St. Peter's gates. I've done . . ." Flashes of blood on his hands, of his fallen brothers' mutilated bodies covered in grit and sand flashed in his mind. To *her*, eyes filled with betrayal and tears.

Nova's fingers slipped through his and squeezed, yanking him back to the present—a lifeline in his inner chaos.

"I'm not like you, Nova. No part of me is good."

She blew out a breath, eyes dropping to her black, chipped nails. "My ex, Brooks, was my first and only Dom. He was . . ." She tipped her head back, staring out the window, her eyes glassy as if she was far off in her memories. "He was my everything. I fell hard and fast. He showed me all these new and exciting things. We went to a few BDSM clubs and play parties. He made me feel on top of the world when I had his attention, which was when I was the obedient submissive he wanted. And I had no one to talk about it in real life to. No one would understand us. That was what he told me when I tried a few times."

The idea of her so connected to another man brought a sour burn to Jude's stomach.

"I lost myself in our dynamic. I thought my needs and boundaries didn't matter. And he assured me that by not having them, by letting him dictate what I ate, what I wore, who I hung out with . . . how my body was used and who used it." Nova curled in on herself, crossing her arms over her chest. "That made me a good submissive even if I didn't want that myself because he knew what was best for me and I just needed to trust him."

Jude's hand clenched in anger. That was not what a Dominant believed. Brooks was a predator. Submissives were the ones who drew the boundary lines and a Dominant made sure to color inside them. A good Dom had their submissive's best interests at heart.

"That's not how it's supposed to work." Jude's voice scraped from his throat.

A small, sad smile curved up the corner of Nova's mouth as she looked at him. "I know that now. And the fact that you do too proves you're a good guy."

He looked away, unable to hold her trusting gaze while she continued.

"What I regret most is that I didn't say something sooner, that I didn't stand up for myself. I'd let him strip me of all my self-worth. I was nothing but a slave to his whims. A toy he could control. And no one in my life knew. I was utterly alone." Her jaw tensed. "Then he died while he was deployed."

"He was in the military?" The comments her family made suddenly made sense.

She nodded. "And the day of his funeral, I met a woman I didn't know. The man I was going to marry had a whole other life while he was away on his *'trainings.'*"

He gritted his teeth.

"She had his collar on, just like the one I was wearing." Her voice came out a whisper.

A collar in the BDSM community was a big deal. Many believed it more a commitment than even marriage. His chest squeezed. The betrayal Nova must have felt.

"Luckily, my brother had some tools in his truck. Ricky didn't ask me any questions—just helped me get it off. I threw it in his grave." She laughed but there was no humor in it. "That's not even the kicker. I'd just found out I was pregnant the week before the funeral."

Her words were like a sucker punch to his gut. The immense situation she'd been put in was heart-wrenching.

"I was trying to figure out how I was going to raise a whole-ass child while I was just trying to pick up the pieces of who I was. Who I'd lost. He'd taken over so much of my life I didn't even know how to exist without him." Tears shone in her eyes.

Jude squeezed her hand. "You don't need to tell me this."

She nodded. "I do. I need to finish it. I've never told

anyone this. And you showed a piece of yourself to me last night. I know that makes you feel unbalanced. Maybe knowing this part of me will help you not feel so alone."

And just like that, she'd stolen the very air in his lungs. Everything he thought he knew about Nova, all his intel that made him question her motives was gone. This woman was genuine. She'd been through hell, been victimized, and yet she was strong enough to take back everything that had been stolen. She was a warrior—a survivor. *Just like Sal.*

Jude wrapped his arms around her, pulling her onto his lap and cupping her face as he stared into her teary eyes. Even now she was fighting, trying not to let those tears fall. He wished he was worth it—and he could be. He'd be a better man for her. And he'd start, right now. He might not have done right by Sal but he could for Nova.

"I'm listening," he encouraged her.

"I couldn't be a mother. Not when my life was falling apart. Not when I would look at the child and see the man who'd cut me so deeply. And I know what it's like growing up with your father's shadow." Something dark rose in her watery gaze. A glimpse of old bone-deep pain erupted and her face contorted before she shook her head and closed her eyes. A few beats passed before she opened them again, only a shadow of her hurt still lingering. "I couldn't do that. I'm not as strong as my mother—biological or adoptive."

She'd never mentioned her biological mother. And there hadn't been much in her file on her either besides the fact that Cynthia Addo was deceased. He should press for more, find out the information that could help him—but this was about Nova. She needed him to listen. If he took advantage of her now, was he really any better than her ex?

"Do you regret your choice?" he asked, carefully.

She blinked, a lightness coming to her eyes. "No. I don't . .

. I've never wanted to have children of my own. That isn't my path in life. And I know what it's like to grow up in the system. I mean, I saw a short stint of it, but that was . . ." She swallowed, staring off into space like memories were playing through her mind. She winced. "Bad enough. I would never have put a child there. Some might think me selfish, but it was my decision and it was the best choice for me. I don't regret it."

"I'm proud of you."

"Why?"

"Because despite that predator doing everything he could to break you down, you rose from the ashes. You took back control of your life. You're so much stronger than you realize."

She sniffed, twin tears finally breaking through. "I was betrayed by the man who'd promised me forever. By the man I gave everything to. And I still feel broken. Like I can't connect with anyone like that again . . . but you . . . you wake up a part of me I'd thought long since buried. You remind me of all the good that comes from letting go and being in that dynamic. It wasn't all bad—not in the beginning. You make me want to try again, and that scares the shit out of me."

"Me too. Me fucking too." He wiped her tears away, leaning his forehead to hers. "Thank you for telling me this. For this gift of knowing you."

"We all have things we're ashamed of in our past, Jude. But we can choose differently every day. It's not too late for you to walk another path too."

He wanted to believe it. She gave him that courage—that warm hope that bubbled inside him.

I should tell her. Ask her what I need to know. Nova would understand.

Would she though? She'd just told him how betrayed she'd been by a man who'd promised her commitment of the highest order, both in life and their dynamic. If she found out why he'd come here and what his original plans were—she'd shut down. She'd push him away, and then he'd fail *her*.

"Such an optimist, Freckles."

She chuckled and swatted his chest playfully. He embraced her, and breathed in her scent from the crook of her neck.

"Whatever you say, Daddy." She giggled.

The use of the honorific tugged at something inside his chest. It was time his plans changed. Jude needed to find a way to tell her the truth. To show her he wasn't like Brooks. If it was just him on the line, he'd tell her now. But this was much bigger than both of them. And Jude had a mission to accomplish. There wasn't much room for feelings or getting soft. Not when everything hung in the balance—not when it was life or death.

20

NOVA

Nova dusted her hands off on her shorts, leaving dirt streaks behind. She stood, stretching her stiff back. Weeding was hard work, especially with the hot sun beating down on her. She wiped her sweaty forehead with her arm.

Musical tones from her phone sounded. She pulled her cell out. *Unknown caller.*

She clicked the answer button.

"Hello?"

A hum of background noise greeted her, but no one spoke.

"Hello?"

Still no answer. Nova's skin pricked as her gaze wandered to the woods on her side. She ended the call and put her phone back in her pocket. *Probably a wrong number.*

"Here. Drink this." The deep voice came out of nowhere.

She jumped, clutching her racing heart. "Jesus! Do you have to sneak up on me like that?"

She whirled around, her mouth instantly dry. Jude stood, bare chested. His smooth brown skin was shiny with sweat, high-

145

lighting each dip and ridge of his toned stomach. A trail of dark, curly hair led from his navel down the center of the deep *V* of his abdomen, disappearing into cargo shorts hanging low on his hips.

"Nova?"

"Hmm?" She bit her lip hard.

"Drink." He forced the water bottle into her hand.

"Why are you so worried about my hydration?"

"Because you don't do it nearly enough."

"I drink plenty."

"Water, Freckles, not soda or hot chocolate or sweet tea. You need plain old water."

"Yes, Daddy." She smiled as she took it, unscrewed the cap, and downed a few gulps. The ice-cold water a complete contrast to the heat of her body, yet it did nothing to quell the fire of desire he stirred up in her.

"Good girl." He gave a satisfied smirk.

She grinned as she flung her water bottle forward, still holding on. Icy water flew out of the top, splashing over his chiseled chest.

Jude flinched and then glared at her. "What was that for?"

She shrugged. "You looked hot."

He wiped his face with his forearm, a sly smile curving the corner of his mouth. She had yet to see a full-on smile. That was a challenge she wanted to win. This guy needed to loosen up.

I know just what to do.

"How much more work do you have?"

"Just finished up with your dad. Thought I'd come see if you needed any help?"

"I have a delivery to make. Why don't we go shower really quick and then head out?"

"Okay."

She nodded and headed for the house.

"Hey, Freckles?"

She stomped her foot and spun around. Admittedly, the nickname didn't really bother her, but it was a matter of principal. "Yes, Daddy?"

The heat in his gaze was enough to put the August sun to shame. "Don't think I'm letting that little display of water fun slide. You'll pay for it later."

She tried, she really did. But it was too fun to push his buttons. And it wasn't like he'd made a move to do a single damn thing about her taunts to date.

"Promises, promises. More big talk and no follow-through." She winked and sauntered into the house, his gaze burning a hole through her the entire walk back.

She swallowed as she closed her bedroom door, her skin flushed and tight, but it wasn't from the summer day. No, Jude woke the submissive brat inside her, and that was the most dangerous thing of all. She was never more vulnerable than when that secret part of her emerged. She'd locked that piece of herself away for so long, but maybe it was time she was let out to play.

* * *

An hour later, Nova walked into the Shattered Cove retirement community's recreation room. Everyone in there was old enough to be her grandparent or even great-grandparent. The women outnumbered the men two to one, and that made for some interesting love triangles. This was one of Nova's favorite places to visit. She didn't have any grandparents, but here, she'd been taken in and treated like family by every single person, especially the four women she'd lovingly dubbed "the Golden Girls." She'd even won over Roger, the meanest grump here.

Nova led Jude into the center of the space. Off to one side, a few couches surrounded a blaring TV with Mary in front of it. The place smelled of fresh flowers and Old Spice—an interesting mix, but it worked. A few comfortable seats were spread around the room, as well as a card table and other spaces for games.

"Clara, hold your pearls, our favorite girl has brought us some new man candy," Loretta said, adjusting her pink curls on her head. She pivoted in her chair at the card table, moving away from her best friend, and gave Nova an open-armed welcome.

Nova hugged her.

"I think I might need some extra insulin for this one." Clara looked wide-eyed at Jude as he surveyed the room.

"Oooh, who's the new guy?" Betty skirted over, playing with her long beaded necklace over her magic shroom T-shirt.

"I called dibs!" Loretta elbowed Betty.

Nova laughed. "This is my friend Jude. Jude, this is Betty, Loretta, Clara, and Mary is over there by the TV. But she's hard of hearing, so you'll need to shout for her to hear you. These are my Golden Girls."

Jude gave them a nod of greeting.

"Oh, he's the strong, silent kind. Just my type." Betty winked.

"You don't have a type except breathing and willing to put up with your wrinkly ass," Loretta teased.

Betty shook her head and looped her arm through Jude's. "Don't mind her, handsome. She's just jealous I stole her date on Friday."

Jude looked to Nova as if to ask *what the fuck is going on?*

She giggled. "Betty and Loretta are both dating the same man—Alfred."

Jude's eyes widened.

"I think we've stunned him speechless. You think us old gals can't handle a beefcake like you? I might be retired, stud, but I most definitely am open for business." Betty smiled up at him with humor in her gaze.

"I appreciate the offer. But I kinda already have a girl of my own." Jude slipped his other arm around Nova.

Nova gulped as butterflies erupted in her belly. *It's just pretend.*

"Awww. Our Nova finally got herself a real man! She's all grown up." Loretta beamed.

"Who got a man?" Mary stood up from the TV and joined them.

"Nova did," Betty answered.

"No one did? Then he's up for grabs and I call dibs." Mary joined them, using her cane to steady her walk.

"Nova! He's Nova's man!" Loretta shouted.

Mary shook her head. "Why didn't you say so in the first place? Unfair to get my hopes up. You know I have a bad heart."

Nova giggled. "This is Jude!"

"He's a Jew? What's wrong with that? I'm a quarter Jewish myself. My grandson had me do one of those DNA tests," Mary added.

Nova's smile widened as she looked up to Jude. A part of her hoped he'd find the group as entertaining as she did. And maybe another part had brought him here to test him. Brooks never would have been comfortable with this.

"Who's shouting about a man? Do I have new competition?" Alfred asked, walking in from the back patio, the scent of cherry cigars following him as usual.

"Hey, Alfred." Nova gave him a hug.

"Hey, how's my favorite girl?"

"I thought I was your favorite girl?" Loretta teased.

"What is she talking about, Alfred?" Betty asked, less pleased.

Alfred blushed, his papery, pale skin taking on a reddish hue. "Ladies, you know I don't have favorites."

"Why do you call them the Golden Girls?" Jude asked.

"Because one day she brought her yummy cookies and we all ate them and watched reruns of the show on the TV. We were giggling and having a grand ol' time when she lovingly pointed out that I resembled the intelligent and witty Dorothy character," Loretta explained.

"Naturally, I was the stylish and suave Blanche." Clara ran her hand through her short brown afro with a wink.

"And since I am the most exciting and already named Betty like the talented actress who played Rose, it made sense." Betty beamed while clapping her hands.

Nova leaned closer to Jude. "And Mary is Sophia because—"

"Because I'm the oldest and wisest." Mary winked, her red-painted nails shimmering as they tapped on the cane.

"Well, well, what do we have here?" Roger asked, walking inside, his Vietnam veteran hat covering his bald head.

"Roger!" Nova ran up to him, giving him a tight squeeze like she hadn't just seen him the week before for her last delivery.

He patted her back, giving her a smile before he looked at Jude, his expression growing hard once more. "Who do we have here?"

"This is Jude."

"Her boyfriend," Clara supplied as Betty and Loretta scolded Alfred off to the side.

"Boyfriend, huh?" Roger scrutinized Jude from his boots all the way up to the black baseball cap on his head.

"Jude's a former SEAL," Nova supplied.

"Navy, huh?"

"Yes, sir," Jude answered.

Roger turned to Nova. "He treat you good?"

Nova swallowed and glanced at Jude. "Very."

"Good. She needs someone who will make sure she stays out of trouble." Roger locked eyes with Jude.

"That she does." Jude gently squeezed the back of Nova's neck.

"You man enough for the task, sailor?"

Jude looked at Nova as if debating something before he returned his focus to Roger. "Yes, sir."

Roger nodded and extended his hand for Jude to shake. Jude took it.

Nova's mouth dropped open. Roger wasn't one to welcome anyone new in. He still hated more than half the residents of their private retirement community. It had taken Nova a lot to win him over and get his grumpy ass to even come to the rec room. How on earth had Jude won him over with a few silent looks and a handshake?

"Close your mouth, Freckles. You're likely to catch flies." Jude tapped her chin.

She snapped her jaw closed.

"Oh my, ladies, did you hear that? He called her Freckles. Isn't that the most adorable thing you've ever heard?" Clara waved her hands excitedly.

Nova hadn't thought the group would be so interested in her love life. She hadn't planned to include them in her lie. But Jude had let the cat out of the bag and now she had to run with it.

"I brought you all a fresh batch of cookies." Nova held up the basket of individually wrapped baked goods.

"Ohhh, just what we need." Mary eyed the basket eagerly.

Nova handed out the cookies. She had a dozen left she'd drop off to the houses of the members of the retirement community who weren't there later.

"You're drugging grannies?" Jude asked in a low voice.

She chuckled. "Only the ones who want it, and don't worry, their doctors know and approve."

"I'll have a batch of shrooms ready next week if you want some." Betty told Nova with a wink. "Remember the fun we had last time? Maybe you can bring this cutie along and we'll have a real party."

Nova laughed. "I'll let you convince him."

"What do you think, big guy?" Betty linked her arm with Jude's. "You interested in a wild ride with yours truly? It's a trip." She winked. "If you catch my drift."

Jude's lips curved up into a smile at the older woman attached to his hip. "Sounds pretty enticing. I think I'll have to pass on partaking, but maybe I'll come along to watch out for you both."

"Oh, look at that. He definitely passes the vibe check, as my great-granddaughter would say," Betty said.

"Who's got a vibrator?" Mary asked. "I need a new one. Mine finally died."

Nova burst out laughing. This was why she loved these people. They were unfiltered and didn't give a shit about proper social etiquette.

"You should get one of those flower ones. It charges on my bookshelf and looks like a decoration. It's pretty and can make you feel like you died and went to heaven in less than a minute. Boy, it's a rush. The first time I used it, I thought I was having a stroke and my family would find me naked with the toy." Clara started laughing so hard she could barely talk. "I thought, Lord have mercy, my son will never forgive me for this."

The others burst into laughter with her.

Clara had tears pouring out of her eyes, she was laughing so hard. "Can you imagine?"

"You'd better calm down or you'll pee your pants again," Loretta said.

Clara wiped her eyes and took a few deep breaths. "Not since I've been doing those pelvic-floor exercises. I told you to come with me. They help you tighten up your snatch."

"Mine's tight enough, thank you very much." Betty gave a friendly wink. "But for research purposes, how would I go about getting one of those vibrators?"

Clara pointed to Nova.

"You deliver drugs *and* sex toys to them?" Jude asked, astonishment in his voice. He leaned in and whispered, "Like a dirty Red Riding Hood."

"First of all . . ." Nova held up a finger. "Weed is not a drug. It's a medicinal plant with health benefits. Second of all, who else is going to? They can't ask their children or grandchildren how to use the Internet or where to go. Just because they're older women doesn't mean they aren't sexual beings deserving of quality adult toys."

"You tell him, sister!" Betty encouraged.

Jude chuckled, and for the first time, his face split in a genuine smile. He held up his hands as if in surrender. "Oh, I'm not against it, Freckles. You just never stop surprising me."

"I hope that's a good thing?"

Dozens of emotions shone in his eyes as he regarded her. "It's definitely not bad."

Well, that's not confusing at all.

"But does that make me the Big Bad Wolf?" A glint of mischief flared in his eyes.

"I fucking hope so." She smirked. *I'd let him chase me through the woods and fuck me against a tree any day of the week. Yes, please.*

"Wow, it's getting hot in here with the way you two are looking at each other. How about a game of pinochle before you head home?" Loretta asked, fanning herself.

"Come on, Jude. Let's go outside and have a cigar while the ladies do their thing." Alfred motioned to the back porch.

Nova turned to Jude, silently asking if he was okay with this.

He squeezed her shoulder and kissed her temple. His warm lips grazing her skin sent a bolt of energy shooting through her. Dazed, she couldn't peel her eyes away from him as he followed Alfred outside. Roger finally blocked her view, trailing behind them.

"Oh, she's got it bad," Loretta said, sitting at the card table before dealing in the ladies.

"I don't blame her. There isn't much I wouldn't let a man like that do to me," Betty agreed, taking a seat beside Loretta.

"Is he hung too?" Clara asked, sitting opposite Nova.

"Clara!" Nova burst out laughing again. Her abs got the best workout from all the laughing when she came here. She took a seat.

"Well, is he?" she repeated.

"Is he what?" Mary asked, standing by Nova's side.

"CLARA ASKED IF NOVA'S BOYFRIEND'S GOT A BIG JOHNSON!" Betty yelled for Mary to hear.

Nova cringed. There was no way Jude hadn't heard that.

She cleared her throat. "I'm not telling you that."

"My first husband had a tiny penis," Clara admitted, holding up her pinky finger. "But that man had a talented tongue."

Nova struggled with another bout of laughter. "Okay, enough about cocks. How about you tell me how your appointment went on Monday?"

Clara waved her hand dismissively. "You don't want to hear about my boring old doctor's visit."

"I sure do. Did he say why he thinks the pain has gotten worse?"

"Because I'm getting old. I told him I was a spry seventy-eight, but he didn't find it half as amusing. So I'll need a little extra of your best stuff."

Nova pulled out a jar of the gummies from the basket she'd been experimenting with. "Okay, I mixed some sativa and indica for this one. You'll have to let me know how they work. Each gummy should be about ten milligrams each, so eat half to take the edge off and work your way up to find your dose."

"What do I owe ya?" Clara asked.

"You know I'm not taking your cash." It wasn't legal in New Hampshire yet without a proper license. But more than that, these people had become like extended family to Nova. She wanted to help. "You give me some of those bread and butter pickles and we'll call it even."

Clara nodded. "That I can do."

"It's about time for my stories," Mary said, taking a bite of her cookie. "Gonna go relax for a bit. All the excitement wore me out."

Nova gave her a hug before she returned to her spot in front of the TV.

"Let's play." Betty arranged her cards.

Nova's attention drifted to the back patio. Was Jude okay out there? Alfred's laugh drifted in through the screen door. Anxiety swirled in Nova's belly. She released a breath. *Jude's a grown man. If he doesn't want to be here, he'll tell me.*

Brooks certainly wouldn't have even come along. But Jude was welcomed into their quirky fold, and seemed to fit right in.

It helped knowing people she respected and admired had also taken a liking to him. It made it easier to trust the little voice inside that told her Jude King was a good man.

But is he my man?

Do I even want one?

Only time would tell.

21

JUDE

Jude sipped his craft beer, staring out the window to the back deck. Nova tipped her face to the full moon, the light of the fire dancing over her features. Every time he thought he had her figured out, she threw him another curveball. He hadn't expected to walk into a retirement community and have her pass out weed cookies. He'd definitely learned more than a few things about Nova while they were there.

The way the ladies flitted around her, stuffing her arms with goodies they'd made themselves and asking after her, made it clear they cared for her like family. The men weren't much different, asking Jude questions about himself—something they'd only have done if they were looking out for their adored Nova. Roger especially. The old man had asked him about his time in the service. Before Jude left, Roger had threatened him with bodily harm if he mistreated Nova in any way. Jude's respect for the man had gone up a notch. Nova had a lot of people looking out for her and who genuinely cared about her. However, he had a feeling she didn't even realize it.

Nova isn't who I thought she was.

Nova lined up a few Mason jars of sealed water on the edge of the deck and set her colorful stones on each one and some surrounding them.

Jude slid open the door to the deck and stepped out. The night had cooled down. There was a little chill in the air now that the sun had gone down.

"What's with all the rocks?"

She spun around and rolled her eyes, coming to sit by the fire. "They're not rocks; they're crystals. And I'm charging them in the full moon and making moon water."

"What now?"

"You're always so concerned with my water intake. I thought you'd be happy."

"You're going to drink this moon water?"

"Mmhmm."

"And then what? Do you turn into a werewolf?"

"I wish. Then I could have a fated mate." She smiled and relaxed into the couch.

Jude took a seat next to her, eyes on the fire. "I'm not even going to try and understand what the hell that means."

"It means we'd be destined for a happily ever after, and I'd know for sure he wouldn't ever betray me." She snorted before she lit up a joint.

"I see."

"Oh, come on. I have the best book for you to read. Suzanne Wright wrote one of my favorite series ever. *Feral Sins* is the one to start with. I have a copy on the bookshelf if you're interested . . ."

"In a book about werewolves?"

"It's more than that. And they're called shifters. There's a grumpy hero and at first they hate each other. But then they get to know one another, and the sex is pretty amazing too. There's biting and scratching and—" She shrugged and then pressed her mouth closed.

"Don't stop now. Sounds like you were just getting to the good part."

She waved her hand dismissively. "Sorry, I know I can ramble on."

He turned to her. Orange flames flickered in front of them, shining on her skin. With a background of shadow, she seemed to almost radiate light.

"I like when you ramble." Jude tucked a stubborn curl behind her ear.

Her eyes widened as she looked at him like he'd truly surprised her. "Really? Or are you just fucking with me?"

He shrugged. "Makes up for my silence."

The corner of her mouth curved up. "Thanks for being a good sport today at the rec center."

"It was amusing."

"Roger seemed to take a liking to you fast. It took me months to wear him down."

"He's not so bad." Jude took a sip of his beer. "He had quite the career in the Air Force."

"I think you two would have a lot in common actually . . ." She took a long drag from her joint and blew it out. "Did you know your grandparents?"

"No."

"Me either."

"Really? As close as the Emersons are, I'd figured . . ."

She shook her head. "No, Mom's dad died before I was born, in Ghana. Her mom also passed on. And Dad's parents are also both gone."

"What about your bio family?" he asked, testing the waters.

Nova stiffened. She took another drag from her joint and blew out a cloud of smoke. It was sexy how her lips wrapped around the end of the joint. The image of those same plump lips wrapped around his cock appeared in his mind. He took another pull of beer to try and calm his body down.

"My bio mom and Renita share the same father. I have no idea what happened to my birth mom's mother. She just wasn't there growing up."

"So you had somewhere to go after leaving that foster house?"

She nodded, taking another inhale from her weed, and then put it out in an ashtray.

"Are all your brothers adopted too?"

"No, just Ricky and me."

A beat of silence passed. Nothing but the cadence of cicadas trilling in the background and a few squeaks from bats. Somewhere in the distance an owl hooted.

Jude took a deep breath. "I didn't know my dad, and my mom wasn't someone you could rely on. She was . . ." *How to sum up everything Cindy King was?* "She was an addict. And she didn't care about anyone but herself."

"I'm sorry. That had to be really tough to grow up with . . . That's why you left for the Navy so early? To get out?"

Tell her. He might not be able to give her everything, but he could start.

"I didn't really have much choice at the time. I needed to get out of there and gain an income. Joining made the most sense. It gave me my independence." *And so much more.*

"That's really brave to set out on your own like that at such a young age."

"I had to forge my mother's signature." He chuckled, but there was no humor in it. He'd never told anyone that.

"Ballsy." She smiled.

"It was survival."

She met his gaze, understanding emanating from her. "We do what we have to in order to survive. It's what separates us from the victims. The lengths we're willing to go to for freedom. The pain we're willing to endure for hope of a better future."

"What did you have to survive, Freckles?" He used the pet name to lighten his question, but he wanted to know what had occurred before Brooks. What had happened when she was in that foster house.

"I got lucky," she said cryptically, picking up her phone, tapping the screen. Music bled from the outdoor speakers, a steady pulsing beat. She stood, her body swaying to the sounds.

"I love this song." She sang along.

Her body moved fluidly with her eyes closed. Her hips swayed seductively as she raised her hands, singing about fading. She smiled, moving around the fire pit and twirling in a circle, her movements becoming wider with the increased space.

Jude sat back against the couch, entranced by the way she so freely twisted and writhed with not a care in the world. Her head nodded along to the steady beat. She was so free. He wished he could capture just an ounce of the energy she radiated—the joy and presence.

"Come on. Dance with me?" She took his hand, trying to tug him to his feet.

He shook his head. "I don't dance."

Nova bit her lip. She picked up her lighter and a fresh joint from the case on the table, climbing onto his lap.

His hands went to her hips. "Nova."

"Do you trust me?"

He hesitated, searching her eyes. Nothing but openness stared back at him in her amber gaze. She was pure goodness wrapped in curves and tied with hopefulness. She called to a part deep inside him. Her presence weaved around Jude, anchoring him.

"Yes." His voice grated.

She smiled, and the fact that he'd been the one to put it there sent a burst of pride to his chest.

She lit the joint, pulling in a drag, but no puff of smoke escaped this time. She leaned forward, melding her lips with his. She blew out into his mouth. He breathed her in, lost in her spell, inhaling her exhale. The smoke filled his lungs. He breathed out, a puff of smoke spreading between them as his tongue dipped in her mouth, taking. His fingers dug into her hips. Nova ground against his cock. He tensed, a groan escaping. She pulled back, a knowing, mischievous smile on her face as she moved off him.

She was teasing him.

"Brat."

She shrugged. "Come dance with me."

Jude's eyes felt heavy as he stood. His control was in broken pieces laid at her feet. His little witch danced as the music switched to a different song. This one was more upbeat than the last, but it was still slow. A thuddy bass dropped. Nova twisted her body, her hands in the air. One glided down the other, skimming over her neck and breasts as she spun around. Her ass shook from side to side as the beat dropped again and she twisted, making a *come hither* motion with her hand.

Jude moved closer, his feet taking on a mind of their own to do her bidding, under her spell. Her arms wrapped around him, leading him. Jude's nose dropped to the top of her head. He breathed in as hazy relaxation drifted into every cell. But he was still very much cognizant—he wasn't as out of control as he'd been with the cookies. With the one hit, Jude was more relaxed. A floaty buzz pulsed through his blood, his head nodding along to the music as she danced against him.

One hand drifted down the back of her neck, the other coming to cup her face and tilt it up.

She looked up at him with her big brown eyes. So fucking trusting and open.

But he couldn't do this—not without her knowing the truth.

His thumb smoothed up the hollow of her throat. "We can't do this."

She winced, clearly taking his words for outright rejection.

"It's not like that. I need to tell—"

"What do we have here?"

Jude didn't even blink before he thrust her behind him. His body revved, alert for a fight—ready to defend and protect her.

Instincts honed over years had him reaching for the weapon in his pocket. The knife flashed in the firelight as four figures moved from the shadows.

Nova gave a sigh of relief and then pushed past Jude, scowling into the dark. "What are you assholes doing here?"

Her three brothers and Everett walked into the light. Jude relaxed, putting away his weapon.

"Nice to know he's not just pretty to look at. Those were some quick reflexes, bro." Roman nodded in approval.

"Yeah, but he didn't hear us until we were right on them," Ricky said.

"The music was blaring," Nash said.

"And they were a little preoccupied," Everett added with a wink to Nova.

"Why the hell are you here? Don't you have families to keep you busy?" Nova whined.

"It's guys' night," Nash said, as if that meant something.

Roman stepped closer, wrapping an arm around Jude. He stiffened. This was a touchy-feely family.

"Guys, no. Jude is still getting settled—"

"Come on. We gave you more than a week. That's pretty gracious if you ask me," Roman said.

Jude surveyed the group of her brothers and soon-to-be brother-in-law. He'd known this time would come sooner or later. He'd have been surprised if it hadn't.

"You can't take him—"

Jude moved out of Roman's reach to pull Nova into his arms. "It's okay, Freckles. I'm sure they just want to make sure their little sister is being taken care of."

Guilt weighed heavily on his shoulders. If they knew why he'd come, they might actually rip him apart.

She was stiff against him, her guard back up from their misunderstanding. He needed to fix that.

"We'll finish this talk later, okay?" Jude asked.

"I think you made yourself pretty clear," she whispered so only he would hear. Her tattooed arms slipped from his chest.

He gripped the back of her neck, pulling her in as he bent low to kiss her. She wouldn't pull away or make a scene with her brothers there, and he took advantage of that. He'd never said he was a good guy.

Her mouth held firm, resisting his kiss. He nipped her bottom lip. She bit back harder.

"Okay, bro. She's our sister. Take it easy, would ya?" Nash grumbled.

Jude grazed his teeth over her lip once more before pulling

away and staring into her eyes, hoping she would understand. *I want you too much. That's the problem.*

"I'd better not get a call from Bently to bail your asses out of jail," Nova called after them.

"Don't worry. We'll go easy on him, sis," Roman assured her.

Ricky clapped Jude's back harder than necessary, a dark glint in his eyes. "What fun would that be?"

Jude allowed the four men to lead him around the house to a parked truck. He cast one more look over his shoulder before he climbed in, but Nova wasn't there.

If he survived this night, he'd make this right between them. She would know without a doubt that he wanted her more than he should.

But that in itself might put her in even more danger.

22

JUDE

Jude pulled his legs together, trying to make more room for the two other large men in the backseat with him, one on either side. Ricky drove with Everett riding shotgun. That left Nash and Roman sandwiching Jude.

"Put some metal on," Nash said as Ricky switched on the radio.

"God, no. I don't need a splitting headache before we get there," Roman complained.

"I'm driving, so I get to pick." Ricky switched the station until the latest hits played through the speakers, just loud enough to give them some background noise.

"Asshole." Nash smacked the back of Ricky's head from behind the seat.

"Hey! No fucking around when I'm driving," Ricky snapped.

Everett chuckled. "Some days I'm glad I only have a sister."

"What about you, Jude? You got any siblings?" Roman

166

asked as the truck jostled from the potholes in the dirt drive before they turned on the main road.

"Christ, take it easy, will ya? There isn't room to fucking breathe back here," Nash complained.

Jude took advantage of the distraction. "Where are we going?"

"Where do you think we're going?" Ricky asked, his eyes flashing in the rearview mirror.

"I'm assuming this is where you take me to a remote location and threaten me bodily harm if I fuck with your sister," Jude answered honestly. It was best to get this over and done with.

Silence blanketed the car before three out of the four men started laughing. Ricky was the only one that remained stoic.

Roman wrapped his arm around Jude's shoulder. "Nothing quite as nefarious as that. We love our little Akua, but she would have our balls if anything happened to you."

"Speak for yourself. I think we should have done that," Ricky mumbled under his breath.

"Ignore him. We're all just a little shocked our baby sister was hiding you for so long, and then bam! Meet the family, and you're already moving in while there's a murderer on the loose," Roman explained.

Ricky took the next turn, heading towards the main part of Shattered Cove.

"Not to mention we dropped the ball last time," Nash added, guilt heavy in his tone.

"You mean with Brooks?" Jude asked.

Ricky's eyes met his in the mirror for an extended beat before he focused back on the road. "How much do you know about that asshole?"

"Enough."

A few beats of silence passed with nothing but music for

noise. But growing up as Jude did, he'd learned to read body language. The way Ricky's grip tensed on the steering wheel spoke of long-held anger. The drop of Nash's shoulders conveyed his guilt. And Roman had stiffened at the mention of her ex.

"We didn't do right by her last time. We were so consumed with our own issues we didn't look out for her. And she doesn't make it easy," Roman explained.

"Your sister is good at pretending everything is okay." Everett placed his hand over Ricky's, pulling it into his lap. Ricky's whole demeanor relaxed.

"Still. We owe her. And we're gonna do right by her this time." Nash straightened as much as he could in the tight space, determination lighting his voice.

Something snapped into place. These guys felt responsible for Nova's heartbreak with Brooks in some capacity. Even if they didn't know all the details, they understood they'd been absent when she needed them.

They knew what it meant to fail someone they loved. *Maybe we have more in common than I thought.*

"So . . . what are we doing, then?" Jude asked again.

Ricky turned the blinker on, pulling into The Shipwreck bar, and parked.

All heads turned to Jude, matching smiles on their faces.

Everett spoke first. "We're gonna ply you with alcohol and get to know you."

"Let's go shoot some pool," Roman said, opening the door and hopping out.

Jude followed as the other men piled out of the truck.

A man with a scarred face stood outside the venue, checking IDs of a group of young women.

"Hey, Mason," Roman greeted as they approached.

The bouncer smiled and waved them through. "You guys have fun tonight, but not too much."

Roman chuckled and held the door open for the rest of their crew. They walked into the bar. The interior matched the name. They'd entered what looked like the belly of a ship. A dim blue glow lit the dance floor and fish tanks decorated the walls. Upbeat music bled from the speakers near an empty stage with a pool table off to the side. A dozen people swayed to the beat. He located the exit in the back, scanned the room, and took stock of the space.

Jude followed the brothers and Everett up to the bar. They passed a table with a life-size skeleton with a pirate hat and a lei wrapped around its neck.

"Hey, Finn." Ricky slapped palms with the bartender and then knocked his fist against the other man's in greeting.

"Guys." Finn nodded. "What's the occasion?"

Finn was a few inches shorter than Jude, but he had some muscle on him. The way he carried himself, much like the man outside, made Jude assume he'd been in the service at some point.

"Guys' night. And we've got to break Nova's boyfriend in," Roman answered, pointing over his shoulder at Jude. "How's Charli and Jamison?"

The hard lines of Finn's face softened with the mention of those two names. He smiled, a proud gleam in his eyes. "She's doing fantastic. Jamie loves being a big brother."

"Oh, shit, I forgot she had the baby. What did you guys finally settle on for a name?" Roman asked.

"Rose Charlotte Reed."

"That's gorgeous," Everett remarked.

"Thanks." Finn's smile just got bigger as he wiped down the busy bar.

He had an expression of pure joy and contentment on his

face. *What would I give to have just a taste of that—* Was it because of this Charli, his wife, Jude assumed, judging by the silver band on his ring finger.

"What can I get ya?" Finn glanced at Jude.

"I'll take a beer. Something local."

"I got some Sand Dune?"

That was the kind that Nova bought. "Yeah, I'll have the Midsummer IPA if you've got it."

Ricky clapped his back. "Come on, let's get a real drink. How about a round of vodka shots?"

"You're supposed to be the DD," Nash pointed out.

"For everyone but me," Ricky corrected.

"Then we can order our own drinks. No vodka. I'll take what Jude's having," Roman added.

"I'll have a Jack and Coke." Nash motioned to Everett.

"Guess I'll go for a beer too," Everett said.

"Make it four beers. I can have one and then I'll switch to soda." Ricky pulled out his wallet. "I've got the first round."

The men waited for their drinks. Finn was quick and efficient. Ricky paid and they found a table on the left side of the bar.

"We've got next," Ricky said to the two players already at the pool table next to them.

The other men gave a nod and resumed their game.

"Is Finn the one who lost his memory?" Everett asked.

Ricky nodded. "Yeah, after he got out of his last deployment, he and Charli got pregnant with Jamison. He went on a fishing trip with his friend and a drunk driver hit them. Woke up thinking he was like seventeen and still dating his high school girlfriend." Ricky winced. "That I conveniently had a small interlude with, not knowing they were still *technically* together."

"Wait, he forgot he had a wife and a kid on the way?" Jude asked.

Ricky nodded.

"Musta been hard for Charli. She's a tough woman, and they didn't have an easy road. But they found their way back to each other just in time," Roman added.

A beat of silence passed at the table. Each man there had that same contented happiness Jude had recognized in Finn.

"So, where should we start?" Everett asked.

The meanest-looking brother, Nash, glared at Jude. "I just wanna know what this fucker's intentions are with my sister?"

23

JUDE

It took a lot for Jude to feel intimidated, but the opinion of the four men Nova cared about mattered.

Nash's question was straight to the point. Jude had to respect him for that.

"I don't want to hurt her. My intentions are to get to know her better. Every day I learn something new."

Nash gave an approving grumble.

Jude's skin felt tight. He'd never cared what anyone thought—anyone except Sal. But for some reason he cared what Nova's family thought about him. He took a gulp of his beer, needing the liquid courage to help him relax now that the calming buzz from the weed was wearing off.

"Alright, what do you like about her?" Roman asked.

Jude's mouth curved up. "What isn't to like?"

"Ha! Now I know you're lying." Ricky slapped the table. "We love our sister, but we know her. Which means we understand she takes a level of patience most men do not possess."

"She's vicious," Jude agreed. "And she can be a bit of a brat. But I don't see those as negative qualities."

Ricky tilted his head, studying Jude.

"I like his answer." Everett peeled the label from his beer.

"You plan on sticking around?" Nash asked.

Jude turned to look him in the eyes. "As long as she lets me." It was the truth.

Nash nodded in approval as the men at the game table behind them waved, setting their sticks down. "Alright, let's shoot some pool."

Roman sat out the first round. They made small talk and joked as they played. Once in a while someone would ask him a question about his life. Jude kept his answers vague but as close to the truth as he could. By his fourth beer and the third round of pool, they were laughing like he had with his military buddies. It was bittersweet.

"Fucker's gonna take all my money. Take a break and let someone else win for a change." Nash shoved him away from the game, but it wasn't with malice. It was the same way Nash showed affection for his brothers.

Jude's chest tightened. Even Ricky had loosened up, if not glaring at him the whole time counted.

"Beers? And a soda for Ricky?" He checked with the guys.

"I'll take a water actually," Nash said.

"Sure." Jude headed for the bar, pulling out a wad of cash while he waited for Finn.

Someone pushed into Jude, knocking him off-balance. He caught the bar to steady himself but not before crashing into the guy on the other side of him.

"What the fuck!"

Shit. Jude turned. Fucking Chad stood there, rubbing a wet mark on his silky white shirt.

"Sorry, man."

"Do you have any idea how much this shirt costs, farmer boy?"

The room was packed, and a few heads turned at Chad's outburst.

Jude gritted his teeth and took a deep breath. *Don't punch him.* The last thing Jude needed was to land himself in jail. He couldn't afford to deal with that shit, much less for a pissant like Chad.

"I'm sure Finn can get you some soda water." He lifted two fingers to get the bartender's attention.

"Unbelievable. You see what this bastard did?" Chad asked as the five guys around him, all wearing different styles of polo shirts and khakis, stood. They looked like they belonged to the same rich-asshole club of trying too hard.

"What can I get you?" Finn asked Jude.

"A couple waters, a Pepsi, and two beers, and some soda water for this guy." Jude pointed to Chad.

"I don't need anything from you but the money I paid for this shirt," Chad sneered.

Jude's hackles rose. That dark part of him was fighting toward the surface, but he tried his hardest to tamp it down.

"Fucking loser. Probably can't even count that high."

Jude shrugged like Chad's words didn't bother him.

"That's why Nova will come crawling back to me when she tires of slumming it with you."

A red haze settled over Jude. Anger roiled inside him. *Fuck.* His skin itched with the pent-up rage. He fisted his hands to keep from doing something stupid.

Stand down, King. Stand the fuck down.

"You never mentioned how long you've been dating. You know me and her had a thing a couple months ago?"

Jude's jaw was going to crack. What the hell had Nova seen in this douchebag? Did she want someone with money? Someone with an affluent family? She didn't seem shallow. So why this idiot?

Finn set the drinks in front of Jude. Thankful for the distraction and something to do with his hands, he gave Finn the money and a nice tip. "Thanks."

Finn nodded to him, glancing at Chad and his friends.

Jude picked up the drinks and turned. Chad's friends had him surrounded.

"Sweetest pussy I ever fucked." Chad's cocky smile burrowed into Jude's skin. "Better than when I had her in high school. Seems she can't get enough. Always comes back for more."

Jude forced a smile, hatred and rage thrumming through his veins. He needed to get himself under control. Nova's history was none of his business. He had one too, and he'd be a hypocrite to judge her for that.

"Sometimes we all make poor choices. Now that she's got a real man, there won't be any need for your . . ." Jude made a show of scanning the man from head to toe and scowled. ". . . less than adequate interference."

He turned his back on Chad and shoved past his buddy blocking his exit.

He's not worth it. Walk away. Be the bigger person.

Before he could take another step, Chad said, "I think we both know you're the one who isn't adequate. She begged for my cock like the little whore she is. She asked me to be rough with her. Gotta love a girl with daddy issues. They're the best lay. Willing to let you do just about anything to them."

Time stopped. His thoughts raced as his guts gave a violent twist. A split-second decision was made. All that crushing darkness that he'd held at bay? He set it free, fully embracing the monster inside him. Jude's pride might not have been worth losing his shit for. But Nova's? She was fucking worth it—even if it was six against one.

Jude spun around, throwing the drinks at Chad, and

laughed at the shocked and outraged expression on the asshole's face.

"You fucking did it now. Laugh it up, farmer boy." Chad motioned to his friends.

A couple of the guys took Jude's arms.

"No fighting in here!" Finn yelled over the rising chaos.

"Show him where he fucked up, Brent." Chad spoke to the man on Jude's right.

"What's wrong? Worried you'll break a nail doing your dirty work for yourself? Daddy's money can't buy you a pair of balls, can it?" Jude laughed.

He saw it in Chad's eyes—the moment he fell for the bait. Chad's arm swung. Jude braced himself for impact. Pain lit up his cheek, but the man's form was as soft as a child's.

Jude turned back to look at him. Chad's victorious smile dimmed, and Jude could only assume it was due to the satisfied gleam in his own eyes or the wild and unhinged smile on his lips.

"Now we can have some real fun." Jude moved as he'd been taught. He swung his fist into the guy on his right. His arm was released immediately, elbowing Brent to grab the guy on his left before kneeing him in the gut.

Groans drifted up as Jude swung his fist at Chad. Those wide blue eyes froze as his fist connected with Chad's cheekbone, sending the asshole flying to the wet ground. Arms grabbed Jude, tearing him away before he could get another shot in as Chad's other friends joined the fray. Pain slammed into his gut the same time something sharp sliced up his forehead. He was shoved to the ground littered with broken glass.

Crushed under the weight, he fought with all his might as Chad recovered, staggering to his feet.

A moment later, a whir of movement blocked his view as Ricky knocked Chad down a second time. The weight holding

Jude down was gone as Nash, Roman, and Everett joined in. Fists flew. Pained grunts joined the music as complete chaos erupted in the bar.

The music cut out.

"Enough!" Mason, the bouncer from outside, bellowed a moment later. He and Finn jumped in the middle of the group, shoving the men apart. The Emerson brothers held up their hands and backed away with Everett. Ricky yanked Jude's arm, pulling him with them. Jude went as Finn and Mason shoved the other men out the door, shouting the whole time.

Everyone in the bar stared at them. Warm liquid slowly oozed down from Jude's eyebrow. He picked his hat off the ground and put it back on.

Voices rose around them, the rest of the patrons resuming their conversations now that the drama was over.

"Damn, that was fun." Ricky smiled.

Jude turned to the men he'd come with, fully expecting anger. But they all had smiles except Everett, who brushed a hand over his flushed face.

"Thanks for having my six," Jude said.

He hadn't expected backup, but it was a nice surprise. He'd missed having a brotherhood to rely on. And these guys had given him a taste of that tonight.

"No problem." Roman nodded.

"Never liked that asshole anyways," Nash agreed.

"Who was he?" Everett asked.

Ricky eyed Jude as he spoke. "An ex of Nova's. Douchebag too."

"Is he the one that couldn't find her clit?" Everett asked.

"Eww, bro. That's our sister," Nash grumbled.

"What did he say to set you off? Bring up their history?" Ricky asked, his voice casually deceptive.

"He insulted her."

A beat passed. They all looked at each other exchanging looks.

Ricky was the first to break. He walked up to Jude, clapping his shoulder. "I think you might just fit in with our crazy family after all. Smart, letting him swing first."

A burst of surprise quickly morphed to pride in Jude's chest at Ricky's approval.

The door to the bar opened and Mason and Finn walked back in, angry expressions on their faces.

"You guys need to leave." Finn motioned to the door. "The other guys already left. I already told them they can't press charges because he threw the first punch and it's on camera."

"But we can't have fighting here." Mason gave them a hard look.

"Don't worry. We've had enough excitement for one night. Come on, guys. Let's get home." Roman headed for the exit.

"Thanks for not banning us yet." Ricky waved goodbye.

Jude followed the guys out to the car.

The ride home was similar to the ride there except the conversation went to Jude's fighting ability.

"You'll have to spar with me sometime," Ricky suggested. "I've got a key to the gym. We can go whenever you want."

Jude nodded. "Sounds fun."

They pulled into Nova's driveway. All the lights in the house were still on, but that didn't mean anything. She usually forgot to turn them off.

Hesitation gripped him as he reached for the handle. Would she be mad he'd gotten her brothers into a fight?

"You should probably get a few stitches in that eye," Roman pointed out.

Jude touched the wound just above his eyebrow. His

fingers came away sticky with dark blood coating them in the dim lights of the truck cabin. "It's just a scratch."

Roman laughed and winced, holding his jaw. "Shit. You sound like Nash. Get out of here so I can go explain to my wife how I got hurt and let her kiss it better."

Jude opened the door and climbed out, then turned back to the guys. "Thanks for tonight."

Nash nodded. "You're one of us now. We've got your back and we expect the same."

They shut the door and drove off as Jude stood there, speechless.

He let out a long exhale and turned back to Nova's house.

Movement from the living room window snagged his attention. Jude adjusted his ball cap.

It was time to face the music.

24

NOVA

Car lights flashed in the driveway Nova had been not so subtly peeking at every few minutes since Jude had left. She pulled her fingernail out of her mouth and shut the book she hadn't been able to focus on. Shifting the living room curtain, she moved closer for a better look. Her brother's truck was parked outside but no doors opened.

They wouldn't actually hurt him . . . much. But there was only so much a man could take. And Jude didn't owe her anything. What if he told them the truth? That she'd lied to all of them. That they weren't really dating?

Disappointment welled within her. She was just getting to know him. She liked having him around. Not to mention that moment they'd had earlier before her brothers had come over and ruined it.

Or maybe they saved me from further embarrassment.

Jude had shot her down twice now. She usually had no problem being passed on. But the man was a walking mixed signal. Everything he said and did showed her he was attracted to her. But when it came down to it, she was rejected.

Two times was enough. She definitely wasn't going to risk opening herself up like that again. Bossy ass had had the nerve to tell her they would talk when he got home. Well, she was ready. She was going to let him know exactly what she thought of him.

Jude climbed out of the truck and headed towards the front door as her brothers drove away. She moved from the window, scrambling back to the couch and reopening her book, trying to make it look like she hadn't been waiting up for him.

Wait, this was too obvious.

Abandoning that idea, she darted upstairs as the front door opened. She leapt onto her bed, opening the book as she caught her breath. Holy shit, she needed to work out more.

Her phone rang. She jumped before pulling it out of her pocket.

Unknown caller.

"What the fuck?" She tapped the screen. "Hello?"

Nothing but the sound of running water was in the background, only this time heavy breathing accompanied it.

The stairs creaked under Jude's weight.

"Stop calling me, asshole." She hung up the phone and set it on the sleep mask on her bedside table.

Her attention darted to the door. Would he come in? Would he go to bed?

Footsteps thudded, getting closer until they stopped outside her room.

She held her breath.

The creak of the door sent a thrill charging through her. Nova stared at the book in front of her, unseeing, masking her face and hoping no emotion but boredom showed.

"Back so soon?" She kept her voice even, not looking up.

"Enjoying your book?" he asked, not answering her question, which rankled her even more.

"Very much."

He walked in, the energy in the room shifting with his presence. Her mouth went dry. With a deep inhale, Nova tried to calm her racing heart.

"Didn't know you could read upside down."

She could hear the smirk in his voice. *Sonofabitch.*

Anger flooded her vision as she finally turned to him. Her mouth froze half open at the sight of Jude.

Dried blood trailed from underneath his hat, down the side of his face to his cheekbone. His hazel eyes were dark and tumultuous. A light bruise discolored his cheek.

"Oh my God." She tossed the book and scrambled out of bed. "My brothers did this to you?" New anger flooded her veins. "This is all my fault."

Two strong hands clamped over her arms, injecting her with instant calm. It was jarring just how much control he had over her emotions.

"Relax. It's not what you think."

"You're hurt." Her voice wavered.

He blinked as if taken aback. Did he really think it was that unbelievable that she could care about his wellbeing, even if she was angry with him? She wasn't an asshole.

"Did my brothers do this?" she asked again, taking his hand and dragging him into the bathroom.

She pulled out her first-aid kit and sat on the sink counter, trying to get level with his injury.

"No."

She breathed a sigh of relief, but it was short-lived.

"Your ex did."

That stopped her short. "Claudia?"

Jude's brows drew together in question. "Claudia?"

"An ex-girlfriend. She's a boxer."

"Wrong ex."

"Who—" Her eyes widened. "Chad?"

"You dated women?"

She snorted. "Yes, I am bisexual."

"I didn't know that."

"There's a lot we don't know about each other."

Jude's jaw turned to stone. She opened the kit and pulled out alcohol swabs and butterfly Band-Aids.

She lifted the tip of his hat, inspecting the damage. A slice arched from his brow close to his temple with crimson drips.

"I think you might need stitches."

"No. You fix it."

She arched her brow.

"Please?"

With a nod, she placed the alcohol swab over the slice. He winced, stepping between her parted thighs. She held the side of his face steady as she swiped it again.

"You gonna tell me what went down?" She cleaned the debris carefully.

Jude sighed, placing his hands on either side of her thighs, his hot skin scalding against hers. "He insulted you."

"So you defended my honor in front of my brothers like the good fake boyfriend you are?" she asked sarcastically.

His thumb brushed against her cheekbone. Her eyes met his as she set the alcohol swab down.

"No. I showed a spoiled little frat boy what happens when someone insults what's *mine*."

Nova swallowed. Arousal bloomed within her from the gravelly possession ringing in that single word. *Mine.* She laughed awkwardly, shaking her head as she picked up the butterfly bandages and placed them over the injury, pulling it closed. "That's pretty good. Almost had me fooled."

Jude grabbed her wrist roughly. Desire shot through Nova like lightning—swift and bright. Energy thrummed through the small bathroom, sucking up all the oxygen.

"I wasn't done." His voice came out deep and gravely. Her legs instinctively tried to squeeze together and offer her some relief, but his body blocked her. Instead, her knees pulled around his hips.

"I'm all ears." She tried to sound unaffected, to hold her armor up. She wouldn't fall for his act a third time. She couldn't risk the rejection. If he wanted her, he'd have to take the lead.

"I didn't like the idea of another man's hands on you—especially his."

"I hate to break it to you, but there's quite a few men who've had their hands on my body." Nova knew exactly what she was doing. She'd push and push, and eventually, Jude would break. He'd either give her what she wanted or walk away.

A dark and possessive shadow eclipsed his eyes as they homed in on her. His hand wrapped around her throat, squeezing the sides just enough to give her the rush she so desperately craved. She bit her lip, holding in a moan he didn't deserve.

"I don't like the idea of someone else getting to see how your beautiful brown skin flushes when you orgasm." He moved so his face was only centimeters away from hers. His breath coasted over Nova's lips. "Or the sounds you make as you ride the edge."

"Why not?" she asked, dazed with his show of control.

"I already told you, Freckles. Because you're *mine*."

Jude's mouth crashed against hers. Unforgiving and

uncontrolled chaos erupted between them, dipped in twisted desire. She opened her mouth, giving as good as she got. Nova bit his lip.

He groaned, the hand around her neck tightening as his other gripped her hip with bruising force, yanking her against him. They were two opposing forces, colliding with the magnitude of a storm. He ground his hard cock against the seam of her pajama shorts. She cursed the thin cotton. She needed to feel him sliding inside her.

His hand left her hip, sliding under her T-shirt and up her rib cage, sending tingles of awareness shooting through her. Nova gasped.

He smirked against her mouth as his warm fingers pushed beneath her bra, cupping her breast. He seemed to hesitate, pulling his hand back out.

"If you chicken out now, Jude, I won't ever forgive you."

A dark chuckle rumbled in his chest as he pulled away. Disappointment flooded her.

Jude flipped his hat backwards as he stared at her. "Oh, we're just getting started, baby girl."

She smiled. "Then what are you waiting for?" She pulled off her T-shirt, tossing it onto the floor.

"Is this another one of your rocks? . . . In your bra?" He held up a chunk of black tourmaline.

"It's a crystal."

His eyebrow quirked. "In your bra?"

"It protects me from negative energy. This is really not what I want to talk about right now."

"Oh? And what would you like to talk about?"

"Nothing." She pulled the other three crystals from her bra, setting them on the counter. "I want you to use that mouth for more important things."

Jude's eyes glittered with devious promises. "I want that too."

"Then what are you waiting for?"

His gaze dropped to the ground and then back to her. "There's a lot you don't know."

"I don't need your secrets, Jude. Just your cock—and that mouth."

Instead of the half-smirk she was expecting, Jude leaned in, taking her face in his hands as he stared into her eyes. "This is your last chance to walk away because if we do this —you'll be mine. No matter what comes, no matter what—" His mouth pressed together in a thin line. "No matter what," he repeated. "I told you from the beginning I'm not the better man. This is your last warning. The decision is yours."

"That sounds an awful lot like commitment." Nova laughed, but she was nervous. She wasn't looking for a pledge of loyalty—just some fun. However, she and Jude had a connection that she hadn't found with anyone else—not even Brooks. What if she could have happiness like her siblings had found? What if this was her chance?

"I know you don't like commitment, Freckles." He kissed her cheek, then moved to kiss her other one and then her nose. "So I'll promise you today. And then tomorrow, I'll do the same."

That seemed . . . less scary.

"I can do today."

He gave a pleased smile, his white teeth flashing against his rich brown and pink-tinged lips. The hard edges of his face were a complete contrast to the fleeting softness in his eyes. "That's all I'll ever ask for."

Jude kissed her like today was all they had. Like he'd infused every piece of himself into the way his lips melded against hers, the way his tongue slid into her mouth, tasting, savoring, and taking all at once.

She wrapped her arms around his neck, holding on as his hands wandered to the back of her bra and deftly removed the clasp. He slid it off her arms, adding it to the growing pile of clothing on the floor. She tugged his shirt up. Jude broke the kiss to pull it over his head and dropped to his knees. His long fingers hooked under her pajama shorts and pulled them down her legs.

"No panties?" He shook his head. "You've been a very bad girl, Freckles. Did you play with this pussy while I was gone?"

"Someone had to. You left me all wound up."

Big hands clasped her knees, spreading her wide. "Next time you record that for Daddy to watch later."

Her eyes widened, surprise cascading down her as he adjusted his backwards hat and dove between her thighs. His tongue lapped up her center.

Nova's legs tensed. "Ohhhh. Fuck!"

"That's it, sweetness. Let Daddy hear you."

Black spots filled her vision. Her fantasy was coming to life. Her back arched as he sucked her clit, bobbing his head directly over that spot. His lips encircled her sensitive bud as his tongue flicked the end.

"Jude!"

His rough beard scraped against her thighs, adding a rippling sensation before his tongue dipped inside her hole.

He lapped and laved, his warm, slick tongue sliding through her wet pussy.

"You taste like fucking heaven."

"Unh." She dug her hands into his shoulders, hanging on for dear life.

He slid two fingers inside her. She gasped. His tongue teased her clit as his fingers fucked her. She was right there—

"I'm gonna come!"

"Scream for Daddy." He added a third finger and sucked her clit.

Nova let go, her scream tearing from her lungs as her orgasm lit her whole body in flames, sending her rocketing into a space where nothing else existed but pure decadent and depraved ecstasy. Her back arched, her head pressing into the mirror behind her.

He sat up, pulling his fingers out slowly. Standing, he lifted them to her lips. Nova opened as she straightened. He slid his fingers into her mouth and she sucked them clean, swirling her tongue around them as if it were his cock.

He smiled, leaning in. "Good girl. You make Daddy so happy."

Nova beamed, his praise filling her with the golden warmth of joy. Jude kissed her, her essence on his lips. But there was a desperate edge to his touch as he gripped the back of her neck.

"Are you up for more?" he asked, his voice ragged, like it was taking everything for him to hold himself back.

But Nova didn't want his self-control. She wanted him wild and reckless. Unhinged and depraved. She wanted the real Jude—the one no one else got to see. Something told her she'd be safe with that Jude.

"I want it all," she confessed. If today was all they had— she'd make the most of it. "Fuck me, Daddy."

Jude didn't ask again. He didn't hesitate. Nova's demand seemed to be permission enough as whatever was holding him back before seemed to snap like a guitar string.

His hands shot to his jeans, unzipping them and dropping them to the floor. He stepped out of them. His hard, long cock jutted up, thick and veiny with pre-cum dripping at the tip. Nova's mouth watered. Jude grabbed a condom from his wallet and slid it on. She opened her mouth to remark on the fact that he, too, was not wearing underwear, but one look at those stormy hazel eyes stole her voice.

Dominance radiated from him as he clamped his arms around her thighs, lifting her. She wrapped her legs around him, her breasts sliding against his heaving chest.

Jude's beard scraped her cheek, his voice rumbling in her ear as he spoke. "You should have run while you had your chance, Freckles." His teeth sunk into her shoulder.

Pain lanced her neck. Jude slammed inside her, forcing her to take every inch of him at once. Pleasure and pain collided. She exploded, digging her nails into his back. A dark laugh rumbled in his chest as he pulled out of her. He carried her into the bedroom. Every step jostled his cock against her sex, teasing Nova with just enough pleasure to keep her on edge.

He dropped her on her feet at the end of the bed. Big hands spun her around and bent her over the end of the bedframe. He manhandled her, and she couldn't get enough. The wood dug into her hips, but it wasn't painful—just uncomfortable. He drove his hips forward, filling her with his cock until his balls hit her ass. She arched her back, a cry of pleasure falling from her lips. He grabbed the back of her hair, tugging enough to turn her head to the side so she could meet his eyes.

"I warned you I'd punish the brat right out of you." The dangerous glint in Jude's eyes sent a shiver of fear through her.

Nova swallowed, her pussy even wetter. *I'm so fucked up.* But who wasn't? She'd learned long ago not to be ashamed of her kinks. And judging by the massive amounts of romance she read, she wasn't the only one with disturbing fantasies. But this wasn't a book. This was real life. And Jude was still very much a stranger to Nova in many ways. Maybe she was in over her head. Perhaps she shouldn't have baited him so much. What did she really know about Jude anyways?

His cock was pretty damn amazing—she could say that much. She could feel his thick, pulsing veins as he buried himself to the hilt and held, pressing his dick against her cervix.

She could always tell him to stop. Call the whole kinky-dynamic thing off. Tell him they could fuck but she didn't consent to any punishments.

But what would the fun in that be?

Nova smiled back at him, fully understanding of what would come next. "So far, I'm hearing a lot of talk and not much action."

It was like a flip switched. Jude's eyes glinted with barely contained violence and need for control.

He was a worthy adversary.

"Oh, little brat, you're going to regret that smart mouth."

Nova held her breath. Excitement and fear wound together like a cyclone inside her until every sense heightened. She braced herself for what was to come.

And then, it all went black.

25

JUDE

Jude slipped the sleep mask over Nova's head, taking away her ability to see as he ground his cock into her tight pussy from behind. He gritted his teeth. She felt so fucking good. So warm and wet.

Her heart-shaped ass was angled over the wooden bedframe, just waiting for his handprints. He wanted to turn it dark enough that she wouldn't sit right for a week without remembering exactly why she was in that predicament to begin with. But they hadn't talked about her limits yet, and the last thing he wanted to do was fuck this up before they'd had a fighting chance. Because he'd spent all his life alone and lost. He hadn't even realized he'd been going through the motions. Hadn't known there could be more. In less than two weeks, Nova had shown him the possibility of more. She'd given him a taste of what it meant to be alive—to have peace. And there was no way he was letting her go. Not then. *Maybe not ever.*

"You want me to stop? All you have to do is beg me for *mercy*," he told her.

"Won't happen, sailor. I don't beg."

He slapped her ass—hard.

She hissed, her pussy clenching around him. "Is that the best you got?"

He chuckled. "This is gonna be fun."

"I won't give in easy." Nova's voice came out breathy.

He leaned down until her back brushed against his chest. He reached in front of her to play with her clit. "I'm counting on it, baby girl. I like the challenge."

Her gasp turned into a moan as he slid his cock in and out of her while swirling her clit with his fingers. She'd already come once—her body must have been ultra-sensitive. Jude would take full advantage.

"Jude—"

"Giving up so quickly?" He pinched her clit.

Her legs drew together as she arched her back, her head against the crook of his neck with his hand collared around her throat.

"You're not allowed to come until I say."

Her breasts bounced as he slowly thrust in and out of her, teasing, drawing out her pleasure.

"What if I—" Nova's pussy clenched around him. Her hands turned white, gripping the wood frame. She must have been right on the edge.

"If you come without my permission, I'll pull out and spank that ass until you beg me to stop, and then I'll jerk off and come all over my work." It wasn't an empty threat.

Sweet, desperate whimpers fell from her lips, the most addictive sounds. Maybe she liked that idea. His balls drew up. *Fuck.* He was close, especially with that image in his head. It had been too long. And she felt too fucking good—like her body was made for his.

Gritting his teeth, he pulled out. She let out a moan of protest.

"Addicted to my cock already?" He smiled and smacked her ass. "Come here."

He moved to the mattress, taking a seat on the comforter. Her movements were clumsy and slow as if she moved through a haze, unfocused. She stood, shoulders back and unashamed. Her tits pushed out, piercings glinting in the low light. Fuck, he loved her confidence in her body. She moved in front of him, her luscious curves on full display.

He seared this image into his memory, from the wild mass of short curls on her head down to her voluptuous breasts and dark nipples with silver barbells. Jude leaned forward, capturing one in his mouth. He smoothed his hands down her soft and warm stomach as he pulled her closer, gripping the flare of her wide hips. He fisted a handful of her ass while sucking on her tight bud. The steel of her piercing tapped gently on his teeth. She lifted the hat from his head and tossed it before threading her fingers through his hair and tugging. Pain lit his scalp—he couldn't get enough.

"Fuck, you're perfect." He groaned, licking the stretch marks on the side of her stomach, bending to nip the ones on her hip.

She jolted and gasped.

Jude's hands glided down her strong, thick thighs to her muscular calves. He pulled back to capture her full expression. "Now this is what's gonna happen. You're gonna lie on Daddy's lap and take the punishment that we both know you've earned—that we both know you need."

Her lips parted, her tiny pants increasing in speed. The corners of her mouth tilted up. She climbed over his lap wordlessly, arching her back so her ass was in the perfect position for him, her hands on the bed to support herself.

She likes that idea.

"So you *can* listen," he teased.

"Sounds like a good time."

He shook his head. "That smart mouth is gonna get you in a world of trouble."

"Tryin' to break me of the habit?" Her ass wiggled seductively—a tease.

"Nah." *Smack!* "What fun would that be?" *Smack! Smack!*

Nova moaned. "Is that the best you got?"

"I was trying to be nice and warm you up, get the blood flowing. But I think a harsher punishment is needed today. What's the word to make it stop?"

Nova bit her lip.

Smack! Smack! Smack! Jude put more weight into his swing, aiming lower for the back of her thighs.

Nova hissed and tensed in his lap. Her ass jiggled from the force of the impact. His other hand threaded through her curls, tugging so that he was in control, pinning her to his thigh.

"What's your safe word, Freckles?"

"Mmmm." She pressed her lips together.

This woman didn't make it easy on herself.

Smack! Smack! Smack! Smack! Smack! Jude pushed her limits, adding more force with each slap of his hand until his palm was stinging.

"Oh, fuck!" Nova's whole body shook.

Jude kneaded the sore and reddening ass with enough pressure that would provide both pain and pleasure. "What's the safe word?"

"Mercy! It's mercy."

Satisfaction rolled through him, a dense fog of power settling over him as he slipped into Dom space. The control was addictive. It was an honor having her trust him so fully, having earned her submission.

"Good girl. See? That wasn't so hard, was it?" He slid his

palm to cup her pussy. "Look how wet you are. Your cunt is dripping."

Nova presented her ass again grinding on his hand, a silent plea. Jude was rock hard, her belly pressing against his cock.

"More." She wiggled her ass again.

"Ask politely." He slid a finger inside her tight pussy, angling to sweep against her G-spot.

"Fuck, Jude, please?"

He leaned in, biting her ass as he added two more fingers, fucking her while his thumb hit her clit.

"Ohh! Shit, that feels so good." She whimpered and bucked against him. "I'm so close."

Jude sat up, admiring the mark his teeth had left as his hand rained down a series of slaps on both cheeks, alternating in a rhythm that made it unpredictable for Nova. Switching from left to right, he gave both sides of her ass and thighs brutal attention. Her nails dug into his leg as she held on. Over and over his hand came down, harder every three hits and then every two. Jude alternated rhythm and intensity as her cunt leaked on his thigh. Every gasp, every whimper that he tore from her throat, he wore like a badge of honor. His cock was as hard as granite from how fucking hot it was, spanking her. He loved the way her body tensed in between hits, preparing for the next one. The way her ass flexed with each strike. The whimpers that fell from her lips, turning into moans. Nova's hard nipples brushed against his thigh. Her face twisted with pain as she fell deeper and deeper into a state of hazy surrender.

Her half-open eyes grew foggy with an expression of pure bliss and relaxation. Most people didn't question marathon runners who pushed their limits to find the runner's high.

Society didn't bat a lash at their endurance of pain to achieve a euphoric state.

Nova's masochism clearly brought her the same high. Her ability to endure different levels of pain brought her into subspace, and with it came peace and grounding. And Jude was the lucky bastard who could give her that gift.

They balanced each other out. He got off on bringing her pleasure through pain. He got his own high off providing that hurt but only because she wanted it—craved it.

Jude's palm rose and fell with the strongest force yet.

"Ahhhh fuck!"

Her scream made his cock pulse with the need to bury himself inside her. Not yet. He wanted to give her what *she* needed—this release.

Jude stopped, his chest heaving. His every muscle was taut and filled with a euphoric rush.

Nova's body tensed, braced for more impact. Instead he gently ran a finger down her spine. She flinched, her shoulders shaking. Fuck, he loved it. He gently massaged her shoulders, coaxing her into relaxation. His hands skimmed down her spine and rib cage making strong, sweeping motions over her lower back to her butt. The skin on her flushed ass and upper thighs puckered up, hot to the touch.

He kneaded her ass cheek, then squeezed hard. A dark flush bloomed on her searing-hot skin.

She moaned, her voice coming out as a whisper. "Please?"

"What was that?" He dipped his finger in her pussy once more, dragging it up to her ass and using her own juices as lube as he fingered the outside of her tight hole.

Nova sucked in a breath. "Please? Please let me come?"

"Who does this cunt belong to?" he asked.

She hesitated.

Smack! Smack! Smack! Smack! Smack! Smack! Smack! Steady,

consistent, and intense slaps rained down on the sensitive flesh between her ass and upper thighs.

"You! It's yours!"

"Close, but not the answer I want, Freckles." *Smack! Smack! Smack! Smack! Smack!*

"Daddy's! It's Daddy's cunt."

Pride filled his chest. "Are you going to listen to Daddy?" *Smack! Smack! Smack!*

"Yes!"

"And are you going to watch that smart mouth around me?"

"Probably not."

Smack! Smack! Smack! Smack! Smack! Jude put more strength and weight in his intense swings, aiming for the space between her ass and upper thighs, where it would sting the most.

"Fuck! Okay! I'll try! Yes! Anything, just let me come. Please!"

A rush of euphoria crashed into him. "Fuck, I love when you submit to Daddy."

Jude released her hair and slipped that hand underneath her, swirling her clit while he resumed spanking. This time, he kept to steady, thuddy swings he hoped were just enough to send her over the edge with a delicious bite of stinging pain.

"Come for Daddy." *Smack! Smack! Smack! Smack!*

"Oooohhhhhhhhhh." Nova's whole body locked up, her thighs pressing together and trapping his fingers inside her like a vise. Her back arched, her eyes rolling up as she rode her pleasure to completion, rocking her hips in a frantic, needy rhythm. Her lips parted as she moaned, not holding anything back. Her eyes wide and glassy with heady pleasure.

Jude snapshotted the look of complete ecstasy on her gorgeous face in his mind, wanting to remember this moment forever. "You're so fucking beautiful."

She relaxed against him in a limp puddle. He picked her up, twisting them on the bed so her back was against the mattress.

"Stop trying to hide what a sexy little slut you are. Open your legs and show me what's mine now." He spread her legs apart, lifting one over his shoulder while tucking the other around his hip.

He adjusted the condom on his cock and slid inside her, his eyes rolling back at how hot and wet she was.

"You feel so good. Please move. I'll do anything for you to fuck me right now," Nova pleaded.

"Beg me, gorgeous."

A flash of defiance sparked in her eyes, but her need won out. "Please, Daddy? Fuck me hard."

More pleas fell from her seductive mouth as he thrust his hips, driving his cock deeper and harder. He fucked her with everything he had.

Nova screamed, her nails digging into his forearms, drawing blood. The sight made him feral with need. Sparks and shimmers appeared in his vision. Urgency roared inside him. His balls drew up. His spine tingled as pleasure coursed through his every nerve ending. Nova's pussy clamped and fluttered around him as she came again and again. Need drummed in his chest. His thrusts became jerky and frantic as he chased his sweet release.

"Look at you coming for Daddy." Jude dropped her leg to the bed, moving within her, chest to chest, framing her face with his arms. He continued to fuck her, bending to lock his mouth with hers. She kissed him with equal desperate hunger.

"Please, I want your cum. Give it to me, Daddy." Nova sucked his tongue and raked her fingernails down his back.

Jude groaned, his vision going white. His ears rang as ecstasy shot through him. He gave a shout. His cock pulsed, hot cum shooting out to fill the condom as his orgasm barreled through him.

Nothing but the sound of panting breaths remained as Jude stilled over Nova. Their eyes locked, breaths synced—they were still connected in the most intimate way.

Mine.

"Wow." She smiled, dreamily. "That was . . ."

"See what happens when you do what you're told?" He smirked.

She swatted his arm playfully. "See what happens when you finally give in to me?"

He chuckled and shook his head, pulling out of her. He sat up, removing the condom. Jude walked to the bathroom, took care of the latex, and cleaned up the mess of clothes they'd left before returning to her. He handed her the jar of her moon water by the bed.

"Thanks." She took a sip and gave it back to him.

"Thank you for trusting me," Jude said, climbing back in the bed next to her and pulling down the covers for her to join him.

This might be one of his favorite parts—the aftercare. After he'd broken her down, he'd hold her and care for her with gentle hands. He'd help her come down and be there when she picked up the pieces and put herself back together. It was both the most powerful and humbling experience all at once.

Nova hesitated, glancing between him and the door.

"If you're thinking of kicking my ass out, you're gonna get yourself another spanking—only this time it won't end with an orgasm."

She chewed on her lip. "You don't have to stay. I won't read into this or anything."

He sighed. "Let me help you go pee and then we'll get your cute ass back under these covers with me."

She huffed but obeyed, climbing out of bed. She swayed, a little unsteady on her feet.

"You need help walking?" He tried and failed to hold back his smirk, wrapping his arm around her waist to support her.

She chuckled. "Don't let it go to your head."

Jude helped her to the bathroom, but she stopped him at the door.

"I'm fine. Really. Stay here." She disappeared into the bathroom, shutting the door for a few minutes before she reemerged. He helped her back to the bed and climbed under the covers, sliding in next to her. Jude moved his arm under her, pulling her back against his front and holding her tight against him.

His cheek rested against the side of her head. "I promised today—we still have a few more minutes."

"And what about tomorrow?" She made a brave effort, her voice sounding almost normal except for the vulnerability bleeding through it.

"I told you. You're mine now."

Silence descended. Her breathing evened out. Was she asleep?

Jude savored the feel of her warm, naked skin against his. The way she molded so perfectly to him.

"Jude?"

"Hmm?"

"It's tomorrow."

He glanced at the clock and smirked. If she thought she was gonna push him away after what they'd just shared, Nova was dead wrong. It was clear she was used to keeping lovers at a distance. Leaving emotions out of it—much like Jude. But he wasn't letting go. When he wanted something, he went after it. It was how he became a SEAL, that determination. He'd ignored those instincts once before with Sal, and it had cost him everything. He wouldn't risk it again and make the same colossal mistake.

"It's never tomorrow, Freckles. Only today." He kissed her cheek and snuggled her closer, letting the weight of sleep drag him under.

For once in his life he wasn't afraid to close his eyes. Her presence would keep the monsters at bay like it had last time. Nova's peace soaked into his skin like cool, calming moonlight as he too drifted off to sleep.

Hours later, when the moon was high in the sky and Nova was lost to the dream world, Jude's eyes snapped open.

What had woken him?

He rolled out of bed, careful not to wake her. He searched the house for any sign of an intruder and found nothing. Jude grabbed his phone from the bathroom counter, opening it to check in with his friend, but he already had a message.

> Reaper: Boys staked out the other leads all week. Nothing to report. I'm gonna bring in someone else who we've worked with in the past for tech help. Might help us find something. Hang in there. We need more information from her about Larry Washburn. Work your magic, King.

Jude closed the app, staring at himself in the dark bathroom, only the dim moonlight threading through the bedroom providing any light.

He'd fucked up so much in the past. Nothing but blood and darkness remained back there. He'd cost people their lives. Rage and pain. Suffocating guilt. He'd learned to live with it.

Jude moved to the bedroom. Nova was curled up on her

side, her hand tucked underneath her face. She deserved so much better than him. She might have been surrounded by darkness for pieces of her life, but the woman was nothing but light.

Jude had never claimed he was a good man. He'd destroyed everything good in his life, but he'd be damned if she became a casualty too.

He climbed back into bed next to her. She rolled over facing him. Jude pulled her against him once more. "I'm sorry."

Jude traced the constellations on her face, circling the wishing star on her freckled cheek, and made a wish.

Let tomorrow never come—only ever today.

26

JUDE

J ude heaved a bale of hay out of the loft and down the chute. Tiny bits of dried grass stuck to his sweaty arms in the hot, dimly lit barn. Even with the chute open, there wasn't much of a breeze.

"You up there, Jude?" James Emerson called.

Jude walked over to the open window. "Yeah. What do you need?"

James waved. "Can you help me load some equipment in my truck?"

"Sure." Jude closed the upper opening in the loft and climbed down the ladder, then made his way out to James.

"It's a real scorcher today, isn't it?" James asked, wiping his brow.

"Definitely," Jude agreed. He'd been through hotter climates though.

"It's too hot to work, honestly. Why don't you take the rest of the day off and cool down. I just need a hand loading some equipment from the event barn storage into my truck." James nodded towards the building they held weddings in.

Jude followed him silently as they made their way to the barn.

"How are you fitting in with my wild bunch?" James asked. "I hope my boys aren't too harsh on ya?"

Jude shook his head as they bypassed the edge of the fence. A few pigs snorted from the other side. "They seem like good men."

"Heard you all found some excitement last night."

Jude tugged the brim of his hat down as if it would hide the bandage. Would he be blamed for corrupting James's sons? For being too violent? "That's on me."

James chuckled and patted his shoulder. "No need to get nervous. I'm a father to three grown men and a daughter who can be more devious than the trio of them put together. I won't claim to have seen it all, but I'm no stranger to a tussle."

Jude released a breath as they walked into the barn.

James continued, "The way I heard it, some asshat said something about my little girl, and you taught him some manners."

Jude ran a sweaty hand up the back of his head. He wasn't used to garnering approval for his actions from anyone other than a commander. He nodded, unsure of what to say.

"Thanks for being there for Nova." James's voice was rough, like he was holding back emotions.

Jude turned to him, his hand wrapped around the knob of the storage room door. "You don't need to thank me."

James smiled and shrugged. "Doesn't hurt to show gratitude where it's due."

Jude opened the door, scanning the boxes and bins and various equipment inside. "What do you need?"

"All the wine-making stuff. Those giant glass containers, funnels, box of tubes, and bottles." James pointed to each item.

Jude got to work carrying them out of storage to the truck in the parking lot. It didn't take long with both of them.

James closed the tailgate and wiped his hands together. "Thanks. I'll be glad to get rid of all this and make some room in there."

"Did you guys used to make your own wine?" Jude asked, eyeing the equipment.

James chuckled. "Nova was gonna try her hand at mead once upon a time. She gets these big ideas in that creative mind of hers. Invests a good chunk in her hobbies, and then, after the motivation fades, the supplies sit in storage. She let us know we could get rid of this stuff."

Jude wanted to ask if that happened a lot, but he didn't want to seem like he didn't know Nova all that well. "Right."

"I'm gonna take this up to the Fates sisters' winery. They can always use more supplies. You make sure to take the afternoon off and relax. You've put in a lot of hard work. We appreciate all you've done to help around the farm and for you looking out for our Akua."

Jude wanted to ask why they referred to her as Akua but figured he should ask Nova. "You're welcome. I'm just happy to have the work."

James leaned against the truck. "You have any plans of doing anything else in the future?"

Jude shrugged. He hadn't thought much about the future since everything had gone to hell a month and a half ago. Being a SEAL meant he was in danger more often than not. He couldn't worry about tomorrow—only the now. Being anything other than homed in on the moment was too overwhelming. The panic would return.

"Not sure yet." He winced. Probably not what a father wanted to hear about his daughter's boyfriend.

But James gave him a friendly smile and patted his

shoulder again. "You've got time to figure it all out. And we're more than happy to have you stay on at the farm as long as you're willing. We need all the help we can get."

"Thank you for giving me the opportunity."

"Honestly, son, I feel like I should be thanking you."

The way James casually and confidently called Jude *son* made his heart race. Jude had never known his dad. No one ever referred to him as "son" besides James and Renita. It shouldn't have been a shock to his system at thirty-four, but it was.

Guilt clawed at Jude's insides. Before coming to Shattered Cove, he didn't trust a single soul on this planet. Reaper was the one who came the closest, but even then, their relationship had been born more out of a mix of fear and mutual respect than trust. Reaper wasn't someone you wanted to be on the bad side of any more than, say, his namesake—the Grim Reaper.

Jude's throat swelled with some unnamed emotion as his gaze wandered to the mud on his boots.

James chuckled again, his joy bleeding out from him. The man with dirt under his fingernails and manure on his shoes smiled like he was a fucking king. And in a lot of ways James Emerson was. He had a wife who loved him, if the way those two cuddled and teased each other at every family get-together was any indication. James had four kids who respected him and chose to live close. Those actions spoke so much louder than words ever could. Jude had left home before he was ready, signed his life away to the military just to get free from the horrors of home. When war seemed like a better option than your mother's house? That said it all. Shame weighed down his shoulders for more than one reason.

Jude had gone in to this assignment with a ton of assumptions about this family, projecting his own experiences onto them and looking for deceit, but he'd found none. No evidence he'd uncovered hinted at the Emersons being dishonest.

How many other people have I pushed away who were genuine? Am I just wasting my time here?

"You look a little lost in thought. I hope I didn't scare you away." James straightened.

"No, not at all. Gave me a lot to think about is all."

"Good. I haven't seen Nova so content in . . . maybe never. Anyone who gives her some peace and the love she so desperately deserves is worthy of my respect and loyalty." James held out his hand.

Jude shook it, despite not believing he'd earned the thanks. He'd been deceitful.

"Alright. Go home and cool off. I'll see you tomorrow. Probably get going a little early to beat the heat. You'd think in late August it would be cooling off. Not yet." James waved and climbed into his truck.

Jude turned and walked away as the engine rumbled to life. His mind raced with what James had said and all that had happened in the last twenty-four hours.

Waking up to Nova's body wrapped around his this morning while she snored on his chest had made him smile. He'd wanted to sink into her, waking her up with a few orgasms. But he'd held off. They needed to talk first. With the things he wanted to do to her, to share with Nova, they needed to make sure they were both on the same page.

Jude smiled, an idea forming as he jogged up the hill towards Nova's house. A few minutes later, he climbed the steps, careful not to trip over the Doc Marten boots she usually left in a haphazard pile by the door.

"Nova?" he called.

"Yeah?" she asked, holding an ice pack to the back of her neck.

"You injured?" He crossed the room, taking her in his arms and removing the ice pack to look before she could even answer.

She chuckled and pressed a hand to his chest. "No. I'm hot as fuck. I read ice packs on your neck help with cooling down . . . or maybe it was migraines? Either way, it's helping."

He breathed a sigh of relief and rubbed his chest. "Go put on your sexiest bikini."

Her brows drew together. "Why?"

"Because we're going out after I shower." Jude headed towards the stairs, pulling off his sweaty shirt with her hot on his heels.

"Where are we going?"

"Somewhere you'll need a bikini." He headed for the bathroom.

Nova leaned against the door as he unbuttoned his pants. "Why are we going?"

He shook his head, blowing out an exasperated breath. "Do what I said and you'll find out."

She crossed her arms over her chest, pushing her breasts together. His mouth watered. The urge to throw his plans out the window and fuck her in the shower rose. *No.* Nova deserved better than a quick, hard fuck. If he wanted this to continue, to begin to make up for his own omissions, he needed to show her who he truly was.

Jude stepped up to her, grasping a tiny curl in his fingers and tucking it behind her ear. "Be a good girl and go get changed and stop trying to figure out what the surprise is, Freckles. This is your last warning, and then I'll start tallying this disobedience."

Her mouth parted and her brown gaze flared with heat for

a moment before she rolled her eyes. "You could have just started with *'It's a surprise, Nova.'* Geesh."

He smirked. "Where would the fun in that be? You like when I order you around and we both know it." He didn't miss her happy grin as Jude placed his hands on her shoulders and gently turned her so she was in the hall. He swatted her ass and shut the door.

When he caught a glimpse of himself in the bathroom mirror, he did a double take. Jude had a matching dopey grin on his face.

Shit. He was never going to be the same after this—not after Nova.

27

NOVA

ova's leg bounced with a mix of anxiety and excitement in the front seat of Jude's truck. He ran a hand over his wet, wavy dark hair before placing his palm over her thigh and squeezed, stilling it. The other arm flexed as he steered left towards the beaches, the veins in his hands and forearms just as distracting as his touch.

"So, we're going swimming?" she asked.

He gave her a knowing look, and those kissable lips curved up into a rare smirk. Her stomach dipped. That mouth was talented. Memories of the night before flitted through her mind. Her heart raced as her bathing suit bottoms grew damp. His warm hand on her thigh didn't help to cool her arousal.

She warred with her emotions, not wanting to get her hopes up. She knew better than to try and hold on to a man like Jude. He'd leave one day and the more she got attached, the harder it would be on her. It was best they kept things physical.

"What gives you that idea?" Jude asked.

"Come on! It's not like we can do many other things in a bikini."

He shook his head with a humorous glint in his hazel eyes. "That's part of it."

She eyed the cooler and bags in the truck bed behind her. They'd stopped at the store and he'd made her wait in the AC of his truck while he'd run into the supermarket. She had no idea what was in either container.

"This is fun." He chuckled.

She crossed her arms over her chest, trying to hide her smile as she grumbled, "For you."

He squeezed her thigh and turned into Shattered Cove Beach parking lot.

"It's fun to tease your curious mind." Jude parked in an empty spot.

She grabbed the door handle.

His hand shot out and gripped her arm. "Wait there, Freckles."

Jude didn't wait for her reply before he climbed out of the truck, walked around to her side, and opened the door.

What the hell? She got out, studying him closer. "I can open my own door."

"I know you're capable. But I like doing things for you."

Huh? She looked over her shoulder at the dozens of cars, the scent of sea reaching her nose as a gust of wind blew. A few couples and families moved towards their vehicles from the beach, none of them too familiar.

"Jude, no one knows us here. We're good to just be ourselves."

He put the backpack on, hooked Nova's bag over his shoulder, and grabbed the cooler. His biceps flexed in the spotless white T-shirt that clung to his broad shoulders. "I thought that's what we were doing."

"Since when do you open my door?"

He leaned over and kissed her mouth. "Since this is our first date."

Wait, what? He walked towards the beach. Nova hurried to catch up to him, sputtering. "Th-this is not a real date."

"Says who?" He looked both ways and crossed the pavement towards the sand.

Damn, those basketball shorts fit his ass like a glove. "Um, pretty sure you have to ask me on a date and I have to accept. Not that I would because this thing between us isn't real."

He scoped out the beach as if she hadn't said anything.

"Jude?"

"There's a spot past the sand dune. Come on, Freckles." He walked past the colorful umbrellas and other beachgoers as a few seagulls swooped down onto someone's abandoned blanket.

Jude stepped to the side, narrowly missing a little kid who darted at full speed towards the water. Nova huffed, double-timing it to keep up, but walking through sand in her boots wasn't so easy with her short legs. She didn't have the oxygen to argue.

Waves crashed against the rock wall to the right, smoothing up on the golden beach before washing back out to sea. A seagull cawed before it landed onto an empty beach blanket.

Jude set down the cooler and pulled the blanket from her beach bag, spreading it out. He set everything up and patted the spot next to him.

Nova sat, tugging off her boots and setting them in the sand. Her bare toes wiggled against the soft material that blocked some of the heat from the sand.

The hot summer sun beat down on them, but she'd never had to worry about sunburn. Sun cancer, however, was a different story. She plucked out her sunscreen and sprayed it all over.

"Need me to get your back?" he asked.

She handed him the bottle and he helped her.

"What about you?" Nova asked.

"Nah, I'm good."

"Sailors don't use sunscreen?" she teased.

"I'm allergic to coconut."

Nova blinked and then looked at the bottle. *Coconut breeze–scented sunscreen.* "Oh. Shit. I might have another kind in the bag." She reached for it, but he shook his head.

"I'll be okay. Here." Jude reached into the cooler, plucked out an iced tea, and handed it to her.

So he knew she liked her sweet drinks, but she didn't know he had allergies.

"So what's with all this?" She motioned to their spread.

He gave her a wolfish smile and pulled at the red bikini strap barely stopping her boobs from flashing the rest of the beach. "I told you, Freckles. It's a date."

"And I'm pretty sure we just established you have to ask and I have to agree for this to be an actual date."

He laughed like she'd joked. "We both know you prefer my commands than my requests, baby girl."

Heat—not from the late August sun—burned her cheeks. She cast a quick look around her at the other beachgoers. No one was too close, but still.

Jude palmed her thigh as he reached into the cooler and pulled out a sandwich. "Here. Eat up and then we can cool off in the water."

She took the sandwich from him, staring at it while her mind raced to connect the dots but there wasn't enough information. He hadn't seemed like the kind of guy who got attached after a fuck. Not that what they'd done last night was typical of her hookups. But something always happened when things were going well, and this seemed a little too good to be true. She didn't want to get her hopes up just to be let down.

"Relax, Nova. Just eat and enjoy the view." He picked out his own sandwich and unwrapped it before taking a big bite.

They ate in silence for a few minutes. A few women off to the side checked him out. Nova stiffened, wanting to grab his face and kiss him to let them know he was taken, but she had no right. And those urges were a sign she might be developing real feelings for someone she had no business catching them for.

"Is there something wrong with the food?" Jude asked.

"What? No. Why?"

"You're making a face like you ate something rotten."

She wrapped the sandwich up and reached over him to put it back in the cooler. "So is this like a consolation date?"

"No."

Nova chewed on her fingernail, her chest tightening with anxiety.

Jude's fingers threaded through hers, pulling them out of her mouth. "That's one, Freckles."

"One what?"

"Bite your nails again and it adds to your tally of punishments."

She cast a quick glance around them. No one other than the women looked their way. Honestly, she couldn't blame them. Jude was sex on a stick.

Still ... "Look, you don't need to do this."

"Do what?"

"Pretend like this is more. We're both adults who have

needs and obviously have chemistry. We don't need to make this into more than what it is."

He didn't say a word, but his smile dimmed. Jude stared out at the waves for a few minutes, his hand remaining in hers.

Is he mad? Did I screw this up? Isn't no strings what he wanted too? He made it clear he was leaving after . . . well, eventually. She chewed on her bottom lip. Had she hurt him?

"I can hear that brain of yours spiraling," he said, quietly.

"I wish I could hear what yours was thinking."

"And I wish I had more experience with this," Jude said.

"With what exactly?"

"Dating. Relationships. All of it."

"Surely you've had some."

He shook his head. "This is my first date, and it's obviously heading for disaster." He brushed his free hand up the back of his neck like he was self-conscious.

Nova blinked. *Oh, fuck.* Jude was serious. He wanted this to be a date? "You mean, you really do want this to be a date?"

"I don't play head games, Nova. I say what I mean. I don't do this." He waved towards their beach setup. He pulled his hand away from hers. "Fuck. Let's go. I'm sorry—"

Nova grabbed his hand like it was a lifeline. "No. Stop. I'm sorry. I just . . . I thought you only wanted sex."

"Is that what you want?" He didn't look at her.

She took a deep breath and let it out. "The sex was pretty amazing."

He didn't smile.

"You scare me, Jude."

He closed his eyes and gave a solemn nod like he was accepting his fate. "I see."

"No, I don't think you do. You scare me because for the first time in my life I truly feel safe with a man other than my family. But the last time I trusted someone with . . . more didn't end so well for me."

"I'm not him, Nova."

What had happened to *Freckles*? "I know. You're nothing like Brooks. I didn't—fuck—I'm still figuring this out as we go too. I guess I'm a little rusty myself. I just didn't think you'd want more than our arrangement."

Jude turned to her, taking her chin in his fingers. "I'd be the luckiest bastard on this planet if you gave us a real chance."

The energy shifted between them. Salty winds blew against them, almost as if Mother Nature herself was trying to push them together. And maybe this was a sign from the universe that she should trust Jude—trust that this really was the start of something new without worrying that the other shoe would drop.

"I think you're far better at this than you realize." She kissed him, wrapping her hands around his neck and pulling him close.

He slid his tongue inside her parted lips in a sensual dance before he pulled back and trailed kisses across her freckles.

"I've been meaning to ask you something," Jude said as she straightened.

"What's that?"

"Why does your family call you Akua?"

"It's my Ghanaian middle name. In my birth mom and Renita's culture they have names for girls or boys born on certain days. I was born on Wednesday, like my birth mom. When I changed my name in the adoption process, I wanted to keep a piece of her with me. So I'm Akua Ketewa, which means *little* Akua in their first language, Twi," Nova explained before taking a drink.

"That's really cool."

"I think so."

"Can I show you something?" he asked, pulling his backpack on his legs, his hand waiting on the zipper.

"Sure."

Jude opened the bag and pulled out the sketchbook he'd wanted to keep private before. He set it on her lap.

She looked at him for permission. He nodded and she lifted the cover. She gasped. Swirls and shapes formed by graphite covered the page in the most hyper-realistic drawings and portraits she'd ever seen. The first page had a few skulls and rotting decay in a field with shaded patches she assumed were blood. It was dark, but it was beautiful—much like the man beside her.

She turned the page, and a picture of a phoenix looked as if it were going to fly off the page. Nova pressed her hand to the flat surface. "You drew these?"

"Yeah."

"Jude, these are incredible." Page after page, his drawings progressed. Soldiers playing cards in the jungle. A desert landscape with bodies and war. Dragons, and wolves and—her. Nova stared at her own reflection. Her face in startling detail with fierce anger in her expression. She looked powerful. Was that how he saw her?

"I drew that the night after running into you with your flat tire."

"You drew this from memory?"

He shrugged, rubbing the back of his neck again. "I finished it after we moved in together."

She turned that page, and the next, and they were of her, though with much less clothes on the farther she flipped. The way he drew her… she looked beautiful.

"Jude ..." The pages blurred as tears marred her vision.

"Shit. Are they that bad? I didn't mean to make you cry." He took the book back and shoved it into his bag.

"Not at all. Those were beautiful. You're amazingly talented. I want to frame them." She wiped her eyes.

He brushed off her compliment, staring at the striped beach blanket.

Nova leaned against his shoulder. Jude tucked his other arm around her, staring at the waves.

"How did you learn to draw?"

"It's just pencil and paper, Freckles—nothing special."

"Fuck that. You could make money with that kind of talent. Pencil and paper," she scoffed. "I wish I had a quarter of that creative talent." She peeked up at him, catching the quick tilt of his lips. "You ever thought of doing something with your art?"

"I was planning on getting an apprenticeship at a tattoo shop in Michigan, but then . . ." Jude's jaw hardened as pain flashed in his eyes. "Then I came out here."

"I could talk to my tattoo artist in town. She's amazing and might be willing to take on an apprentice. Cleo was looking to have another artist or two join her shop."

Hope brightened those hazel orbs making them look green like the sea, but then Jude shook his head. "It's kind of stupid to start a career at thirty-four."

"Don't say that. It takes most people until their thirties to start to understand who they are and what they really want out of life. Don't knock yourself because you're going after a dream. That's fucking brave, to start fresh, if you ask me." Nova snuggled closer. "Vera Wang didn't even design her first wedding dress until she was forty, so you're getting an earlier start than she did. Stan Lee didn't create his first comic until he was almost thirty-nine."

Jude chuckled. "How can you remember these facts and forget what you walked in the room to get?"

She shrugged. "That's ADHD for you."

He kissed her forehead. "I like that about you."

Butterflies swirled in her belly. "I like that you're a big softie under all the grumpy scowls."

"After last night, you still think any part of me is soft?"

Nova smiled and looked up at him. "I had a lot of fun last night."

"Me too. No one's ever . . . never mind."

"Tell me."

"I've never been called Daddy before." Jude picked up a handful of sand and let it spill out back onto the ground beside him.

"First date and first time being called Daddy. You're on a roll." She laughed.

"You bring a side of me out I've never thought existed," he admitted quietly.

"I have a confession, too." She grinned, picking up his hand in hers. "I've never called anyone that honorific before either."

"Good." His smile was smug as he gave her hand a playful squeeze.

"How does it make you feel, being called that by me?"

"Like I could take on the world." Jude's statement stole her breath.

Nova sat up so she could face him better. "It turned me on too."

"I know." His grin grew.

She slapped his chest playfully. "Cocky."

He laughed, the rusty sound far too unnatural. She wanted to change that.

"Did everything we do . . . was it okay?" he asked.

"You took it kind of easy on me."

"We didn't talk about limits."

And that statement right there was why she trusted Jude. Why she hadn't worried he would hurt her or cross her boundaries despite all his commands. He was the polar opposite of her ex, and somehow she'd known what he'd just confirmed. Yet still, a piece of her held back.

"I'm not entirely afraid. I think our conversation after the cookie incident would show you that. Your needs seem to fit mine."

His hand slid up her sweaty legs, drifting under her cut-off shorts. "It would seem that way."

She tucked a curl behind her ear. "How did you get into this lifestyle?"

"My buddy in the SEALs brought me to a club when we were in Germany. What I saw there . . . things kinda just clicked. I could make sense of some of my desires and not feel like a total outcast in a room full of people who were into some of the same things."

"Clubs and dungeons can be fun." She wiped sand off her knee.

Jude curled his finger just under the line of her bikini bottoms, teasing her covertly. "What's one of your most out-there fantasies?"

"Oh, that's a fun question. I've always wanted to know what it would be like to be chased. Like, hunted down and overpowered. I would still fight back of course."

"Wouldn't expect anything less from you," he murmured, a smile still on his face.

"But it would be hot to be taken like that, pain and fucking raw in our most primal energy."

"Raw?" he asked.

"Pausing to put on a condom during that might be diffi-cult." She giggled.

"I got checked before I was discharged, and I haven't been with anyone since a while before that."

"I'm clean too." She swallowed, her gaze dropping to his mouth. She fanned her face. "Fuck, I think I might need to go for that dip sooner than later."

"Let's go." He got to his feet, pulling his shirt over his head, and tossed it on the blanket next to their shoes. He held his hand out for her. Nova took her time, admiring his abs as she slid off her shorts and slid her palm into his, interlocking their fingers. They walked to the edge of the water and she dipped her toes in the cool ocean waters. Waves lapped at her feet.

"It's cold."

"It's New England and the Atlantic Ocean. What do you expect?" Jude picked her up against his front.

Nova squealed and wrapped her arms around his neck, her legs around his waist. "What are you doing?"

He trudged into the water, the waves getting higher and higher. "You said you needed to cool off."

She braced herself as he continued farther in. The water wasn't terrible once you got used to it. This was the warmest it would get all year.

"I hope you're looking for sharks. I don't usually go out this deep." She clung tighter to him as they swam past the break and the water reached her neck. She looked around in the greenish-blue water.

His chuckle vibrated against her hardened nipples. "Don't worry. I'll pee to mark my territory."

She burst out laughing. "I don't think that's how it works."

"You're beautiful, but when you laugh like that? Christ,

Freckles." His hands dug into her ass as he pulled her closer against him. "You make it hard to breathe."

Her mouth dropped open as their bodies shifted with a wave. She stared into his eyes on the most handsome face she'd ever seen. "Don't say shit like that to me unless you mean it."

"I meant every fucking word." He leaned in, his lips sliding over hers as if he was making love to her with his mouth.

Damn, this man could kiss. Nova gripped his shoulders, sliding her tongue against his. His cock pressed against her core as she pulled back.

"Looks like not even icy ocean water shrinks that bad boy."

"It's you. I've had a constant hard-on since I met your sassy ass," Jude grumbled.

"Now that can't be true. You hated me in the beginning."

"Not at all true. I was mighty inconvenienced by my attraction to you."

Oh. "Why did you walk away from me the night in the hot tub, then?"

Jude took a deep breath as a seagull swooped and cawed overhead. "Because it wasn't fair to you, and I knew I'd be lost if I touched you. I wasn't quite ready to jump off that cliff."

"And now?" she asked, holding her breath.

"Thought I'd made that clear, Freckles." He nuzzled her neck.

She tilted it to the side to give him better access. He moved so her back faced the beach, the water lapping at the bottom of her breasts. Jude adjusted her, one of his hands slipping underneath her bikini bottoms.

She gasped, looking around them, but no one was close by this far out. "Jude—"

"No one's gonna see. You just need to be quiet and let Daddy have some fun with my pussy."

"Oh fuck." She moaned as his finger swirled her clit.

"Shhh. If you make noise and draw attention, I'm gonna have to stop."

Pleasure built within her as he played with her clit. It was like the man had a map to her body, knowing just how to turn her on. Nova gritted her teeth together, trying to hold in her moans of appreciation. Her thighs clenched around him, her feet digging into his ass. Fuck, she was so close already. Everything else fell away. The heat of the sun was replaced with the sticky warmth of Jude's skin against hers, still no match for the flames of desire he stirred within her. Water lapped at their bodies in a seductive rocking motion. Two fingers were buried inside her, his thumb swirling around her clit, and they were just a handful of yards away from the other unsuspecting beachgoers.

"I'm so close." Her voice was all breath, drowned out by the rushing sound of the waves or her own blood ringing in her ears—she wasn't sure. Nothing else mattered right then but the building sensations swirling through her body like a whirlpool of forbidden want and dark need. Tingles raced over her skin. She caught fire with raging urgency taking her right to the edge of her orgasm. A hairline fracture of her control remained, Nova slipped from the edge. She wouldn't be able to hold on much longer—

"Come for Daddy." Jude's soft command in her ear sent her over. He squeezed her sore ass at the same time that he spoke, pain melding with pleasure and making her fly even higher.

Nova bit his shoulder to stifle the scream in her throat.

"Fuck. You'd better leave a mark, baby girl."

She bit harder. His cock jerked against her. Euphoric bliss

cascaded through her limbs. Her body relaxed, as fluid as the water around her. Jude pulled his hand from between her thighs.

She leaned against the shoulder she'd bitten, enjoying the warm, hazy pleasure coursing through her body.

Jude kissed her cheek. "Thank you."

"I should be the one thanking you."

"No, Freckles, you can thank me for pain, but your pleasure is my greatest fucking honor. I'm the lucky bastard who gets to make you come."

"Jude?"

"Hmm?" His cheek pressed against the top of her head as he rocked her side to side in the cool water.

"This has been a perfect first date."

Nova didn't need to see him to know her words had made him smile. She could sense his energy shift as he squeezed her tighter.

And for the first time in a long time, those voices in her head that told her how many ways a relationship could go to hell—they were silent.

It seemed maybe she had gotten a little of that luck her brothers seemed to have after all.

But he doesn't know all of it. He doesn't know who I am, what I've been through. Who I come from.

The old familiar shame she'd carried like a weight around her neck since she'd learned the truth returned. But Nova pushed it away. Jude would understand. If anyone would, a man who'd been through what he had would get it. Trauma recognized trauma after all.

Nova was not going to let her past hold her back any longer. Not when she had Jude King holding her in his arms like he didn't ever want to let her go. She was going to jump in with both feet this time. Life was short. Nova might have a murderer after her. Her family had welcomed him into their fold. Even Ricky had warmed up to Jude.

So what do I have to lose?

My heart.

But who better to protect something so vulnerable and fragile than a fucking former Navy SEAL who happened to be her Daddy Dom?

28

NOVA

Nova relaxed on the Adirondack chair around the bonfire in the field by the event barn. Laughter and conversation came from all directions. Her niece and nephew ran around in a game of tag with the puppy, Pepper, chasing and barking every now and then as Ariel giggled. Bailey hunched over her phone, sharing whatever was on the screen with Elise as they pointed and scrolled, smiles on their faces. The scent of fresh-cut hay mingled with campfire. Cicadas trilled from the edge of the field.

Everett, her brothers, Isabella, and her dad had roped Jude into a game of volleyball. They'd been laughing and talking smack with Jude like he'd been a part of their family unit all along. Something light and warm expanded in Nova's chest.

"Come on. I thought you had skills, old man." Ricky's cocky grin was aimed at Nash.

Nash scowled back. "I was up all night with Alba. Shut your face."

Alba squealed from her grandma's arms in the chair beside Nova.

Handing the toddler a marshmallow from the s'more supplies beside the chairs, Nova smiled at Alba. "Who's your favorite aunty?"

"Mmmm mmm." Her tiny hands opened and closed as she repeated the sound.

"That's right. It's a marshmallow."

"Oh, Lord, you're gonna get her as addicted to sugar as you are." Mom shook her head with a humorous glint in her dark eyes.

"That's okay. It just makes us sweeter, right, chica?" Nova handed the treat over.

"Tank." Alba gobbled it up.

"Oh, look at you with your manners. You're welcome." Nova smiled at her.

Ding! Ding!

Nova pulled out her phone and checked her messages.

> Cleo: I can make room for an apprentice if your guy is serious. The sketches you sent over are pretty amazing. He's got talent. I'd be happy to pay it forward for a fellow veteran and show him the ropes.

Nova did a small happy dance in her chair. She couldn't wait to surprise Jude.

"What's got you smiling over there?" Mom asked.

Nova tucked her phone away. "You remember Cleo?"

Her mom's brows drew together, studying the ink on Nova's arms and legs as she pushed purple locs off her shoulder. "She's the owner of the tattoo shop in town you get your work done at, right?"

"Yeah. Well, I asked if she would be willing to take on an

apprentice." Nova's gaze darted to Jude. Sunlight from the low sun made his skin glisten golden brown. His black hat shaded most of his face. His muscles flexed with each movement as they volleyed the ball back and forth.

"Nova?" Her mom's voice drew her attention back to a knowing look.

"Hmm?"

"I asked if you were abandoning cannabis to start tattooing?"

"Me?" Nova shook her head. "No, for Jude."

"He wants to become a tattoo artist?"

Nova leaned in. "He's private about it, so don't say anything. But he's really good."

Her mom nodded. "You must really care for him if you're trying to help him make career connections in town."

Nova swallowed. And for the first time, she didn't need to lie to her mother about her feelings. "I do."

"It's nice to know you have another person looking out for you. Especially one so . . . ." Her mom eyed Jude up and down with a smirk. "Capable."

Nova burst out laughing so hard she snorted. Jude ran off the makeshift volleyball court.

"Come on, get back here, King, so we can finish beating your ass," Ricky called.

"Watch your mouth around the kids!" James chastised, playfully smacking Ricky on the back of the head.

"An ass is another name for a donkey," Eli helpfully added, stopping just in time for Ariel to tag him.

"It's also another name for a butt." Ariel giggled. She'd been finding potty humor especially hilarious lately.

Jude opened the cooler. "You know what they say about pride, right, Ricky?"

"I prefer to think of it as confidence." Ricky chuckled.

Jude walked over to Nova, sliding his hand over her shoulder as he drank from the bottle of water. He'd been doing that since their date at the beach three days ago. Finding ways to touch her, be near her. They'd spent hours talking about sexual boundaries as well as real-life limits. Jude's thumb grazed the back of her neck. She shivered and wrapped her fingers around his wrist over the corded survival bracelet he always wore.

Jude handed her the water, leaning down and whispering in her ear, "Drink up. I've got plans for later."

She couldn't hold back her smile as he pressed the cold drink into her hands.

"I'm not thirsty." She set the bottle on the ground, smirking.

Jude's left eyebrow lifted as his other drew down—a silent warning.

"Let's go, King! No use in delaying your loss," Ricky taunted. "Best to just rip off the Band-Aid."

Her grin grew. "Sounds like you're needed on the field."

Jude trailed his finger over her cheek. "That's four, Freckles."

"How are we already up to four?" she asked with a pout.

"You skipped breakfast, didn't drink enough water yesterday, and bit your nails." He kissed her nose and spun around without giving her a chance to respond.

Jude walked back to the volleyball game, shirtless and barefoot. Excited butterflies wrapped in the most delicious heat swirled in her belly. It was such a mind trip to know he had a tally going of her not listening to their agreed-upon rules. Would it be three spankings? Three was hardly enough. Perhaps he'd wait until the count was higher. Maybe he'd refuse three orgasms and edge her into desperation?

Jude stood next to Isabella and Nash, lifting up the volley-ball in his strong, capable hands.

"He fits right in." Her mom set Alba down.

The tot's sticky fingers opened and closed as she stared at them and then shoved one in her mouth. Pepper, the dog, took her opportunity to run over and lick Alba's other hand clean.

Alba giggled and screeched. "Puppy!"

Nova laughed and then returned her attention to the volleyball game as Jude served. Back and forth the players volleyed until Ricky hit the ball straight down over the net. Jude dove, saving it just in time. Isabella spiked it back over the net and right past Everett's reach, scoring the win.

"Yes! That's my wife!" Nash picked Isabella up in a princess carry as she smiled and laughed, holding up her hand to high-five Jude.

Jude's eyes lit with a new emotion she hadn't seen from him, and it looked a hell of a lot like gratitude and belonging.

"How the fudge did they beat us?" Ricky scowled.

"You know sports are not my forte." Everett shrugged.

"Right. You're lucky you're cute." Ricky grabbed Everett's face and kissed him.

"Better luck next time." James patted Ricky on the shoulder.

"How about another round?" Ricky asked. "Best out of three?"

"My tired old bones need a rest. Besides, there isn't much sunlight left." James walked towards Nova and her mom.

Nova got up. "You can have your spot back. I need to stretch my legs."

She walked to Jude. "Good save."

"Thanks, Freckles." He turned his head, scanning their surroundings, and adjusted his baseball cap backwards. "You wanna go for a walk while the sun sets?"

"Ohhh, that sounds romantic," Elise said.

Nova stuck her tongue out at her and then turned to Jude. "Absolutely."

He took her hand and led them up the path leading through the fields towards the woods.

"Don't wait up for us for s'mores," Nova hollered to her family as they headed up the well-worn trail. Instead of turning towards her house, though, they made their way towards the hill with the bend that overlooked the giant field filled with late summer wildflowers. Crickets began to chirp, joining in the late summer symphony coming from the long grass. The blue sky dimmed into a burnt orange-yellow tinged with indigo as they approached a wooden bench at the top of the hill overlooking the fields below and the barn in the distance.

Jude tugged her hand, leading her away from the bench. "Let's walk in the woods."

"Okay." It had cooled off some with the setting sun, but as soon as they entered the canopy of trees, the temperature decreased noticeably.

A light breeze rustled through the leaves. Speckles of sunset hues dappled the forest path through the breaks in the trees.

"Having fun?" Jude slipped his hand onto her shoulder.

"It's nice to get a break from the craziness." She took a deep breath and let it out.

"They're not that bad."

"I'm glad you think so too." Her lips quirked in a playful smile.

"So this path leads to the pond, right?" Jude asked, pointing to the split in the trail.

"Yeah, left will take you to the pond. And right takes you

towards the maple sugaring shack, and if you keep going, it leads up to the knoll." *Where they discovered Ana's body.*

He nodded as they turned right and tracked farther than she'd thought they would've as it got darker. He took her hand in his.

"So, are we sneaking off so you can give me my three spankings?" She licked her lips.

He chuckled. "Three is hardly enough for a proper spanking."

"That's what I thought."

"You still want to try sex bare next time?" he asked, picking up a stone from the path, tossing it in the air, and catching it in his palm.

"If you're comfortable with it. I have an IUD and we already talked about being clean."

"So we're good?"

"Definitely."

They walked a little farther in silence. Squirrels and chipmunks chattered, scampering through the forest.

"I'm not sure I'll be able to see the path on the way back," she said.

"I got you. There's something I wanted to show you, and we're almost there."

"You mean you've been out here?"

He hesitated, his hand slipping from hers. "Yeah. I've explored a bit on my runs, getting the lay of the land. Let's go this way." He motioned to a space in between the trees with no path.

She stepped carefully over the dead leaves and scrub. A branch snapped under her foot.

"We don't have shoes on," she pointed out.

"Don't need 'em. It's not too far. Keep going straight."

Nova concentrated on ducking beneath branches and not

tripping over her own feet. They must have been a mile from the bonfire.

"This better be good, Jude. Walking is one thing, fuck, hiking on a trail is a possibility, but this is not great for someone with spatial and balance challenges." She laughed.

Another rustle of wind through the creaking trees above her was the only reply. Maybe he hadn't found her joke funny. She kept going, focusing on avoiding branches and thorny bushes.

She pushed a long branch out from her path, holding it so it didn't swing back and hit Jude. "You might want to hold this."

No hand came to replace hers.

She turned, but he was gone. "Jude?"

Nova squinted in the dim woods, searching all around her. "Jude?"

No answer.

Chills raced up her limbs. The tiny hairs on her arms stood on end.

"Where are you?" She spun around. Which way had she come from? *Shit.* She was lost. It was getting dark and—

She grabbed for her phone in her back pocket, but it wasn't there. Nova smacked her forehead. Had she left it on the chair after checking the message from Cleo? *No. I know I put it back. Shit.* She'd lost her phone.

"JUDE!" Nova yelled.

Nothing.

Her heart picked up speed as another branch cracked. Fuck, she really didn't like the dark when she was alone.

A low growl came from behind her. She spun around, adrenaline rushing through her veins as her fear morphed into panic. Nova took off, racing through the woods with no idea if she was heading in the direction of her home. Branches and twigs caught on her exposed skin and hair. She ran, calling Jude's name. Where the fuck was he? Had something happened to him? She sucked in a breath. She wasn't far from where the killer had buried Ana.

Turned out a wild animal in the woods wasn't her biggest worry. Had the killer come for her and taken out Jude first? *No. He would have made a noise. Yelled for me to run or something.*

Stop screaming. If there is someone out here, I'll be like the ditsy blonde in the horror movies who dies first because I led the killer right to me! She swallowed.

Another twig snapped. She whirled around, sliding her hand into her pocket. She pulled out her knife with a shaky hand.

She stood frozen, her chest heaving and her heart racing. If Jude was out there, she couldn't leave him.

Something heavy dropped to her left. She whirled around, knife ready.

A hand clamped over her mouth. Instinctively, her arm swung, aiming the knife at the arm that held her.

If this was the end, she wasn't going down without a fight.

29

NOVA

Nova swung the knife with all her might. Before it connected, her wrist was wrenched in the opposite direction and twisted. It didn't hurt, but that didn't make it any less terrifying. A large, strong hand squeezed her fingers open until her weapon dropped with a dull thud, useless.

She scratched at the hand and arms holding her in place as something halfway between a growl and a scream erupted from her mouth. The scruff of a beard scraped her cheek. Teeth raked across her ear. A hard cock ground against her lower back. Fingers tangled in her hair and tugged, forcing her face to tilt up against her will with the burn of pain.

Nova froze. Her belly flipped with butterflies. Her panic morphed into something darker, hotter.

Jude.

"I can't wait to hear you scream for me." His hand slid under her crop top and gripped her breast over her bra, squeezing hard.

She moaned with the bite of pain, her nipples hardening.

"I'm not stopping even if you beg. You know what you did. You know why we're here. And there's only one word that will stop this. What is it?" His hand dropped from her mouth, collaring her neck instead and squeezing hard—his warning clear.

"Mercy."

"If you utter that word, everything stops. Anything else, and I'll consider it *more*. And *harder, Daddy*. Understood?"

"Yes."

His nose brushed behind her ear, trailing down her neck before his teeth sunk in.

"Ahh! That fucking hurts!"

His dark chuckle vibrated in his chest. "You wanted to see the real me, Freckles. You wanted to test my boundaries. Now run, little one, before I change my mind and fuck you right here."

His hands dropped—Nova took off. She crashed through the trees, the dim sunset still lighting her way just enough. She jumped over a log and turned. Her heart raced with a mix of excitement and danger. Sweat broke out on her forehead. All her senses zinged on full alert. Her legs ached and her lungs burned. The man was silent and stealthy as an assassin. He could have been right behind her and she wouldn't even—

A dark figure burst out of the woods to her side. Nova screamed. The shadows of the forest were a primal painting across Jude's chest, his abs flexing with each feral breath ripped from his lungs. His sharp, white teeth were highlighted in the shadows of the forest. His eyes gleamed with something dark and predatory. The man before her was Jude but he wasn't at the same time. Her Jude was a grumpy, scowly guy who used his calluses to cover his soft center. But this primal version of the man was more like a wolf—stealthy, intimidating, and craving violence. There would be no mercy.

Nova gulped. What had she gotten herself into? And why was she so fucking turned on?

"Giving in already, Freckles?"

She shook her head. "No." She backed up one step and then two, her eyes not moving from his.

He didn't come closer, but his dominant, depraved energy reached out, wrapping around her, holding her captive. Her knees trembled. Another step back on lead feet and her back hit the rough bark of a large fallen tree behind her.

His mouth curved up. "There's nowhere else to run."

"I—"

His hands wrapped around her throat, cutting off the blood supply to her brain. She pushed him away but it was no use. He was too strong.

The bark cut into her back as he leaned her over the trunk. Nova scratched down his arms, her stomach flipping. Would he drop her on her head?

She gasped as her body was wrenched from the tree, thudding onto the soft ground. Jude's weight settled over her, his thighs on either side of her hips.

A dark laugh erupted from him. Nova's heart drummed, her thoughts quieting until all that was left was *fight*.

He pinned one of her wrists to the leaf-covered earth. Jude grabbed for the other. Nova swung her hand, connecting with his cheek with a hard slap. Her eyes widened as his grin grew feral.

"Fuck, I love it when you fight back." Jude's deep, hungry voice sent shivers through her.

"Good. Because I'm not giving in." In a move she'd practiced with Ricky a hundred times, she planted her feet, knees up. Using all her strength, she pushed her arms wide and whipped her elbows to his knees on either side of her rib cage. In the same instant, she lifted her ass in the air, throwing him off-balance. She tucked and rolled to her feet, sprinting into the trees. A smile of triumph lit her face as sadistic laughter echoed through the darkening woods.

"Run all you want, little one. Catching you will be that much sweeter," Jude taunted from somewhere close behind her.

Nova darted to the right, jumping over a bush to a small creek. The pebbles were rough on her feet, but she didn't slow, ducking under a half-fallen tree covered in dense moss. She kept going, darting around trees, zigzagging as her chest burned from all the exertion. She stopped just to catch her breath. She turned to look behind her, fully expecting Jude to grab her again, but he wasn't there. She wasn't naive enough to believe she was alone this time. He was watching her. She could feel the heat from his gaze searing her skin. Nova licked her lips, scanning the moving shadows in the woods. She backed up a step, a small twig snapping under her weight. She froze. Still, nothing moved. She took another step back and hit something solid—no *someone*.

Fight returned as she spun. But it seemed Jude wasn't underestimating her this time. His chest rumbled with a satis-fied sound. He probably thought he'd won. But Nova wasn't done yet.

She swung her fist. Jude blocked her with a swipe of his arm. He grabbed her and forced her down on her belly. She gave in, hoping he believed she was ready to surrender. She huffed, gulping in breaths of sweet oxygen as his hips settled on both sides of her waist. Those rough hands pressed hers to the ground—again. She bit back a smile. Hadn't he learned anything?

Jude bent, inhaling the juncture of her neck, and dragged his teeth along the exposed flesh. She hissed. The bite of pain only added more endorphins to the delicious cocktail of hormones rushing through her body.

Nova just needed him to let his guard down. She exhaled, relaxing her body as if accepting defeat. "You're fucking heavy!"

He chuckled but shifted his weight away from her ribs. "How does it feel to know you're at my mercy?"

"Cocky," she retorted, lifting her left knee to the back of his at the same time that her right arm punched forward, knocking him off-center. She pushed up, rolling them, her back to his front and then she spun to face him, fist swinging towards his cheek.

But Jude wasn't an average Joe. He was a former SEAL. He grabbed her fist, spun her around, and lifted her before she could take another breath. Her body met a hard tree, arms hugging it. Jude's front caged her against the rough bark.

She struggled but it was no use. He fiddled with something near her hand. Something thin tickled her wrist as his hot breath puffed against her temple.

"Let me go!"

"Never," he snapped.

Something cinched around her wrists, pulling tight.

"What the—"

Cool air met her back as Jude walked around the tree. She tried to pull away, but that cord in his hand held her in place.

His eyes gleamed and his lips curved into a feral grin as he continued tying the thin rope.

When had he had time to grab that? Her focus dropped to his wrist. That survival bracelet he always wore was gone, leaving only a light tan line where it used to be. *Inventive.*

Jude pulled her knife from his pocket and cut the end, using her own weapon against her in a sense. He bent, grabbing her calf roughly.

"Oh, no you don't." Nova kicked with her other leg. It did nothing but make her lose her balance. Bark scratched against the inside of her arms, her wrists screaming in protest at the weight on them from her fall.

Jude finished tying one ankle to the tree and moved on to the other, giving her ass a shove and a smack. "Behave."

"Fuck you!"

The cord tightened around her ankle. She gasped. Jude stood, locking eyes with her. "Oh, little brat, I'm going to really enjoy making you scream for me."

Jude gripped her shorts, tugging at the button until it popped open. He yanked them down her legs, shoving them as far as they could go until they reached the binds on her legs.

"It's hot how helpless you are."

Cool air teased her wet pussy. Her inner walls clenched.

"Now, let's see, how many were we at? I think we'll go with ten to start."

"Ten what?"

"Wouldn't you like to know." He walked away from her.

"That's why I asked, asshole!"

"Fifteen."

A snap sounded somewhere behind her. Steady footfalls came closer. Her heart rate increased the closer they got.

Something hard and cool traced over her lower back, sliding down her bare ass. She gasped.

"You like nature, don't you, Freckles? With your colorful rocks and moon-blessed water. Well, what if I told you I planned to mark this smooth brown flesh with welts and bruises from the gifts of the earth?"

Nova whimpered partly in excitement and partly in fear. Her body trembled with anticipation. That warmth in her belly swirled, but it wasn't an innocent fluttering of butterflies.

No, this was stronger, darker—a murder of crows taking flight, making wide arcs in her stomach and soaring from her mouth in a moan of want.

"My little pain slut wants it. Don't you?"

She pressed her lips together, not ready to submit fully. She still wanted that push and pull.

The smooth tip of the switch he'd plucked from one of the trees lightly swatted her cheek. Her eyes widened as she met his hungry gaze.

"Let's warm you up."

She opened her mouth to taunt him.

Stinging fire lit her ass in a thin strike like a whip. A whimper escaped her. Hot pain lanced across the other side of her ass. His strikes were relentless. But not too much—just enough to hurt, not overpower. He alternated from one ass cheek to the other. Every once in a while, he'd increase the force. Nova whimpered and hissed. Gritting her teeth, she took everything, closing her eyes and surrendering to the pain —it was the only way through.

Jude groaned, his long fingers tracing the hot lash marks on her ass. A moan escaped her at his gentle touch, a complete contrast to the painful switch.

"Look at you, wearing my marks. Such a good little whore. I think you deserve a reward."

She gasped as his thick fingers swirled around her clit. A needy whine slipped through her clenched teeth. Nova arched her back, seeking more. She shamelessly rubbed her pussy against his hand, seeking pleasure to inoculate her from the stinging pain that would no doubt come.

He laughed. "Mmmm, you like that, don't you?"

"Yes," she confessed.

"Yes, what?" He teased her with gentle swirls and light strokes.

"Yes, Daddy." Her pussy clenched in anticipation of those thick fingers sinking into her core, filling her. God, she ached for him.

But Jude withdrew his hand, sliding her arousal over her burning ass. The air cooled it, drying it on her skin.

He gripped the back of her neck. "That was just the warm-up."

Nova whimpered, mentally trying to prepare herself for more pain.

"For every strike of the switch, you'll count. Failure to do so results in us starting again." His hand clamped over her jaw, holding her in place as he leaned in. "Now be a good girl and scream for Daddy."

30

NOVA

Nova screamed as stinging pain lit up her ass much harder than any of the other hits before.

"Five!"

Jude's warm hands massaged her aching skin. Her ass was on fire, all the blood rushing there from his rough ministrations. His hand replaced the switch, slapping her hard, but it was a dull hum of pleasure compared to the thin branch. His palm thudded against her again and again. Nova's toes curled, her nails digging into her palms. The pain dulled into hazy pleasure. She slipped into subspace.

Jude groaned. A thrill lit her blood on fire. She needed to endure his pain just to draw more of those delicious sounds from him.

"God, you're beautiful with all these welts. Taking it like a good little whore."

The switch tapped the back of her thigh and she gasped, her whole body twitching and clenching in anticipation. He fucked with her mind the way he did her body. She never knew when to expect the next hit, and that kept her off-balance. She had no choice but to trust.

Thwack! Thwack! Thwack!

"Ahhhh! Fuck! Six, seven, eeeeight!" Her ass radiated with pain that walked the fine line of being overwhelming. Her safe word was at the tip of her tongue—but then those wicked hands massaged her ass. Nova took a breath, enjoying the small reprieve before he began again. The pain lessened, but her ass burned like it was on fire. She leaned into his firm, comforting movements but Jude had other plans.

Thwack!

"Nine!" she cried, barely able to speak. But the last thing she wanted was him starting over.

"So you *can* follow directions," he teased.

Nova gritted her teeth, biting back her retort. Her ass clenched in anticipation of more pain. If she hadn't called him an asshole, she'd only have to endure one more. There was no way she was tempting fate with another comeback.

"What's wrong? No comment?" He laughed again at her expense. He slid his fingers into the back of her hair and tugged, his lips caressing her ear as he spoke. "So she can keep her mouth shut too."

Nova's teeth felt as if they might break under the pressure of her holding back her retort. Six more. She could do it.

Thwack!

"Ten."

Thwack!

"Eleven." Jude groaned. "Fuck, you look so hot like this. Tied up at my mercy. Ass turning a beautiful copper and covered in so many welts. The way you flinch when you think I'm gonna strike you again."

His warm hands slid over her sensitive backside like a lifeline of relief. "The way your ass shakes as it absorbs my hits. You're a fucking living, breathing work of art."

Her mind went fuzzy with his appreciation, the blooming pain sinking and transforming to a blissful buzz humming through her every nerve ending. His groans of approval helped her morph into one of the highest highs she'd ever experienced. The urge to take everything he had to give her like his good little slut overrode the primal instinct to flee the pain. Instead, the hurt melded together into the most euphoric feeling of subspace.

His grip at the base of her head tightened. She sunk deeper into this warm pool of bliss. Pleasure swirled, flames licking her belly. Arousal leaked down her spread thighs. Her pussy clenched, begging silently for something to fill her.

Thwack!

Thwack!

Thwack!

"Ahhhhhhhhhh!"

Thwack!

Nova detonated. Ringing filled her ears. Her body locked up. She was no longer aware of the bruising scrape of the bark, or the pain coursing through her ass—only the crash of her orgasm as it stole her breath and sent her flying. She gasped.

Warmth met her back. With gentle touches, Jude cut her hands and ankles free. She slumped against him, sinking into the relaxing warm euphoria her orgasm had brought.

"Twelve, thirteen, fourteen, fifteen," she gasped through the haze, not wanting to disobey and start over, but also because she didn't want to disappoint him.

He kissed her temple and her forehead, her nose and cheeks while massaging her wrists. "You did so good."

She caught her breath. Orgasm from intense pain was like

getting the wind knocked out of you—sudden and over-whelming. But in a minute or two—maybe three—it passed. And then Nova would be ready to go again. But Jude didn't know that.

He cradled her gently in his arms like she was made of glass. Like she was precious. His tender care was a complete contrast to his rough treatment before. She wanted vicious Jude back. She wasn't ready for this beautiful scene to end.

Nova rolled to her knees.

"Nova—"

"Just give me a second." She wobbled to her feet, kicking out of her shorts and panties.

Those assessing eyes raked over her.

She smirked at him in challenge. "Is that all you got?"

Nova didn't miss the flash of surprise in his hazel gaze before she turned and sprinted her bare ass into the woods once more. She didn't make it far. She stumbled over a branch and her leg gave out, still jelly-like from the orgasm and stiff from being tied to a tree. Jude caught her before she could hit the ground. He picked her up and laid her back against another large fallen tree. His hand wrapped around her neck, pushing her further onto her back, bruising her skin. Her nails dug into his forearm, clinging so she wouldn't slip. Not that she believed he'd let her fall, but it was instinct. And if he could leave marks on her, she'd make sure to do the same with him.

"Jude—" Nova kicked.

He dug his hands into her thighs. Pain lanced through her soft flesh, and there was no doubt in her mind that the bruises and marks from tonight would last for a long time. That only turned her on more.

Fuck, her pussy was so wet and hot, but more importantly —so empty. The way Jude took control mixed with the adrenaline from the chase made for the perfect aphrodisiac cocktail. She hissed and stopped fighting.

"You're gonna do what I tell you when I tell you, little brat, because you're MINE."

Fuck, did he just growl?

He yanked her legs farther apart and stepped between them. Cool air brushed against her sensitive folds. Her sore ass rubbed against the bark. She arched into him, needing friction.

Jude slid his fingers through her pussy lips, swirling around her clit. "Fuck, you're already dripping wet? Of course you are, my pathetic whore. You getting off from pain is the hottest fucking thing I've ever seen."

Nova whimpered. Her body wanted this so much. Desire surged through her veins, spinning and gathering in power. She craved this. Needed him to strip the control from her. "Don't—"

He sunk two fingers inside her pussy. Her stomach clenched, and her eyes rolled back with the most heady rush of pleasure.

"Stop." Her pathetic plea only added to the forbidden fantasy playing out.

His fingers slipped out of her.

Smack!

Smack!

She gasped as stinging waves landed on her exposed pussy.

"This cunt is mine. And I'm gonna do whatever I want with it."

His palm returned to her pussy, and he was fucking her hard with three fingers while the other hand on her neck slid down to pinch her nipple through her bra and shirt. The piercings added an extra layer of pain.

"Oh, oh, ohhhh!"

"And there's nothing you can do to stop me. You're gonna take it like my good little slut." Jude yanked on her shirt. The sound of ripping fabric filled the woods.

"Fucker! That was one of my new shirts!"

"You're gonna pay for that little outburst." He growled, slapping her pussy before he sunk three fingers back in and started fucking her with them again.

Jude unhooked her bra clasp in the front, not bothering to take it all the way off. Nova held her breath, bracing herself for the pain. His mouth descended on her breast. Teeth clamped on to sensitive flesh. She screamed as sharp pain lit up her nipple when he tugged.

"Fuck, I love these pierced." He licked the spot, the warmth of his tongue soothing the bite just a little. Jude backed away, nibbling a trail down her stomach. He sucked her thigh, his sharp teeth dragging across the sensitive flesh.

"Jude!"

"I love how you suffer so beautifully for me."

She whimpered, her legs reaching out to wrap around him. She kicked against his thigh, but his grip was too strong. The movement scraped her back against the tree.

"I wish I could tell you this wasn't going to hurt, but I'd be lying." He smirked.

Fire heated her blood. Uncontrolled masochistic want sunk into the marrow of her bones. Hot, wanton energy pulsed between their bodies, feral and wild like the rush of wind just before a summer storm. Nova was going to combust.

"Hurt me good, Daddy."

Jude stood. One minute, Nova was balancing precariously over the fallen tree, and the next she was pulled to her shaky feet, facing Jude.

He backed her up in the other direction and pinned her

arms to another tree with his hand. "Open your legs like the little whore you are."

She pressed them closer together in defiance. His dark chuckle sent shivers down her spine.

Jude's lips brushed against hers. His hazel eyes were dark in the shadows, black as midnight with a new moon.

"Good girls don't come. Now be an obedient little whore and open your legs for Daddy to use you." He nipped her jaw. "This is what you deserve."

She tilted her chin up. "Make me."

He licked his lips, violence shining in his eyes. "You're fucking perfect."

She sucked in a surprised breath, his words shooting straight past what was left of her defenses to her heart. Jude plied her legs apart with bruising force and hiked them over his hips. Nova's legs wrapped around his waist. The bulge of his cock rocked against her core. She moaned, her head tilting back against the tree.

"Your pussy doesn't deserve to be dripping with my cum. Beg for it."

"I don't beg," she snapped, her will fading with each thrust against her exposed pussy.

Jude pressed her wrists harder into the bark, his other hand undoing his shorts. They dropped to the ground, his cock springing free. Each drive of his hips forced the tip of his cock through her slick folds. Fuck, she was dripping. Her arousal slid down the back of her thighs.

"Tell me you deserve this," he commanded, his free hand wrapping around her throat once more.

Her lips clamped shut.

Jude ran his nose under her jaw and nibbled on her ear. "Tell me what a dirty whore you are. How you deserve to have

Daddy fuck your cunt whenever I want. These sexy tits?" He pinched her nipple with the bite mark.

She whimpered.

"They're mine too. And I've got all night to break you. Make you cry pretty tears. No one will come looking for you. I already texted your mom from your phone and told her you'd decided to call it an early night."

Her eyes widened. He'd picked her phone from her pocket? *Sneaky and sexy.*

"We're far enough away that no one will hear your screams. It's just you and me, my aching cock and sadistic mind." He snapped his teeth near her ear, menacing and vicious.

She had no idea what he was capable of, but she trusted that if she said one little "mercy," the soft side of him would come out and he'd be gentle and caring with her and start the aftercare they'd agreed on.

But Nova didn't want gentle—she wanted fire and flames. Raw, unbridled power emanated from the man, and he wanted *her* to be the vessel for it. To submit to him in every way. Lust thrummed in her veins. A need like no other intoxicated her, making her drunk. A fog settled in her mind as she drifted into subspace at the safety his absolute control offered. The sensation of his firm grip on her wrists, binding her in place, made her wetter. The rough cut of the bark at her back took her deeper into submission as she surrendered to the pain. The insistent drive of his cock against her clit brought her closer and closer to the edge of her orgasm. All she had to do was give in, surrender, and trust that he'd catch her.

Tears of desperation, of giving in, dripped down her cheeks. "I deserve this. I'm a dirty whore. Punish me, Daddy. Use me. Fuck me. Please? Please, I'll do anything."

Jude's thumb swiped the tear off her cheek, his eyes glittering with satisfaction before he sucked the saltwater from his finger. A pleasured sound rumbled from his chest.

Pride surged within Nova. His mouth crashed against hers in a tangle of teeth and tongues. This wasn't a kiss—it was a conquering. Jude fucked her mouth with his own, greedily taking all she offered and more. Her back arched. She ground against his cock, trying to slip it inside her.

Without warning, he pulled away, setting her down on her knees. Leaves and small twigs bit into her legs. And then he was behind her. He twisted her hair in his fist, holding her up as his cock slammed into her.

"I'm gonna go deeper and you're gonna take it like my good little pain slut, aren't you? You're gonna let Daddy mark you inside, too, aren't you?"

"Yes, Daddy!"

He fucked her without mercy. His big cock plowed through her tight hole, hitting her cervix. She broke apart, screaming as all that frantic, needy energy combusted into a cyclone of euphoric rapture.

Darkness edged her vision. Pain and pleasure melded, as did their bodies, until they became one with a violent crash like thunder and lightning. A storm of sadistic, chaotic bliss exploded with each drive of his hips. Jude's erotic grunts and groans only made her fly higher.

She wasn't able to do anything but dig her nails into the earth beneath her. Her pussy clenched around him as every molecule surrendered to the torrent of pleasure that wracked her body, drumming through every breath, encompassing every gasp and moan that filtered through her lips.

"Fuck!" Nova cried out. Her hands gave out. Her cheek pressed against the cool leaves and earth turned up from their struggle, a complete contrast to the wildfire raging within her.

Their slick, heated bodies slammed together with a force she'd never known.

"You like this because you're a little brat who needs to be punished, don't you?" He tapped her hand. That was her nonverbal cue. Despite her not being gagged, he was checking in on her, making sure she was still in this—still wanting to continue.

Nova gave a thumbs-up gesture.

Jude pressed his hand to the back of her shoulders, pinning her down, ass in the air as he continued to fuck her. He hiked one leg over his hip. "I don't care if you can't take it anymore—I'm gonna fuck you anyway. You feel too fucking good to stop."

Stopping was the last thing Nova wanted as her eyes rolled back and white-hot pleasure blinded her. She didn't care about anything other than the feel of his veiny, thick cock pounding her pussy. The moans and slap of flesh were the only sounds in the otherwise quiet woods. Her nails dug into the earth, holding on for dear life as she was fucked harder and faster.

More. More. More.

There was something so primal about the weight of his body pinning her to the forest floor, the scent of dirt and leaves and pine soaking the air around them while she was ruthlessly used in the wild of the woods.

"I'm gonna come in this tight little pussy. Ready?"

"Yes, Daddy!" Nova screamed as her body locked up. Another wave of pleasure exploded through her, tearing her world apart until only one thing was certain—she would never be the same after this. Jude King had ruined her for all others.

"Nova!" Jude's cock pulsed inside her, filling her with his hot cum.

His weight descended on her again, his hand releasing her shoulders, sinking into the dead leaves beside her head. His chest heaved against her back. Their mingled sweat stung the cuts on her back. A heady warmth floated through her boneless body as a small sob tore from her. She didn't have the ability to speak—there was nothing left of her but a puddle of bliss.

Jude's arms wrapped around her as he sat back, still inside her. He held her in his arms, moving and cradling her sideways across his lap.

She tilted her face upwards, tracing the line of his strong jaw to the night sky above. A few stars poked out in the indigo sky between the tips of the trees overhead that swayed in the warm breeze.

Jude's soft lips pressed against her temple. He cupped her face, his forehead leaning against hers. "Thank you for trusting me."

Jude plucked a twig from her hair and tossed it onto the ground. He wiped the tears from her cheeks, looking at her as if she were the greatest treasure. Like she was worthy of so much more than she believed.

"Thank you for making my fantasy come true." She kissed him, soft and slow, a complete contrast to the rough fucking they'd done.

Their dynamic wasn't traditional; it was taboo. It was exactly what she needed—what she craved. Excitement and freedom. This was a part of her only Jude would ever see.

He pulled back. She couldn't even see his face now that it was so dark in the woods. She shivered in the coolness of the forest. Her body was breaking out in gooseflesh. His warm limbs wrapped around hers like a furnace.

"Let me grab our clothes. Your phone's in my pocket. I'll carry you home and run a bath. Then I'll clean your cuts and get you some food. I'll hold you while you fall asleep. We can talk about the scene we just had tomorrow."

She nodded, unable to form words as her eyes filled with tears once more. Only this time, they were tears of overwhelming emotion, gratitude, joy, release, excitement, and something that felt an awful lot like the beginning of love.

Nova didn't protest as Jude gathered their things, helping her into her bottoms before he pulled his own pants on.

"I'll replace your shirt." He lifted her, holding her against his chest as he made his way through the forest, seeming careful to turn and take the brunt of the slap of branches so none would harm her.

"Worth it."

And so was Jude.

31

JUDE

Jude's whole body reverberated with need. Hot, delicious licks teased the crown of his cock. The image of Nova planted on her knees with sunlight dappling her smooth brown skin in the forest painted the back of his eyelids as he shifted to the floaty space between asleep and awake. But whatever he was lying on was far too comfortable for it to be the ground.

And that hot little mouth that sucked his cock was far too real to be a dream. He cracked his eyes open. Loose brown curls tumbled onto his naked thighs. Nova's head bobbed up and down on his cock while that devious little tongue flicked over the tip and then traced down the sensitive vein to the base. He groaned, fisting his hand in her hair. Her ass lifted, giving him a brilliant view of the healing scratches from their scene in the woods the night before. Seeing those temporary marks—his marks—on her otherwise smooth skin almost had him coming.

"Fuck, Freckles. You tryin' to kill me?"

She hummed around his cock in answer. Abs tensing, Jude

sat up on one elbow to get a better view of the angel in his lap. She sucked harder, and he guided her head faster—deeper. Her throat constricted around him in response. Fuck, she was perfect.

"You like making Daddy come, don't you?"

She nodded, sucking him harder as he fucked her mouth.

"That's my girl."

One of Nova's hands wrapped around his balls, massaging, while the other landed on his bare thigh, chipped black nails digging in and scraping mercilessly like the little firecracker she was, leaving angry red marks in their wake. Pain and pleasure gathered at the base of his spine. His balls drew up.

"I'm so close." He pushed her head down, holding his cock in her throat, cutting off her supply of oxygen. *One . . . two . . . three . . .*

She hummed. His eyes rolled back. A rush of euphoria burst through him, his cock spurting hot cum as he released his hold. It took all his strength to pull back out of her sexy mouth so she could breathe again.

Nova stared up at him, eyes half-lidded, honey brown with lust burning in their depths.

The trust, the awe, the gratitude in them floored Jude. *And what have I done to deserve her?* He needed to open up more, tell her why he'd come there. Why he'd sought her out. And how it had all changed once he'd gotten to know her.

Nova smiled and licked her lips as if savoring every drop. A groan left him, uninhibited. He clasped her face and drew her up on top of him, kissing her. Her mouth parted on a gasp, like she hadn't expected it. He slipped his tongue inside, sharing his taste. He fucking loved it. Loved that he'd marked her on the inside and out. Loved that she tasted like him. Smelled like him. Wore his marks. Fuck, he loved—*wait. No.*

He couldn't love her. Two weeks was hardly enough time to fall for someone. Wasn't it?

Nova pulled away, giving him one more quick peck on the lips. She snuggled to his side, lying on his arm. "Did you think you were dreaming?"

A humorless half-chuckle escaped him as he shook his head. "For a minute I did, baby girl. But I don't usually dream. All I've ever had were nightmares or nothing at all." He turned, facing her on his side, staring into her understanding gaze. "You're my one and only sweet dream."

She smiled, biting her lower lip like she was self-conscious. "But I'm not a dream."

"I fucking hope not."

She giggled. Her joy lit up the room more than the sunshine filtering in past the opaque curtains blowing in the breeze from the open window.

Jude dragged his knuckles over her cheek, memorizing this moment. Her tangle of curls dripping over the silk pillow and his arm. The freckles splattered across her face like a galaxy of wishing stars. The way she looked at him as if he was her savior. A sweet dream indeed.

Her pert little button nose scrunched, those adorable little wrinkles forming. "What's wrong?"

"I don't want to lose you." He gave her the truth. He might not have been in love, but he knew a treasure when he found it. Jude wasn't an idiot. And for the first time in his life, he had hope that maybe he could have something good and not fuck it up. Someone who wouldn't be scared off by his past, by what he'd done. By the blood on his hands. His failures. And his sadist tendencies.

I'm going to tell her everything.

Her expression softened. She cupped his face. "I'm not going anywhere."

"I need to tell you something." His voice came out like gravel. His chest constricted, his heart thudding against his rib cage like a war drum.

"Oh, me too." Excitement bounced off from her in waves as she wiggled against him like she could barely contain it.

"You first." He wanted her to keep this joy just a little longer before he tore it all apart.

"I talked to my friend Cleo—she owns the tattoo shop in town. I, um, well, I showed her a few of your designs—I hope you're not mad."

"You showed her my drawings?" he clarified, vulnerability lighting his body on alert.

"Yes, and she said she'd love to have you as an apprentice. Isn't that amazing?"

He blinked.

"You hate me now, don't you? I overstepped?" All the joy left her expression, the room dimming along with her as if the very sun had slipped behind a cloud, depending on her joy for its radiance.

He felt a lot of things in that moment, but none of them were anger. Jude traced a finger over her forehead and tucked a stray curl behind her ear. "I would normally be livid. Feel betrayed."

Her eyes dropped to his chest. Jude tipped her chin up, forcing her attention back to him, but she closed her lids.

"Look at me," he commanded softly.

She squeezed them shut tighter.

"Freckles," he warned. "That's one."

Her eyes popped open, watery and unsure. Her steel walls were already being rebuilt.

"Don't do that."

"Do what?"

"Hide from me. Not after what we shared."

She blinked, searching his face as if trying to understand him.

"I'm not mad. I'm . . . touched. Overwhelmed. So fucking grateful. No one's ever . . . believed in me the way you do." Emotion rose, clogging his airway. Jude's eyes burned. He cleared his throat. "A week ago, I'd have been mad. You should have asked my permission."

"I'm sorry."

"But I feel like I know who you are. I know you'd never do anything out of malice. You're petty but only ever in response to someone doing you or those you love harm. You're not calculating."

Her throat bobbed. "So you're not mad?"

"Let me show you how I feel."

A beat of silence passed before she gave the slightest nod. Jude leaned in, softly capturing her lips with his in the sweetest soft kiss. He savored her taste, the feel of her in his arms. He pulled her tighter against him as he rolled over until he was on top of her, his weight on his elbows on either side of her head.

Jude pulled back, pressing tender kisses over her freckles and her closed eyes.

"Watch me, baby girl." *See what I can't say with words.*

Those brilliant brown orbs obeyed, staying on him as he backed away, taking in her gorgeous naked body beneath his. Bite marks and hickeys decorated her throat and breasts. He kissed each one in gratitude. His palm stretched over her throat. She would look even more beautiful with his collar there. *Fuck. I've never been interested in collaring someone before. Because I'd never met Nova. It's just her I want.*

"You're so fucking sexy." His hand splayed over her soft stomach, his mouth pressing to each silvery stretch mark zigzagging over her flesh. He kissed every mark on her body made by him, nature, or her yesterdays as if he could take it all, possess every piece of her past, present, and future.

"Jude?" Nova's voice shook as he bent to the apex of her thighs.

Tears welled in her eyes, but they didn't fall. It was as if she were still holding back. But Jude was a selfish bastard and he wanted it all, whether he deserved it or not.

"It's okay, baby. I've got you." Jude bent, licking through her warm, wet slit. His lips brushed her pussy lips and the neatly trimmed hair. His tongue swirled around her clit.

"Mmmm," she hummed, blinking once. Twin tears slipped down her cheeks. She wiped her face and glanced at the wetness with wide eyes as if she, too, was surprised by the emotion stirred up between them.

"Let go. I'll be there to catch you," he promised, licking her, gentle and exploring. Teasing her to the brink. More wetness dripped from her sweet pussy, and he lapped it up, groaning his pleasure. "You like how Daddy eats you out?"

"Yes." Her voice was nothing but breath.

"Let me hear you, little one. Don't hold back. Never with me, understand?"

She nodded, her eyes rolling back as he slid two fingers inside her.

Whimpers and moans fell from her sweet mouth like an erotic symphony. Jude was the conductor finding the right tempo, the specific pressure and pattern that sent her into cries of ecstasy. Over and over again. He ate her like a man starving because he was. And Nova Akua Emerson was his redemption. She'd been there at his fingertips the whole time. And he'd been too much of a blind asshole to realize it.

He would tell her everything after he'd wrung out as many orgasms as she could take, and then—and then it was time he gave her the truth. He hoped it was enough and that he wouldn't repeat his past mistakes and ruin everything he cared about.

Nova's scream sunk into his flesh, burrowing into the marrow of his bones.

She was worth every risk.

"Tell me who you belong to," he demanded, mercilessly forcing another orgasm from her.

Nova arched her back, her hands gripping the sheets, her legs tangling in the blankets at the base of the bed. She tried to wiggle from his grasp but he held firm. His palm matched the handprints and the purple bruises on her thighs, but he didn't hold back.

"Say it!"

"YOU! I belong to you."

Jude added a third finger, fucking her and lifting her hips to suck her clit into his mouth. Her thighs locked around his face, blocking his ability to hear as she clenched him like a vise.

Nova was his. And just like that, he became hers. Even if Nova hated him for his lies, Jude wasn't letting her slip through his fingers.

His hand fisted her ass, and he gave her another lick as she came down. He smirked, tasting her essence on his lips. She'd marked him too—right down to his soul. And he was never letting her go. Not if she begged, or pleaded, or cried for mercy. She was his. And Jude—he had a feeling he'd been hers for far longer than he wanted to admit.

Jude crawled up her body, kissing her, brutal and unforgiving. She bit his bottom lip, tugging playfully with a hint of pain.

He smiled down at her hazy and sated expression. "Mine."

32

JUDE

"We have to leave the bed at some point." Jude brushed his fingers up and down Nova's spine, taking care around the small scabs he'd cleaned after their shared bath the night before.

Nova groaned against Jude's chest. A puff of warm breath coasted over his skin, his tiny hairs standing on end.

"Let's take the day off. What's the benefit of being self-employed if we can't play hooky once in a while?"

"Only one of us is self-employed." He chuckled.

"Right, well, as your boss, I'm telling you to take the day off."

"Oh, really? You're telling me what to do now?"

"Mm-hmm."

"Don't let the power get to your head," he teased.

"Trust me, I like when you wrestle it from me." She winked.

A whole-body laugh erupted from him. "That sass is one of my favorite things about you."

"You have more than one?"

"Freckles, I've got a whole damn list."

Her eyes lit up. "Oh, I want to hear!"

"And you will. But first we need to get some sustenance and go over the scene we had. I need to know what you liked and what you didn't like. What we could do better next time."

She waved her hand, setting it on his chest. "That's easy. I liked all of it. Repeat it, but maybe chase me a little longer. Oh, maybe we could do it again at night under a full moon. You could pretend to be the Big Bad Wolf and I could get a red cape."

"That sounds hot. You want me to chase you, and what happens when I catch you?" he asked.

"I thought that was obvious. You get to eat my cake." She laughed.

He shook his head. "I do like your cake." He slid his hand down to cup her sex.

A small gasp left her parted lips.

"Sore?" he asked.

"A little, but don't let that stop you. It feels better when it hurts."

"Come on." Jude used all his self-control to roll out of bed.

She groaned in response. "But the bed is so comfy."

"I'll make you cheesy scrambled eggs and bacon, and you can even have a cup of that horrible sweet stuff you like in the morning while you text Cleo back and give her my number." He dangled the reward in front of her.

"I'd rather have you for brunch."

He smirked, blood rushing south to his cock at the thought. "Trust me, I would like that too, but we need to get you fed and then we need to have a conversation. Besides, it's past brunch and into late lunch at this point."

Nova's gaze drifted to the clock and her mouth formed an *0*. "Damn. Okay, but I get you for dessert later."

"You won't hear an argument from me." Jude picked out a crop top from her drawer and a pair of cutoffs, and tossed them to her.

"What about a bra and panties?"

"I like easy access." He grinned.

Her clothes would cover most of her marks. But the ones on her neck would stand out. Jude liked the thought of her walking around town on his arm, his marks keeping every other man envious of the queen he'd found.

"You seem very pleased with that idea," Nova said.

"Because I am. Now get dressed before I add to that tally."

She grumbled and mumbled something under her breath, but she rolled out of bed and disappeared into the bathroom.

Jude went to his bedroom, grabbed his toiletry bag, and brought it into her bathroom.

She was peeing on the toilet, her eyes widening. "A little privacy?"

"I've gotten to know every inch of your beautiful body, Freckles. Nothing to hide from me now."

She rolled her eyes, wiping before she flushed. Nova walked over to the counter. "I draw the line at pooping."

Jude shrugged. "Agreed."

He took out his things and brushed his teeth as she worked on her tangle of hair. Nova winced through the process.

Jude spat and rinsed his mouth. His hand hesitated as he considered putting the toothbrush back in the bag. Instead he placed it by the sink, right next to hers. A silent statement. A further merging of their lives. It shouldn't have been a big deal, but for the first time ever, Jude considered having roots. He wanted to belong to someone and for them to belong to him. Not someone—Nova. He wanted to stay.

"Fuck. Some days I hate curly hair."

"Let me." He took the brush from her.

She spun around, not even hesitating to trust him. "You'll need to keep it wet with the spray bottle or it will all frizz and break."

He sprayed the hair, finding the knot. Gently, he worked it free.

"You've done this before." She stared at him in the mirror.

He nodded. Images of Sal tore at his chest. Guilt crashed into him, sucking the air from his lungs. How could he be focused on his happiness when she might still be suffering so much because of him?

"Hey." Nova turned around and grabbed his wrist near the hand that held the brush. "You don't have to talk about it if you're not ready. I get it."

Nova would understand.

"I want to tell you. I planned on it today after breakfast."

"Okay, and I'll listen."

She faced the sink once more, taking out a product and squeezing some in her hands before applying it to her hair. She did the same with a bottle of oil on the counter. "Okay, ready. I'll meet you in the kitchen." She stood on tiptoes and kissed his cheek.

Jude took a moment to gather himself. He finished in the bathroom and went to his room to get dressed before making his way to the kitchen.

Nova was already cracking eggs in a bowl. "I've got the bacon in the oven."

"You go sit, and I'll finish here." He wrapped his arms around her from behind and kissed her neck.

"Don't have to tell me twice," she teased, grabbing her sweet tea and setting herself up on the kitchen island. Her gaze seared into his back as Jude turned the stove on and got to work finishing breakfast.

A few minutes later they both had plates of bacon and cheesy eggs with toast. They dug in. Nova's stomach rumbled.

She laughed. "Guess I was more hungry than I realized." She took a bite of the eggs and one bit of bacon. "These are so good. Thanks for cooking."

"It was a team effort."

They ate in silence, mouths full to refuel after their adventurous twenty-four hours.

"I'm so tired. I forgot how draining a scene can be the next day," she mused, pushing her plate away. Only the crust from her bread remained.

"I was thinking of going to the café for a treat and then maybe we could stop by the bookstore and you could show me some of your favorite books."

Her joyful expression lit up her whole face. "You want to read one of my books?"

"Maybe get some inspiration for this wolf fantasy of yours."

She clapped her hands together excitedly. "We don't even have to leave—I have the books here. But I'll never pass up a trip to the bookstore."

"It's a date . . . *after* we talk."

"Right, what—"

Ding-dong!

Nova and Jude's attention snapped towards the door at the same moment. She got up and he followed her.

"You expecting anyone?" he asked.

"No, but my family doesn't exactly make appointments." She pulled out her phone and clicked on an app. "It's the mailman."

She opened the door. A guy about their age held an envelope and a scanner in his hand. His eyes tracked down Nova's body and then back up. Jude slipped beside Nova, wrapping his arm around her waist possessively. "Can we help you?"

The mail guy's attention flicked to Jude, and he blinked. "Yeah, I've got a registered letter for Nova Emerson I need signed for."

"I'm Nova." She held out her hand.

The guy held up the device. "Just need you to sign here with your finger."

She did. The mailman glanced at the mark on Nova's neck. His pale skin turned a light shade of pink before his gaze flicked to Jude and then to the device.

"Here ya go." The mailman tucked the device under his arm and handed the envelope over along with the rest of her mail.

"Thanks."

Nova carried the mail inside as Jude stayed in the doorway, waiting until the guy returned to his van and headed back down the drive. Jude closed the door and joined Nova by the bar in the kitchen. Her fingers ripped open the letter frantically.

"What is it?" he asked, coming to stand in front of her.

She pulled out a letter. All the blood drained from her face before panic seized her expression. Jude's body went on alert.

"What is it, Nova?" he repeated, moving to read the letter.

Remember when you used to scream for me? I'll have to refresh your memory when we meet again. Enjoy what's left of your time because it's running out.

You're gonna pay for everything you've done to me.

It was just a few lines, yet somehow a dark evil poured out from it as if the paper itself was inked in malice.

Jude ripped it from her hand, like he could somehow protect her from its vicious taint.

"I need to call the FBI." Nova's voice trembled almost as

much as her hands as she pulled the phone from the charger on the counter.

Someone was coming for Nova. Threatening *his* woman. Jude saw red and he let it envelop him. Violence buzzed through his veins, darkness swirling inside him. The need for blood and vengeance soared to the forefront. He couldn't lose her too. Not when he'd just found her.

"Tell me what happened in that house."

Nova fumbled with the phone, dropped it on the counter. She picked it back up but he pushed it down to the marble countertop.

"Did that bastard touch you?" he pressed.

She turned to him, blinking rapidly. Her fingernail slid between her teeth. Jude pulled it out of her mouth, holding it in his tight grip.

He stepped into her space. "Tell me, Nova, did that fucker touch you or Sal?"

Nova's panicked eyes widened. If he'd thought she was pale before, now she was a ghost. Shit, he was scaring her. He needed to tone it down.

"You . . . you know Salem?" Her words were a punch to his chest. The air was sucked from his lungs. He'd wanted to tell her, but not like this.

"I can explain."

"No." She shook her head, pointing her finger at him. "You called her Sal. Only her friends called her that." Nova backed up, looking at him as if he were a stranger. "Who are you, Jude?"

He stepped forward. "Nova—"

She flinched back. Pain streaked, jagged and spiked through his chest. Was she afraid of him? Nova's focus darted to the door and then back to him like she was finally seeing the real Jude King and trying to find the nearest exit. She looked at him as if she was finally witnessing the evil that lived inside him. The blood on his hands. The violence in his past. Like he was a monster.

Nova had every right to be afraid.

She should be terrified.

Because those suspicions were right.

Jude was a killer, and he was out for blood.

33

NOVA

Nova's lungs burned as if she'd inhaled pure fire. That could be the only explanation for the utter destruction wreaking havoc under her ribs. Pain suffocated her as she stared at the man she'd let into her home. The man who'd saved her. The man who'd torn down the walls she'd held up since she could remember. The man she'd been stupid enough to fall for. Jude King—if that was even his name. *Is he the killer?*

He'd had so many opportunities to end her life if that had been his plan. But the killer clearly wanted her to suffer, and what better way to observe her agony than with a front-row seat to Nova's dumpster fire of a life?

Wary, Nova stepped back until her spine met the cool marble countertop. Her hand itched to grab on to something to protect herself.

I thought I knew him. That he'd bared his secrets to me. But Nova should have known better than anyone how deep and dark a person's secrets could be. There were things she'd never told a living soul, not even the woman who'd adopted her and become her mother after her own had passed. What did she really know about Jude?

His words flooded her mind, haunting her like ghosts from her recent past.

I'm the one who has so much to atone for.

I've killed a lot of people.

After I've truly taken everything you have to give will I revel in the mess I've made.

Nova's stomach roiled, vomit climbing her throat.

I should have known better. She sucked in a breath, clinging on to the pain. It would help her through this next part—their inevitable end. Would he try and kill her now? Could she fight him off?

"Who are you?" Her voice was a whisper, but it cut like a knife as she drew back, putting more distance between them.

Regret poured off him in waves. Those hazel eyes, so full of life and hope only minutes before, were now empty and soulless. Maybe they'd always been that way and she'd clung to the delusion that she could actually have a second chance. That she could have her own happily ever after. Yet there she was with another liar. What should she have expected? She'd come from a monster; it was no wonder she was attracted to them. That was her penance for existing. Her fate written before she'd breathed her first breath.

"You know who I am." Jude's voice grated.

She shook her head, a humorless hysterical laugh eking from her body. "I know bits and pieces pulled from you while you were stoned out of your mind. But what's truth and what's a lie?"

"It's all truth. Just not the whole of it."

She scoffed, stepping to the side, testing him. Would he block her exit?

Jude held his palms up. "Let me explain. I was just about

to tell you everything—"

"Liar!" Her vision blurred. She angrily swiped at her eyes. He would not see her break. She would not give him that power ever again. "Are you here to kill me too?"

He flinched. "You think I'm capable of that kind of evil?"

"Ten minutes ago I would have said never. But now? Now I'm not sure of anything."

He winced, his hands lowering to his sides as his shoulders slumped. He almost looked genuine. But it seemed even now, Nova's intuition was wrong.

"It's not me. I would never hurt you or any other woman like that, Nova."

"So how do you know Salem?" she demanded, her hands fisting at her sides to keep from showing him how much she trembled. No one would be able to save her if he was here to kill her. No one would be near enough to hear her scream before he silenced her or overpowered her. He knew how she'd try to evade him from their time in the woods. *I was so stupid to trust him.*

"Salem's my sister."

"You said you didn't have any siblings."

He grimaced. "Because I was afraid you'd notice the resemblance."

Nova blinked. Memories of her short time in the house from hell assaulted her, leaching from the cage she kept them in.

Salem's jet-black hair and dark eyes flashed in her mind. "Salem's white."

A humorless laugh left Jude. "I would think you of all people wouldn't buy into that 'all families match' bullshit."

She stared at him. "You have the audacity to chastise me right now?"

His chest rose and fell, an emotionless mask sliding over

his face. "Salem and I share the same bitch of a white mother. Salem's dad was Latino. She's just white passing."

"You should leave."

"No."

The word slammed into Nova. She flinched.

"I'm not here to hurt you."

She scoffed. *Too late for that.*

"I was about to tell you everything before you got that letter."

"Are you kidding me?"

Jude slid his fingers under her chin. "Freckles, I—"

She slapped his hand away. "Don't you ever fucking touch me again. And my name is Nova. Not Freckles. Not baby girl or little brat. Not anything else to *you*."

His mask slipped for a moment. Pain and regret speared through his eyes.

"Nova." His voice came out gruff. "Please just let me explain?"

"Now you're the one begging?" Done with retreating, she stepped into his space. She'd promised herself after Brooks that she would never lie down and take abuse of any kind. That she would fight tooth and nail for herself even if she was breaking apart inside.

She tipped her chin, looking him dead in the eyes. "I don't want to hear you spin more lies to try and mess with my head and gaslight me."

"This is what I was trying to tell you—"

"How do I know that?" Her chest heaved. "How do I trust anything you have to say to me?"

"That's rich coming from you." He growled, not backing down. "You lie to everyone that gets close to you just so you don't have to deal with confrontation. That's why I'm in this goddamned house to begin with!"

She blinked, looking up at him. Rage and pain churned in the inch of space between them.

"I never lied to *you*." Her voice came out as a whisper.

"Just your family, so that makes it okay?"

Yes, it was hypocritical of her. But damn it! She'd let that man into her heart.

"Why did you come here?" she asked.

Soul-crushing, all-encompassing grief bled from him, coating her skin, sticky and heavy like tainted oil. "To find out what you knew about Salem. How you were connected to all of this." The truth of his words was like a javelin, piercing her already shredded heart.

"Why didn't you just come and ask me?" she asked. Why the secrecy?

His eyes dropped to the floor.

Oh. Wow. "You thought I had something to do with it."

He gave one stiff nod. "Either that or you'd stonewall me."

"I would have helped you."

"I know that now. But where I come from, people don't do anything out of the kindness of their hearts. They always want something in return."

"So that's why you pretended to be nice? Why you saved me from those men? Why you agreed to this fake relationship? Why you stood up to Chad? Why you fucked me!" She fumed, but the remaining light inside her flickered. The hope she'd had for a future. For her happily ever after. "You wanted something. You—you *used* me."

His arms lifted as if he was going to reach out to her and then he dropped them, hands balling into fists like he'd thought better of it. It was a good call. She wanted to scratch those sad eyes out. Sink her teeth into his lying lips.

"None of that was a lie. That's why I held back. I didn't

want to start something when I wasn't giving you the whole truth. When I wasn't in it for the right reasons."

"I guess that went out the window, huh? You fucked me over and then fucked me."

Jude's hand collared her throat, pushing her back against the counter. He didn't squeeze—just held her in place so she couldn't move.

Her nails dug into his forearm. "Let me go!"

"Don't you *ever* reduce what we shared to a quick fuck," he commanded with a deep voice. His eyes were wild and unhinged; she stared into his soul. Death and grief. Pain and blood. Regret and despair. Darkness spun from him like a web of shadows. "I had no ulterior motives at any time when it came to watching you get yourself off in the hot tub. That's why I held back that night."

Could it really be?

"When I laid you out on the sink and feasted on your sweet pussy it was because I wanted *you*. When I chased you through the woods to fulfill your fantasy, and this morning, when I took every piece of you you offered up, it was because I wanted *you*, Nova. I wanted to bring you the highest pleasure and the sweetest pain that you—that *we* crave."

"How do I know that isn't just another lie?"

Jude's chest rose and fell. "Because you're the only person on this planet that I've let in. Despite my objective, I chose *you*. Somehow, while searching for my redemption, I found you." He leaned in, his nose brushing up the side of her face as he inhaled her scent. "My actions have never proved otherwise."

Nova's eyes fluttered closed, her emotions blurring. She hated that she was weak to him. That everything inside her screamed to give him a chance to explain. To work this out. But she couldn't afford to chance it. She'd never risk being vulnerable again. He'd broken her for good.

She rebuilt the wall, brick by brick. Every second, she reinforced what was left of her crumbling, tattered attempt at keeping herself safe.

"I told you I wasn't a good man. I told you I was a monster, and you didn't listen. You pushed and pushed."

He was right about that. Damn her weakness. This was why she didn't let new people into her life. They fucked her over and abandoned her when they'd had their fill.

Jude pulled back enough to look her in the eyes. "I told you I was a monster, yet you still gave yourself to me, little one. I'm never letting you go. You're *mine*. And I'm yours. We will work this out one way or another."

"Excuse me? You've got some balls if you think you get to tell me what to do." She stood her ground.

"No. I have hope. You gave me that."

"I can't believe I was stupid enough to trust you before. If you think that will change now, you will be sorely disappointed."

"I didn't lie to you—I omitted things. But I've always been the real me when I'm with you. You know me more than my own fucking best friend."

Her mouth opened. "I didn't realize you even had friends. So I guess maybe you're wrong. I don't know shit about you except you're a lying asshole!" She shoved him, but his body was like granite—unmovable. "Let me go!"

He sighed and dropped his hand, giving her space once more. But Jude was still too close. "My friend Reaper is who I was staying with before I came here."

Nova blinked, her stomach twisting. "You weren't living in your truck?"

Jude's eyes dropped to the floor. "No."

That one word had such finality, like a nail in a coffin. Her skin prickled like tiny spiders crawled up her spine and down her limbs. Sweat broke out on her forehead, hot and sticky and then icy cold the next moment. Her chest constricted.

The killer had just delivered another threat directly to her door.

Jude King was not the man he'd claimed to be. He'd been playing her the whole time. What was truth and what was a lie?

It was too much. Overwhelming pressure crushed her chest. She didn't have time for a panic attack.

He won't see me break.

Nova closed her eyes. She took all the pain raging inside her like a hurricane and shoved it into a box. She mentally locked it and buried it into the deepest recesses of her soul until she felt nothing. Numb, she blinked. Staring at the fridge, she left her body. Her armor slid into place just where she needed it. *But how long will it hold?*

"I never wanted to hurt you." Jude's voice was soft and coated in honesty.

Lies. Fuck, he was good. Better than Brooks. So much so that her bleeding, tattered heart believed him. You'd think that glutton for punishment would have learned its lesson by now.

She motioned to her phone on the counter. "I need to call the FBI and tell them about the letter and warn the other girls. Then I'll tell you what you want to know so you can leave."

She grabbed the phone and pushed past him, heading for the stairs.

Gentle fingers gripped her hand. "Nova—"

She yanked it back. "I told you not to touch me."

"I'll make this right. I promise."

She didn't bother responding.

What were more words worth when they were soaked in lies?

34

NOVA

Nova spat out the toothpaste in the sink in an attempt to remove the taste of vomit from her mouth. She stared at herself in the mirror, unable to recognize herself. Her usual liveliness was gone. A shadow of the blissful reflection she'd experienced only an hour before stared back at her. Nova ran a hand over the pale skin of her cheek, under her dim eyes. She'd bought herself a few minutes, calling the agent in charge of the case, Mallory. The agent had asked her questions and was on her way with her partner to come gather the evidence and fully question Nova.

Would they offer to take her into protective custody? Would she have to leave her family? Would her brothers and parents be safe?

She closed her eyes. *Why is someone after me? And who?*

The shrill ring of her phone interrupted her thoughts. She gasped, nearly jumping out of her skin.

Unknown caller.

Nova's hand trembled. What if this wasn't some random prankster? What if this was the killer calling her? Her thumb hovered over the answer button. Her mouth was bone dry. Still, she tried to swallow. Could she face whoever was on the other end of this line? If she mouthed off to them, would they hurt someone else she cared about?

The ringing stopped.

Her foster father's blue eyes flashed in her mind, making her skin crawl and bile rise in her stomach once again. She needed to tell her family. She had no choice but to warn them.

She texted Ricky.

> Nova: Everyone needs to be on extra alert. Don't let the kids go anywhere unsupervised, and no one go anywhere alone. I'm safe, and I swear to God, if anyone shows up on my doorstep, I will lose it. The FBI are on their way. I'll update you once my interview is over. I just need an hour at least before you tell everyone else.

> Ricky: What the fuck? I can't keep that a secret! What happened?

> Nova: You owe me. I'm calling in my favor.

> Ricky: You already called in that favor . . .

> Nova: I'll never ask you for anything else in my life. Do this one thing for me. I need an hour.

> Ricky: Is Jude with you?

Nova sighed, pain threatening to escape the confines of the cage she'd buried it in. She shoved it down, taking steady breaths until the numbness took over again.

> Nova: Yes.

Ricky: You've got one hour.

Nova: Thanks.

She pulled up her texts and clicked both Carrie's and Amanda's names to send them a group message this time. She didn't have the energy to do individual updates. She didn't need the letter in front of her to remember the threat—it was burned into her brain.

Remember when you used to scream for me? I'll have to refresh your memory when we meet again. Enjoy what's left of your time because it's running out.

You're gonna pay for everything you've done to me.

Nova's stomach churned as she shut her phone off and slipped it into her pocket. But the sender listed on the envelope had been Salem Cade—Jude's *sister*.

Nova walked into her bedroom, her attention falling on the rumpled sheets of her bed. The room still carried the faint scent of sex. *How could the situation between us change so quickly?* The last time she'd been this ungrounded was when she'd found out the truth about Brooks and had had the rug ripped from under her. Nova marched up to the bed, fisted the covers, and tore them off it. She stuffed them into the washer, her hands shaking with rage, and took one last deep breath before veering for the door.

Time to rip the rest of my life apart.

Jude was waiting on the center of the couch, back hunched, head in his hands. His elbows rested on knees spread wide, like he carried the weight of the world on his shoulders. Nova shouldn't have pitied him, but she couldn't help hating the sight of Jude in pain. It only made her angrier.

She tipped her chin and sat at the farthest seat from him on the couch.

He straightened, turning to her immediately. His eyes were bloodshot and glassy. Brown tufts of hair stuck out from his head in disarray, like he'd been pulling it repeatedly. Dark shadows had sunk into the hard lines of his unfairly handsome face.

She focused on her hands, picking the skin around her nails. "Salem was at the house before I was."

He stiffened. "How did you get there?"

She shook her head. "I don't owe you that."

He swallowed, his Adam's apple bobbing. "Go on."

"We lived with our foster parents, Larry and Kim Washburn. When I got to the house, there were already six other girls living there. Their niece, Amanda, whom they had taken in, shared a room with Anastasia, the first victim. Then Simone, Hannah, and Carrie shared the room next to them. Two of them were dead now. Lastly, there was Salem and me. She was the youngest in the house and I'd never had a sister before. We just clicked."

Nova fought against the reminders of her past that tried to rise like a tidal wave. If they did, they would sweep her into a world of pain and trauma she didn't want to revisit. Still, it was like cutting Nova's feet on shards of memories like broken glass.

"My first few nights were fine. The girls were quiet for the most part around Kim and avoided Larry altogether. Except for Carrie." She smiled. "That girl was a bitch to everyone. She hated being there and made her feelings clear on the subject to all of us."

"So Carrie and Amanda are still alive?" Jude asked.

"Last I checked. I just sent them a message letting them know about this letter." Another beat of silence passed. She was thankful Jude didn't press her, letting her go at her own pace—it was the least he owed her. "She talked about you, you know? Salem, I mean."

His jaw pulsed. His shoulders hunched further, as if the weight over them had increased. Jude's mouth opened and then snapped shut like he was afraid to ask a question.

"She told me about her big brother who was supposed to come and rescue her from that place."

The room dimmed as if a cloud of guilt had swept into the space.

"I failed her so many times." His voice was seeped in regret, nothing but gravel.

"I was with her when she got your phone call. When you told her you were being deployed."

Pain etched onto his face, carved into the marble of his profile. The lines at the corners of his eyes were like scars of past regret.

"I didn't have a choice. If I'd known—"

Silence descended, sharp as a knife, accusatory and unforgiving.

As a teen herself, Nova had been angry at a boy she didn't know in support of her friend. But as an adult, she understood that life wasn't as simple as she'd once believed. Justice was hardly ever granted. To love was to open yourself up to pain. To live was a game of survival.

"The first Saturday I was there was different than the rest of the days I'd stayed. Kim left for her weekly bible study. Larry called us all down to the living room."

Nova's chest burned like acid, fighting against the memories. His calculating eyes had raked over the girls. They'd landed on her that first night. Her skin crawled, the memory of feeling his oily flesh on hers.

The couch shifted. A warm hand covered her own.

"You're hurting yourself." His voice was as gentle as his touch.

She looked down. Crimson blood pooled in the bed of her nail. She took a shaky breath and let it out. Facing Jude, she spoke her truth. "He called us to the living room like what he was doing to us was completely normal and didn't need to be hidden." She sniffed. "Larry was a monster. He said that we were *his* girls. His to protect from the world. And in return, we would keep his secrets. If we didn't, we'd be called liars and no one would believe us. No one would ever take our word over his, a man of the community. A leader in his church. A loyal husband. We were the broken ones. And it was his job to cleanse us. If we didn't obey, he'd send us somewhere worse."

Jude's skin heated. His breathing turned ragged, but his hold on her never tightened. His eyes never wavered from hers.

"He'd make us watch." Nova took a breath, trying to steady the tremble in her voice. "He'd chosen Ana that night." Her eyes crashed shut. The scene replayed in front of her. Bile rose in her throat.

"Nova, you're safe. You're not there anymore. We can stop. You don't need to—"

She pulled away from him, standing and walking to the fireplace. "This is what you came here for." Nova wrapped her arms around herself, as if by some miracle it would protect her. But she knew better. She needed to get this out. She'd never told anyone what had happened, except the police. They hadn't believed her at first either. She would rip the scab off and bleed, let it all out finally.

"You don't have to—"

She shook her head, filling her lungs with a deep breath.

"He said we had to pay for our sins. Amanda pleaded with him for us. She begged him to take her instead of Ana. Every

Saturday, she'd step in and beg. Sometimes he listened, and other times, he'd just make her join in."

"I'm going to kill him." Jude's voice was lethal and sure.

Butterflies swirled in her belly. The idea that someone wanted to protect her, was willing to take a life to end the nightmares that plagued her—but no. Jude wasn't there for Nova and she needed to remember that. He was there for revenge for Salem.

She cleared her throat. "The week he chose Salem . . ."

"Tell me."

She looked at him. Why did he want all these details? She didn't need to ask. *Because he's punishing himself.*

The guilt he carried—it was for Salem. Sure, a lot of it was for the men he'd lost, brothers in service. But the obsidian shadow that hovered over him, bearing down on his shoulders —that was for his sister.

"So you can punish yourself more? You said yourself you had no choice. You were enlisted, just finished boot camp, and had orders to deploy. You had no idea what was happening because of Larry. You're not at fault here," she said.

He might have lied to her, manipulated his way into Nova's life, but the things that had happened in that house were not his burdens to bear. Salem wouldn't want that for him. She loved her big brother.

Jude shook his head, shooting to his feet, towering over her like an avenging angel. "It is my fault!"

"Why did you enlist at seventeen, Jude?"

"To make a better way for my sister and I. She wasn't safe in that house with our poor excuse for a mother who had men coming and going. The older Salem got, the more their gazes lingered. I was powerless. I couldn't support us. Enlisting gave me options. I never wanted her in the system, but my mother fucked up like always and Salem wasn't safe at home. I'd hoped after boot camp—" He pressed a fist in his mouth.

The urge to comfort him rose, but she held her ground. He'd still betrayed her. But his reasons were understandable. *I'd do anything for my brothers.* She shook her head. She couldn't be weak. Not right then.

"Unlike the other girls, I grew up with a mother who loved me and did everything she could for me. I was taught how to speak up for myself. My mother never wanted me to be a victim like she—"

Jude's intense and perceptive gaze pinned her in place.

"Like she?"

Nova hadn't meant to let that slip. She stared at the floor, squeezing her arms tighter against herself.

"Nova—"

"I guess it makes sense that I fall for the depraved. That I crave it. I'm the product of one of the most violent and unforgivable acts of immorality and sedition. My biological father raped my mother. A white man who thought he could take what he wanted without repercussions—and he was right. And in return he gave her AIDS." The confession scraped from her throat. She was unable to stop it. Spewing her truths over the room like they couldn't be contained anymore.

From what Nova filled in from what Renita had told her, Nova's mom, Cynthia, was the product of an affair—an embarrassment Nova's grandparents wanted buried.

"She endured so much shame because of her assault. The cops treated her in horrific ways when she tried to report him. She never got an exam. Never got tested. It ate away at her. She grew sicker and sicker until it was too late." Hot tears dripped down her face.

Jude's strong arms wrapped around her. She tried to push him away, shaking her head, but he only held on tighter. His woodsy scent filled her nose, grounding her. She hated it. Hated that he could still make her feel comforted despite having ripped her heart to shreds.

"It wasn't your fault."

"I wouldn't be here if not for her greatest suffering. I was the constant reminder of that. A burden she was sidled with on top of the disease, as if a death sentence wasn't enough." She scoffed. "I'll believe I'm innocent of blame as soon as you do." She looked up at him through blurry eyes and shoved him away harder.

He let her go but still stood close, his body thrumming with barely contained violence. But Nova wasn't frightened. She understood it wasn't aimed at her.

Her skin itched like she wanted to crawl out of it. Decades of old pain lit every cell as her stomach churned. But she still had a story to tell. If not for Jude, for Salem—anything to help find her old friend.

"I told the social worker after I stole a voice recorder from the pastor's office at church. I set it in the living room as Kim left for her group meeting. That night, he chose Salem."

"Christ." Jude pulled the ends of his hair. Agony streaked across his face.

If Nova was a vindictive person, she could have hurt him with the details. She could have made him hurt like she was. But Jude was already in pain. The few times he hadn't been, hadn't carried that shadow with him, were those intimate moments they'd shared.

Could he be telling me the truth?

"Tell me," he grated, his hair sticking out at all angles, curls knotted. Those bloodshot eyes speared through her down to her very soul.

The image of a terrified Salem with empty eyes, like she

was already far away from the room of horrors, flooded Nova's mind.

"NO!" Nova pulled the younger girl behind her.

Larry tipped his head to the side, a sick smile twisting his thin lips. "Oh? Do you want to be cleansed tonight instead?"

"You're a fucking monster!"

Larry's laugh reverberated through the room.

Carrie scowled at her, her fists angrily shaking at her sides. "You're just going to make it worse!"

What was worse than this? Nova shook her head. Salem's body shook behind her, rattling Nova's teeth.

"Uncle Larry. Please don't. I'll do it. Just let them go," Amanda begged.

Larry didn't even look at his niece. "No. This one needs to be taught a lesson. She needs to be cleansed. Bring me the straps, Amanda."

He came at Nova, twisted glee morphing to excitement.

"NOVA!" Jude framed her face in his hands. "Look at me, Freckles. Come back to me." His voice was like a lifeline, pulling her from the memories. "I'm going to kill the mother-fucker. He will never touch you again."

How she wanted to hear those words. Have someone looking out for her—a partner to have her back so she could finally let her guard down. She'd thought she'd found that with Jude. He made it so easy to just give in and let him take the lead. But she couldn't betray herself like that again by settling for less than she deserved. Accepting half-truths and secrets.

She shook her head. "No, he won't. I made sure of that. I got my evidence. I hurt him before he could hurt anyone else again. When he tried to shut me up, I bit his fucking dick. When the police came, they could match my teeth marks to his injury. So they could hear the recording to back up my testimony." She shoved her finger at her chest. "*I saved me.* Just like I will again."

"Nova—"

She moved to the other side of the couch, out of reach. She grabbed the checkbook from her purse. "No, Jude. I gave you what you wanted. I gave you the truth." She scribbled a sum on the check, barely able to see through the tears welling in her eyes once again. Nova forced the emotion down.

"Here." She handed him the check. "For your work."

He glanced at the paper in her hands. "I don't want your money."

"So the fuck was enough of a payment? Got it." She pushed him away the only way she knew how.

He blew out a breath like he was trying to maintain his sanity. "I'm not going anywhere. You're alone and vulnerable."

"Don't act like you fucking care."

"I do. I do fucking care, and that's been the problem since the moment you blew out a tire on that fucking dark road."

"You used me!"

"Like you used me to lie to your family?"

"That's different—"

"How? How is it different? You lied to protect the people you loved, to save them from seeing you as a disappointment."

She flinched. His words had hit their mark.

Jude stepped closer. For every step he took she moved back until her shoulders hit the door behind her.

"But guess what, Freckles? I lied for the same intention. To help find my missing sister and either rescue her or avenge her death. To find the bastard who thought he could get his slimy fingers on someone I cared for. The only person I loved until—"

"Don't!" She shook her head. "Don't say that. Not now. That's low, even for you."

"It's the fucking truth. You gave me yours and I'm giving you mine. I fell in love with you, Nova. From your scuffed Doc Martens to your black, chipped nails. To your addiction to sugary treats you try and pass off as breakfast. To your chaotic and disorganized and creative mind."

"Stop." Her protest came out in a whisper.

"Ask me anything in this world. For the blood of someone who hurt you, or a head on a platter. Ask me for the moon you dance under. But don't ask me to stop loving you. Don't ask me to leave you unprotected."

Nova sucked in a breath tainted by his intoxicating scent. The air crackled between them. It was filled with so much pain, rage, and trauma. But there was something else tinged along the edges, wrapped in warm, cloying hope.

"I don't need you." It felt like a lie on her tongue, acid burning through her layers of protection.

"I've spent most of my life trying not to need anyone. I was successful until you, Nova. I can't let anything happen to you. It would destroy the threads of what's left of me."

The weight of his statement stole her voice and punched her gut. It sounded too good to be true.

"I don't want anything else to come between us." He walked over to the end of the couch where his backpack lay and pulled out a folder. Jude handed it to her.

She scoffed, flipping it open. "What's this?"

Her own photo stared back at her. Information about her life was printed all over the pages with notes scribbled in Jude's masculine scrawl on the sides. Realization slammed into her, locking down any softness his confession had stirred. The depth of his betrayal shook her to the core. He'd researched her. Targeted her. Manipulated her.

Yet . . . still, after all this, all the hurt and the emotion roiling inside her, her intuition didn't stop telling her to give him a chance to explain. Or maybe she'd confused red flags for butterflies.

I can't breathe. She needed space to think. To break down. *Away.* She needed to get away from the pain—from Jude.

"Get out."

"Nova—"

"Get out!"

"I'm calling in my favor. We made a deal. We need to work together to figure this out. Just listen to me. You know this makes sense."

She threw the papers at his chest. They scattered to the floor like all her hopes. "Fuck. You."

"Be angry at me all you want, sweetheart. I deserve it and much more than your pure heart is capable of." He leaned in, his hand by her head, resting on the door. "But I'm not leaving until we catch the son of a bitch and I know you're safe."

"I hate you," she said in a harsh whisper, but she might as well have screamed the words by the shuttering of his expression. The pain that lit his eyes seemed to cut down to his very soul.

Jude nodded in resignation before he turned and walked away, taking what was left of her heart with him.

Damn him for making her feel again. For making her hope. For messing with her head and her heart.

And fuck her for still caring about the bastard.

35

JUDE

Jude flexed his fingers under the table. His knuckles ached from the tree he'd taken his anger out on. He and Nova sat opposite Agent Mallory and her partner, Agent Green—a string bean of a man with circular lenses and a balding head. Renita sat on Nova's other side with her dad at her back. James glanced at Jude before he set his hand on Nova's shoulder. Jude's back was weighed down with guilt. James had tasked Jude with protecting his daughter and Jude had failed, even causing her more pain—not that James knew yet.

Jude regretted how this was going, but he was there to help find his sister, dead or alive, and to make the person who'd taken her pay.

His phone buzzed in his pocket as Agent Mallory took down notes, her gaze barely leaving Nova and him. The severe bun pulled all the hair from her face, highlighting her pointed chin and narrow cheekbones.

The floorboards creaked from the pacing Nova's brothers were doing outside on the back porch after the agents had banned them from the room. The thin screen door allowed them to hear what was spoken about as long as they promised not to interrupt again.

"And I want to confirm you still haven't had contact with Mrs. Washburn since you left their home?" Agent Mallory asked.

Nova shook her head, her arms still crossed over her chest.

"But Kim Washburn did threaten her during the proceedings outside the courthouse." Renita's hand moved to Nova's knee in a comforting gesture.

Mallory's attention homed in on Nova. "If you keep information from us, Ms. Emerson, you're making our job harder. We want to find this person before they can do any more harm."

Protective anger engulfed Jude. "Don't—"

Nova shot to her feet, her hands slamming on the table. Her voice cut like a knife. "You think I don't want to find them too? You think I like living my life knowing there is someone out there hurting people I knew? Hurting people I love now? Knowing my family could be in danger?"

"We're just trying to help," Agent Green added.

"Then stop accusing her of withholding information!" Jude glared at them.

After an extended pause, Mallory nodded. "Please tell me what your mother meant."

Nova remained on her feet. "It actually happened twice."

Renita's eyes widened as if surprised. It had to hurt her, knowing her daughter had kept something that important from her.

Nova turned to her mother. "I didn't tell you about the first time because I didn't want to cause you any more trouble. I wasn't sure . . ."

Renita got up and pulled Nova into a hug. "It's okay. We

were still getting to know each other. You'd been through something traumatic after losing your mother and your home. I don't blame you for being scared."

Nova exhaled, leaning into her mother's embrace. Jude was glad she was finding some solace in all of this. He wished he was able to give it to her; instead, he'd caused her more pain.

Nova nodded and pulled back, taking her seat once more. "In the women's bathroom before court. She accused me of lying and ruining her life. She said if I didn't tell the truth and let them know I'd made the whole thing up, she would make me regret it."

"And then what happened?"

Nova's attention dropped to her hands. She picked at the skin around her fingernails. The sight of crimson pooling in one corner was a contrast to her chipped, black polish. Jude couldn't resist. He slipped his hand into hers. She stiffened, digging her nails into his flesh. But the bite of pain was worth it as she stopped hurting herself.

"Ms. Emerson?" the agent asked again.

Nova's voice trembled almost as bad as her hands. "Then I went to court and gave my testimony. Answered their questions. Sat through being accused of lying and making the whole thing up. And then they showed the evidence I provided to back up the truth." She took a breath, glancing at Renita over her shoulder. "After court is when she approached my mother and me. Yelled at me and repeated many of the same sentiments until my mother shut her up."

Both agents turned to Renita.

"How exactly did you do that?" Mallory asked.

Renita tossed the purple locs behind her shoulder and shrugged. "I told her that while she may care what other people think, I don't give a fuck. And I would beat her skinny white ass in front of everyone if she didn't leave Nova alone."

Agent Mallory's expression remained stoic, but her head gave the slightest nod. She focused back on Nova. "Is there anything else you haven't thought to mention before? Threats? Run-ins? Messages?"

Nova hesitated. Jude narrowed his eyes on her as she nervously looked around at everyone.

"I thought it was nothing, but . . ."

"But what?" Mallory demanded more than asked.

Nova shifted nervously in her seat. Jude rubbed his thumb against the back of her hand, hoping to bring her some comfort during such a difficult time. He braced himself for whatever she was about to share.

"I've been getting some phone calls from a private number," she admitted.

"What?" James asked.

"Fucking A." Ricky pulled his hat off and threw it on the ground before he started pacing the porch again.

"When?" Jude asked.

Her glare sliced through him before she faced the agents once more. "Three calls from an unknown number. The first time I figured it was a scammer or something and hung up because no one answered. Second time it sounded like they were by water and I could hear their breathing. I, um . . ." She looked sheepishly at the agents. "I yelled at them and told them to stop calling me."

"Did they ever say anything?" Agent Mallory asked as her partner scribbled notes down.

Nova shook her head. "No. But I got a third call a little while ago. I didn't answer because I thought . . . with the timing . . . Do you think it's Larry?"

It hurt knowing Nova had kept this from him, and yes, it

made him a fucking hypocrite because he'd kept a lot from her. But this was life or death, and the thought of Nova in danger and not even telling him someone was harassing her made him see red.

"I can't divulge information in an active federal investigation." Mallory closed the file in front of her. "I'll need to see your phone."

Nova handed it over. Mallory tapped it and looked closer, tilting the cell for her partner to see. Agent Green pulled a laptop from the bag across his shoulder and a cord, hooking Nova's phone up.

"Surely you have something you can tell us," Jude insisted. "Who is your suspect if not this predator?"

"I can't discuss an active investigation," she repeated, giving him an unimpressed glance before she focused back on Nova. "However, I would advise you be vigilant. It seems you have a lot of people who care about you and can help keep an eye out."

"You're not going to give her protection?" Jude demanded as Green typed quickly on the keys.

Mallory narrowed her eyes on him. "I don't have the manpower because of budget cuts. Would you like me to take someone off the case looking for your sister, Mr. King?"

"What?" Renita asked, her head whipping towards Jude.

"Your sister is missing?" James asked.

"Salem Cade," Jude answered, hoping he hadn't just blown this whole thing up even more for Nova. He faced Mallory and her arrogant smirk. "I want you to find her and the bastard who took her and is terrorizing Nova. I want you to do your fucking job and end this."

"Do you have any information to add that could enable us to do so?" Mallory asked.

Jude gritted his teeth. "No."

She nodded. "I believe we're done here. I will reach out to local law enforcement and ask they do some drive-bys a few times a day, but I'm not sure how much manpower they can spare."

"Bently will help," James said, sounding sure as Mallory stood.

"The phone calls are untraceable. Looks like they used a different burner phone each call. I've got the info and will run it through some software at the office and see if our tech guys can find anything useful to help us." Agent Green handed Nova back her cell. "Do you mind if I use the restroom?"

Nova shook her head and pulled her hand from Jude's grasp to take her phone and then point towards the downstairs bathroom. "Go ahead."

Green walked by Jude.

Mallory tipped her head to the side staring at Jude pointedly. "Can I speak to you for a moment?"

Jude got up, moving around so Nova was still in his line of vision, but that forced Mallory to turn her back on the kitchen table.

"Is there anything you want to share?" Mallory asked.

Jude shook his head. Movement over Mallory's shoulder caught his eye, but he stayed focused on the agent, not wanting to give Nova away. Nova pulled her phone out, reaching for the file Mallory had left on the table, and flipped it open. *Smart girl.*

"I've shared everything I know with your office. Kind of hard to have intel when I haven't been stateside most of the last seventeen years. I told you my sister cut off contact with me a long time ago. If it wasn't for your call, I wouldn't have known she was missing." The confession grated from his throat, scraping old wounds open with the weight of shame.

I should have tried harder.

Mallory's eyebrow rose skeptically as Nova placed the folder back and faced her parents, speaking in low tones. "And you expect me to believe it's pure coincidence that you're now dating another woman involved? The woman under direct threat by this killer? Or that this threat came with your estranged sister's name as the sender?"

Jude took a deep breath, his hands fisting at his sides. Anger pulsed through him. "You think I have something to do with this?"

She shrugged. "I keep an open mind. But I don't believe in coincidences. You have to admit, it's quite interesting that you and Ms. Emerson are seeing each other with your entwined histories. And even more interesting that her family didn't seem to know that connection."

Jude bit the inside of his cheek. "Maybe instead of accusing people who are suffering because of your inability to do your fucking job, you should find more evidence and look closer into the Washburns. Women are dying and you're looking more and more incompetent with each passing day of dead ends."

Mallory sneered at him. "I'll catch the killer, don't you worry about that."

"We'll see, won't we?"

"Ready to go." Agent Green popped back around the corner.

Mallory scanned Nova and her family. "Please call me with any news or changes, or if you notice anything out of place—I mean *anything* that seems off. And let me know if you have any more unknown callers. We'll try to get to the bottom of this."

Nova nodded.

Nash opened the sliding door and her brothers filed into

the room as the agents left. "What the fuck? They're not gonna give you protection?"

Nova rubbed a hand over her face. "Guys—"

"That's bullshit," Roman cursed.

"We have to do something," Ricky agreed.

"We can take shifts—"

"Just stop!" Nova yelled.

Everyone's attention turned to her.

"You already have every inch of this property set up with motion-activated cameras. My house has an alarm. I live with a fucking Navy SEAL. You're all close by. You need to be with your families. Keep them safe. I'm covered."

"Shit, I need to check on Bella and the kids. They're supposed to be getting home from the library. You call me when you figure out how we can help." Nash darted to the front door.

"Ariel's with Elise alone at home. I need to fill her in and make sure they don't go anywhere without one of us." Roman was the next to leave.

"Everett's at work until five, so I'm free. Let's brush up on your self-defense, Nova," Ricky said.

"Enough. Please. I just want you all to go home. We can't live like this. I'm safe here with Jude."

She's letting me stay? Jude's chest filled with warm hope and pride that she felt safe with him after all of this. He wrapped his arm around her protectively. "I swear to you, I won't let her get hurt."

"You stick with her twenty-four seven. If you need to so much as go for a run, you call me and I'll come over and stay by her side," Ricky ordered.

Jude nodded. He liked that she had all these people who cared about keeping her safe. Salem had deserved that from him, and he'd failed her. "I swear it."

Ricky gave his sister and mother a hug before he left.

"So are you going to explain how you ended up dating Salem's brother?" Renita asked. Jude admired the woman for never pulling her punches.

"Honey." James placed his hand on his wife's shoulder.

Renita turned to him. "What?"

"I think Nova's been through enough questions for the day. Let her rest and process. We can reconvene later," James suggested.

Nova pulled out of Jude's arm to hug her dad. "Thank you."

"Alright. But we need to get to the bottom of this," Renita said before giving her daughter another hug. "You lie down and rest. We'll chat later. I'll bring you some dinner so you don't have to worry about cooking."

"Thanks, Mom."

Renita pointed her finger at Jude. "You take care of my daughter, you hear?"

"Yes, ma'am," Jude answered.

He hung back as Nova let her parents out. She closed the door. Her shoulders slumped with the click of the door, like she was carrying the weight of the world on them. She pressed her palm to her forehead and turned. Dark shadows hung in half-moons under her glassy eyes. Even her once bouncy curls seemed limp. The usual spark of her attitude was nothing but ashes.

Jude stepped closer, gently gripping her shoulder to pull her into a hug. But Nova shoved him away, anger flicking her tired gaze aflame with determination. She pushed past him and grabbed a small backpack from behind a chair. She headed to the kitchen where she began filling it with bottles of water and iced tea, tossing in bags of food before zipping it up. She slipped on her boots and double-checked the knife was in there.

"What are you doing?"

"I'm done waiting for shit to happen. If this killer wants me, they're gonna have a hell of a fight. I'm done being toyed with and manipulated." Stormy brown eyes slammed into his, giving him a death stare in challenge. She grabbed the keys off the counter and walked to the front door.

"Where are you going?"

She didn't even turn back to reply. "To find answers."

Adrenaline coursed through his veins. Jude needed to make this right—starting with giving her the rest of his truth. He'd do anything to keep her safe. It was the least he owed her. The front door slammed behind her like the walls she'd erected between them. He didn't have time to waste gearing up.

It was now or never.

36

NOVA

Nova turned down the blasting music. She'd kept it up for the whole drive, not giving her asshole passenger the chance to speak. But the last thing she needed was to have eyes on her as she drove into the suburban neighborhood.

She never thought she'd be back there. She never thought she'd do a lot of things again, like trust a man enough to let him fool her. But there she was.

Salem's face flashed in her mind. Jude was her friend's big brother. If something were to happen to any of her brothers, she would do anything to help them. She couldn't fault Jude for his loyalty. *I just wish it would have been to me.* But that was a sign she was in too deep. She'd opened up to Jude like she'd never done with anyone else—not even her ex.

Green pruned trees lined the street with cookie-cutter suburban homes. She pulled over behind an SUV on the side of the road and parked. The blue house catty-corner from where she sat looked the same as it had the day she'd left, as if nothing at all had changed. Colorful flowers lined the porch and walkway. Kim Washburn's special talent was making something look beautiful on the outside, no matter what horrors were locked within.

"What's your plan?" Jude asked, eyeing the kids riding bikes down the sidewalk beside them.

He didn't ask where they were, so he obviously knew.

"What happened with Salem after shit went down and Larry went to jail?" Nova asked instead of answering. "My mom tried to foster her, but we were told she was placed with family."

He kept his attention on the blue house, but she got the feeling that he was looking at her too.

"I got emergency leave. Tried to make it work, taking care of her. I was able to get custody of her, but it took a while. I found a woman she could stay with while I finished my deployment. She wasn't happy I was gone so much. She got into trouble at school. We fought a lot." Regret shadowed every word he spoke. "I should have tried harder. Not reenlisted after the four years. But it was money, and I'd started making friends and finally felt like I'd found where I belonged. It was like a family in a lot of ways. But by doing so, I abandoned the one family member I had left." Jude sighed, turning to face her this time. "I failed her. It's my fault she's missing. It's my fault no one knew until it was too late."

Nova stared into eyes burdened by guilt. She wanted to reach out and comfort him. But that would make her weak, wouldn't it? "So you just stopped returning her calls or something?"

"She blocked me, actually."

Nova's eyes narrowed. "Why?"

"She was with this guy who was a loser and an asshole to her. I told her she needed to leave him. That I'd pay for her own apartment, support her to finish college." He swallowed, turning back to the house. "She told me I was always trying to throw money at her problems. That at least her boyfriend was there for her when she needed him. That he hadn't abandoned her." Jude's inhale was shaky. He cleared his throat.

"I was so mad because all I could see was the work I'd put in to get her out of that shit hole and then she turned around and found a man just like our mother . . . I couldn't see she was crying out for my help. That she needed me to show up. Instead, I told her she was just like Mom and hung up. By the time I pulled my head out of my ass and tried to call her a couple weeks later, it wouldn't go through."

Nova would have to be made of stone not to have her heart gutted by that story. Salem was a quiet girl, from her memories, who'd idolized her brother, seen him as a savior. Kind of like Nova had because of their connection. She'd thought Jude was her second chance at a happily ever after.

"Sometimes it's easier to push the people you love away rather than having to own up to how far you've fallen and become someone you aren't proud of." Nova slid her foot under her thigh on the seat.

"I would do anything to go back in time and make a different decision. And now, it's probably too late—" His voice caught, emotion bleeding through as he blinked rapidly, clearing his throat.

She reached out and took his hand on impulse. The warmth of his palm was a contrast to the chill of the AC in the car. "Look at me, Jude."

His jaw pulsed, and then he locked eyes with her. His body remained stiff like he was expecting a blow, his guards up like they'd been when she'd met him. And that hurt more than anything. She didn't like this version of Jude. And for the first time since she'd found out he'd lied to her, she realized just how far they'd come. Like an onion, they'd both peeled back layers and layers of self-protection and pain. They were more alike than she'd realized.

"Salem wouldn't want you to blame yourself. She loved you. Siblings fight. And despite how dark it looks right now, we don't know she's gone. Don't give up on her yet."

A beat of silence passed. Jude's hand trembled before he wrapped his fingers around hers. "Thank you."

She nodded, pulling back and facing the blue house once more. "The plan is, we wait. If they're still following the same schedule as when I lived there, tonight is date night. They'll leave and be gone for hours. I'm going to go in and see what they're hiding."

"Breaking and entering?"

She shrugged. "I learned a few other things from your sister in that house too."

The corner of Jude's mouth turned up as he shook his head. "She was a sneaky little thing."

"*Is.* She *is,* Jude. And she's a fighter. When faced with the worst of the worst, she did what she had to in order to survive, and I can't lose faith that she's out there fighting. It's time we find her."

"Right. I've got my friend Reaper and his motorcycle club using their resources to find information on the Washburns' financials, to see if they have any other property, or member-ships—hell, even extended family. The boys have been checking out leads all over New England, but they've been dead ends," Jude explained.

Right. Jude wasn't homeless and alone. He'd come with a plan and resources. "Why did you pick me?"

Jude wiped a hand over his face, taking what seemed like a fortifying breath. "Amanda and Carrie, the two other girls alive from the house, have been followed, had their financials checked. Nothing came of it. But since you're familiar with the Pirates MC in town, I knew you'd recognize them. And with your brother being accused of killing Anastasia when she went missing, I couldn't afford to take a chance. I didn't know if you'd protect him if you knew, or if you—"

"If I was behind it?"

"I didn't know you then, Nova. You were a name and a picture in a file. I made assumptions trying to find my sister. I regret that. I wish I'd come up to you and explained who I was and that I needed your help because I know now that you would do everything in your power to help me find Salem." He shook his head. "I'm not trying to make excuses. But no one in my life has been noble for no reason. Even Reaper, a man I consider my best friend. Our friendship came at a cost."

"What do you mean?"

"I mean that no one has ever wanted to help me just to help me. No one's ever cared for me that much. And here you and your family come, like sharing love and loyalty is how the world works. It's not—"

"I know it's not. You think our life is perfect?" she asked.

"That's not what I meant."

"Nash's fiancée went missing and for years most of the town turned on him, claiming he was the killer. Some still think he is. He almost fucked up his second chance with Isabella because he couldn't accept the fact that he deserved something good."

Jude stared at her.

"Roman lost his high school sweetheart. Came home one day to find his daughter no longer speaking and his wife dead in their home. When Elise came along, he did his best to push her away too. And Ricky," she huffed. "That man fought his happily ever after tooth and nail from the closet he'd locked himself in. He and Everett almost died because he couldn't accept the fact that he deserved to live his truth. None of them thought they were good enough—could protect their loved ones enough—or whatever bullshit narrative they decided to tell themselves." Nova's skin prickled as she shook her head. "And I did it too, for years. I told myself that I shouldn't let anyone else get close to me because I was doomed to be unloved and betrayed. And look where I am."

"Nov—"

"No. Let me finish. Maybe I'm the one that's been holding myself back. Maybe I had the power all along to change my reality, and I just needed to start believing in myself. Not making myself small. Hiding behind half-truths and white lies. I need to own who I am and what I've been through. Because it's a lot." Hysterical laughter bubbled up in her chest, pouring out of her throat. "I'm so fucking tired of living like this. It's exhausting, molding myself to make everyone else more comfortable. Make myself smaller and quieter." She shook her head, wiping her eyes. "No more."

She glanced back at the house and froze. Larry exited a car from the driveway and made his way to the front of the house with a bouquet of flowers. Nova's stomach twisted. Bile climbed up her throat. It had been more than a decade since she'd seen him. His sandy hair, now grey. He dressed the same way, with a pale green button-up and khakis.

Nova's arms and legs felt like they had pins and needles before they went numb. Images flashed through her mind that she wanted wiped away forever. The pleading for him to stop. The sound of his zipper. The smell of his sweat and expensive cologne. She was sucked into a black hole of warped memories where Nova was powerless once again.

"Nova?" Jude's voice shook her from her spiraling.

She blinked at the empty porch. Larry must have already

gone inside. Nausea tipped her stomach side to side like a ship in a storm.

"Nova, baby, please?" Jude's strong arms wrapped around her and pulled her onto his lap.

She didn't even try to push him away. Fighting to stay in the present took all her energy, and Jude's touch was a lifeline. She gasped for breath. Why did it feel like someone was squeezing her rib cage? Why couldn't she breathe?

"I can't—"

"Don't try to talk. Just breathe with me." Jude locked her in his embrace, his chest rising and falling with big even breaths like a guide for her to follow. They were chest to chest, heartbeat to heartbeat. Nova gave in, relaxing in his arms, tears falling despite her eyes being closed.

"Feel my arms around you, holding you safe."

She leaned into his touch, desperate for an anchor to ground her.

"That's it, baby." His fingers gently massaged the back of her neck. "You got this."

His chest expanded and hers followed. She was breathing in sync with his deep inhales before they exhaled as one. Warm fingers coasted up and down her spine through the thin material of her clothes, bringing her farther into her body.

"Good girl." Jude's voice was as rough as the man himself.

She shouldn't be taking comfort from someone who had hurt her so deeply. But that was the thing about relationships —they weren't black and white. They were complicated and messy and entangled. She might not have been able to trust Jude, but Nova was protected and cherished in his arms for this one moment in time.

After all, there was a fine line between love and hate.

37

JUDE

The loss of Nova from Jude's arms was painful. His lap felt several degrees cooler. His arms, achingly empty. *Was that the last time she'll let me touch her?* Had he truly ruined the one good thing in his life?

The glow of her phone highlighted the frown on her expressive face. She tapped a message as the streetlights turned on.

"Did Amanda or Carrie share any new information?"

She sighed and tossed her phone on the console. "No. Amanda wants to meet up. So we're waiting on Carrie to tell us what day and time works for her."

"Might be good to get together and see what everyone else knows."

Nova crossed her arms over her chest and stared at the blue house catty-corner across the street from them. Her leg bounced anxiously under the steering wheel. "Yup."

"Are you planning on confronting him?"

The bouncing stopped. Her whole body went rigid. "No."

"I won't let anything happen to you."

Two beats of silence passed as she stared ahead. Was she sucked back into the memories again?

"Nova?"

Her mouth pressed in a firm line before she nodded. "I believe that. I probably shouldn't, but I do."

Her words gutted him. How could one statement bring both hope and torment?

"Nova—"

Her phone rang in a wedding march tone. She picked it up, sighing at her mother's name on the caller ID. She ignored the call, opening her messages instead and typing a quick reply before tossing the cell in the cupholder.

"She's just going to keep calling."

"I know. I told her not to bother with dinner because we wouldn't be home. And I am done lying to make other people more comfortable, but if I told her where I was, she would lose her fucking mind. So I'm not saying anything except I'm out with you. She'll know I'm safe." She cut Jude a glare. "I've realized how much worse my little white lies will hurt her. And thanks to the revelation made by the FBI regarding your connection, she's got a million questions, and I'm gonna have to face the consequences of my choices and hope she forgives me."

"She will."

Nova turned her glassy gaze to him, soul-deep pain and the fear of rejection shining in it. "What makes you think so? You've known her for like two weeks. You can't know anyone in that amount of time."

He winced at the obvious dig. "People's actions always speak louder than their words. Your parents . . . they're good people. They gave me a chance to prove myself. They let a perfect stranger move in with their only daughter because they trust you, and they want the best for you. They love you,

Nova. She'll understand why you did what you did when you explain it."

His phone vibrated in his pocket. He pulled it out and smiled. He clicked answer. "Hello, Mrs. Emerson."

Nova's eyes widened as she drew a line over her neck with her finger, glaring at him.

"Jude, how many times have I told you to call me Mama E?"

"Sorry, ma'am."

"Alright. Is my girl with you?" Renita asked.

"Yes, ma'am."

"And you're keeping her safe? Not letting her do something that could get her hurt more?"

He cleared his throat, buying himself time. "I'm taking care of her. I promise I won't let anything happen to her."

"Alright. Don't think we aren't having a conversation when you get back about that little bomb the agent dropped."

"I'll tell you anything you want to know about me."

"Good. Alright. Keep her safe. Have a good night. We'll see you tomorrow," Renita said.

"Goodnight." He ended the call.

"What was that?" Nova asked, her full lips pursed.

"I couldn't ignore your mom's call. She would worry."

"And you care about my mother's feelings?"

"I do. And your dad's. They're good people who showed me kindness when they didn't have to." But would they be able to forgive his lies? He wasn't their son—their family, like Nova. Even if he could somehow convince Nova to forgive him and give them another chance, would her parents or brothers forgive him?

That small ember of hope left inside him dimmed. The cab of the truck grew cooler. A light flicked on at the blue house. The porch light illuminated the front yard as the door opened.

Nova ducked behind the steering wheel. She grabbed his shoulder and tugged him down with her.

Larry went around to the passenger side of the sedan, opening the door for Kim before climbing in the driver's side. The car turned on, and a minute later they backed out of the driveway. Nova and Jude ducked completely down as they drove past.

She slipped her head up first, looking both ways down the street. Those red taillights must have slipped around the corner because she bolted from the car.

"Shit." Jude slipped his phone in his pocket. He closed the truck door and raced after her down the dim street.

"What's the plan?" he whispered.

"Taking back control." She moved past the house, slipping between the garage and the fence to the backyard. Jude focused, on alert, adrenaline pumping through his veins. A dog barked from a few houses over. A car honked. A few teenagers shouted plays with the distinct thump of a basketball in the property behind them over the fence. This was risky. The moon moved out from behind a cloud, illuminating the garden in the backyard that stretched all the way to the fence, rows and rows of plants, some he recognized, some he didn't.

Nova kneeled on the back porch by the door. She pulled something from her pocket, the metal glinting in the glow of the moon. Now was not the time to be noticing how hot she looked with that determined focus in her expression.

The click of the door opening put Jude even more on edge. He instinctively looked around, making sure no nosy neighbor had seen them.

"I think we're clear," he said.

Nova opened the door and wordlessly crept in. Jude was right behind her, closing the door as quickly and quietly as possible.

Nova stood immobile. The house reeked of flowers. An overpowering floral scent assaulted his nose like this was a goddamned flower shop. Bouquets in vases decorated every flat surface.

"What's with all the flowers?" Jude asked aloud.

Nova didn't answer. Her shoulders were pulled up to her ears. Jude slid his hand over her and she flinched.

"Go check the basement. I'll take upstairs." Nova headed through the living room towards the steps.

"We should stay together," he argued.

"You wanted to tag along, then listen. I'm the one calling the shots here. The quicker we get this place searched, the faster we can get the fuck out."

She beelined for the stairs.

Jude kept an ear out for a minute. Just her footsteps creaked through the old house. Jude cursed and searched the bottom floor, checking every door until he found one leading to the basement. He flicked his phone light on, searching for trapdoors, locked cabinets, anything. Nothing but gardening supplies, bins with holiday decor, and a bunch of crap. A light flickered in the small ground-level window that faced the front of the house. *Headlights.*

"Fuck."

They were home already. They must have forgotten something. Jude darted up the stairs, searching for any sign of Nova.

"Nova?" he whispered harshly, as he ran up the second-story stairs.

The front door squeaked open as he frantically searched the upstairs rooms, making his steps as light as possible.

Nova walked into the hallway. He grabbed her arm, tugging her into the closet in the nearest bedroom.

"What—"

He slammed his hand over her mouth, backing them as far into the closet as he could. The scent of mothballs and horrible perfume mingled, burning his nose. Shit, the last thing he needed to do was sneeze.

Nova pinched his arm.

"They're back," he whispered.

She froze in his arms, her body going ramrod straight. Her heart slammed against her ribs, reverberating against his arm. She was clearly terrified. He hated that she was in this position. But if he'd held her back from coming here, she would have hated him more and found a way to do it on her own.

The breaths from her nose puffed rapidly against his fingers like she was fighting to breathe. She pulled his hand away. A small gasp filling the closet sounded as a sonic boom. Her panic would give them away. He'd do anything to free her from it.

Jude pulled her tighter against his chest. She was still facing the doors as the hall light flicked on. Footsteps thudded closer up the stairs.

He coasted his lips near her ear and whispered, "If he finds us, I'll kill him before he even gets the chance to look at you."

Her breath hitched as she stared through the tiny slats of the closet door.

"You're safe with me. I won't let him touch you again."

Her chest rose with a deep breath as the man who haunted her nightmares and stole her innocence walked into the room, flicking the light on.

Nova trembled against Jude. The panic was setting in. He

did the only thing he could think to distract her. Jude covered her mouth again, his other hand sliding down her belly.

"Don't give him any more of your fear. It's mine. Your fear, your pain, your pleasure. Trust Daddy." Jude unbuttoned her shorts, sliding his hand between the fabrics, and cupped her pussy.

She tensed in his arms but didn't fight.

"Look how strong you are, focusing on even breaths. You gonna be quiet for Daddy?"

She gave a slight jerky nod, but her body relaxed against him. He could give her this one gift. She may hate him later, but in this moment when she needed a distraction most, he would help her reclaim her power back.

"Where is it?" Larry mumbled. The sound of a drawer creaking open preceded shuffling sounds as if he was rummaging through the dresser.

Nova stilled.

Jude slid a finger inside her, his palm nudging her clit. Wetness slid over his finger as he fucked her with it, slow and steady.

"Good girl. Look at you taking this for Daddy. Don't make a sound. Just take the pleasure. Fall into it. Get lost in it."

Nova's head tipped back, resting on his bicep as she stared up at him. Her hand covered his across her mouth. Blunt nails dug into his skin as her hips rocked in motion with his finger thrusting inside her, a silent plea for more. Light bled from the cracks of the closet door, illuminating the depraved desperation in her eyes. He added another finger.

Her hot wet cunt squeezed around him. Fuck, she was so sexy like this. Scared and desperate, yet trusting him. A heady, powerful feeling clouded his mind. Jude's cock hardened. He was a sick fuck.

He slid his hand down from her mouth to cup her breast.

"Got it." Larry slammed the door closed and tucked a square brown wallet in his back pocket before shutting the light off and exiting the room.

Nova didn't even seem to notice. The way she was riding Jude's hand never faltered.

Keeping his senses alert, he fingered her until the front door closed, and headlights flashed in the window. They were gone. Which meant Jude didn't need to be so quiet anymore.

"Look at you, pathetic little slut, getting off on fear. You're a fucking goddess, Freckles. So beautiful. Come on my hand."

He pushed his palm against her clit with every rock of her hips. "Take it. Take your power back."

A whimper escaped her lips. The sound was an oasis in a desert. Dark and desperate. Forbidden and taboo. He might have been fucked up, but she liked this. She got off on her fear. If that wasn't the most badass power move, he wasn't sure what was.

"That's it. You're so close, aren't you? Soaking Daddy's hand with your need. Aching for my cock. I bet you want me to lay you out on his bed and fuck you, don't you?"

"Ahhh!" Nova screamed as she came, clenching around him, shaking and trembling, but it had nothing to do with fear. Her head was thrown back, an expression of complete ecstasy visible thanks to the dim moonlight filtering in the cracks.

Jude slowed the pace of his fingers, sliding through her wet folds one last time as he kissed the smattering of freckles he knew was there despite the darkness. "Good girl."

She slumped against him, hazy and limp. Jude buttoned her shorts back up and then opened the closet door, going first.

Nova stumbled from the closet. He wrapped his arms around her, but she pulled away.

Pain lanced through every cell at her rejection.

He searched the floor, then they made their way carefully downstairs. He went first to the living room. "You find anything?"

She shook her head and veered for the door they'd come in through. Cool night air brushed against his skin as he exited the house. He inhaled a breath of fresh air untainted by the sickly sweet flowers inside. The backyard seemed more like a garden than flowers for the most part in comparison. A small shed stood in the far corner.

"Let me check here." Nova darted toward the shed.

Jude surveyed the area once more. The basketball still bounced with voices in a heated game of horse behind the fence. A rush of wind made the leaves on the giant oak trees hovering above them shiver and rattle. Goose bumps broke out on Jude's arms.

"We need to go."

"Let me just check. Give me your phone." She held out her hand.

Jude placed his cell in her hand, his senses on alert.

Nova shone the light in the shed and sighed. "Nothing." She handed him back the phone.

"Let's get out of here." He led the way.

Nova moved to his side. She stumbled, falling before he could catch her.

Jude bent low, grabbing her hand. "You okay?"

Nova didn't make an attempt to get up.

"Nova?"

"Jude . . . these plants . . ."

"I know. The woman has a serious obsession."

"No." She pointed to a small growth of yellow flowers, climbing to her feet. "I think these are Gelsemium."

"Now's really not the time to stop and smell the flowers. We need to go." He tugged her arm.

"No, you don't understand." She pulled away. "These cause paralysis, even death."

"Don't touch them." He yanked her against him.

Nova's big brown eyes reflected the moon as she stared up at him. "What if Kim is the killer? Or they're working together?"

His brows drew together. "Why—"

"The FBI files I took a photo of? All the victims except Ana had traces of Gelsemium in their system, though her remains would have been too old for a blood or urine sample."

Jude eyed the cluster of yellow flowers. He needed to call Reaper and fill him in, have him look into Kim and Larry again. They had to be missing something.

But first, Jude needed to get Nova home safe. "Let's get out of here."

38

NOVA

Nova ducked just in time to miss the punch aimed at her head. She grunted and rolled, sweat dripping down her forehead. Her limbs ached, screaming in exhaustion under the heavy rays of the sun. She licked her dry lips and held up her hands in a T shape.

"Time out," she wheezed, out of breath.

Ricky immediately backed off. "That was a good escape maneuver, but you should have blocked."

Nova wiped the sweat from her brow and stumbled to the back porch, dropping into the nearest spot on the couch. "Hard to do when your arms feel like noodles."

"Ha!" Ricky jogged past her into the house. Asshole had barely broken a sweat in the two hours they'd been out here.

Nova sighed, lying back on the couch. Everything ached. It had been too long since she'd used those muscles or sparred with her brother. But it was also a great way to relieve some of this excess anxious energy constantly making her stomach twist with nerves and her heart skip.

Ricky returned, handing her a bottle of water with a yellow sticky note attached.

Drink me.

Nova rolled her eyes and tore the note off, letting it fall to the table in front of her. She almost wanted to not drink it out of spite. Jude thought he could still order her around after everything? He was delusional. *And yet I let him touch me. Make me come while the man who'd assaulted me was right there.* A hot flush seared her skin.

"I think I have heatstroke." It was the only explanation. She sure as fuck couldn't want the bastard after he'd manipulated her.

"It's like seventy-five degrees." Ricky chuckled, sitting in the spot next to her. He opened his own bottle and took a few sips.

"Still."

"Drink your water before your boyfriend comes back and finds out I didn't make sure to keep you hydrated." Ricky motioned to the bottle in her hand. "The man is a little obsessed with your water intake."

She scowled at it. "Why do you care what he thinks?"

Ricky shrugged. "I kinda like the guy. He's also a scary fucker when he wants to be. You should have seen him at the bar, taking on that dumbass and his lackeys."

Nova unscrewed the cap angrily before gulping down the icy water. Despite the relief to her parched throat, her anger simmered. Had that little display been to win her brothers over, or had Jude genuinely been standing up for her? Now she'd question everything—like was he serious when he said he'd kill Larry before the fucker had a chance to look at Nova again? The vehemence in those whispered words had stolen the very air from her lungs.

"I'm surprised he called me to take over so he could go out to the fields with Dad." Ricky set his drink on the coffee table in front of them.

"Yeah, well, there's always work to do. He's not my babysitter. You don't need to be either."

"It's not babysitting, Nov. We don't want you getting hurt. We love you."

"I know. But it doesn't make this easier." She closed her eyes and sighed. "I'm sorry this has thrown a wrench in your wedding planning. Not easy to plan one of the happiest days of your life when your sister's life is being threatened."

Ricky wrapped his arm over her shoulders. "This isn't your fault."

The sliding door opened and a sweaty Jude walked through, shirtless. His golden-brown skin shone under the late summer sun, like he was a bronze warrior. His abs flexed with each even breath. His gaze locked on to Nova. He scanned her from head to toe like he was searching for injuries before his attention flicked to the water bottle. An approving tilt of his lips made her belly flutter. Nova scowled, turning to face the backyard. The green trees swayed in the breeze as the wind picked up. She inhaled a deep breath. Maybe it would storm.

"Hey, you all done in the fields?" Ricky asked Jude, getting to his feet.

"Yeah. I'm gonna go shower and then my friend was going to join us so we could go over what we have."

Nova stiffened.

"I've got to get Bailey to Hope. Everett has volunteered us for the carnival fundraiser. You guys staying home tonight?" Ricky asked.

"Yeah," Nova said. "You can go. I need to clean up too." Nova got to her feet. Every muscle protested.

She didn't spare Jude a glance but wrapped her arms around her brother. "Thanks for today."

"Anytime." Ricky squeezed her back. "We'll get this bastard, sis. Just hang in there."

She nodded and gave him a smile she hoped didn't look as forced as it felt. "I know. I'll give him hell if he shows up."

"And I'll send him there," Jude growled.

Her traitorous pussy clenched at the promise in his voice. God, would her body ever get the memo this man was off-limits? *I guess it will be a cold shower.*

Nova pushed past the men into the house, heading upstairs where she locked herself in her bathroom. She took her time, washing up. Her teeth chattered in the cool water, but oddly enough, it eased her anxiety. She dried off and brushed her hair, putting some product in it to keep it moisturized. As soon as she stepped into her room, she sensed she wasn't alone.

Her mother sat on her bed, smoothing her hand over the wrinkles Nova hadn't bothered straightening.

"I hope you don't mind—I let myself in. I just needed to know my baby girl was okay," her mom said.

Renita Emerson had the biggest heart, but it took a lot for her to get emotional. The unshed tears welling in her eyes were spears through Nova's chest.

"It's fine." Nova smiled. She went straight for her drawers, pulled out shorts and her usual comfy crop top. Renita turned towards the table beside her bed, picking up the copy of the latest romance novel Nova was reading, giving her privacy as she changed. After she was dressed, Nova made her way to her mother's side and sat on the mattress.

"Is this any good?" Renita asked, lifting the book with the blue alien on the cover.

"Very. I'll drop it off to the house once I'm done."

Her mom placed the book back and twisted to face Nova. Her brown eyes scanned Nova much like Jude did, but where Mom's gaze was filled with maternal concern, his had been possessive.

"I'm sorry, Mom."

"For what?"

"I only wanted to make you happy. You and Dad have done so much for me. Took me in when I had nothing and no one. You believed me. You protected me."

Renita wrapped her arms around Nova and pulled her into a hug. "You are my daughter. From the moment I found out I had a half sister who'd passed and left behind a child, you were *mine*."

Tears dripped down Nova's cheeks and she didn't stop them.

"Nothing you do could ever change that." Her mother squeezed her tighter and then backed away and cupped Nova's face. "Jude came over this morning. He told us that he hid why he came to town. That he manipulated you into going along with it."

Nova sniffed. "He did?"

She nodded.

"And somehow you let him live?" Nova joked.

Her mother gave her a knowing look. "I know my Nova doesn't do anything she doesn't want to do. You're intelligent enough to find a way out of things. Like making up a fake boyfriend for a year so I would stop setting you up with locals."

"Y-you knew?"

Renita rolled her eyes. "You're a terrible liar anyways. Your voice goes up in pitch. You should never pursue a career in acting."

"Mom—"

Her mother shook her head. "I love you, and I only want what's best for you. I did my best to push your brothers towards their happiness, but I should have known you'd take your own route. After Brooks . . . I felt like I lost my only daughter."

"I'm sorry."

"No. You don't have anything to apologize for. You were so happy at first. But I saw how you were disappointed by him over and over. He didn't try to get close with your brothers or us. He didn't show up for family activities. I was afraid if I stepped in and said something, he'd take you from us too."

"Oh, Mom." Nova shook her head. "I was lost. He had a hold on me . . . I never want to be that vulnerable again."

"The thing about love is . . . you can't let it in without showing your most tender pieces. It's the scariest thing." She smoothed her hand over Nova's. "Sometimes strength means wearing armor to protect yourself, but other times it means stripping yourself bare and being vulnerable."

Nova sniffed. *Wise words.*

Her mom continued, "To love is to surrender all and trust the other person won't use the opportunity to hurt you. And they, in return, do the same. Two people giving and taking in a synchronistic partnership."

Nova fiddled with a crease on the comforter. "I'm not sure I have much left to give."

"Oh, sweet girl. You have the worth of the entire universe inside you. And you've chosen the right person to keep all your tender parts safe."

Nova shook her head. "Jude isn't . . ." She searched for the words to explain.

Her mom placed her hand on Nova's knee. "He makes you smile in a way I've prayed to my ancestors to see."

"It was all lies." The confession was scraped from Nova's throat.

Her mother studied her under a keen, knowing gaze. "Then maybe you're a better actor than I'd thought." Renita patted her knee and stood. "Jude and his friends are waiting in the kitchen. Your dad and I brought over dinner. Take a minute and join us when you're ready."

Nova closed her eyes as her mom's lips pressed to her forehead.

"Your mother would be proud of the woman you've become. Don't forget you have her strength running through your veins. I wish I'd known her, but I'm so blessed to be able to know you, Akua Ketewa."

"Thank you, Mom."

Renita gave a nod and left the room, closing the door behind her.

Nova exhaled and flopped back on the bed, staring at the white ceiling. Her mother's words repeated in her head.

Then maybe you're a better actor than I thought.

Nova wasn't. But the truth was far more insidious. She was in love with a man who had lied to her and used her.

Had she used him too? *Yes. But at least he knew I was using him. We had an agreement.*

She sighed. Her mind a jumbled exhausted mess. She hadn't slept well at all the night before, tossing and turning. She had closed the door in Jude's face. And after he'd made her breakfast, she'd stayed in her room out of principle, her stomach growling at the smell of the bacon and eggs.

It wasn't until Ricky had knocked an hour later that she'd come out to find Jude gone, a plate of breakfast left on the table with one of those yellow sticky notes attached.

Eat me.

A puff of air snorted from her nose as she shook her head, fighting off more tears. Now was not the time to fall apart.

Because if Nova did, she might never be able to find the pieces to be put back together.

39

NOVA

Nova sat at the kitchen table, moving the food on her plate. Usually, she gobbled up her mother's lasagna. But tonight, it tasted like ash on her tongue. Her parents' concerned gazes landed on her like rough fabric scratching her already raw and exposed nerve endings. Jude's solemn, stoic expression never changed; he remained cold and emotionless. He didn't look at her once. Maybe he was trying to give her distance? Or maybe he'd gotten what he'd come for and now had no use for her? A stabbing sensation tore through her rib cage.

She shivered, a chill sinking into her bones as the other guests at her small table stared unabashed at her. Where Jude's gaze seemed cold, Reaper's dark eyes were frigid and empty, almost as if he didn't possess a soul. If people thought Jude was scary, he had nothing on his friend who looked like the Grimm Reaper himself. No wonder he'd gotten that nickname. The air hummed with violence around him. Nova inched away from him, taking a drink of her water just to have something to do.

"So, Reaper and his friends are part of a motorcycle club in Dark Cove," Jude said.

"The Pirates? I think we might have run into your club at Hope Facility." Her dad nodded. "You rescue women from domestic violence situations and bring them to a safe haven. Escort them to court. Things like that, right?"

"Yeah. I'm Casanova. My silent and stoic friend here let us know about Salem and Nova's predicament. We've been following leads and investigating on our own ever since." Casanova thumbed toward Reaper, poking his shoulder. The two friends were like polar opposites. Casanova seemed friendly and easygoing while Reaper lived up to his namesake.

Reaper brushed a hand over his thick beard. His umber fingers tangled in the curly strands. He rested his elbows on the table around his finished lasagna plate. "We've tailed Larry Washburn since we got the call about Jude's kid sister. He goes to work, to church, and even finds time to volunteer for a charity once a week. He goes out every week with his wife for date night. Other than that, he's home."

"What about his wife?" her mom asked.

"We've had someone tailing her since I got the call last night. She works at a private school. Their financials are clean. They have a lake house in upstate Maine. We cleared it already. No sign anyone's visited in quite some time," Casanova answered.

"And what about the other girls? We're supposed to meet them tomorrow at the café and see what they know," Nova said.

"I've got my guys keeping an eye out for them, taking shifts. They won't even know they're being followed. We also checked their financials, social media, backgrounds. Carrie did a couple small stints in jail. Assaulting an ex-boyfriend . . ." Casanova leaned forward with his hand next to his mouth as if he was telling them a secret. "Though from the police reports and background on that loser, he deserved it."

Reaper scowled at his friend, though friend might have been too kind of a word for their dynamic. "Drug possession, and a stay in a mental institution after she tried to take her own life seven years ago."

Just before Ana was killed.

Reaper continued, "Since then she's lived in Massachusetts, working as a waitress while pursuing her degree part-time. She's single with a few steady friends who comment on her posts and she interacts with outside of work."

Nova swallowed. It was weird hearing about another woman, her life broken down into a few sentences summing up where she was after the horrors they'd shared in the foster home together. *Maybe I should have reached out sooner.*

Reaper crossed his arms over his chest and leaned back in the chair.

Casanova leaned towards Nova. "Amanda doesn't have much on social media until she moved to Dark Cove five years ago. Works for a production company. She's dating Mathew Reyes, who works on an oil rig."

"What does your intel say about me?" Nova asked, glaring at Jude.

His jaw pulsed, but he didn't react otherwise.

Casanova's gaze flicked between Jude and her and then darted to the last few bites of food on his plate.

Reaper's attention, however, was aimed directly at Nova. It was enough to drop the temperature in the room a few degrees at least. "Nova Akua Emerson. Age twenty-eight. Adopted by Renita and James Emerson at age sixteen. Cannabis farmer. Fiancé killed in action while deployed in the Army. Lives alone on her parents' farm. Three siblings, one of which was engaged to the first victim, Anastasia. You're the one who put the bastard Larry Washburn in jail."

Nova flinched. She braced herself for more, but nothing came. Jude must have given him private information. Everything Reaper said had been in her file—the one she'd thrown in Jude's face. But Reaper shifted his attention to Jude. "I've got my tech guy researching the photos your girl took of the FBI files, seeing what he can find with the info on there." Reaper gave her a small nod. It almost looked approving.

"What about the poison plants?" Nova asked.

"We can't do much without proof she or Larry used it. Neither can the Feds. So we're following her, gathering information."

Nova let out a frustrated breath. "So more waiting, sitting here useless while Salem is missing."

"You got a better plan?" Reaper asked.

"Reap—" Jude warned as a rumble of thunder sounded in the distance.

"Make him confess." Nova slammed her hand on the table.

Violence glinted in Reaper's black eyes as a sadistic smile curved his lips up. "That's two votes."

Huh? Two votes for what?

"I said no. It's too risky." Jude's tone left no room for argument as he glowered at his friend.

What's too risky?

"Listen, I think it's best if we let Nova get some rest." Her mother's warm hand pressed over hers. Nova flinched. Renita offered her a comforting smile. "Try to eat and get some sleep. We can talk about this tomorrow. You're safe and, for now, your other friends are too. The Pirates will make sure of that."

Nova nodded more to appease her mother than in agreement.

Her parents stood and began clearing their plates.

"I've got that." Jude's chair scraped across the wood floor as he gathered everyone's dishes except Nova's, which she'd barely touched.

Rain pelted the windows, adding a steady patter to the background noise of dishes clinking in the otherwise silent room.

Her parents thanked him and then gave her a long hug before waving goodbye and letting themselves out the front door. Dishes clinked in the sink.

Nova turned to Reaper. "What did you mean that was two votes?"

"I'll walk you out," Jude barked before he nodded toward the front of the house.

Reaper stared at Nova. She didn't drop his gaze even though her skin prickled like she was in danger. The tiny hairs on the back of her neck stood straight. Every instinct screamed at her to drop eye contact and defer to him.

"Ask your boyfriend." He stood. His full height had to be somewhere near six foot eleven. He towered over her, his head almost grazing the light over the table.

"He's not my boyfriend." Lightning flashed followed by another rumble of thunder.

Reaper's cheek pulsed as if he were biting back a smile, though she really couldn't imagine this man smiling. Tearing into the necks of his enemies, smeared with blood, some of it dripping from his chin as his mouth curved up with sadistic glee—yes. Smiling—not even close.

"Nice to see you too, King." Reaper left.

Casanova took Nova's hand and pressed a kiss to her knuckles with a wink. "Nice meeting you."

"You too."

"Not the time, Cass," Reaper called behind him.

Casanova chuckled. "There's always time when there's a beautiful woman in need of cheering up."

Jude actually growled, following behind Casanova, and shut the door behind him. Silence blanketed the house once more except for the steady rain that showered outside. Droplets of water pinged off the furniture on the back porch. It was loud even though the sliding glass door was closed.

Somehow her spacious open-plan house seemed impossibly smaller with four less people.

"What did he mean that was two votes?" she asked for the third time.

Jude approached the table warily as if she were a skittish animal. His hands landed on the back of the chair across from her and squeezed. "You should try to eat."

Nova shoved the plate across the table at him.

Jude caught it as it slipped over the edge. He sighed. And for the first time since the truth had come out, she looked at him—really looked at him.

Dark shadows underlined his eyes, making his sculpted, chiseled bones look more skeletal. Had he slept at all last night? Had he had more nightmares? His sister was missing, kidnapped by a monster. If that had happened to one of her brothers . . . she'd be sick with worry.

I've been selfish. What he did was wrong, but for good reason.

She opened her mouth to apologize. "I—"

"Reaper is the enforcer for the Pirates. He likes to get a little creative when it comes to men who lay their hands on women and children," Jude said without looking at her. His shoulders drooped farther, as if he'd been beaten down.

Nova stood and took a step further away from Jude, crossing her arms. He winced as if it caused him physical pain. He took her plate and carried it over to the sink. The urge to walk up behind him, wrap her arms around him and tell him they'd find a way—that everything would be okay—was overpowering. She stumbled forward with the force. But what if she had read him wrong? What if he was here out of obligation now? Or simply to find the person responsible to exact his revenge? And he'd still lied to her, betrayed her trust.

"We can't risk him interrogating the Washburns. Not without knowing where Salem is." Jude's voice dripped with defeat.

At the end of the day, Jude was only human. And if she believed him, he'd done all this to rescue his missing sister. She walked up to him, taking a chance that the Jude who'd weaseled his way into her heart was the real Jude. How could you be so angry with someone and then crave comforting them the next? It was too similar to how things had been with her and Brooks. She backed up a step. Jude's shoulders sunk even more. The muscles in his back bunched under his T-shirt, as if strained with the mountain of stress they were under. But Jude wasn't Brooks. He didn't gaslight her. He was searching for his missing sister, and he was doing whatever it took to give her justice.

Nova pressed her hand to his shoulder. His muscles turned to marble under her palm. "Jude?"

He turned, guarded, bloodshot eyes locked with hers. Raw unbridled pain emanated off him in waves, making Nova's knees weak. She swallowed, staring up at the man who'd both protected and hurt her. The man who'd both betrayed and given Nova the sweetest gift of her power back over the scum that had damaged her. Jude was all sharp edges and hard lines. It was no wonder she'd been cut. He was both the blade to her hunger for pain and the balm that made it all better. She'd offered herself up to him in the most intimate way. Shared pieces of her that had never seen the light of day.

Somehow, in two weeks she'd felt safe enough to bare her soul to him.

Maybe it was time she examined her own narrative. What if she wasn't shit at choosing men? Perhaps she'd been so desperate for love and undervalued herself and she'd settled for scraps and breadcrumbs with Brooks and Chad and every other partner she'd allowed to treat her like less than she deserved. But that could stop there. She wasn't dead yet. She could still change. Was it too late for her and Jude?

Her gaze fell to his lips. She knew what he needed—what they both needed. She could have sex without emotions, just like she had in the past. But that was before Jude. Before she knew what it meant to touch souls with someone. To show your deepest, darkest self and have the other person revel in your shared depraved desire.

Nova gripped his face, pulling him closer as she slammed her mouth against his. She kissed him with all her pent-up energy like a storm rising within her. Thunder cracked from the heavens above. The house rumbled with its vibration. Energy thrummed all around them, cocooning Jude and Nova in an electric embrace.

He didn't kiss her back at first, but his hands clamped around her head, cradling her while also pinning her in place. She dragged her teeth across his bottom lip, spurring him on. Teasing. Enticing. Pushing his limits for that need of control that he so clearly harbored. She could sense it now, rising between them like a black fog. She breathed it in, getting higher with each lungful of his scent.

She'd bare herself once more—give him the chance to show her this had all meant more than just him using her. If she took the risk, would he be there to catch her? Or had this been pretend?

Nova's hand slid around the back of his neck, her nails

digging into his skin for purchase as she pressed against him. The thin fabric of her cotton crop top separated her breasts from his chest. Her other hand smoothed down his shirt, over taut, defined abs covered with soft material. She gripped the button on his jeans.

Long fingers clamped over hers, tugging them behind Jude's waist.

"Nova, wait."

She was raw, with every nerve ending exposed. Nova's heart stuttered, squeezed by an invisible fist.

She gasped, looking up at him. Lightning flashed, reflecting in his stormy hazel eyes.

"We shouldn't do this. Not—"

Nova winced, the full impact of his words hitting her like a sledgehammer. She yanked her arm away and stepped back, pain merging with rage and boiling inside her. This almost felt worse than when she'd found out about his lies. She'd put herself out there—*again.* "I see I'm only good to fuck when you want something from me. It's not fun anymore that I know the truth, huh?"

His expression darkened.

She should feel like she'd won, getting that jab in. So why did it feel like she'd lost?

"Nova." His voice was a growl—a threat.

Nova had never been good at backing down from a fight. She retreated another step, holding up her hands. "It's okay. Really. Glad we know where we both stand." She turned, her eyes stinging. She wouldn't let him see her break. She darted for the stairs.

"Stop!" Jude's footsteps thumped after her as the storm raged outside.

Wind whipped and the house creaked. Thunder cracked and lightning flashed as if feeding off her energy.

"No!" she yelled, grabbing on to the banister. Her foot landed on the first step. Jude's strong hands wrapped around her wrists, pressing her to the wall. She gasped. One of his hands pinned her wrists to the wall. The other gripped her chin with bruising force, giving her no choice but to look in his eyes. Jude's imposing form blocked her in.

"If you think for one fucking second I don't want you, you're dead wrong." He growled.

"Aren't you the one who told me actions speak louder than words?" she sneered, unafraid. "Maybe I should see if Casanova is still here. He seemed interested."

Lightning streaked. Jude's white teeth flashed before his voice came out like a rumble of thunder. "I warned you that mouth of yours was going to get you in trouble."

Her lips parted with a retort, but the wind was knocked out of her as he heaved her over his shoulder like a sack of potatoes and climbed the stairs.

Nova pounded on his tight ass with her fists. "Put me down!"

A stinging slap landed on her own ass. "Behave!"

Her eyes widened as she growled and pounded even harder with her fists. "Who the fuck do you think you are? I said, put me—"

She gasped. Her stomach dropped in free fall before her back hit the soft mattress. She scrambled up the bed, away from Jude.

He stood, feet braced apart. His hands dropped to his belt buckle. The clank of metal sent a shiver through her bones.

"W-what are you doing?" she asked, her mouth dry.

The dark slashes of his brows drew together. Only the dim light of the hallway highlighted his silhouette. Rain pelted the windows, faster and harder, turning to tiny balls of hail. Lightning flashed, making Jude's hazel eyes glow as if he himself embodied the storm.

She swallowed, her chest panting in anticipation as the leather slid from his pants.

Thunder boomed, louder than before. She flinched. He folded the belt in half twice, hitting the other end over his hand with a *thwack*.

"Jude?"

His head tipped to the side, cracking his neck, before he took a step closer to the mattress. "Mercy won't save you tonight, little one."

40

NOVA

Real fear lit Nova up inside and exploded as if she'd swallowed the whole damn Fourth of July celebrations. *What the hell have I gotten myself into now?*

Jude snapped the belt on the mattress. "Come here."

Nova gritted her teeth together. "Make me."

Jude's sadistic smile curved his stupid kissable lips as excitement glittered in his gaze. The storm continued to rage outside but it was no match for the energy swirling between them, writhing and powerful. Violent sedition and chaotic urgency whipped around them. Lust and need pulled and cinched her to him like chains, binding them together.

"I was hoping you'd say that, Freckles."

She barely had enough time to register his words before he was on her. She kicked and writhed and fought, trying to push him off. Nails scraped flesh. Teeth snapped. His movements were strong and steady, pushing her limits but not outright hurting her. Nova didn't give him the same courtesy and hold back though. If he couldn't handle all of her—then he would have none of her.

Jude's weight pinned her down, hips against hips. Her legs held between his. A big hand locked her wrists above her head as she snarled and snapped at his face. He'd caged her in. Taken her prisoner in her own bed. And she'd never been fucking wetter.

"Do you give up?" he asked.

"Never," she panted.

"That's my girl." He kissed her nose, just missing the snap of her teeth.

The clank of his belt preluded the smooth leather binding around her wrists. She struggled, but it was no use. He was stronger. She saved her energy, biding her time for the right moment—

A bolt of light streaked across the sky, illuminating Jude hovering above her like a vengeful god, promising punishment.

He sat up, his weight still pinning her hips to the mattress, and dropped his hands to his lap.

Nova tugged her hands, but they didn't move. She looked up. He'd tied them to a metal O-ring attached to the head-board. That was new. *When had he—*

"See? I knew this day would come." Jude reached over to her bedside drawer and pulled out a length of rope. He tossed it on the end of the mattress.

Nova began to struggle again. If he tied her feet too, she'd be completely helpless. "Don't you dare!"

Jude's hand collared her throat, squeezing the sides. The pressure in her head rose the tiniest bit, making her feel floaty and hazy. She squeezed her legs together, trying to quell the building ache.

He leaned in, inhaling her neck before backing away to lock eyes with her. "I told you that I was no good. That you deserved better."

She licked her lips, her chest heaving, her hard, sensitive nipples grazing his chest through the thin fabric of her crop top. "I should have believed you."

"Ahh, but you didn't. You chose to beat down the door I kept closed between us until you broke through. Until I had no choice but to let you in."

Arousal and excitement tangled with fear and anticipation, winding around in her belly like a cyclone. The pounding of hail on the roof grew almost deafening.

"Now there's no way out for you." Jude boomed over the thunder, as if he was the source of the frantic, destructive energy raging outside. Her very own Thor—the god of thunder.

Jude was beautiful like this. Brown curls mussed from their struggle. Dark eyelashes framing his hazel eyes, illuminated with each flash of light.

The hail rescinded until the pitter-patter of rain resumed.

His hand tightened on her neck. "Beg me for mercy and I might consider it. But know this, Nova, you are *mine*. I like your sharp nails, your disrespectful mouth, and the steel walls covered in barbed wire around your heart." His other hand slid under the material and cupped a bare breast, gently tugging her nipple piercings between his fingers. She arched her back, a whimper slipping free. She ground her teeth until she tasted blood.

"I see you, little brat. Afraid that if anyone saw the real Nova underneath, they'd run scared. They'd laugh and judge you. They'd abandon you." Jude leaned in until their noses touched. His lips coasted over hers as he spoke. "But I'm not them. I'm not going anywhere. No matter how hard you push. How sharp you cut me. I'll only want more. And I'll give you what you need in return. A soft place to land and protect you.

But also the whip that guides you." He twisted her nipple harder.

Nova arched her back, her nails digging into her palms. Pain turned her on—something she'd been ashamed of once upon a time. But not with Jude. Never with him. Not when she knew he thrived on it. Lived for it. Craved it.

"Are you going to break me now like you promised?" she asked.

"The more reinforced your walls are, the sweeter the victory will be when I have you in pieces underneath me where you belong—writhing from the pleasure and shuddering from the pain." His deep voice skittered across her flesh, sinking into muscle and bone until every piece of her tuned into the sound. The storm raging outside was background noise until Jude swallowed up her entire attention.

"And why would I let you do that?" she asked.

"Because you don't have a choice. You exist for my pleasure. My cock. You're nothing but a toy that I can pick up and play with, hurting you as I please or bringing you pleasure for the simple reason that I want to. That I can. And you'll let me, like Daddy's good little slut, won't you?" His fingers slid from her neck to her jaw, squeezing. "Answer me, little one."

A *yes* bubbled up in her throat. But she pressed her lips together to keep it in. She had some dignity, after all.

He tsked and his smile only deepened. "I still don't hear you begging for *mercy*."

"I'll never beg you for anything again," she spat the words at him, the lie bitter on her tongue.

"I fucking love when you fight me. It's gonna make this punishment that much sweeter." Rough hands unhooked her shorts, yanking them down her legs along with her panties. "Let's see if your cunt is that defiant."

"Don't you da—ahh!" Nova moaned as his fingers dragged through her slick flesh.

His thick finger dipped into her tight pussy. The obscene wet sounds his movements made while he fucked her gave her corrupted desire away.

A rumble drifted up from his chest, morphing into a satisfied chuckle. He withdrew his fingers from her and Nova's pussy clenched around nothing, leaving her wanting. She managed to hold back a whimper at the loss. But when Jude's long pink tongue slid out of his mouth to lick her juices from them, she lost the battle.

His eyes closed half-lidded as he sucked his fingers clean. "Fuck you taste good, baby."

"Jude?"

He ignored her plea and reached back into the drawer, pulling out a dual-action vibrator. He slid the silicone dildo through her pussy lips, teasing as the suction piece grazed her clit. "Don't even need lube you're so wet for me."

"You're a sick fuck!" She made a half-hearted attempt at wiggling her legs to get away, rolling to her side, her wrists still tied to the headboard.

Jude's hand splayed over her naked hip, shoving her to the bed the same time as he thrust the dildo inside her, the buzz on the curved end hitting her G-spot the same moment that the suction grabbed on to her clit.

"Fuuuuuck!" She gasped as forced pleasure licked her nerve endings, flickering and growing with each gentle hum of the vibration. Jude clicked a button and the vibration increased, making her toes curl. Her orgasm crested. "Right there—"

A warm hand wrapped around her ankle, tugging it straight before the smooth rope cinched around it.

"Don't even think about it—"

"Come for me, Freckles. And don't stop." His eyes glinted with triumph as he clicked the button again.

After that, speech was no longer possible as overwhelming pleasure shocked through her. The strong suction on her clit and the vibration against her G-spot worked in tandem, leaving her powerless. She writhed, arching her back, trying to fuck herself on the toy. But he secured her other ankle. He had her at his mercy now. Helpless and tied up. Unable to fight back with anything other than her mouth. But the relentless toy made it hard to breathe, never mind speak.

Jude grabbed the vibrator, pushing it harder against her to the point of pained pleasure. Lights burst behind her eyes and Nova clenched up every muscle, her eyes rolling back into her head. Nothing else existed in this space but pure unadulterated, relentless pleasure.

He ripped the toy from her body. She sucked in a breath, filling her lungs with delicious oxygen.

Slap!

Nova screeched. Stinging pain radiated from her oversensitive pussy.

Slap!

Slap!

Her arousal gushed out of her, soaking the comforter beneath her.

Two thick fingers plunged inside her. Jude leaned over her, his other hand shoving her crop top up under her armpits, exposing her breasts. His mouth descended, sharp teeth scraping her tender flesh, alternating with his soft, warm tongue. She arched into him, wanton and reckless.

"Don't act like you don't crave my depravity. Your body doesn't lie."

Slap!

Slap!

Slap!

"You want this."

Nova screamed as pain streaked through her with each smack of his hand on her pussy. The heat bloomed like a flower, budding into something much sweeter. The hazy fog of subspace slipped into her mind as she gave in to the pain, surrendered to it. *More. More. More.*

As if he read her mind, Jude slapped her breast, three fingers diving into her pussy this time, stretching her wider as his thumb swirled around her tender clit.

He rained down slaps on her tits as the water dripped down the windows outside her room. Calm settled over her, filling her limbs with the warm, golden light of steady bliss.

"Look at you, taking it like Daddy's good girl." He pressed a gentle kiss to her temple.

Her whole body exploded. If she'd thought she'd known pleasure before, his approval was nothing compared to the euphoria crashing against her walls now. His presence shadowed everything else. All her fear and anger. The powerless feeling she'd had since this all started. When she gave him her trust, when Nova surrendered to him, she was the farthest thing from powerless. She was the essence of empowerment.

She'd never been more confident than she was right then, in the eye of the storm, tied to her bed, with absolutely no control over what he did with her body. Sure, she knew if she uttered that one word—*mercy*—he'd give it to her. But she didn't want his *mercy*. Nova wanted his punishment. She craved his approval and groans of pleasure. His rough touch just as much as his gentle kisses. This was him showing her he could meet her needs. That he wouldn't be scared away.

Slap!

Slap!

Slap!

Each wave of pain steadily increased like a battering ram against the walls she'd rebuilt around her heart.

"You're mine. This cunt—this body—the very air in your lungs . . ." He collared her neck again and squeezed. ". . . are a gift for me."

"Please?" she begged, arching into his touch, presenting her breasts to him to abuse and mark.

"So fucking gorgeous when you give in." Jude plunged his fingers inside her, fucking her roughly. "You suffer so goddamned beautifully for me."

She shuddered and trembled, cresting the cliff of another orgasm and riding the edge. She held back, punishing herself further.

"Tell me who this cunt belongs to." He released her throat to slap her pussy twice.

She hissed, tears spilling down the sides of her face. "Yours."

"Whose?"

Slap! Slap! Slap! Slap! Slap!

"Daddy's. It's Daddy's." She sobbed. A dam released as emotion poured out of her in a wet, salty mess.

"And who do these tits belong to?" Jude sucked a tender, raw nipple into his mouth, his teeth clinking against the metal barbells as he bit down.

"Daddy's," she gasped.

"That's right, baby girl. Every piece of you is *mine*." Jude leaned in and licked the tears off the side of her face. She shivered, pleasure coiling tighter with each pump of his fingers inside her. The bindings at her wrists and ankles dug into her skin, grounding her further.

"Mine to use." His thumb swiped under her eye, dragging down her cheek towards her chin as if he was smudging her makeup. She must look a complete mess, but the way Jude stared at her with such pride and awe, like she was the greatest gift, stole her voice. More tears spilled down her face.

"Mine to make suffer and punish." He palmed her breast again only this time more gently. His words were at odds with his touch. "Mine to protect."

She held her breath as he locked eyes with her. Jude leaned in, his hand collaring her neck once more. Hesitation flashed in his hazel eyes but then it was gone, replaced by a grim determination that made her skin prickle and her pussy clench around his fingers.

"Mine to love." His lips collided with hers as he pinched her clit.

And just like that, with a creak and shudder, those walls blew up as a tortured scream scraped from her throat. He swallowed it with his mouth, taking everything from her. Her orgasm exploded, shattering her into a million little pieces shooting from the earthly plane. She was riding her pleasure like a rocket shooting towards the stars and burning just as hot. A supernova spun around her in blinking lights and swirling euphoria.

The corners of her vision dimmed until the room around her disappeared and she sunk into the darkness.

But she wasn't afraid, because despite everything that had happened, she trusted Jude would be there to guide her way back.

41

JUDE

Jude's chest heaved as he balanced his weight over Nova's sweat-slicked body. Those hazy eyes of hers blinked lazily up at him, uncertainty creeping in at the edges. He wanted to keep her in the moment just a little longer.

Jude leaned down and pressed a single kiss to her forehead. "You did so good."

He untied her wrists first, massaging the reddened skin. She'd given him one hell of a fight. A small smile curved his mouth. He wouldn't expect anything less from his little brat. God, his dick was hard as a fucking rock. But this was about her and what she needed.

Jude reluctantly rolled off her and sat up to untie her ankles. He repeated the same gentle massage from her heels to Nova's calves. "How do they feel?"

"Fine." Her breath evened out, slowing as her eyes drooped.

"Come on. I'll help you to the bathroom." Jude climbed out of bed.

Nova rolled to her side and closed her eyes. She would be asleep in less than a minute but she'd regret not going to the bathroom first.

A soft little snore came from Nova as she curled into herself. He hated to disturb her finally getting some rest, but he also understood the importance for her to pee after he'd had his fingers and toys inside her; it was part of their agreed-upon aftercare.

Jude slipped his hands under her body, picking her up and cradling her against his chest. She clung tighter to him as he moved into the bathroom.

He gently set her on the toilet. She gave a little mewl of protest. He bit back another smile. His ferocious little brat who took the world head-on seemed so much more fragile asleep. It reminded him of the quote he'd found and painted on one of Salem's childhood bedroom walls—something about letting her sleep because when she woke up, she would move mountains. That fit Nova to a tee.

"Come on, little one."

"Tired."

"I know. You'll get to sleep after you go the bathroom."

She sighed, her head leaning against him. A moment later, she relieved herself. Jude helped her back to the bed and handed her the glass of water on her side table.

"Take a few sips."

Nova grumbled, but did as he asked before lying back down. Jude covered her with the soft comforter. He returned to the bathroom to clean the toy before drying it and returning the vibrator to her drawer.

He climbed into the bed, pulling her into his arms. She snuggled into him, her head on his shoulder and palm over his chest. Jude didn't dare close his eyes. He savored this moment, her closeness. He'd taken a chance, having a scene with her with everything going on between them. He'd checked in with her and she'd never safe-worded. That was progress.

He'd gotten to know Nova quite a bit over the last couple weeks. She pushed people away for a reason. He just hoped she'd see he wasn't going anywhere, not when she needed him.

"I'm sorry I lied. That I hurt you so deeply." He pressed a kiss to her head and dragged his fingers up and down her hip. "I let my past experiences cloud my judgment." He took a deep breath and let it out. "I won't let it happen again."

Nova's hand coasted across his chest, her thumb brushing over his nipple in soothing strokes.

"I believe you." Nova's voice was barely above a whisper.

He froze. He'd thought her asleep, but this was good. "You do?"

She tilted her head, honey-brown eyes locking with his like a sucker punch. He held his breath, praying to whatever higher power that would listen to give him one more chance with this amazing woman.

"If something happened to one of my brothers, I would do anything to find them. The fact that you would go to these great lengths for your sister shows what a good brother you are."

Shame thrashed inside of him, rejecting the notion. "I wasn't. But I'm trying to be. I want to be better. For Sal . . . for you . . . and for me."

Her gaze dropped to his chest. "I don't know if I can trust you again."

Nova's words pierced his chest like a spear, ripping and shredding everything in its path to reach his heart. His eyes burned and his grip tightened on her hip as if his will alone would keep her with him.

"Do you want to?" he asked.

She looked at him, her gaze conflicted. "Honestly, a big part of me does. But then there's this other piece that says you're just going to hurt me again."

So there was still a chance? A small coal of hope lit inside Jude, and he breathed life into it, stoking the ember to a flame. As long as there was a possibility, he would do whatever it took to show the woman he loved that he was a safe place for her to land. He'd never lie or omit parts of the truth from her again. And he'd keep her safe from harm.

Jude just needed to show her what he already knew to be true. Nova belonged to him as much as Jude belonged to her.

He cupped the side of her face and tipped their foreheads together. "I fucked up and, because of that, you were hurt, and I will do everything in my power to fix this between us and show you that no matter what happens, I'm gonna be the one person you can count on above all others."

"That's a pretty high ambition."

He chuckled and tucked her against his chest once more. "Good thing I've got some experience in perseverance and patience."

A small puff of air left her nose in a sleepy laugh.

"You nervous about meeting the women tomorrow?"

She nodded, curling tighter into his embrace. His chest puffed up a little at that, warm hope glowing brighter inside him. She might not think she could trust him, but the very fact that she was snuggled up to him, turning to him for comfort amidst her anxieties? Well, that spoke much louder than her words.

Jude held her tighter. "I'll be with you every step of the way, Freckles."

"I was thinking . . . if I'm who the killer wants, maybe we could use that to find out where Salem is—"

"Absolutely not. We're not putting you in danger of this psycho."

"But—"

"I said no."

She huffed and pushed him away to roll to her side. Jude curled around her, his front to her back, wrapping her protectively in his arms.

"We're dealing with someone who gets joy from other people's pain. Losing one woman I love to this psycho is enough to make me lose my mind with grief. I can't lose you too."

Maybe that makes me a terrible brother.

"But it's not your choice." Her voice rose.

This was not how he'd wanted to end their night. He'd wanted her to drift off to dreamland without worries or stress, riding the high from their scene, not argue with him over putting herself in danger.

"You're right; it's not." The words scraped from his throat.

Nova turned to face him, surprise lighting her features.

"I just want you safe, baby girl. So much so that the thought of you in danger for even a second lights my blood on fire and calls to every primal instinct inside me to protect you . . . but if that's your choice, when the time comes, I'll have your six."

Nova blinked at him through watery eyes, her lips parting as if she was going to say something, but they pressed together instead. Doubt shuttered her expression before she rolled back over, facing away from him. Nova snuggled tighter into his arm, tucking it over her chest. His palm rested on her belly. At least this was progress.

They had a long road ahead of them to rebuild trust, but he'd hold out hope. When she was ready, he'd be there for her. He wouldn't run. He wouldn't abandon her. And as strong as his need to protect her was, he would never try and control her. Nova's free spirit and headstrong willpower were some of the beautiful things that made her who she was. And Jude would never diminish her identity—not even if it meant he had to let Nova go.

42

———

JUDE

Jude opened the passenger-side door, offering his hand to Nova. But she ignored it and climbed out of the vehicle on her own. He moved to her left, on the sidewalk by the row of cars. Things weren't fixed between them. But at least she seemed open to forgiving him. He just needed to show her he wasn't running away, no matter how hard she pushed. Nova and he were not so different—both fearing abandonment from anyone who really, truly got to know them. But maybe there was someone equally fucked up for everyone. *I sound like a cheesy romantic.* Jude snorted aloud.

Nova turned to him as they walked down Main Street.

"Still nervous?" he asked, not wanting to share where his thoughts had strayed.

"Yes," she answered.

Jude slipped his fingers through hers, and when she pulled away, it was half-hearted. He gripped her tighter and she gave in, holding his hand.

"I'm still mad at you." Nova looked through the large bay window of the Stardust Café as they stopped outside.

"I know. But we will find a way to work through this together." Jude dragged his knuckle down the side of her face. "I'm not going anywhere, Freckles."

Nova gave a quick nod, as if acknowledging his words but not yet able to let herself agree. *That's okay, baby. I'll convince you.*

"Ready?" He gave her hand a squeeze.

Nova released a loud exhale and headed for the door. Jude grabbed the handle and opened it for her, his right hand settling at her waist to guide her in.

The bell above the entrance chimed as they entered. The scent of fresh-roasted coffee and sweet baked goods enveloped them and made his mouth water. His skin prickled in the air-conditioning as he scanned the room. A few tables to their right were filled with people working on laptops. Nova walked to the main counter in front to a smiling barista with a young teenage girl next to her behind the counter. The two looked too much alike to not be related.

"Well, hello, my favorite people." Nova smiled warmly at them.

"Hey, Aunt Nova. Can I get you something?" the young girl asked as the barista studied him over Nova's shoulder.

"You sure can, Lyra. I'll have my usual and the big guy here likes his coffee as black as his soul," Nova teased.

Jude chuckled, sliding his arm around her shoulders and tucking her to him as his attention wandered to the tables on the left side of the counter. Amanda and Carrie sat in the corner. Carrie scowled, her arms crossed over her chest.

"Jude?" Nova elbowed him in the gut.

"Hmm?"

"I was introducing you to my cousin Remy. She owns the café and this is her daughter, Lyra," Nova said.

"Sorry. It's nice to meet you." Jude pulled out his wallet and dropped some cash on the counter.

"Thought you passed through town. Haven't seen you here in a while." Remy filled a cup with coffee as her daughter busied herself, cashing him out.

Jude glanced at Nova. "Nah. I plan on sticking around."

Remy's eyes volleyed between him and Nova as she bit back a smile. "I'm sure Aunt Renita is in heaven."

Nova snorted and grabbed the iced drink she ordered, topped with whipped cream and speckles of red. She closed her eyes and sipped from the straw. "Perfection."

"I'm glad you talked me into iced spicy hot chocolate for the summer. It's been a hit," Remy said to Nova, wiping down the counter as Lyra pulled out his change.

Jude waved his hand. "Keep it."

Lyra's smile lit up her face. "Thanks."

"As much as I'd love to stay and chat, I'm meeting a couple of people." Nova tipped her head to the back corner where the ladies sat, still not seeming to talk to one another.

"Oh, don't let us keep you. We're thinking of coming to next week's cookout at your mom's. It would be great to catch up." Remy glanced at Jude again, her intention clear.

"That sounds fun." Nova waved as she headed towards the table where two people from her past waited.

Nova stopped abruptly.

Jude balanced his cup of hot coffee so it didn't spill. "You okay?"

She didn't answer. He gripped the back of her neck, stepping in front of her. She looked up at him.

"What if they hate me?" Her voice trembled.

"You think it's your fault their lives are being upturned?" he asked.

She nodded, her chin wobbling. A couple of men by the table next to them glanced up and then resumed their conversation in the mostly quiet café.

He gently squeezed her nape. "It's not your fault. It's whoever's behind this. They're the ones to blame. You're a victim as much as the other girls are."

She blew out a breath. "I never wanted to be a victim again."

"And you won't be. Because you're going to go over to that table and share the information you have with those women to help them be prepared while you take your power back. This fucker thinks you're all easy prey? Prove him wrong."

Nova's eyes flashed. There she was—the fighter he loved so much.

"Jude?"

"Yeah, Freckles?"

"Thank you."

He swallowed, his throat thick with emotion. "I'm the one who owes you gratitude." Jude kissed her forehead and then they both faced the waiting women whose gazes were aimed at them.

"Here goes everything," she said under her breath before walking the rest of the way to the table.

Amanda's lips curved up in a smile, but the warmth wasn't there as it had been with Remy. Though she didn't have much to be happy about these days, with a killer gunning for them.

Carrie's scowl didn't change. If anything, her frown deepened. She eyed Jude warily, stiffening.

There wasn't much he could do to make himself less imposing as a six-foot-nine man. So he grabbed an unused chair and set it at the end of the table, not trying to crowd anyone's personal space.

Nova took a seat next to a hostile-looking Carrie.

"Wow." Amanda blinked, her eyes growing watery. "It's so weird seeing you both after all these years."

"I'd rather this reunion didn't happen. Can we just get it

over with?" Carrie asked. "And who's the bodyguard?"

Nova straightened, her shoulders back. Pride swelled in Jude's chest at her courage.

"This is Jude. He's Salem's brother."

I'm more than that to you. He almost growled, but this was not the time to get possessive.

"I'm so sorry to hear about your sister. She was special. A fighter," Amanda said, swiping at her eyes with her left hand. A sparkling ring caught in the light of the café. "I'm sorry. This is really hard, to bring this all up after so long. It probably doesn't help I just found out I'm pregnant too." She smiled.

"Oh wow." Nova's eyes widened. "Congratulations."

"Thanks." Amanda lifted up the same hand, showing off the large square diamond. "And I just got engaged. So this killer thing is really ruining the vibe." She laughed.

Carrie rolled her eyes. "Yes, because only you would see missing and murdered people as an inconvenience."

Amanda's expression shuttered. "You're right. That was selfish of me. I just . . ." She sniffed, tears dripping down her cheeks. "Sometimes I laugh so I don't cry, you know?"

Nova handed her a napkin from the table.

"Thanks." Amanda cleaned up her face, facing them once again with a smile that didn't reach her eyes. "I'm just overwhelmed and terrified that now that I've finally found my happiness, it will all be ripped away from me."

"Well, I'm grateful to both of you for meeting me here. We"—Nova motioned to Jude, including him in the conversation—"thought it would be best to come together so we can share information to make sure we're all being as safe as possible. Has the FBI been to visit you?"

"They sent some lackey to ask me a few questions. But I don't know fuck about anything. After I left that house, I never looked back. Life hasn't been all roses, but I'm not looking for any more trouble. I don't want to be involved in any of this. And if that piece of shit comes after me, he's gonna get his balls ripped off," Carrie seethed, glaring at Amanda. "No one got anywhere sniveling and whining like a little baby."

Amanda's pale cheeks flushed pink. Anger flashed in her blue eyes before it was gone. "How dare you judge me for how I survived? I—I did my best to keep—" Amanda glanced at Jude.

"He knows about your uncle," Nova said.

"Unfortunately, we can't choose our blood relations," Amanda said, sitting back, but she didn't drop eye contact with Nova.

"No, we can't." Nova shifted uncomfortably in her seat. Did Amanda know how close her words had hit for Nova?

"Can we just get this over with?" Carrie griped.

"I think that's for the best." Nova agreed. "I'll start." Jude studied the other two women as Nova relayed the information she had, keeping nothing back. Carrie sipped her coffee, staring out the window as if disinterested, but her fingers tapped nervously on the table and her reflection in the glass remained focused on the two other women at the table.

Jude's skin prickled still. It was an instinct honed from his need to survive in dangerous environments his whole life—at home, growing up, and then on missions. His gut was never wrong. But why was his internal alarm blaring at him that something wasn't right? The hair on the back of his neck stood on end. Jude scanned their surroundings, but nothing seemed out of the ordinary. *So why does it feel like we're being watched?*

Nova continued recapping what she knew and the details they'd gathered while Jude scanned the café once more and then back outside. Movement across the street caught his eye.

A hint of blond hair under a red baseball hat and designer sunglasses reflected the sun from the man staring directly at Nova. *Chad.* What the hell was he doing here? Was he stalking Nova? Was he the killer? Nova had doubts, but what if this asshole had used his daddy's resources to dig up the information about Nova's past? What if he was targeting her for dumping his ass? Had the other women's murders been to fuck with her head? Or a delusional attempt to have her turn to him? Jude shot to his feet.

Nova grabbed his arm, questions swimming in her gaze.

"Does the bodyguard have anything to add?" Carrie asked.

Jude glanced at her—it was only for a second, but when he returned his attention across the street, Chad was gone.

"Jude?" Nova asked, tugging his hand.

"Sorry. Thought I saw someone watching you."

"Who?" all three women asked, turning their attention out the window.

"He's gone. But it was Chad."

Nova whipped her attention back to Jude. "Chad? You're sure?"

"Positive."

"Who's Chad?" Amanda asked as Nova scanned outside.

Nova grimaced. "An ex—if you could even call him that."

Amanda clasped her chest. "Oh. Do you think he has something to do with this? Maybe it's not—"

"Anything is possible at this point, but I really don't think he's capable. And most of all, he has no motive." Nova massaged her temples as if fighting a headache.

"I should go see if I can find him." Jude pulled his arm from Nova but she dug her nails in.

"Please stay. It's not like I don't know where Chad lives."

Jude sat despite everything in him telling him to chase the

fucker down. Nova needed him, though, and that was his priority.

"Maybe this ex is trying to get your attention," Carrie suggested.

"What?" Nova asked.

"I once had an ex who killed the neighbor's cat and left it on my doormat. He'd thought the poor animal was mine. And when I wouldn't return his calls, he got creative." Carrie shrugged. "I didn't think he was capable either, but he's in jail for it. Luckily my neighbor had a Ring camera and caught him."

"What a monster," Amanda said.

"We can't focus on all the unknowns because there are just too many of them. We have to use what we know—stick to the facts," Nova insisted.

"She's right," Jude agreed.

Amanda fiddled with her ring. "I haven't gotten anything in the mail. Or any phone calls. I live alone most of the time. My fiancé, Matt, works on an oil rig, so he's gone for months at a stretch. He was going to try and finish up this last contract and take some time off, look for something closer with the baby on the way." She placed her hand on her stomach. "I pretty much just go to work at the studio in the city and come home."

"Has uncle dearest contacted you since he got out of jail?" Carrie asked.

Amanda's eyes darted to the table. "Yes."

"You always were his favorite," Carrie sniped.

"Carrie," Nova warned.

Carrie shook her head. "I guess not much has changed over the years. Nova's still trying to protect everyone. Amanda is still a crybaby with no backbone—"

"That's enough!" Jude's voice lashed out like a whip. All

three women stared at him. He even garnered a few looks from other tables. Jude lowered his voice and leaned in. "The fact is some sick fuck is out there killing women who lived in that house. All evidence points to Larry or Kim Washburn, and we can't rule Chad out. The FBI isn't doing much about it. So if you want to live, you need to take this seriously and work together."

"He's right," Nova said. "We need to put the past aside. Keep each other informed. Check in."

Amanda sighed. "Uncle Larry reached out after he got out of prison. He said he wanted to apologize but I ignored him. I moved without telling anyone where and started my life over. I haven't heard from him since."

Carrie pulled on her short brown hair. "I ran into Kim at one of the restaurants I worked at as a server in Boston two years ago. Bitch made a scene and got me fired. So I keyed her car and found another job farther away from their reach. That's it."

Nova pulled up her phone, tapping the screen and turning it to show the women. "Have you seen this guy around anywhere? This is Chad."

Both women glanced at the photo.

"Never seen him. Pretentious smirk like that, I'd remember him." Carrie shook her head.

Amanda leaned forward, squinting her eyes. "I might have seen him in the studio before with some friends."

"Really?" Nova asked.

Amanda clutched her chest again, with wide eyes. "Oh my God, does that mean he's targeting me next?"

"We don't know anything for sure, but if you see him, call one of us and don't ever be alone with him," Nova instructed.

Amanda smoothed out her pink dress. "Okay."

"Had you heard from Salem in the last few years?" Jude

asked, trying to get them back on track.

"No," Amanda answered quickly.

Carrie shook her head. "The last time I saw her was in that house."

This meeting wasn't really giving them the answers he'd wanted. Disappointment settled in his gut.

"What about you?" Carrie asked him.

"My sister and I . . . had a falling out and haven't spoken in a while," Jude confessed. If they were all willing to drag up their painful pasts, then he could be honest.

"And you said the latest letter was addressed from her with registered mail? Don't they need to, like, be in person to do that?" Carrie asked.

"Yes. The FBI said they were following up on that lead. See if the post office cameras can give them anything I would guess," Nova answered.

"Wasn't Ana dating your brother? I thought I remember seeing her engagement in the paper to an Emerson," Amanda pointed out.

"She was."

"So this all comes back to you." Carrie glared at Nova. "I knew it."

"Knew what?" Nova asked.

"No good deed goes unpunished." Carrie sighed.

"What about Kim? What happened after the court stuff?" Nova asked Amanda.

"Aunt Kim was deep in denial. She stayed with him throughout his imprisonment. She threatened me—said she'd make my life a living hell if I didn't tell everyone it was all a lie." Amanda shrugged. "I was put in the system and lost touch." More tears streaked down Amanda's cheek. She didn't bother wiping these away. "I know how much they both hurt us. But they were the only family I had left."

Nova reached out her hand to the woman and Amanda took it. "Something I've learned is that chosen family can be even better because they choose to be in your life and love and accept you for who you are. Just like you have with your fiancé."

Amanda frowned and stared at Nova for a beat before she nodded. "Yeah, you're right."

Carrie drained the last of her coffee. "Look, as much as I've enjoyed this trip down memory lane, I've got to head back home before my shift starts."

"You'll let us know if anything doesn't feel right? If you get any messages or anything seems off?" Nova asked.

"Yeah. But don't expect me to be Chatty Kathy in the group message."

"Let's check in every day just to let each other know we're alive," Nova suggested.

"A bit morbid, but okay," Amanda agreed.

Jude stood, giving the women space to get up from the table. Carrie grabbed her things and waved. "No offense, but I hope we don't have to meet again. Not because any of us is dead, but because I prefer to leave my past behind me and pretend it doesn't exist."

Nova snorted. "I hear ya."

Carrie left as Amanda gathered her purse.

She sniffed and smiled at Nova. "I never got to thank you for what you did for us."

"You really don't have to—"

"Well, I hope I get the chance to thank you properly. Maybe we can have dinner together sometime?" Amanda glanced at Jude. "It can get pretty lonely with Matt gone on the oil rig."

"I think once everything settles down, I'd like that," Nova answered.

"I'm really sorry about your sister, Jude. Salem was . . ." Amanda's expression shuttered again. "She was a kind soul."

"Is," he corrected.

"Hmm?" Amanda asked.

"She *is*. There's no proof she's dead yet."

Amanda smiled. "Of course. It's really encouraging to see how you care for her." She tucked a strand of blonde hair behind her ear. "Well, I've got to get back to the studio. You two have a wonderful day."

"Thanks, Amanda," Jude said.

Amanda left, the door chiming as she exited. Nova sat back in the chair and took another sip of her half-empty drink.

"You okay?" Jude asked, sliding his hand over hers.

"I don't think I've been okay for a long time. But I want to be. I want that so bad." Nova's dejected voice hit him square in the chest.

He stepped closer and wrapped his arm around her, pulling her cheek to his belly as he rubbed his hand in slow circles on her upper back. "I'm gonna make it okay for you. I promise."

She sighed, leaning into him as if taking refuge.

Jude wasn't one to promise anything. But he'd move heaven and earth if he had to in order to give Nova even a moment's worth of peace.

"I need to get home. I've got a meeting with clients at the barn in twenty minutes." She stood, drink in hand.

Jude cupped her face, tilting her chin up as he stared down at her. He placed a chaste kiss on the tip of her nose before pulling her into his arms and holding her there. "I'll make this right."

Her small hands smoothed up his back, pulling him closer, sharing in this intimate moment despite the few people tapping keyboards and having quiet conversations in the busy café. Everyone else fell away with the feel of her willingly clinging to him in the safety of his arms—a gift he would cherish until his last breath.

"Let's go before I'm late, or I'll never hear the end of it from my mother." Nova laughed, but it was forced.

"Not many people have managed to scare me in this world, but your mama is one of them." Jude tried to lighten the mood as he released Nova. She walked beside him as they waved to Remy and Lyra before exiting the café.

"You definitely don't want to get on her bad side. And if we're not on time, I'm blaming you," she teased.

Jude smiled. Happiness that he was able to distract her from the seriousness of their situation burst in his chest, filling his limbs with warmth. "I'll take one for the team."

"The team, huh?" she asked as they reached his truck.

Jude opened the door for her. "That's what we are, Freckles. A team. Which means we win together or lose together. I'm not partial to failing myself."

She chewed on her bottom lip before a cautious smile tilted the corners of her mouth. "I think I'm starting to see that."

Jude waited until she climbed in the car. He reached over, grabbing her buckle and snapping it in place. He traced the curve of her jaw. "Just you wait, little one. I've got a whole lot more to show you. It might take a lifetime."

Her eyes widened. Jude smirked and shut the door, his steps a little lighter. Because for the first time since everything had gone to shit, real hope shone in those dark brown orbs of hers.

Maybe he could earn her trust back after all.

And just maybe he could find his own future with Nova.

43

NOVA

Nova waved goodbye to the engaged couple, her smile disappearing with the click of their car doors. She dropped the mask, rubbing her aching face. Sometimes it took every bit of her energy to deal with people. Not that this couple was more demanding than any other. But when a psychopath was after you, one only had so many spoons. Normally being busy was good—it helped distract her from everything going on. But not so much today. She'd barely been able to concentrate on what the couple said half the time, her mind a million miles away, sifting through all the evidence and past memories, trying to find a connection— trying to find the killer.

"All done?"

She spun around. "Everett?" She scanned the empty field next to him. "Where did Jude go?"

Everett ran a hand through his jet-black hair with a warm smile. "Your dad needed his help with the tractor. He asked me to stay with you."

Nova chewed on her fingernail. "He went with Dad alone? Or was Ricky with him?"

Everett's knowing gaze locked on hers. Having a youth counselor as a friend was nice, except when he turned those psychoanalyzing skills on her. "Just your dad. They said they'd meet us at your parents'."

Nova sighed and shut the barn door. "Figures." She dusted off her hands on her jean shorts. "Let's go face the firing squad."

Everett's jaw dropped open and then a belly-shaking laugh erupted. "I never thought I'd see the day."

"Are you feeling okay? Has the heat gotten to you?" She pressed her hand to his forehead.

Everett shook his head, his eyes sparkling with mirth. "I'm just surprised you're not running to your truck with some excuse to avoid facing your family. Especially after the truth about Jude came out and your parents want answers."

Nova winced. "Yeah, well . . . the cat's out of the bag now. I talked to Mom a little already."

"I think it's more than that."

She crossed her arms over her chest. "What is that supposed to mean?"

"I mean every other time you'd run out of here like your ass was on fire, but you're not. You avoid conflict like the plague. Yet, with every interaction I've seen with you and Jude, you haven't backed down."

Nova blinked. *I guess I haven't, have I?*

"What makes him so special?" Everett asked.

"I didn't have any expectations to live up to when he was a stranger."

"But he's been more than that for a while, hasn't he? I've seen you two together. No one's that good at pretending."

"Who said I was pretending?" she backtracked. Shit, it

was hard to keep track of who she'd told what to—and exhausting.

One of Everett's eyebrows rose. "Do you honestly think you're good at lying?"

She rolled her eyes. "He's . . . I can be myself with him."

"Remember when we talked about love in my apartment on Valentine's Day?"

"You mean when my brother was being a scared little bitch?" she quipped.

Everett chuckled. "Yes. You said you wanted fire. Someone who wasn't afraid of the deepest, darkest parts of your soul."

Nova closed her eyes, the memory washing over her. "I wanted someone who wasn't afraid to get in the trenches with me when the shit hit the fan. Someone who knew what it was like to go through hell and come out the other side, having conquered their demons with dirt under their fingernails from clawing their way out."

"You wanted someone who would stick by your side when trouble came. Someone who saw you and loved and accepted you for who you are. Someone who wouldn't hesitate to do what you needed, despite the consequence," Everett added.

"Someone to protect me." Nova took a deep breath, staring at the black-eyed Susans growing at the edge of the barn. The yellow petals fluttered in the breeze.

Jude had been that for her, hadn't he? He'd protected her from the moment she'd run into him with that flat tire. He'd played along with her wild idea of being her fake boyfriend, even if he hadn't been completely honest. But they didn't know each other. And as soon as they began opening up, he'd shown her the most vulnerable parts of himself—his shame. And though things didn't go as she'd hoped, when the full truth came out, he'd given her all the information. He'd protected her even when she hadn't wanted to look at him.

When she'd said hurtful things to him and pushed him away. He'd stayed. He'd fought for her—for them.

"He hurt me," she confessed. "But I hurt him too."

"It's interesting how you avoid conflict with every other person, but with him you meet it head-on. You don't back down," Everett mused.

"Because I know if he wanted to walk away . . . I'd be heartbroken, but I'd survive." She wiped her arm across her forehead, realization making her stumble back a step. "And I know I'm safe with him. I don't have to change myself when I'm around him. He accepts every piece of me."

"That's because you are not codependent. You can love him and understand you're both your own people with your own needs and wants. You have boundaries. You aren't molding yourself into someone you think he'd want. You're authentically you in this relationship and so is he. We're human, so it isn't perfect. But that's the start of a very healthy relationship."

"You think so?"

Everett nodded, before picking a dandelion from the grass at his feet.

"I think I do love him." The confession tore from her. "But that's what scares me. Our love isn't perfect—far from it. But it's ours. I'm just still not sure it will last. With everything going on . . . what if something happens and it tears us apart? What if Salem doesn't make it? What if we never find her? Will that hang over our heads? In a way, it's because of her that we came together. What if after the dust settles, that's all we had?"

"What-ifs can be dangerous as much as they can be hopeful. We have to focus on the now. What is happening? What choice is best for you in this moment?" Everett asked.

Nova took a deep breath and exhaled. Images of Jude

bringing her water, making sure she ate filled her mind. Cleaning, organizing, cooking, helping her be on time for things. Showing her new systems she could put in place to meet her goals. There were other things, too. The way he supported her career instead of treating it as a hobby or a joke. The way he took interest in her thoughts and opinions. How he so perfectly slipped into the Daddy role she craved, giving her a level of connection, release, joy, and trust she'd never known. The way he didn't let her push him away. He took the brunt of her temper and pushed Nova to dig deeper, but also gave her space when needed.

But is it fair to Jude to start something when I could be taken away like his sister?

"I see those thoughts taking a turn." Everett slipped his arm over her shoulder and tugged her against his side before handing her the small yellow flower he'd picked. "You've got the potential for something amazing here. No matter what you decide, you know you have your whole family to support you."

The reminder of her family made her flinch. "You think they're going to forgive me for lying to them?"

"I think your boyfriend will take care of that."

"What do you mean?"

Everett smirked and led her down the hill towards her parents' house. "I should have brought popcorn for the show."

"Oh, God." She clutched her stomach. "I think I should smoke first—"

"Nah-ah. Let's go. They're waiting on us."

"All of them? Oh, shit. Poor Jude. We need to go rescue him." She jogged out of Everett's arms and stumbled. "Fuck."

"Let's try to arrive in one piece. I don't need Jude kicking my ass for not keeping you from harm—even if it was self-inflicted." Everett laughed. "Don't tell Ricky this, but I'm pretty sure your boyfriend could take him in a fight. As hot as watching those two spar without shirts on would be, I don't want my fiancé having a black eye for our engagement photos next week."

Nova shook her head and marched up the hill beside her friend. "That would be pretty hot, wouldn't it?" The image of Jude's muscles, sweaty as he took her annoying brother down a peg or two, was kind of amazing.

"Maybe we save that for after the wedding." He winked.

"Only if you promise," she teased.

"Aunty Nova! Quick! Uncle Nash and Uncle Ricky are wrestling with your boyfriend!" Ariel came running out of the house, eyes alight with excitement and mischief.

"Fuck." Nova took off running into the house with Everett's laughter echoing behind her.

It was time to face the consequences of her choices.

44

___

NOVA

Nova rushed into the house, scanning the living room for Jude.

"They're out back. I told them if they were gonna break something in this house, I was going to lose my mi—"

Nova rushed past her mother, ignoring the rest of her sentence. Heart racing, she opened the back door and froze.

Jude smiled at her through blood-stained teeth. "Hey, Freckles."

"What the fuck is this?" she yelled, stomping down the stairs. She grabbed his jaw, tipping his head to get a better look before she glared at Nash, Ricky, and Roman. "Which one of you did this?"

Jude placed his hands on her shoulders. "It's okay—"

"This is the farthest thing from okay! They hurt you."

"Baby—"

"He deserved it," Nash growled.

She whirled on her oldest brother, pointing her finger and

jabbing his sternum as she yelled at him, "No he fucking did not deserve it!"

"He lied to us—to you," Ricky added.

Nova turned on him. "Like you've never lied? Your whole life you've been lying to us and yourself!"

Ricky had the good sense to look chastised.

"And you!" She spun back to Nash. "You ever lay your hands on my boyfriend again and I will make it my mission to make your life hell."

"What about me?" Roman asked. "I'm starting to feel left out."

She rolled her eyes and focused on him. "We all know you're not out here throwing punches. You're here to make sure these two hotheaded idiots don't go too far—which I appreciate, but you could have stopped it before Jude got hurt."

"Freckles, look at me," Jude ordered in a laughing tone.

"Why are you smirking like this is all a joke?" she asked as his hands wrapped around her waist.

"It's not a joke. But I deserved it."

"How—"

"Fuck, it's really hot seeing you all feisty like this for my sake."

Her brothers groaned in unison.

"Come on, bro," Ricky complained.

Nova ignored them. She cupped Jude's cheek. His lip was a little swollen, but it wasn't bleeding anymore. "They hurt you."

"I offered them a swing. You really think I wouldn't be able to take them on?" he asked, one eyebrow quirking up in question.

She scanned her brothers.

Ricky stiffened, puffing his chest as if in challenge. "I could take him in my sleep."

Nash snorted.

Jude pulled her closer so that they were chest to chest.

"Are you telling me this was some masculinity contest?" Nova asked, looking up at him.

"I'm saying I deserved it for lying to you. And it was only fair I take the time to clear things up with your family as well. I lied to them too."

"Because I asked you to," she whispered.

"And we're certainly going to talk more about that," her mother called through the open back door. "Get in here and get some ice on that mouth of yours, Jude."

Nova cringed. "You'd better go."

"It's just a scratch. Your brother has weak form."

"Hey!" Ricky yelled. "Fucker. I'll show you weak form."

Nova smiled as Jude chuckled.

"Name the place and time, Emerson." Jude pressed a kiss to her forehead and walked into the house, closing the door behind him.

"He's good for you," Roman said.

Surprise shocked Nova. Her eyes widened as she focused her attention on her three brothers standing side by side. "Why does this feel like a trick?"

Ricky wrapped his arm around her shoulders and pulled her into his side in a half-hug. "Our little sister, always so suspicious."

Nova pinched the skin under his arm.

"Owww!" Ricky jerked away from her.

"That's what you get for punching Jude," she hissed and crossed her arms over her chest.

Roman laughed, and Nash's lips even quirked up.

"Oh, man, I never thought I'd see the day." Roman clutched his stomach, his eyes dancing with happiness.

"What day?" Nova asked.

"The day our baby sister met her match." Roman smirked.

The impact of his words socked her in the stomach and stole Nova's breath. "Y-you guys aren't mad that we lied?"

"We?" Ricky tipped his head to the side, his smile slick. "That's not the story Jude told us all a little bit ago."

"What do you mean?" she asked.

"I'd rather hear what you were about to say." Ricky narrowed his gaze on her.

Nova sighed. "It doesn't even matter anymore. Jude . . . is a good man. He's far from perfect. But so am I. I'm just not sure . . ."

"Listen, all the times you were there to curse me out when I fucked things up with Bella, maybe you should take your own advice and tell him you love him."

Nova held up her finger. "First of all, you proposed without doing that. Our situations are not the same. I have no desire to get married." She lifted another digit. "And second, since when do you actually encourage me to be with a partner, much less a guy? You've always tried to chase them away from me."

"Brooks was an asshole. We told you that from the beginning." Ricky shook his head as if disgusted.

He wasn't wrong.

"Claudia was sweet, but she liked you more than you liked her," Roman added.

"They weren't the one for you," Nash said.

"And Jude is?" She tried to give an air of indifference, but her brothers' support of Jude made her heart lurch with hope.

"Anyone loyal enough to take the blame for your crazy

ideas with Mom and Dad is worth giving a second chance to," Roman said.

"What crazy ideas?" Nash asked.

Roman slipped his arm around Nova's shoulder and pulled her into a hug. "Look, I know I wasn't really there for you when you were going through everything with Brooks."

"You were grieving your wife and adjusting to being a single father—"

"Still. I should have tried to talk to you about your situation." Roman's voice dripped with regret.

"We all should have been looking out for you better," Nash added.

"I'm sorry we were too wrapped up in our own shit to see you needed help." Ricky's shoulders slumped.

Nova squeezed Roman back and then released him to face all three of her brothers. "I don't know that I would have listened to anything you had to say back then." She laughed, but there was no humor in it. "I think we all needed to take our separate paths and find what we were looking for. It was pretty dark for a while, but we made it out. We learned and now we can do better. We can enjoy the rewards of getting out of our own way."

"Always with the little drops of wisdom," Nash teased.

"That's why we keep her around. Lord knows it isn't for her organizational skills," Ricky joked.

"Hey!" She went to smack Ricky's arm, but he dodged her.

"Seriously. You were the one who convinced us to break into Nash's house that day he fucked things up with Isabella—"

Nova raised her hand. "The door was unlocked. Technically, we didn't break in."

"And you gave me shit when I was being an asshole with

Elise. Told it to me straight when I needed to hear how much I'd fucked up." Roman shook his head as if he still couldn't believe how stupid he'd been.

"And you helped me break out of the hospital to see Everett . . ." Ricky narrowed his eyes at her. "Even if you made me do it half-naked. You also kept him company on Valentine's when I should have been man enough to confront my feelings for him."

Nova beamed. "So what you're saying is, I'm the best sister ever and you all owe your happiness to me? I hope you know I'll be collecting favors in perpetuity for that."

Her brothers laughed in unison. Their deep chuckles stirred something warm and bright in her chest.

"Don't ever change, Nov," Ricky said, placing his arm once again over her shoulders.

"Except maybe put the guy out of his misery and tell him how you feel," Roman said.

The back door creaked open. Her mother walked out, crossing her arms as she gave Nova a knowing look.

"So, I need to get Ariel and get back home . . ." Roman left Nova to give their mom a kiss on the cheek and then disappeared into the house.

"I gotta go too—look at the time. Everett's waiting for me out front." Ricky gave Nova a wink and then followed Roman.

"After all that, you guys are just abandoning me? What happened to loyalty? Having my back?"

Nash shook his head. "It doesn't trump what we have for that woman right there."

"You mean fear! Scaredy-cats! All of you!" Nova yelled as her last retreating brother said goodbye to their mother and left.

"Are the theatrics over? Can we sit and talk now, Akua?" her mother asked.

Nova swallowed the ball of anxiety and gave a quick nod. It was time to put the truth on the table. She climbed the steps to the back door and followed her mother inside. The home that had always felt so warm and welcoming made her sweat and her heart race. It was like the first time she'd arrived all over again. She'd been scared that if she did something wrong, her new foster parents would send her back to the hell she'd come from. But they never had. They'd only ever supported and loved her. And how had she repaid them back? *By lying.*

Her shoulders slumped. Deep inside she was still that sixteen-year-old girl afraid of her adoptive parents rejecting her. Nova tipped her chin up. *That doesn't have to be my story anymore.* It wasn't fair to her mom and dad either. They've proven time and time again that they were there for her—no matter what.

Nova could be brave and tell them the truth—even if it came at a painful cost.

45

NOVA

Nova walked into the dining room. Jude held a bag of frozen peas to his mouth, sitting beside her father. Nova sat next to him and Renita took the empty chair across from her.

"You okay?" Jude whispered as if she was the injured one.

She licked her lips and gave a brief nod. Her body was strung tighter than a rubber band about to snap.

Nova eyed the pitcher of lemonade. "Can you pass me a cup of that please, Daddy?"

As if the moment couldn't possibly get any worse, Jude and her father both reached for the pitcher at the same time.

Nova's eyed widened as her face flamed. *For all that is holy. I'm never going to be able to look my parents in the eyes again. I'll have to move—change my name—*

"Nova?" Jude asked.

"What?" Her voice cracked.

"Here." Jude passed her the cup.

She took it and downed the liquid, not even tasting it. She

risked a glance at her mother, who seemed the safer option at that moment. Boy, had Nova been wrong.

Her mom's eyebrow was arched with an unimpressed look.

Death would be better, right now preferably. Where was a freak lightning strike when you needed one?

Nova's stomach soured. How could she even think that at a time like this? When people were actually dying and the true damage that would do to her loved ones was insurmountable. *God, I'm selfish.*

"I'm so sorry. For all the lies. For the trouble I've brought to you time and time again. You both deserve a better daughter and I'm . . . not her. I've tried to be. I just . . . I'm sorry."

"Is that really how you feel?" her mom asked. "Even after our chat the other day?"

Nova tipped her chin up to face the woman who had welcomed her into her home and family from the very beginning, without even knowing everything about her history. She nodded.

"Oh, Akua Ketewa, that makes my heart hurt so much." Her mom got up, walked around the table, and sat next to Nova. She took Nova's hands in hers.

Nova turned to face her mom.

"You were the greatest gift to me. I thought I was doomed to be in a house full of boys and testosterone. And then I got a call from the state, letting me know the half sister I'd found out about only six months prior and never had the privilege of knowing, had passed. But that she'd also left behind a daughter." Her mom sniffed, emotion shining in her eyes. "I knew at that moment my sister wanted me to find you and make sure you were safe. To bring you into our home and love you like the daughter you are to me. I wish I had more pieces to the puzzle of her life just so I could give you more answers to the questions I know you have."

Tears dripped down Nova's cheeks.

"I never expected you to be anyone other than who you are. Because you're enough, Nova. Whether you find a partner or not. Whether you give me grandchildren or not." Her mother blinked. "I think my attempts to help push you to move beyond the pain of your past maybe weren't the right way to go about it."

"You just wanted me to have the same happiness you and Dad have. That all my brothers were able to find." Nova glanced at her dad.

James spoke. "Sweetheart, we just wanted you to have the companionship and love that you deserve. We want you to be happy."

Nova shook her head, but her mother gripped her chin, forcing Nova to face her once more.

"I wish I'd realized before."

"Realized what?" Nova asked.

"That you were carrying such a heavy burden all these years."

"What are you talking about?" Nova wiped her eyes.

Renita tipped her head to the side as if studying her. "It's not your fault."

"What?"

"What happened to your mother—Cynthia. What happened to those girls and you in that house. None of that was yours to bear."

Nova shook her head. "If it wasn't for the man who—I wouldn't be here. I was created with violence. By the worst of the worst kind of human."

Renita shook her head. "That doesn't have to be your story. I may not have known your mother, but her actions speak far more than anything. She loved you, Nova. She wanted you. She held on as long as she could to give you the best chance in life."

"But I was also her greatest source of pain."

"The man who raped her was. Not you—never you. You were only an innocent child in all of this. I won't try and pretend I understand the complicated relationship of a mother to a child of a product of that horrendous act. I won't dismiss your experience as her daughter either. Or try and say it wasn't painful for her in some ways. But I want you to know first of all none of that was your fault. You were created from an act of violence, yes. But look at what you've used this life to do. Look at how you've taken that darkness and turned it into light."

Nova's mind raced to all that she'd done in her time alive. Her brothers' gratitude for helping them with their partners. The elderly friends at the retirement community who lived with less pain because of her medicinal cannabis treats.

"You were the first one to suggest we learn sign language for Ariel when she wouldn't speak anymore," her dad said.

"You saved those women from that foster home. You saved my sister." Jude spoke up, his hand spreading out on her thigh. Comfort surged through her at his touch.

"You saved me." He leveled those hazel eyes on her, nothing but honesty shining through them. "You gave me hope when I had none. You showed me what real love is."

"Took them long enough." Her dad laughed.

"What?" Nova asked.

"When you two showed up in the office with this crazy story of Jude being your long-distance boyfriend moving in, it took everything in me to keep a straight face." Renita smiled.

"You knew?"

"Of course we knew," her dad said. "It's not like it was the first time you'd fake dated someone. At least this time you chose a man who was actually interested in women. And you're also a terrible liar."

"That's what everyone keeps telling me," she mumbled. "Why did you let it go on if you knew?"

"It was entertaining." Renita laughed. "And also your dad ran a background check on Jude. We knew he had a clean record. We missed the part about his sister though. We'll have to take that up with Bently."

"You had the sheriff look him up?" Nova asked, baffled.

"You think we'd let a stranger move in with our daughter without doing the necessary checks? Especially when there's a killer on the loose?" James asked. "We try to give you kids space to make your mistakes and learn from them, but there is a line."

Nova blinked, glancing between her parents. "You knew the whole time . . . but you never treated me or Jude differently."

"We knew you'd come around eventually. You just needed the shit to hit the fan first. You always did like the dramatics," her mom teased. "However, do you think you can put the lies behind you now? You're almost thirty, for Christ's sake."

"I guess there's no reason to continue. I just . . . don't like disappointing you both," Nova confessed.

Her mom patted her left knee. "There's nothing in this world that would make me not love you."

"Thank you, Mom." She turned to her dad. "And you. You guys gave me a home and love that I never expected. Thank you for your forgiveness and for pushing me when I needed it."

"Don't expect any of that to change." Her dad gave her a wink before turning to Jude. "Now, about you."

Nova instinctively reached for Jude's hand on her thigh.

Jude stiffened, shoulders back, chin raised, his whole body braced as if ready to take a hit. He squeezed her hand back. "Yes, sir?"

"You plan on staying in the farming career path?" her dad asked.

"I . . . hadn't really thought that far ahead with everything going on."

"He's got an apprenticeship with Cleo at Squid Ink in town if he wants it. Jude is a wonderful artist." Nova beamed with pride.

Her mother gave Nova a knowing look.

"Is that right?" her dad asked.

"I do okay." Jude shrugged. "But I'm also happy to help out at the farm as long as you need me."

"Welcome to the fold, Jude." Her dad held out his hand to shake Jude's.

Her mouth dropped open. Jude's eyes flared as if he, too, was shocked, but he took her father's hand and shook it. "Thank you."

"Renita wasn't too sure about you in the beginning—"

"Because I never thought she'd give another military man a chance," her mother butted in.

Her dad's attention locked on to Jude. "But I recognized that look in your eyes the first time we met."

"What look?" Jude asked.

"Loneliness. You needed to find your people. And now you have." Her dad held up his hands, motioning around him. "That night I asked you to watch over Nova in the back of the truck? I could see the struggle you faced, getting too close. You needed to make a choice . . . and I might have tried to help you along."

"Then I owe you more of a debt than I could possibly

repay," Jude said, turning to level the weight of his full attention on Nova.

Her heart fluttered like a damn whirlwind of butterflies had erupted inside it.

I love you. She hadn't meant to. Never thought she'd be able to open herself up again after Brooks. And when Jude had betrayed her, she'd never thought she could forgive him. But here she was, still here. And so was he.

"So how about we start over? Jude, welcome to our crazy family. We're a mess, but we love hard and are loyal to a fault." Her mom smiled at him.

"Thank you, ma'am—er, Mama E."

"Welcome home, Jude. No matter where you came from, you're one of us now—if you want that—and you promise to treat our daughter like the gift that she is," her dad added.

"You have my word." Jude looked both her parents in the eyes and then turned to her.

Nova must have been a saint in a previous life to have earned this level of happiness and love. *Or maybe I take a page from my mom's book and believe I deserve it.*

"I'd like you to take my hunting rifle, keep it at the house just in case. Nova's got a safe in her room under the bed. You can store it in there in case the kids come over." Her dad got to his feet.

Mom turned to Nova. "Bently said he'd make sure his team are patrolling nearby, but I don't want you going anywhere alone. I want someone with you at all times." Her mom left no room for discussion. That was an order. "We can't lose you." Her mother's arms wrapped around her.

Nova stood to give her a better hug. "I won't take any more risks. I promise."

"Good."

Nova didn't fight the extended embrace. She soaked up

her mother's scent. Cocoa butter and sugar cookies. Her purple locs tickled Nova's neck before her mom pulled away.

"You need anything, you call us."

"I will," she promised, but she didn't miss the tinge of fear in her parents' expressions as she moved to give her father a hug goodbye.

She hated that they lived in fear of something happening to her. What if the killer went after them?

"You won't go anywhere alone either, right?" she asked.

Dad pulled Mom to his side, his arm wrapping around her waist. "Won't let her out of my sight. Your brothers and Everett are all doing the same with the kids and your sisters-in-law."

"Good." She nodded stiffly.

Nova and Jude made their way silently out the front door. Her mind spun the whole time they walked towards her home. Everyone there was living in terror because of this monster lurking in the shadows. But whoever it was only seemed to want her—to make her pay.

Maybe everyone would be better without me.

Not that she didn't want to live—but what if she ran away? Left for a little while, just to give her family a reprieve? Or would the killer hurt them regardless?

"Nova?" Jude's voice cut through her spinning thoughts.

"Hmm?"

"You okay?"

"I—I just need some space to think."

Jude nodded, his palm warm on her lower back as he guided her up her front porch and inside. She didn't miss the concern etched into his handsome face. She massaged her temples, trying to ease the growing ache there.

Strong, capable fingers pressed into the base of her neck, massaging as she stood in her living room. Jude shut the door with his other hand. "Come on. Let's go lie down in the bed and I'll rub your head."

Nova didn't have the energy to argue. If Jude wanted to help care for her, she'd let him. She wanted him to. Nova needed her Dom to take away the growing ache consuming her whole body. The overwhelming pain grew with each breath. She just needed a break—a short escape into her Daddy's safe arms.

Nova climbed the stairs, barely seeing where she was going. She leaned against Jude, using his guidance to find the soft comforter of her mattress. She slid beneath the blanket. His warmth joined her a moment later. The bed sunk under his weight as she shifted, tucking her to him as he rubbed her temples as promised.

She closed her eyes, no longer fighting the darkness but welcoming it. She'd reached burnout. Everything was shutting down. If only this were one of her romance novels, where the darkest hour came before the dawn.

She was too tired to even cry. Instead, Nova surrendered to sleep.

46

JUDE

J ude relaxed into the chair in the living room as Nova flitted around the space. She'd woken from her nap and they'd checked on her plants in the grow houses before they'd shared a quiet dinner. A trail of smoke drifted from the bundle of herbs she held in her hand. Her full lips moved as if she were speaking, but her words were too light for him to make out. Something about the elements and protection.

"Are you a witch?" he asked.

The corners of her mouth tilted up as she finished circling the room. She put the bundle of tied herbs down in a bowl in the kitchen.

"Ahh, but what is a witch?" She closed the sliding door and joined him on the couch.

Her nap had helped, but the dark shadows under her eyes remained. The usual feisty spirit in her expression had dimmed with bone-deep exhaustion of the soul.

Jude grabbed her ankle, pulling her foot into his lap. He massaged, starting at the arch of her foot.

"Ohh, that's so good," she moaned, relaxing into the corner of the couch.

"Someone who practices witchcraft?" He answered more like a question.

Nova chuckled. "Yeah, that's one way of looking at it. Back in the day it was simply women who didn't fit into society's expectations. Women who shunned the patriarchal rules of that era. Women who slept with who they wanted without worrying about their reputation. Women who didn't adhere to the rules, like going to church. Some were even arrested just for using herbs to help heal others."

"Interesting."

"They were punished and even killed for their knowledge and the threat that their freethinking posed to a patriarchal and religious society."

"Insecure bastards made that call. Cowards," Jude said.

"Yeah." She laughed and then tipped her head to the side, leaning against the couch cushion. "I consider myself a spiritual person. I focus more on energy and intention. Yes, I could identify as a witch." She smiled mischievously. "I promise not to hex you unless you lie to me again. How about that? And if you do, I'll turn you into one of Roman and Ricky's bees. Sound good?" It was nice to see the spark back in her eyes.

He laughed. "Sounds like a deal." He switched to her other foot. "Speaking of . . . I wondered if you were willing to talk about us?"

Nova's chest rose like she was taking a deep breath. Her warm brown gaze landed on him as if she were trying to read him. "Okay."

"All my life I've been let down by the people who were supposed to be there for me no matter what." Guilt sliced him. Hadn't he done the same to Salem? Did he have any right to ask Nova for forgiveness?

Her feet slipped from his lap. She crawled closer, climbing to straddle his waist. She cupped his face, staring into his eyes. His hands immediately went to her hips, holding her in place.

"Don't go there," Nova said.

How did she know? He closed his eyes, stuffing the pain down to the darkest depths. The slick oil of regret tainted his soul.

"How can you stand to touch me like this—with so much kindness—after everything?" He was desperate for her answer, focusing on her lips, not wanting to miss a single word. Starving for something—hope of some kind.

"I could say the same."

His grips on her hips tightened. "You're nothing but goodness. A survivor that made it through the fires of hell and came out the other side. You have *nothing* to be ashamed of."

"That's how you see me. But I see it differently. And maybe that's the problem for both of us." She brushed a stray curl from his forehead. "We have a choice. We can focus on our past. On our failures. On the things we regret, the things we wish we could change. But where does that get us?"

"Nowhere good. But it's the truth."

"Maybe it's one side of the truth. The older I get, the more I realize life is about perception. I can look at how I was created and feel guilty. Sink into the feelings of unworthiness, of self-hatred. Or I can choose to look at it as something that shapes me. I can turn the energy of that pain and trauma into something better. The drive to help make the world safer for women like me. Empathy for people in different situations."

Jude couldn't look away from the goddess on his lap. He pinched one of her wild curls between his fingers just to assure himself she was real. Her silky-smooth tresses slipped through his fingers like a gentle caress. Those big honey-brown eyes were filled with so much genuine sweetness and light, as if she glowed from within.

He dragged a finger over the smattering of freckles on her cheeks. "I wish I could see the world through your eyes."

"You can. It's a choice. A constant, daily choice. Your experiences shape your life. But every day we have the decision to let those experiences empower us to do better for ourselves and the world around us, or to let the negative energy take over. That's what I've learned from this."

"You're so fucking beautiful—inside and out."

She beamed at him, and that burst of joy shook his world off its axis. Nova truly was too good for this life. She was the embodiment of everything pure all wrapped in a curvy, feisty package. She was perfect—for him.

"And what about my omissions? What good can come from those?" He swallowed, both dreading and eager for her answer. He held his breath, everything riding on that moment.

Nova exhaled. "It hurt. I felt like I opened up to you and gave you everything—showed you the parts of me that I'd kept hidden for so long."

Darkness shrouded Jude at the pain he'd caused her. If only he'd manned up sooner.

Nova brushed her hand over his five o'clock shadow. "Were you really going to tell me?"

"Yes. Right before that fucking letter arrived."

"I'm not sure it would have hurt much less, but it would have felt better coming from your mouth."

"I'm so fucking sorry. I regret so many things in my life, but that's in the top two." The fact that Salem could be dead or suffering because of his actions was hard to beat, but hurting Nova was a close second.

"I believe you."

Jude sucked in a breath. Hope burned in his gut, the

brightness of it unfamiliar to his chemistry. "I know you don't believe in absolutes. But if we do this, I swear I will never lie to you again. I'll do whatever it takes to rebuild your trust." He smoothed his hand over the side of her neck, cupping her nape. "I was never one to believe in love, never mind fate." He chuckled, the smile on his lips disappearing as he locked eyes with her. Jude needed her to hear the truth in his voice—to know he meant every word. "But I think you might just be the match to my soul. When I'm with you, you make me want to be a better man. You make me want to grow and challenge myself. To be worthy of you."

Her eyes fluttered closed, tiny lines appearing on her forehead. Jude pulled her closer, tipping his face so their foreheads pressed together. His nose brushed the side of hers, his mouth breathing in her sweet breath.

"The only way I know how to fix this is to show you. To choose you—every time, in every way. I promise you today—because that's where we live. Yesterday is gone. Tomorrow will never truly be here because it's always the future. And if you let me, I will spend the rest of my todays making you happy. Giving you what you need and want forever."

"Forever?" she asked, her lips brushing his in a tempting caress.

"I know marriage isn't your thing. We don't need a piece of paper to show how committed we are to each other. But I swear to you, there will never be another for me but you."

"Jude—"

"I think I've loved you since the moment you pulled that knife from your boot on the two men who thought they could take from you."

Warm tears slid down her cheeks, soaking into his skin.

"Something inside me snapped that night. I didn't want to acknowledge it—I was a coward."

"What was it?" she asked, her voice breathy.

He hesitated, afraid that his answer would scare her.

"Jude?"

He pulled away to look deep into her eyes. "I knew in that moment on some level that I didn't want anyone else to be able to hurt you—except for me."

Her lips parted as if in a silent gasp. God, that sounded so fucked up when he said it out loud. But she understood what he meant. A consensual pain between partners. The level of knowing someone so intimately that they had your complete and unmitigated trust that he'd only ever witnessed in a BDSM dynamic. One he'd never thought himself capable of —until now. Until Nova.

"I knew you were mine to protect. It wasn't until later that I realized it was because I'd fallen in love with you."

Nova wiped her eyes, smudging the eyeliner under them. Her hair was still mussed from her nap. Her cheeks were tearstained, eyes shiny and red. But she was never more beautiful to him.

"I want all that with you too. No one's ever made me feel like you have—as safe and taken care of. You make me believe I can be better too."

Relief poured over Jude like a bursting dam, crashing through his worry, drowning his fear until every part of him was overcome with so much love for her that he couldn't contain it another second.

Jude's lips crashed against Nova's like they were two souls colliding. Finally, he was giving every piece of him to her, not holding anything back.

Her nails dug into his shoulders, her hot pussy grinding on his cock as she rocked her hips. He craved her—needed her.

The sound of her phone ringing was like nails on a chalkboard.

"Ignore it." He shoved his hand under her shirt, pushing it out of his way to cup her breast.

Nova moaned, her back arching, which gave him better access. He sucked one of her bare nipples into his mouth.

"Jude—"

"God, I need you so bad right now."

The ringing died down and started again.

"I have to get that." She grabbed the phone from the coffee table. "It might be important."

Jude's body was wound tight as a drum. Utter need boiled in his veins to connect with Nova in one of the most intimate ways. He hadn't been inside her since before all this had happened.

She picked it up, glancing at the caller. "It's Carrie." All the heat in his body was replaced with cold fury that someone was out there still stealing peace from his woman.

Nova tapped the screen, placed the phone on speaker, and answered, "Hello?"

"He sent me a letter!" Carrie's voice was hysterical on the other end.

Nova's eyes widened, and her mouth dropped open. "What?"

"Why is this happening to me? I've finally got my shit together and now it's all falling apart again."

"What does it say?" Jude asked.

"It says I'm next. God, I can't do this—I can't."

"Did you call the FBI?" Nova asked.

"They're sending someone. A police officer is here with me now. But, Nova—I haven't heard from Amanda. I tried calling her, too, and it kept ringing, and she never answered."

"Oh no!" Nova's face paled.

Jude grabbed the phone from her hand and pulled her

against him. "Carrie, is the police sending someone to look for Amanda?"

"They already did," she sniffed. "They haven't been able to find her."

"Amanda's missing?" Nova gripped her chest as the shocked whisper left her.

Everything inside Jude screamed at him to shield her from this—to take away her pain. He lifted the phone closer to his lips. "You've got someone there with you, so you're safe. Just stay put. And update us with anything you find out. We'll do the same."

"Okay." Carrie's voice cracked.

Nova trembled against him. "I need to go." Red and blue lights lit up the window facing the driveway. "The police just showed up."

"You'll keep her safe?" Carrie asked.

She hadn't seemed happy to see Nova in the café, but these women were bonded from living in that house. She still cared, just as Nova did for them.

"With my life." He hung up the phone and tossed it on the couch.

He tucked Nova into his chest, rubbing her back. He searched for words of comfort, but none came. How could he assure Nova that her friends would be safe?

"I got you, baby. I won't let anything happen to you."

Nova didn't answer and that worried him more than a flurry of words would.

Someone pounded on the front door. "Nova? Open up, it's Bently."

He was the sheriff her parents had used to run a background check on Jude. But Jude wasn't taking any chances.

"Nova? What happened?" James's voice carried through the door before more pounding ensued.

Jude lifted Nova in his arms, holding her tightly as he moved to unlock the front door. He wished he could hide her away from all of this, give her a reprieve, but that wasn't possible. And what about Salem? If another woman was taken, did that mean Salem's body would be found? That was how the last one had been discovered. The women went one after the other.

Oh, fuck. If she was truly dead… He stumbled with the force of the pain slicing through him.

But small blunt nails dug into his neck, that little bit of pain grounding him. He needed to be strong for Nova.

And he would—even if it killed him.

47

NOVA

Nova sucked in a breath as sharp as glass. The weight on her chest got heavier with each inhale. Voices murmured around her, but she hadn't heard a word since Bently had come to confirm the news that Amanda was missing. *Never made it to work this morning. Hasn't been seen since.* The FBI finally had agents sitting outside both Nova's and Carrie's homes. With three dead and two missing women, it was about fucking time they did something. They were just waiting on a search warrant for the Washburns' to come through.

Someone's hand touched Nova's knee. Another arm wrapped around her. But she barely felt them. Numbness sank into her cells one at a time until she felt nothing—nothing but the pain of hopelessness.

Her mother's voice drifted closer, but she still sounded far away, before she kissed Nova's cheek. Nova nodded, needing to do something. The last thing she wanted was to worry her family even more.

"Nova?" Jude asked, his voice somehow reaching her through the thick black fog of her despair.

"Hmm?"

"I've got one of the guest bedrooms ready for your parents."

"What?" She shook her head, as if it would work to disperse the fog hanging over her. "No. Mom, Dad, you should go home and rest. I'll be fine."

"You think I'm going to leave my baby when there's a psycho after her?" Renita demanded.

Nova used her remaining energy and took a deep breath. "Mom, I have a Navy SEAL to protect me. I'm safe here. Bently is staying outside until Deputy Vargas takes over in the morning. My brothers have put cameras all over this place. Bambi couldn't get on the property without someone knowing. Go home. Get some rest. I'm just going to bed."

"I don't care if you're sixteen or twenty-eight. You're my daughter and I will do what I need to keep you safe. I'll give you space, but I'm staying." Her mother's voice was firm.

Nova didn't have the energy to fight. "Fine. I'm still going to bed." She got to her feet. Jude's hand splayed over her lower back. She leaned into him, her only source of strength. He seemed to understand because he swooped her up into his arms and climbed the stairs.

Dishes clinked from the kitchen as they entered her room. Jude shut the door behind them. Nova's eyes burned, but she didn't cry. Was it possible to use up all your tears? She hadn't felt this defeated—this low—since . . . Images of that blue house flashed in her mind. She remembered feeling terrified and utterly alone with a monster while grieving her mother.

A sliver of warmth permeated the ice chilling her bones where Jude's body came into contact with hers. He cupped her face, staring into her eyes and through to her very soul.

Concern distorted his expression. Deep lines creased the center of his forehead, the corner of his eyes and between his brows. His lips turned down before he spoke. "Nova?"

She didn't answer—couldn't. Her voice was trapped inside her. She had no energy to even try forming the words.

Jude cradled her like she was the most precious cargo, gently laying her on the bed. The soft mattress sunk beneath their weight. Jude tugged her shorts down her legs, leaving her in a T-shirt and underwear. Grabbing the back of his shirt, he pulled it over his head in one move. Jude slid beside her, covering them with the blanket before he pulled her against his chest. His warmth enveloped her. She closed her eyes, breathing him in, clinging to his body as if she could hang on to the safety his arms offered forever.

Jude's palm made soothing circles on her back as he held her in silence. Dim light came from the bedside lamp. Time passed as they lay like that. The soft murmur of her parents' voices drifted in occasionally from downstairs.

Heartache lanced through Nova's rib cage. She hated that she'd brought this much trouble to their lives. And then that hurt morphed to anger. How dare this fucker mess with her and her family? How dare they steal those women's lives and peace? And fuck them for hurting Salem! Rage pulsed in her veins, overwhelming and suffocating. She wanted to find this asshole and rip them apart. Nova slammed her eyes closed, her breaths coming faster. *But I can't. Because I don't even fucking know who they are for sure. I'm just waiting while they play this sick game.*

"Just breathe, Freckles. Breathe with me." Jude's chest lifted in an extended breath before he exhaled.

Nova tried to copy him. It helped having him there to do it with her. Her body trembled from a mix of fear, adrenaline, and anger.

His hand splayed out over her chest as he pressed hers to his. "Like this."

She closed her eyes and focused on her breath. *In. Out. In. Out.*

"Good girl, just like that." Jude rubbed her back with his other hand in soothing circles, grounding her. It helped.

"Do you think it's Larry and Kim?" she asked, moving to lie on his arm and look at his face.

"I don't know. But it seems that way. I should have listened to Reaper."

Damn, she'd been so wrapped up in her own shit, she hadn't even taken the time to check on Jude. Salem was still missing. But the killer's pattern had been to reveal a body with every abduction. That meant that Salem could be—

"There's still hope she's alive." Nova pushed the terrifying thoughts away. She had to be strong for Jude. "There've been no messages to me since that letter. That must mean that Salem is still out there, hanging on. We have time to find her."

Jude's gaze clouded with something that looked a lot like how she felt inside—hopeless. "I hate this. I hate knowing my sister was taken by a psychopath. What she must have gone through, being scared and alone—what she could still be going through. If he hurt her. If she's still alive after all that— a month and a half of God knows what. A part of me wonders if we found her alive, if she'd even be okay."

Jude's pain was a tangible thing permeating the very air they shared, thick and rancid with grief.

Nova rubbed his chest in slow strokes, trying to offer him some of the comfort he'd brought to her. "When we find her, we'll give her all the help and support she needs. She won't be alone, and neither will you."

Jude pressed a kiss to her forehead. His index finger

stroked across the line of freckles over her cheeks. "You know this one looks like a shooting star?"

"My freckles?"

He nodded. "I even wished on it when we were in the truck that night after the movie."

She smiled, touched that he'd thought her special enough to hold the power to make wishes come true. "That was before you liked me."

"Nah. Just before I wanted to admit it to myself."

"Jude?"

"Yeah, baby?"

"I'm scared."

Jude drew the comforter over their heads, encasing them in more darkness. The dim light barely made it through—just enough for her to make his features out.

"When I was younger, I looked after Salem. She'd get nightmares sometimes. I'd crawl in bed with her, pull the covers over us like this. We'd pretend the rest of the world didn't exist."

Her chest squeezed as she imagined a younger Jude and Salem curled together, forming their own way of coping with their unhealthy environment.

"She always had a beautiful imagination. She'd come up with whole worlds in her head. Pirate princesses who raided kingdoms. Sometimes she'd be the girl who slayed the dragons; other times they'd become her pets."

Nova laughed. "And did you tell her stories too?"

"Usually I'd start them and she'd take over."

"Show me."

Jude turned on his side, staring down at Nova. "Let's pretend that nothing exists outside this blanket. It's a magical comforter, carrying us to a land far away where no darkness exists, no monsters hiding in the night. Only sunshine and rainbows."

"Is there weed in this new land?" she teased.

"Anything you want. It's a magic land that creates your heart's deepest desires."

Nova swallowed the lump of emotion that welled in her throat. "Then I want you there."

"You couldn't get rid of me if you tried, little brat." He pulled her closer, pressing chaste kisses all around her face. "I will protect you with my life." *Kiss.* "I won't let anything touch you." *Kiss.*

"But you can't be here with me all the time—not forever. Some serial killers are never caught. Some take years—"

"Shhh." He kissed her nose. "I know trust is a lot to ask for. But I'm begging you, please know that I will never let any harm come to you. I can't—I don't think I would be able to go on without you."

"Jude—"

He shook his head, his eyes glistening with tears. Nova's heart slammed as realization sunk in. He'd told her so many times that he cared for her—loved her even. He'd taken care of her over and over again. The way he reminded her to stay hydrated despite her being a brat about it. He'd fed her and comforted her. The last two times they'd been intimate he'd taken nothing for himself, only given to her. Met her needs. Showed her on multiple occasions that he was loyal and trustworthy. If only she could let go of her past pain—the trauma keeping her from going all in. But the way that he looked at her, like she was his everything, rocked her to her core. She was standing on the edge of a cliff. She no longer had any doubt he'd catch her. But would she be brave enough to jump?

"It just feels like I'm holding my breath waiting for the

next shoe to drop. The next call confirming someone I care about is dead."

His mouth hovered over her lips. "Then let me breathe for you."

And just like that, Nova jumped, free-falling into the great unknown of love. It wasn't reckless nor impulsive—it was right. If she only had a little time left of this life, she was going to make the most of it.

"I want you." Her lips pressed to his, seeking and hungry. Need spiraled through her with each drag of his soft mouth against hers.

Jude pulled away. "Neither one of us is in the right head-space to scene right now."

She shook her head. "Please, Jude? I need this. I need you. Make love to me."

"I'll always give you what you want, baby." He leaned down, capturing her mouth with his. Electricity sparked through her skin with his touch, striking down to her very soul.

I love you.

Nova kissed him back, infusing everything she felt into it. The desire to connect with him—to make him feel good rose like a storm gathering energy inside her.

The rough nip of his teeth on her lip sent shivers through her. Nova moaned, her pussy slick with arousal.

Gentle and slow, Jude pushed her shirt up over her head. Nova wiggled out of it, still under the light weight of the blanket. Jude shifted, climbing on top of her, not breaking the kiss as if he, too, needed this as much as her.

His calloused hands caressed her breast, squeezing and kneading. She gripped his shoulders, moving down his back, craving more. He had marble muscles encased in warm, soft skin. His touch was tender and sure. She parted her lips, his tongue immediately sliding through the opening. She sucked. He groaned. Nova tangled her tongue with his, gripping the back of his neck. They kissed for minutes or hours—Nova lost all sense of time. Lost herself in this world under the blanket where nothing else existed but the two of them.

She panted, lust morphing to yearning.

"You're so beautiful." He trailed kisses down her neck and sucked at the base of her ear.

Her exhale was hot, as if she'd consumed fire. It was need for Jude burning her up from the inside out. "Please? I want you."

Those wicked lips nipped and kissed down to her breasts, winding her up even more. Her body thrummed like a heartbeat, pulsing and alive. Anticipation lit up every synapse. With each delicate press of his mouth, she climbed higher. Dragging, searching fingers sent spirals of pleasured sensations rippling through her. His rough facial hair scratched down her rib cage, over her soft stomach.

"I want you inside me," she said.

"Shhh. Just lie back and let Daddy take care of you, baby girl."

Sudden and unbidden tears welled in her eyes. Jude's wide tongue slipped through her already slick folds. She arched her back, pleasure streaking through her as he swirled and flicked and worked her clit in his mouth. One finger pressed inside her, fucking her slowly, curling up to hit her G-spot.

Saltwater slid down the side of her face, falling towards the pillow. In all her life, Nova had never felt this cherished. This cared for. This loved. They weren't just connecting bodies but something bigger—spiritually, on a soul-deep level.

She spread her thighs wider, gripping his hair, digging her nails into his scalp. His groan vibrated against her clit, sending her closer and closer to her first orgasm. But she held back.

She wanted to come with him—for them to leap over the edge together.

"Please, Daddy. I need your cock. I need to feel you inside me."

Jude took one last lick and then nipped her thigh, playfully. "I love how needy you are for Daddy."

He slid off his shorts and lined himself between her thighs. His cock teased her clit. She clenched her pussy, aching for him to stretch her walls and fill her up.

"Tell me who you belong to," he commanded softly before sucking her nipple into his mouth.

Nova arched her back. "You. I belong to you. I'm yours. Make me yours."

"That's my girl." He sunk into her pussy with one thrust, stealing her breath.

"Oh—"

"Shhh." His hand locked around her mouth. "Got to be quiet, little one. Be a good girl and take Daddy's cock. Don't make a sound; those are only for me."

She nodded.

His hips thrust once, twice, stretching her walls with a mix of delicious pain and pleasure without the time to adjust to his size. She wanted more. Nova dug her heels into his ass, pulling Jude even deeper. He knocked her cervix with every thrust and it felt so goddamn good. *More. More. More.*

"Such a good little whore." Jude fucked her torturously slowly.

Everything inside Nova screamed for more and harder, but there was something about this pace, edging her, feeding her craving until she was a writhing mess.

"God, you feel so good in my arms. Your cunt squeezing around my cock like a vise. You're the sweetest fucking thing."

The muscles in his shoulders bunched under her hands.

His expression strained as if it were taking all his self-control not to lose himself in her. It only turned Nova on more.

She tugged his hand away from her mouth. "Don't hold back. I want everything. Every piece of you. The tenderness and rough edges. The care and the hurt. I can take it for you, Daddy. I need it just as much as you."

A decadent, dark smile curved his sinful lips. "Thank you for trusting me with the most vulnerable parts of you, baby."

Jude slammed into her, still slow, but oh so much harder. Her body surged upwards under the force. Pleasure rocketed through her with each drive of his hips. His hand wrapped around her neck, pinning her down as his cock dragged out of her only to force back inside, bottoming out. Nova gritted her teeth, attempting to hold in the moans as her eyes rolled back in her head. He'd wrecked her for anyone else, obliterating all her walls, everything that had ever held her back. Putting the pieces of her heart back together into places she couldn't reach on her own.

"Look at me."

She blinked, trying to focus, but it was hard to do anything but take. Overwhelming pleasure mingled with golden light, growing and merging inside her. Glimmers and sparks of bliss shimmered through Nova. Every sensation was compounded over and over, magnified with each brush of his lips against hers.

"I want to see the moment you fall apart and come for me." Jude's voice was rough with his own blazing need. He hooked an arm under her thigh, lifting it over to join her other. Her hips tilted, her legs squeezing together. She clenched her pussy around him, trying to lock him inside. She never wanted this to end. A feeling of rightness and home and *everything* enveloped her. Jude was *her* everything. She didn't know where she ended and he began anymore—and it didn't matter. They were *one*.

Every brutal drive of his hips hit a spot deep inside her, somehow more powerful than her G-spot. Euphoria swallowed her whole. Vicious need clawed her self-control to ribbons.

"I'm gonna—"

"Come," he commanded.

"Come with me." Her voice dripped with frantic desire.

Jude didn't hesitate, switching from slow, hard thrusts to fucking her with a violent desperation she could taste.

"Nova!" Jude's voice was soaked in hunger.

His hand tightened around her throat, searing her skin like a brand, bringing her higher than she'd thought possible. Unable to hold back, Nova came with an instant force that shouldn't have been possible with human limitations. She flew higher and higher until she no longer existed in physical form. Until their hearts mingled and their souls connected—finally, whole.

Delirium-inducing euphoria rushed over her, drowning her until she had no choice but to breathe it in, taking a lungful of the highest pleasure. Her every cell vibrated with utter surrender and acceptance. Nova floated, boneless, in a sea of warm bliss. Jude's cock pulsed, sending one last spurt of his cum inside her.

Nova caught her breath, his hand sliding from her throat and gripping the hair at the base of her neck. He pulled her closer as he bent and met her in a sensual kiss.

And when he pulled back, the covers fell, illuminating the adoring look aimed at her. How he could take such a low moment in her life and turn it into this—her heart bursting with so much love—she didn't know.

But she wouldn't take another second with this man for granted.

"I love you."

His eyes flared wide with surprise and awe. "I love you too. More than anything."

She pulled the covers over their heads again, needing to shut the world out for just a little bit longer. Tomorrow, the sun would rise, and with it, their problems. But for tonight, she'd stay in their bubble, locked in her Daddy's safe arms, protected from the evils stalking her.

She'd live in the promise of today.

48

———

JUDE

S and coated everything, filling Jude's nose and mouth until he choked on it. The oppressive heat of the desert made it stick to his sweaty, exposed skin. Jude coughed, shielding his eyes—it was suffocating. Just as soon as it appeared, it was gone—replaced with his brothers in uniform surrounding him in a sea of sand and burning vehicles. East, west, north, and south, nothing but sand until it met a purple sky.

Unlike other times, the men weren't lying on the ground. Instead they stood in a half-circle around Jude. Smoke rose all around them from a burning tank and convoy vehicles, but the men looked untouched otherwise.

What the hell?

"Look who's finally awake," Kirk said, Jude's lieutenant.

"'Bout time. This kid can sleep through a damn war." Commander Jefferson shook his head.

"What are you doing here?" Jude asked, surveying the men he'd bonded with over the years in service just to lose to combat.

"Saying goodbye."

"What?" Panic streaked through Jude. He couldn't lose them—not again.

His commander pulled him into his arms and slapped his back hard before pulling back to look him in the eyes. "You gotta let us go, King. She needs you."

"Commander—"

"It was never your fault." Jefferson's words felt like a slap across the face—sudden and unexpected.

"Who else was to blame? I survived. There's no one else to pass the buck to."

"It was a shitty situation. We were ambushed, and you survived. You got the package back safe." Jefferson shook his head. "For whatever reason, this was my path in life. Not yours. You still have so much life to live, King. And if you throw that chance away like a fucking coward again, I will come back and haunt you, motherfucker."

"He never was good at taking orders," Kirk snickered.

God, Jude had missed his friend.

Kirk clamped a hand on his shoulder. "She's hot, King. Way out of your league."

A laugh burst from Jude, unexpected and healing. Bittersweet. "She is. Shit, I've missed you, Kirk."

"You think I'm leaving you? Nah, we won't be too far. You've got a fucking killer crew of us watching over you." Kirk smiled.

"But we do have to go. It's time," his commander said. Jefferson's lips quirked up, tipping his head to the purple sky. "I'll give you one last piece of advice before I go."

Jude swallowed. The other men around them joined in, speaking as one with their commander, over a dozen voices at once: "Don't be afraid to live."

One by one, all but two of the men from his past unit walked away until they got smaller and smaller on the hills of sand and disappeared altogether. Faces from his time in the Navy, and then as a SEAL.

Jefferson gave him one last nod. "I'm glad I got to know you, King."

"Stay?" Jude asked.

"You don't need me anymore." Jefferson turned and left the same way as the other men.

Kirk was the only one remaining. The man he'd known in his first unit. Kirk was the one who'd convinced him to join the SEAL team—his first real friend. "Tell Reaper I said hello."

Jude shook his head. "I'm sorry I didn't jump first."

"I'm not." Kirk shrugged.

"What?"

"When that fucker threw the grenade, I didn't think—I just acted. Instinct took over. It was you or me, and I chose. I have no regrets."

"Why haven't we talked before now?" Jude asked instead of replying.

"Because you weren't ready."

"And now you're leaving too?" Jude asked.

Kirk shrugged. "You finally freed us."

"What?" Jude sucked in a breath. "I kept you here?"

"Until you were ready to let the past go and hope for a future, you were stuck here in limbo. We couldn't leave a man behind."

"Where will you go?" Jude asked.

Kirk smiled. "Where we all go when we die, brother. Back to the beginning."

Jude's brows drew together in confusion.

Kirk laughed and pulled him into a hug. "Watch your six."

"You too."

Kirk smiled as he backed away. He looked at something over Jude's shoulder.

Jude turned, the landscape shifting with him. He was no longer in the desert but back in his mother's filthy apartment.

Salem sat huddled in the corner, her arms wrapped around her knees as she trembled. Her stricken expression stared up at him.

"Sal?" He dove to his knees, reaching for his sister, but his hands slipped right through her. "Salem! No!"

"Help me. Jude? Please? Help me!"

He tried again, but he couldn't grasp her.

"Salem!"

Her head turned towards the opening door, eyes wide as the temperature in the room dropped several degrees.

"It's too late," Salem said.

Jude tried to climb to his feet, ready to defend his sister from whoever was coming through the door, but it was as if his limbs had filled with lead. The room grew darker, his vision going.

No. Open your eyes! Fuck! Salem!

* * *

Jude's eyes shot open. He blinked, his vision adjusting to the dim room. But it wasn't the same. He was back at Nova's. It was all a dream. Which meant—

Jude carefully but quickly pulled his arm out from under Nova's head. His skin itched, and his breathing came faster. He pulled on his shorts, slipped the phone in his pocket, and ran out of the room.

Was Salem dead? Was it all a dream or some kind of premonition?

Jude stumbled down the stairs, ran to the back porch, and sucked in cool night air. Sweat beaded on his brow. The urge to run and scream rose like a tsunami inside him. But he couldn't leave Nova unprotected for even a minute. Her parents were there, but he couldn't live with himself if something happened to her too.

He fell to the ground, holding his head in his hands. His lungs constricted; every breath was a chore. Pain lanced his rib cage, spreading throughout his body until everything hurt.

"I'm so sorry I failed you." Jude rocked back and forth, his fingers threading through his hair and fisting, pulling hard.

Minutes turned into hours. Jude's skin was cold and numb.

The moon moved across the sky. The black sky turned to indigo, lighter in the east where in the next half hour the sun would rise.

Jude pulled out his phone and dialed Reaper.

"Couldn't sleep?" Reaper answered.

"I should have let you grab Larry. Even if he didn't have her—I would have made him suffer for what he did to them."

"You can't talk about this on the phone, King," Reaper warned. His friend was an expert in how to get away with murder. But was it murder if you were killing a monster of the worst kind?

Jude didn't care. "You didn't see anything at the Washburns'?"

"No. You know we can't be there twenty-four seven. We took shifts. He must have slipped out, or there's the possibility that it isn't them.

"Axel has been doing some more digging into Kim and Chad like you asked. His white hat hacker discovered Kim's degree is in botany. Her sister, Amanda's mother, died of what was ruled natural causes. A heart attack at age thirty-five. No history of illness before then."

"Seems like a big coincidence." Jude rubbed a hand over his face.

"Right. And Chadwick Herrington the Third had some interesting financials, including dropping a large sum at the music studio Amanda works at. Looks like he and his buddies are aspiring music artists."

"Of course they fucking are," Jude grumbled.

"He's got the means but I'm not sure the man has the forethought to pull off something as calculated as this. And it still leaves the question why he would choose to go after the women that were part of Nova's life far before he ever ran into her."

Jude fisted his hands, his stomach hardening. Maybe he should pay Chad a visit tonight. "It's one of them. The evidence is too fucking strong not to be." Jude slammed his hand on the grass. "We should have taken Larry weeks ago before the FBI got too involved."

"It's too late for that right now. They've been camped outside his house all night. I'm guessing they're waiting on the warrant."

"No one was watching Amanda?" Jude asked.

"We're not a huge outfit. I've got my guys doing all they can. But there's too many places to be. Washburns took priority. That's why I'm staking out the Washburn house as much as possible."

"I'm sorry. I don't mean to be ungrateful. Salem was—" Jude's throat clogged with emotion. His eyes burned.

"I get it. I won't leave until I have answers from the FBI. Once they're gone, if Larry is still there, I'll get what you need." Reaper's voice cut like ice through the phone.

Jude shivered. He never wanted to end up on his friend's bad side. Reaper showed no mercy—Jude had witnessed that firsthand on more than one occasion.

"The last time I spoke to her she told me she hated me. And I said—" Jude shook his head. "I told her I couldn't do it anymore. If she wanted to ruin her life—then go ahead. Just leave me the fuck out of her mess." He wiped the tears from his face and sniffed. He couldn't afford to lose it. Jude slammed the door on his grief and locked it tight.

"You'll get to make it right. Don't lose hope—"

"I dreamed of her tonight."

"Jude—"

"Kirk was there. He told me to tell you hello."

"It was just a dream."

"I don't think it was. Ever since that op in the desert that went wrong, I've had dreams of our fallen brothers. They're always dead. The first time I dreamed of anything different, it was Nova. But that only happened once." He took a breath, fully knowing his friend might think him absolutely crazy. Maybe some of his little witch was rubbing off on him. "This time they were whole and talking to me. They left, moved on, whatever you want to call it. I just have this feeling that I won't be seeing them again."

Reaper stayed quiet on the other end of the line.

Jude sighed. "After they left, Salem appeared. She was terrified. I couldn't touch her—couldn't save her. I think it's too late."

"King?"

"Yeah?"

"You better man the fuck up. The mission isn't over until we find her—dead or alive. You have to keep your head on straight and not let emotion cloud your judgment. We'll find Salem, even if we have to leave a bloody trail doing it. I've let you run point on this because she's your sister, but you're compromised."

"What do you mean?"

"You're not in the right headspace to call the shots. I'm assuming command. I'll bring her back, brother."

"Rowan?" Jude asked.

"Yeah?" his friend asked. Not many people knew Reaper's first name, and no one used it.

"Thank you."

"Don't thank me yet."

The line went dead. Jude pulled the phone away, tucked it into his pocket, and then turned up to face the purple sky. Dark indigo was fading into a violet like it had in his dream.

"I need you to help me, Kirk. Help me find my sister and

keep Nova safe. I'll never ask another favor if you do those two things."

Jude hadn't been one to believe in life after death. The myths of heaven and hell had never meant much to him. But after that dream—which felt all too real—what was the harm in talking to ghosts?

Jude climbed to his feet, his body stiff from sitting on the ground for so long. He went back inside and slipped into Nova's room. He leaned against the door.

Nova's hair was fanned out over the pillow. Her arms and legs were spread out over the bed like a starfish. Slight snores came from her parted lips. She was so fucking adorable.

Jude stepped forward quietly until he reached the mattress. He leaned down and pressed a kiss to her nose and backed away. She scrunched her face, tiny lines appearing between her brows as she let out a mewl and snuggled closer into her pillow.

"I promise I'll do whatever it takes to keep you safe."

If only he'd made that same promise to Salem.

If only he could go back in time.

If only he knew who the killer was.

49

NOVA

A shrill ring woke Nova. She gasped, scrambling for her phone next to the bedside table blindly while trying to get her eyes to work.

"It's mine," Jude said.

Nova blinked, turning towards him as he clicked the button to end the offending sound. Her heart raced. Who could—

"Tell me you have something," Jude demanded, swiping the speakerphone button.

"They found Amanda in the Washburns' house," Reaper answered.

Nova gasped and sat up. The blankets fell to her lap. "What about—"

"No sign of your sister yet. The FBI raided and the coward shot himself."

What?

Ringing filled Nova's ears as Jude's voice rose, asking about his sister. About Kim. Could Amanda tell them anything?

But Nova was reeling. Larry Washburn had shot himself? The man who'd caused so much pain to so many women was gone?

"Is he dead?" she asked.

"Ax's mystery friend was able to get hospital access. He's gone into surgery. Still alive—for now."

"He needs to stay alive," Jude said.

Nova's mouth dropped open as she stared at him, a mix of conflicting feelings rising. She wanted that bastard cold in the ground.

"At least until we can find out where he put Salem."

Right.

"Salem wasn't in the house? Did Amanda see her?" Nova asked.

"Amanda was also taken to Mass Gen Hospital to get checked out. She had a few injuries, but nothing life-threatening."

"When can we talk to her?" Jude asked.

Reaper sighed. "I'd imagine after the Feds are done with her."

"I'm going to message her and Carrie in the group chat." Nova picked up her phone, typing out a quick message to Carrie separately, letting her know that Amanda had been found, and then one in the group chat, reaching out to Amanda.

"What about the wife?" Jude asked.

"Feds have her in custody too."

"Nothing else about Salem?"

"I'll let you know what I find out," Reaper said.

"I appreciate it, brother."

Silence blanketed the other end and then the line cut off.

"Not much of a people person, is he?" Nova asked, hoping infusing some humor would help Jude smile.

But Jude dropped the phone and rubbed his hands along his face, his shoulders drooping with defeat.

Nova rolled over to sit on his lap and wrap her arms around him. "Hey. Listen, this is good news. We have a lot more information now. We know Larry is the one who took her—he's the murderer. She can't be far."

Jude's hands dropped on either side of her, but he didn't hug her back. She tried not to let it hurt, but it did. This was when they needed to cling to each other the most.

"I should have let Reaper do it. Should have gone to that fucker's house and torn him apart until he gave me answers." Anger rolled off Jude, permeating the room.

"You'd most likely have been caught. You'd have been on their suspect list. Jude, that isn't the answer either. Not when it could put you in jail."

"It doesn't matter!" he yelled.

Nova flinched.

"She's gone!" he snapped, agony streaking over his features. "My baby sister was taken by a monster. He did God knows what to her and then he most likely killed her—buried in some unmarked grave like the others. Salem deserved better than that. From the world . . . from *me*."

She placed a tentative hand on his shoulder. "Jude—"

He moved away, gently setting her back on the bed before he got to his feet. He stood, staring out the windows with his bare back towards Nova. His shorts hung low on his hips. Every muscle was drawn like a bow and arrow, ready to strike.

"I should have never fucking come here. You all would have been better off without me."

Those words were a blow straight to her heart.

"Don't do this," she begged.

Jude spun around. His bloodshot eyes were aimed at her.

Grief and rage poured off him in waves. "I don't know how to live like this. Knowing it's my fault—"

The beating organ in her chest lurched as pain sliced through it. Nothing she could say would make him blame himself any less.

"You take it one day at a time. When even that's too much, you take it one moment at a time." Nova crawled off the bed and stood before him, her chin tipped up to look him in the eyes. "You breathe."

"And what if I can't?"

She swallowed, the weight of his words sinking into her marrow. Nova slipped her fingers through his and squeezed. "Then I'll breathe for you."

Jude cupped the side of her face with his free hand, his thumb brushing over her skin. "What did I do to deserve you?"

She shivered from the intensity of his stare. Her smile was sad. "The fact that you have to ask that makes my heart break."

"It feels wrong for me to be this happy with you knowing she's suffered."

"Survivor's guilt. Maybe when all of this calms down, you could think about talking with someone? You probably met Mason and Finn at The Shipwreck bar? I believe they see a woman named Rebecca Cole. At least that's what their wives mentioned at book club. Maybe she could help you too?"

He took a deep breath and pulled her against his chest without answering.

So many times in her life Nova had been told that people didn't just change overnight. But what they failed to leave out of that assumption was trauma. Trauma could happen in an instant and affect your entire life. It changed everything—the way you saw the world around you. The way you related with people. How you thought about yourself. And those were just the tip of the iceberg.

Nova glanced out the window. They could both use a little sunshine right about then.

Help us find her. Nova pleaded with the universe—to anyone out there who was listening.

They'd finally caught a break, catching the killer. That meant the FBI had to be much closer to finding Salem.

If only their luck could continue just a little more.

50

JUDE

Jude's skin itched as he paced the length of Nova's living room. Rain poured outside, spilling down like even the heavens mourned his sister's loss. It felt like a confirmation that she was gone. That he'd failed her.

The steady tap of rainwater falling from the roof onto the front porch was the only noise in the otherwise solemn house—a stark difference to the near constant music Nova had playing as background noise. Her parents had left an hour ago, giving Jude and Nova some space after Renita and James had cooked a breakfast neither one of them wanted to touch.

The urge to run and not look back made him grit his teeth. He felt like a wild animal trapped in a cage. Powerless.

Nova's worried glances flicked to him every now and then, but she otherwise seemed to give him space. He should be supporting her through this, but he could barely keep himself from falling apart.

"Salem was stripping." The confession grated from his lips. He needed to come clean about everything with the woman he loved.

Nova didn't say a word, but she faced him, giving him the space to gather the words.

Jude cleared his throat. "I found out and lost my shit."

"My brothers would too."

He gave a sad huff. "I suppose they would. She'd always wanted to be a dancer, hip hop, jazz, ballet, something like that. We never had money for her to take classes. By the time she came to live with me, she was a teenager. It was hard to start at that age. It was difficult for her to begin all over. I signed her up for a class, but she wouldn't go back after the first week. She wouldn't tell me why."

I wish I'd pressed the issue. Instead he'd given her space. It had only widened each day after that.

"Years later, I was off on assignment. I got home early, and a few of my buddies convinced me to go to a local strip club. I'm sure you can imagine my reaction when my sister walked on stage in a thong and something she tried to pass off as a shirt."

Nova's lips pressed together. "Did you make a scene?"

"The biggest fucking scene. I walked up there and tried to drag her off. The bouncers got involved and I fought, screaming at her the whole time. The manager came out and fired her for bringing drama." Jude sat on the edge of the couch and scrubbed a hand up the back of his neck. "She tried to tell me she only wanted to dance. And I know how that should have been her choice. But Christ, she was my little sister. I did everything I could to keep her from a life where she had to use her body to get what she needed like our mother . . . I wanted better for her."

Nova's soft hand landed on his shoulder. She scooted closer on the couch. "There's nothing wrong with wanting her to be safe and cared for."

"I should have listened to her. Tried to find a way to help

her and keep her safe instead of fighting and telling her if she wanted to ruin her life, then she should leave me out of it."

"That's the thing about the past. We see it more clearly than our future. The problem lies in spending too much time looking back." Nova's thumb dragged over the side of his kneecap. "It can be mighty tempting to stay there—where everything is certain because it has already come to pass. But if we keep looking behind us, we won't be able to apply what we've learned and shape our future to make it better."

"How'd you get so wise?"

She shrugged, a sad smile tilting the corner of her mouth up. "You taught me that."

He sucked in a breath.

"I was so focused on how much I've been hurt by people that I couldn't let anyone else in. I isolated myself trying to protect myself from ever feeling that pain again. But you made me want to take the risk. And once I did, it's like everything changed. It's still terrifying, but also exciting. Because for the first time in my life, I'm present. I'm living for today rather than yesterday."

Jude was truly humbled by this woman. "You make me want to let it all go too. But it's so fucking heavy. It's embedded in my skin."

"I didn't say it would be painless." She chuckled, and then her face grew serious. "In fact, healing might be one of the scariest, loneliest, and most painful things I've ever had to do in my life—and that's saying something."

Jude wrapped his arm around her and leaned back on the grey couch. She lay on his shoulder, and he stared at the pictures of all the important people in Nova's life on the wall across from them by the TV.

"I'm going to talk to someone, like you suggested. I can find someone through Veterans Affairs. I don't want to live like this—let this dark cloud ruin what we have here. I won't let me destroy us." Jude kissed her temple.

She snuggled in closer to his chest, kissing his pec through his shirt. "That right there—is love."

Ding-ding!

Nova darted for her phone. Her thumb swiped the screen open and tapped. "It's Amanda!"

Jude sat up straighter. "What's it say?"

"She was just released from the hospital. The agent is driving her home, but she doesn't want to be alone. Her fiancé won't be back until tomorrow, because of flight issues. She says she wants to tell me something about Salem." Nova smiled, a cautious hope filling her eyes as she looked at him. "She knows something."

"What time can we head over?"

"An hour."

Jude trembled, adrenaline coursing through his bloodstream. Hope and dread warred inside him. If Salem was alive, why hadn't Agent Mallory called him back to let him know? Unless it meant—Salem was dead. Jude needed confirmation. Because he wouldn't give up on her—not until she was found.

He would never give up on her again.

51

NOVA

Nova walked down the street with Jude by her side. Tall old brick buildings lined each side of the road. Some were in better shape than others, but that wasn't saying much. Nova stepped over a piece of trash and eyed the dark alleyway they passed. The smell of rotting garbage was pungent, wafting from the overfilled dumpsters from the side of the building under a granite brick engraved with the numbers eighteen fifty-seven. *Must have been when the building was constructed.* She turned her head away, trying to gulp some fresh air. She stopped in her tracks.

Jude quickly stepped closer, his arm going around her shoulders as he scanned the side street. "What is it?"

"I'm just really anxious."

"You want to smoke before we go up?" he asked. "Calm your nerves?"

"Yeah, that's probably a good idea." Nova reached into her pocket and pulled out her pen. After she took two hits, she put it away and took one more deep breath. "Okay, let's do this."

Jude turned to their right, walked up the two steps, and opened the door. Nova entered into the apartment building with him trailing right behind her. The smell of curry permeated the entrance, but it was a thousand times better than the garbage outside. She passed a few silver mailboxes and looked for number six—Amanda W. She pressed the call button.

"Hello?" Amanda's shaky voice answered through the intercom.

"It's Nova, and I brought Jude with me."

"I'm on the third floor." A buzz sounded.

Jude opened the door and held it for Nova to walk through first. They passed an elevator with an "out of order" sign.

Jude's hand pressed against Nova's lower back, blanketing her in a sense of comfort. Whatever Amanda had to tell them, neither of them would have to go through it alone.

They climbed three flights of stairs and walked to Amanda's door. Jude was pale. Dark half-moons hung under his eyes. Had he gotten any sleep last night?

"No matter what we find out, that doesn't change things for me. I love you and I'll be here through the good and the bad." She took his hand in hers.

Jude leaned in, kissing her like he was trying to communicate without words. "And I'll be here for you too. I won't run away. I'm not going anywhere, Freckles. I told you, you're it for me. Through the highs and the lows."

A creak sounded behind them. They both whirled around. A woman with grey hair held a garbage bag in her hand in the doorway of apartment seven. She looked between them and beyond to Amanda's door before her eyes widened and she promptly shut her door. The slide of a chain lock sounded right after.

"I think we scared her. Or you did with your giant height and SEAL muscles," Nova said.

"You ready to do this?" Jude asked.

She took a deep breath and faced Amanda's apartment once more. "As ready as I can be. You?"

Jude lifted his fist and knocked.

Timid footsteps approached the door and then it opened. Amanda's dirty-blonde hair was a mess. A pretty big bruise highlighted her right cheek. The corner of her lip was split and swollen. She brushed a strand of hair from her face, her bruised knuckles highlighted in the shitty hallway lighting. *Looks like she put up a fight.*

"Thanks for coming. Carrie's here too. She insisted after hearing I got out." Amanda moved out of the way, ushering them into her apartment.

Other than a few large chests on wheels labeled "sound equipment," the place was pristine. Her white couch sat against a wall, a glass coffee table in front of it. A TV sat on a small entertainment center. Amanda shut the door behind them as Nova walked farther in. Carrie sat at the kitchen island on a stool. The counter was pretty bare with just a few necessities—coffee maker, toaster, and a few utensils.

"Can I get you all a drink?" Amanda asked, walking past them.

"I can do that. You should be resting," Nova insisted.

Amanda shook her head, opening the fridge. She grabbed a bottle of what looked like wine. "No, I need to keep busy. It helps."

She grabbed a few glasses as Nova looked around the room once more. A picture of Amanda with a handsome man smiled at the camera in a restaurant.

"Is this your fiancé?" Nova asked.

"Yeah, that's Matt. He'll be flying in to Boston tomorrow morning," Amanda answered.

"That's good."

"I really appreciate you all being here." Amanda set three wineglasses on the table. "I know I can't partake, but I thought this conversation would be best over some booze. My neighbor's son makes a mead with some local honey and fruit. It's really good—though a bit strong." Amanda broke the seal and uncorked the bottle.

"Should we sit in the living room?" Carrie asked.

"Yes, that sounds good. Sorry I don't have more to offer you; I've been meaning to get to the grocery store. I don't think I can face going out until Mathew gets back." Amanda sniffed and poured the three glasses. She offered one to everyone before grabbing a cup of water for herself.

"Do you need us to make a grocery run?" Nova asked.

The corner of Amanda's mouth quirked up before it flattened again. "That's sweet of you. I would love that."

All four of them moved to the living room. The ladies took a seat on the couch and Jude settled on the floor next to Nova.

Amanda cleared her throat. "I don't know where to start."

"How did he get you?" Jude asked.

"The stress of everything was really getting to me. I had a migraine and I needed a break from the noise at work. I stepped out for a few minutes and he was waiting. He put something over my mouth, and I passed out. I woke tied up and he was—" Amanda sobbed, tears springing from her eyes.

Nova placed what she hoped was a comforting hand on her friend's arm. "It's okay. You're safe now."

"That fucking bastard. I hope he dies," Carrie spat.

"You're right. I'm safe. I made it out. And he won't ever touch anyone again." Amanda wiped her eyes with the sleeve of her sweater. "Let's cheers to that." She picked up her water. "To surviving."

Nova raised her glass, joined by Carrie. She elbowed Jude and widened her eyes at him. *She needs this sense of solidarity.*

Jude sighed and grabbed his glass from the coffee table. "To surviving."

They all took a drink.

"I know it's selfish for me to drag this out." Amanda set her water down. "I don't want to be alone, but I know you want to know about Salem."

"Did he mention her? Did you see her?"

Amanda turned to Jude. "He bragged to me about her—about what he did to all of them. How he strangled Ana. How he kidnapped Simone and used her until he broke her. He strangled her too."

"Did Kim know?"

"She does now. He'd drugged her somehow. When I got there she was passed out on the couch while he . . . well, you know what happens in that living room." Amanda faced Nova with cold, dead eyes.

A chill ran through Nova. The same look Amanda had worn in that room whenever Larry would round them up.

"Jesus." Carrie took a gulp of her mead.

Nova's stomach tipped, anxiety and dread roiling within her.

"He did the same with Hannah. He made me listen to it all, every detail while I was tied and helpless." Amanda turned to Jude. "And then he told me about Salem."

"No." Jude's protest was but a whisper, yet it felt like an explosion. "Tell me she's alive."

Nova grabbed his hand. Whatever Amanda told them, they'd face together.

"She fought the longest. He starved them, you know? She hung on until the very end—I'm sorry, Jude."

Oh no! Nova's stomach roiled and a dull throb began to pound in her head.

Jude grabbed the mead and chugged it. The empty glass clanged against the coffee table. "Tell me where she is."

"He didn't tell me—but she's gone."

"No!" Jude surged to his feet and fell onto his knees. An anguished cry scraped from his throat.

"Jude!" Nova moved to him, but her head swam. The room spun. She couldn't have a panic attack right now—

Her head swirled and the pounding in her head grew. Nova clutched her chest, her heart racing.

"Jude?"

But he didn't answer. Jude lay facedown on the beige carpet. Nova spun around to look for the other two women on the couch, but something heavy connected with her skull.

And everything went black.

52

NOVA

Pain was the first thing Nova registered. A pulsing, splitting headache thumped against her skull, making her teeth ache. Her stomach churned.

This is the worst hangover of my life. What had happened? She hadn't drunk a lot since New Year's Eve. Drinking wasn't usually her go-to. *The last thing I remember was sitting down at Amanda's and then—*

Nova gasped, opening her eyes and shifting forward. She immediately regretted it. The one hanging light bulb in the dank cement room pierced her vision, making her headache rage with vengeance. She tried to cover her eyes but Nova's hands were tied behind her, and her legs were also bound. Moving only caused the binds to tighten on her limbs. She fell back onto the damp concrete floor, pain lighting up her wrists and ankles. She slammed her eyes closed.

I've been kidnapped.

Panic set in, her breaths coming faster. *Is Jude here too?* Nova risked peeking through one cracked eyelid, slowly letting

431

her vision adjust. It hurt, but she pushed through the pain—she had to if she wanted to survive. *Focus, Nova.*

Wasn't Larry in the hospital? Had Kim gotten out of FBI custody? No. That didn't make sense. Someone in that room had to have attacked her—put something in her drink.

Fuck. How could I have been so stupid and let my guard down?

Nova scanned the space. Two women lay prone on a dirty mattress a few yards from her. No sign of Jude. Her worry only intensified.

Spiderweb cracks filled the walls, moss growing through some. There were no windows. Black filthy puddles had formed in the corners of the room, brown stains leading from them. Black mold dotted the ceiling. Cobwebs covered every nook and cranny except around a rusty metal door that looked more like an antique bank vault. And the stench of human waste was rancid and overpowering. The bucket in the corner probably had something to do with it. The room was out of a horror novel.

Nova swallowed despite her throat being desert dry. Someone could walk through that door any minute. She needed to find a way to free herself and give her and the other women a fighting chance.

Nova lifted her feet, kicking and wiggling. The motion sent her stomach churning. Vomit climbed her throat, but she fought against it, barely holding herself together. Her head thumped and the room tilted. She gritted her teeth and forced a deep breath out of her lungs.

The sound of clanging metal hitting the wet cement floor brought tears of gratitude to her eyes. Her lucky knife Ricky had gifted her years ago. She never left home without it.

Because you never know when some psycho is going to kidnap you.

Now was not the time for humor, but it was one way to not completely fall apart with fear.

Nova wiggled and rolled, lining up her tied hands with the knife on the ground. The metal was warm from being tucked in her boot. She gripped it, flicking it open behind her back. She lowered her arms behind her and blindly sawed the binds on her feet.

A moan slipped free from one of the women on the mattress.

Nova stopped what she was doing and rolled to them, pushing through the pain and motion sickness. Carrie was closest, her back to Nova, unmoving.

"Wake up," Nova said, nudging Carrie with her shoulder before sitting up to check on Amanda. But it wasn't Amanda blinking her eyes open. Green eyes met hers, sunken and dull, hidden behind a mass of black hair.

"Salem?"

Salem's eyes widened and darted to the door. Nova's ears rang as she took in the skeletal frame of her old friend.

"Oh, fuck." Tears sprung to Nova's eyes. She needed to get free and get them out of there. "You're alive."

"If you can call this living." Salem's voice rasped before she coughed. Her lungs made a hacking noise. She wasn't tied, like Carrie and Nova. A rusted metal chain rattled with Salem's movement. She'd been starved and chained up like an animal these past six weeks?

"Jude will find us. He's been looking for you. He's got a whole motorcycle club searching. Salem, you have to hold on. We're gonna get out of here," Nova promised.

"Is she dead?" Salem asked.

Nova eyed Carrie's chest as it barely lifted and fell. She was alive but for how long? "Not yet, but she will be if we don't get the fuck out of here." Nova refocused on cutting the ties on her ankles.

The heavy metal door creaked. The wheel in place of a doorknob spun slowly as Carrie stirred.

Salem's back went ramrod straight as she scurried up the end of the mattress, her dirty, boney knees bent as she made herself as small as possible. Her movements were so much like they had been when they were stuck in that hellhole together.

"It won't end like this, Salem. We fight. We survive." Nova tried to encourage her friend, resuming her work on the ankle binds. But the fight was gone from Salem's eyes. The poor woman had been terrorized and possibly tortured based on the marks visible under the tattered material of the T-shirt and shorts she had on and the filth coating her.

Nova rolled to her knees, the knife behind her back, working one strand of her binds free. A burst of satisfaction lit her up inside as she focused on the rest. She held her breath as a blonde head peeked through the door.

"Amanda?" Nova asked, surprised.

Salem's chains rattled as she shook.

Amanda rushed in, her eyes wide and panicked. "Oh my God! We have to go. He's coming!"

Confusion didn't help Nova's pounding head. Chills raced through her as every hair stood on end.

"Untie them," Nova said.

Amanda's concerned face morphed into a sadistic grin, her eyes lifeless and devoid of human emotion once again—dead eyes. "Now why would I do that when I've worked so hard to bring us all together?"

Nova's heart raced. Shards of ice slid through her veins. Amanda was the killer. Amanda had drugged them.

"You bitch!" Nova spat. "Where's Jude?"

"Where he fell." She lifted her arms. "I may be strong, but I can't lift a giant, even with the help of my sound equipment trunks. Couldn't lift him over the edge of them. But that's okay. I think it's better to leave you with the knowledge he'll blame himself. I took you right under his nose."

Bile rose in Nova's throat. *No.* That would destroy Jude.

"I'm going to kill you, fucking pregnant or not."

Amanda laughed. "There's no baby. No fiancé either—"

"No one wanted your psycho ass? What a surprise." *I can't believe this was all an act—and I swallowed it up hook, line, and sinker.*

Amanda stepped forward, glaring at Nova. Nova paused her cutting, not wanting to give away the fact she had a weapon until the opportune moment—when her limbs were free.

"If Anastasia taught me anything, it was that death wasn't the best revenge. Rather anticlimactic actually," Amanda sneered, flicking a switchblade from behind her back. Her eyes gleamed with darkness. "Suffering, however? Now that is satisfying. And I'm going to enjoy every moment of yours."

"Why?" Nova asked. "What did I ever do to you? Or Salem and Carrie? The other girls? I got you out of that house—"

"You ruined everything!" she screamed, slapping Nova hard across the face.

Nova bit her lip, holding back a cry of agony. The pressure in her head built. She squeezed her eyes closed and then forced them open. She couldn't afford to take her eyes off Amanda, not when the other woman had a weapon in her hands.

Amanda backed up and walked to the other side of the room before spinning back around. "I loved staying with my aunt and uncle. It was so much better than my pathetic mother. She was useless. Always in my business. Aunt Kim taught me about plants and gardening. She inspired the idea of using plants to get what I wanted—and I got to stay with them."

"You killed your mother?" Nova asked, appalled.

"And I got to live with Aunt Kim. Do as I like. Kim gave me freedom."

"And that was worth living with Larry?" Nova asked. If she kept Amanda talking, Nova would be able to get free. Her movements had to be slow and measured. If Amanda found her knife, Nova didn't like the odds of fighting without the use of her feet—especially when Amanda also had a weapon.

Amanda smiled wistfully. "Uncle Larry was the best part —he gave me the ultimate control. But Aunt Kim never would have understood. Uncle Larry had needs that were dark like mine. We had a lot in common. Those needs were his weakness. Control the man's needs—control the man."

"All those times you begged him to use you instead of us . . ." Nova's stomach churned.

"It was brilliant, wasn't it? It earned me trust from you all, and made for a great show for Uncle Larry. He became addicted, wanted more of our little games. He's the one that convinced Aunt Kim to take in more girls."

"You're a sick fuck."

Amanda laughed. "Oh, you naive little orphan. You fell for it. Too bad you had to ruin it all." Her lips straightened into a thin line. "Because of your little stunt, I was removed from their home and sent away. I lost everything. I went from his number one girl to just another mouth to feed in a group home."

Nova's stomach churned. "I'd play a violin for your sob story but I don't have one small enough."

Amanda glared with malice. "It's gonna be really fun to break you."

"Go ahead and try, you cunt," Nova spit.

"You always were mouthy." Amanda shook her head. "I wanted you to know I was coming for you. That's why I left the markings." Amanda rolled her eyes. "Those stupid agents wouldn't have connected my work otherwise. I had to help them along of course. I wish I could have been there when you heard the news about Ana's body. And then Simone's. You even helped me out reporting Hannah missing. Sped things up."

"What the hell happened to make you this fucking psycho? Were you born a lunatic?"

"You call it psychosis—I call it brilliance." She clapped and laughed.

"Why now after all these years?" Nova asked, the knife slipping in her sweaty hands. She caught it before it fell, her heart racing. But the tip of the blade stabbed her calf. She sucked in a breath. Now was not the time to be clumsy.

"I had nothing after I was sent away. I couldn't afford college. I had no prospects, no future. And then I saw the engagement announcement for Ana and your brother. I didn't even know he was your adoptive brother until later—that was just the icing on the cake."

"She was innocent."

"Ana was a selfish bitch, just like the rest of you. She didn't deserve to be happy—not when I was still suffering. So I reached out to her, asking to meet up. She turned me down of course, at first. Ignored me like you did." Amanda's eyes narrowed on Nova. "But I guess she got in a fight with your brother and decided to message me. I picked her up from the bar and she told me she knew a quiet place we could go." Amanda stared right into Nova's eyes with glee. "The first time I killed was with my bare hands. She was going on and on about Nash and how she'd cheated and ruined everything. She just wanted the pain to stop. She asked if I ever thought about what had happened in that house, if I was ever able to move on." Amanda's cold expression turned Nova's stomach.

"I was so overcome with a flood of emotion. The pure rage I felt—I drowned in it until my hands wrapped around her throat. For the first time in decades, I was free."

"I hope you die a slow, painful death."

"We're all gonna die one day, Nova. But yours is coming so much sooner than mine. And it will be my greatest work. Just ask Salem here." Amanda motioned to the shivering woman against the wall.

"You leave her alone," Nova ordered.

Amanda gave her a patronizing look and shook her head. "I don't think I will." She walked towards the women on the mattress. The chains rattled louder.

"Don't think Carrie will hang on much longer. She drank her whole glass, after all. Heartbreak grass, also known as Gelsemium, is a plant that is native to both North America and China. It's been used to kill some powerful people. I thought it was fitting to use in this project of mine."

"They're innocent. You want to hurt someone, hurt me."

"Oh, I will. But see, I've learned the way to cut you deepest is to keep you powerless while I destroy everyone around you," Amanda said, smoothing her hand over Carrie's chest, pushing the unconscious woman to her back. The knife hovered in her hand. "That's true power."

Nova sawed the knife against her bindings. "Don't—"

Amanda plunged the knife into Carrie's shoulder.

"No!" Nova screamed, pulling at the restraints on her ankles, but they wouldn't give. Panic raced through her, horror and revulsion.

Amanda pulled the knife out with a wet sound. Crimson red pooled from the wound as Carrie's body jerked before she moaned and blinked her eyes open.

Nova's ears rang. She was unable to believe what she was seeing.

Amanda's expression relaxed into contentment as if she were getting a relaxing massage not stabbing a helpless woman. She ran her fingers through the blood on the blade, holding the knife up in the dim basement lighting. "It's so pretty, isn't it? I should have tried a knife out sooner, huh, Salem?"

Salem whimpered, tucking tighter into herself.

"I've never killed more than one at a time. Maybe I'll paint the whole room red and leave it for your boyfriend to find," Amanda mused before raising the knife again to Carrie's cheek. "This is going to be so much fun."

"No!" A scream ripped from Nova's throat as Carrie thrashed, an inaudible moan slipping from her.

Powerlessness suffocated her. *Help me!*

She still had so much to live for. She wanted a life with Jude beyond today. She wanted to hug her parents one more time and tease her brothers. Watch her nieces and nephew grow up. Nova wanted to *live*.

Jude's face flashed in her mind, the sweet, affectionate way he'd looked at her while he held her in his strong, protective arms. She'd give anything to be back there again. But for the first time in her life, she wasn't sure she would survive the day.

53

JUDE

Flashes of red filled Jude's mind. Explosions rocked him from all sides. One minute he was in the sandy desert all his dreams brought him to, and the next he was soaked and running through the jungle. His heart raced in his chest. His stomach twisted violently. He couldn't stop. He needed to keep going or something bad was going to happen. But what?

Jude looked over his shoulder. Encroaching darkness rushed at him. No. He couldn't stop. He needed to get . . . where? Scanning the thick jungle, he caught a wisp of a shadow ahead of him. A slight bounce of curly hair. A flicker of whiskey eyes. Nova.

Something was wrong, and he needed to protect her. An explosion lit his vision, white piercing light and then throbbing pain in the front of his head.

Jude blinked blurry eyes open. His cheek pressed against a thick carpet as the room came into focus. *Amanda's apartment. Drinks. And then—*Jude surged forward to sitting and groaned as pain pierced his skull like a thousand knives stabbing his forehead.

His stomach sloshed before he vomited all over the floor.

"Nova!" Jude rolled to his knees, going as fast as possible despite how heavy his limbs were, how much the avalanche of visceral pain in his head slammed into him. Nova was in danger. He crawled to the first room, opening the door. A simple blow-up twin mattress sat against the wall with tangled sheets at the foot of it. Otherwise, the room was bare. Jude gripped the doorframe and pulled himself up, forcing one foot in front of the other. His heart stuttered—no doubt from whatever he was drugged with. He needed to find Nova now. The next room was just as empty, a simple bathroom with less toiletries than a hotel. The last room was completely bare. Jude stumbled back to the kitchen. Something was very wrong about this place.

An anguished cry ripped from his throat as he fell to his knees. *I failed her. The fucking killer was right in front of us and we never knew it.*

Jude fisted his hair and pulled, screaming. "I'm sorry! I'm so fucking sorry! I should have known!"

He'd failed Salem and now Nova.

Jude's eyes shot open and he pulled out his phone. Ten missed calls from Reaper. *Shit.* Jude dialed his friend back. He was done waiting. He had nothing left to lose. And he sure as fuck wasn't giving up on Nova—not when she needed him most. *I'll find her.* "Hang on, baby."

"Where the fuck have you been?" Reaper answered.

"She's gone." The confession grated from his throat.

"When?"

Jude glanced at his watch. "Shit. Two hours ago."

"Fuck. Where are you?"

"Dark Cove, apartment six in an old building on Picket Street."

"We're five minutes away. Break it down for me."

Jude took a deep breath and gave his friend the rundown, naming every detail he could remember.

"It has to be Amanda. She gave us the laced drink and didn't partake. The apartment is bare except for the main rooms, which made it look a little lived in."

"Let me up." The buzzer rang.

Jude pressed the button to let his friend in.

Reaper's boots thudded as he scanned the room, giving Jude only a glance. "What was over there?"

Jude looked at the spot on the rug Reaper had motioned to. The crate was gone, leaving deep impressions in the carpet. "Sound equipment."

"That's how she moved the bodies."

The image of an unconscious Nova being rolled into that dark case and wheeled out while he was passed out was enough for more vomit to rise in his throat. He managed to keep it down. Was she already dead?

"Pull it together, King. She needs you to have your head in the game."

Jude nodded and swallowed down his grief until his rage won out. He walked to the kitchen and switched the faucet on. He stuck his head under it and rinsed out his mouth before shutting it off. He wiped his mouth with his arm.

"I was on my way here to pay Amanda a visit myself. Ax's tech person found out her fiancé doesn't exist. The face those pictures belongs to is a married man in California. Had no idea who Amanda was. Ax checked his story out and it's clean. So we dug deeper and got the hospital report from today. Amanda is not pregnant."

Jude picked up the picture of Amanda and Mathew. He inspected it closer. The shadow on Mathew's shoulder didn't continue to Amanda's. *Photoshopped.* "This was all a setup."

Reaper nodded. "This was meticulous and planned."

"It's been Amanda this whole time? She was hiding in plain sight and I let her get to Nova."

"Don't start the self-blame." Reaper grabbed Jude's shirt and slammed him against the wall.

The room spun from the movement.

"Pull yourself together. We'll use all our efforts to find your girl."

"She could be anywhere! We've been searching for Salem for weeks and this bitch outsmarted us at every turn."

Reaper smiled—that psycho fucker grinned like somehow he found pleasure in this. "But we didn't know who we were after. We were looking into the wrong people. Now we know who we're hunting. We know how she thinks and what she's capable of."

"Right." Jude nodded and shoved his friend off him.

"We need to search the building first. With that heavy trunk she'd either need help to move it, or she wasn't going far. Is the elevator really broken?"

"Already have my guys on it. If she's here, we'll find her."

"Then we check the studio where she works. No one would question her unloading equipment there."

"Now you're thinking."

Someone pounded on the door. "Reaper, open up."

Reaper yanked the door open. Casanova filled the space as another man with a black Pirates MC vest knocked on the door in apartment seven.

"What did you find?" Jude asked.

"Elevator works. No one on the other floors have seen anything, so they say . . ."

"Get to your point, Cass," Reaper snapped.

The young guy didn't blink at Reaper's gruff tone. "Most didn't act like they spoke much English. I think they're afraid to talk."

The door opened and the older woman from before peeked out.

"Excuse me, ma'am—" the other member of the MC started but Jude pushed past Reaper and Cass and crossed the hall.

"Please! My girlfriend was just abducted by the lady living here. She took her. Did you see where she went? She would have been in a long black trunk."

The woman's eyes widened as she shook her head. "No trouble."

"No, please, we're not trying to get you in trouble—"

The door slammed shut, the lock engaging.

Jude slammed his fist on the door. "Please! She's all I have!"

"King—"

"I can't lose her too."

Reaper's hand landed on Jude's shoulder. "I know."

"Maybe we should call the FBI," Jude said.

"Not for what we have planned. Let's go check the remaining floors, and I've got Blade and Piper heading to the production company to look there."

Jude didn't need to be told twice. He took off down the stairs, running as fast as he could, passing men in vests knocking on doors. All of them were searching for the woman he loved—the one he'd promised to protect and failed.

The stairway grew darker and cooler as he descended into the basement. The smell of mold, dead rodents, and sewage burned his nose. He stopped in front of a rickety old door and opened it. The room was pitch black. He flicked on his phone light. Reaper caught up to him, adding his. They swept through the dark space. Cement walls lined the space and shelves littered with old broken furniture and bins were covered in dust.

"The floor isn't dirty," Reaper pointed out.

"What?" Jude aimed his light at the ground.

"Everywhere else in here is littered in dust, but there isn't a speck on the floor."

Jude rushed over to the shelving unit, pulling it to see if it was a false wall or covering something. He pulled, and the old wood groaned under the shifting weight.

"Help me," Jude said.

Reaper gripped the other side, and they pulled. The whole shelf toppled over, crashing onto the ground. Spiderwebs crisscrossed the wall behind it. But it was solid cement.

Defeat weighed heavily on his shoulders, crushing his lungs. "She's not here."

"Then we have to search the production building with Blade. They said the company vans have GPS. Maybe we'll get lucky and she used one of those to transport the container with your girl and Carrie. No way she'd fit something like that in her Ford Focus."

"Let's go." Jude turned and ran up the dark steps, his heart lurching almost as if he could sense Nova slipping away. "I'm coming, Freckles. Hold on. Just hold on, baby."

He pulled out his phone and dialed the last man he wanted to face.

"What are you doing?" Reaper asked.

"Her family deserves to know."

"They'll call the FBI—"

"I don't fucking care. We need everyone looking for her. I won't fucking lose her—I won't. I *can't*." Jude looked Reaper in the eyes.

Reaper held out his hand. "You shouldn't be the one to do it."

"I'm the one who failed to fulfill a promise to protect her. So yeah, I'm the one that deals with the consequences."

His friend gave one nod and continued climbing the flight of stairs. Jude pressed the call button and pressed the receiver to his ear as James's phone rang.

Whatever it takes.

If I was a psycho killing these women, where would I take them?

54

NOVA

Nova gritted her teeth until they ached, working the knife behind her as fast as possible to free her feet. At last, the final rope gave way, but there was no time to celebrate. She twisted the knife, sharp point up, and slid it between her wrists, knocking the sensitive flesh there. She breathed through the pain, trying to shut out the screams from Carrie and the sadistic glee from Amanda as she butchered Carrie's flesh. Crimson rivulets streamed down Carrie's pale skin in a violent contrast. Blood seeped into the mattress and splashed onto the filthy floor.

Holding the knife with bound sweaty hands while trying to cut the binds was extremely challenging. Her wrists ached, but she pushed through the pain. If she gave up, they'd all be dead. She needed to distract Amanda, get her focus off the other girls—but she didn't want Amanda to pay too much attention to her either. Not while she was trying to free herself.

"I never thought I could hate anyone more than Larry, but you're a monster! You'll pay for this," Nova said.

"Oh, Larry." Amanda sat up and wiped her brow,

smearing Carrie's blood on her forehead. "Shame he took his life, no? He was weak. Pathetic," she snarled. "When I showed up, offering him one more taste for old time's sake, he was so quick to agree and slip Kim her usual cocktail with a sleeping pill." Amanda's calculating eyes gleamed. "Guess he didn't count on me doing the same to him. After he tied me up, it wasn't long before it kicked in." She laughed. "You should have seen his face when he came to. I was crying—a brilliant act if I say so myself. Screaming to a sleeping Kim to help me. I told him the FBI were outside. How I'd planted evidence in his room. He was so scared, he'd rather die than go to prison again—this time for life."

This woman was sick. She'd fooled everyone, manipulated the whole situation. How could she have seemed so normal?

Carrie gave a weak moan. She'd lost so much blood. She wasn't even screaming anymore.

"There's a fault in your plans." Sweat dotted Nova's head, dripping down her temple as she worked the ties on her wrist, but this angle was nearly impossible to do without injuring herself.

"Oh really?" Amanda's lip curled in what looked a lot like irritation.

"There's no one to take the blame for us missing."

"My dear, stupid girl. That's what Jude is for."

Nova's eyes widened. "You motherfucker!"

Amanda stood, leaving a whimpering Carrie lying on the dirty mattress. Salem had gone completely silent, staring off into space like she was somewhere far away. Fuck, she was in shock at the very least. Salem needed medical attention—they all did.

Amanda crouched in front of Nova, the bloody knife in her hand cool against Nova's throat.

Now would be her chance to strike—if only Nova was

free. The damn wrist ties were tight, and they didn't give her much leverage. She couldn't break through them without sawing the knife. She also couldn't risk Amanda figuring out she was trying to cut her binds. Nova stilled.

Amanda pressed the tip of the blade harder into Nova's neck while glaring in her eyes. "I'm saving you for last. So you can see that everyone you tried to save is dead because of *you*. And your boyfriend will be blamed. It's perfect!" Amanda's excited tone sent ice through Nova's veins.

"You're psycho."

"No, I'm unstoppable. I'm powerful. And I'm going to savor this revenge I've waited so long for. Do you know how many ways I've imagined killing you? How this would play out? I've covered every base. Had years to plan this. And you got caught in my web. Now, there's nothing you can do to stop the inevitable." Amanda tipped her head to the side, drawing the knife to Nova's face. She sliced along her cheek.

Nova gritted her teeth to stop from crying out, speaking through a clenched jaw. "You're going to die."

Amanda shook her head, her lips curling up. "I can't wait to break you of this fight. That will be the last thing I take from you before I kill you. And then I truly will have everything."

Amanda rose to her feet and spun around—another perfect chance for Nova if only she could get cut through these binds. She gripped the knife tighter and pressed harder, ignoring the pain in her wrists. She needed her hands free *now*.

"Maybe I should give Carrie a break and have fun with my old toy." Amanda moved towards a trembling Salem.

"Don't go near her!"

"You forget that I'm in control. And I'll do whatever the hell I want. Things are finally right in the world." Amanda grabbed Salem's arm and yanked. Salem kicked, but she was weak, and the hit bounced off Amanda with ease. "She's been here so long almost all her fight is gone. Pathetic really. Not much fun. But it was worth keeping her alive long enough to see your face, Nova—knowing she's been suffering all this time. Right under your nose. If you'd met me for coffee, you could have seen each other sooner." Amanda sighed.

"Jude will find me."

Amanda laughed. "Jude already walked right by the door. Searched the basement, but the entrance isn't as easy to find unless you know what you're looking for."

"You're lying!" *No.* Amanda had to be lying. Jude couldn't have been so close and yet so far. It couldn't end like this!

"It's the cold, hard truth."

"Wh-where are we?" Nova asked, not daring to take her sight from Amanda.

"In my apartment building. Did you know it used to be a bank years ago?" Amanda opened her arms, motioning to the putrid, dingy room. "This was the safe. Completely sound-proof. And it has a secret access. Your boyfriend searched the basement half an hour ago and walked right past the entrance off the stairs." Amanda's expression shifted to absolute joy as if she'd won the lottery "Although I can't risk a close call again. So it's time to finish what I started and kill them before I take care of you."

"They don't deserve this," Nova tried.

Amanda shrugged. "You should have thought about that before you fucked me over. They're only here because I wanted to fuck with your head. That's true torture. You took everything from me, and now it's only fair I return the favor."

Nova pressed the knife against the rope, ignoring the pain slicing through her fingers. She couldn't let anything happen to the other women—

Amanda plunged the knife into Carrie's chest over and

over.

"NO!"

Blood splattered Amanda's white skin like a violent work of art, arcing and spraying. Amanda hacked into Carrie. Carrie's eyes remained open, bubbles of blood foaming out of her mouth. She gaped like a fish, once—twice, and then she stopped moving altogether except for the sick wet sounds of the knife piercing her body.

Nova screamed until her throat was raw. She yelled until she had no voice left. The smell of iron tainted each rapid inhale she took.

Amanda stood over Carrie's body, covered in crimson. Blood dripped from her face and neck. It soaked her clothes and stained her teeth as she smiled. Her cold, dead eyes dilated, bright with hazy satisfaction—almost as if she were high.

Amanda looked directly at Nova. "You failed her. And now it's Salem's turn."

There is a moment when you are faced with something truly traumatic, when things are completely out of your control. Time slows down and the fear disappears. You're left with an unnatural calm. You understand in a split second that whatever happens next will be out of your control. All those instincts to fight, flee, freeze, or fawn disappear. Your brain fills with chemicals that give you a peaceful feeling of acceptance.

The dominos had already been knocked over. The cards played. Choices made. There was no more avoiding what had to happen next for Nova.

So when Amanda grabbed a fistful of Salem's hair, Nova knew what she had to do.

"You're a coward."

Amanda snarled. "I'm not scared! Look at me! I have all the power!"

"Yeah? So much power that you're killing drugged, defenseless women? Look at Salem, starved to death, and you still keep her chained because you're weak."

Amanda trembled, her nails digging into Salem's shoulder. Salem didn't even make a sound, as if she'd accepted her fate. She looked catatonic.

"You want a show?" Amanda reached into her pocket and pulled out a key. She shoved Salem to the ground. The young woman immediately curled in on herself. Amanda unlocked the shackles around Salem's ankles.

"Happy now? Look at her—she's so broken she won't even try to run away or fight. And that's exactly what I'm going to do to you, Nova. It won't take long—not when you're soaked in your friends' blood and I carve everything I hate about you into your skin."

"You're a fucking dumb bitch, aren't you?" Nova spat. Her mind was clear and focused on one goal—protecting Salem. She just needed a chance.

Amanda whirled around. "Shut up. I'm sick of your incessant mouth."

"Or what? You said yourself you won't hurt me until you kill her. I knew you were stupid and reckless. What's wrong? Daddy didn't love you enough to stay? Had to suck your uncle's cock to get even a little attention?"

Amanda marched straight for Nova, knife raised, but Nova didn't back down. She planted her toes under her, ready to propel herself forward, tied or not. But she wasn't going down without a fight. Nova put everything she had into the binds at her wrists.

"You're pathetic. No one will even remember you. You have no one. No family, no friends. You had to make up a fake fiancé for God's sake," Nova snapped. "You. Are. Weak. And worthless. *Forgettable.*"

Rage filled Amanda's expression as she slashed the knife towards Nova.

Nova pushed up to her feet. Her hands broke free. She shoved the knife forward.

Amanda's eyes widened. Nova's knife landed right under Amanda's rib cage at an angle. But Amanda had managed to land her strike too. Her bloody hand twisted the knife in Nova's stomach. Pain lanced through Nova's abdomen right below her belly button.

"I might die, but I'm sure as fuck taking you with me, you piece of shit." Nova shoved Amanda backwards. The woman was strong, but not trained like Nova. *Thank you, Ricky.*

Nova punched Amanda in the face, sending the woman careening backwards towards the door, taking Nova's knife with her.

Something warm soaked Nova's skin around the knife sticking out of her as she staggered forward. But Amanda had to be stopped.

"You stabbed me!" Amanda screamed in rage.

Nova stumbled towards Salem. "Run! Go get help!"

Salem trembled even harder but her eyes darted to the door to the right of Amanda.

"Sal—" The edges of the room faded with black closing in. Nova clamped a hand around the blade protruding from her stomach, trying to staunch the flow. She couldn't give up now. She had to finish this.

Nova reached for Salem, taking her grimy hand in hers. Salem jolted, her eyes flaring wide.

"Jude is looking for you. He never gave up. Don't give up on him. He needs you to pull through, Sal."

"My brother?" Salem asked, an ember of cautious hope sparking in her eyes. "He's been looking for me?"

"Yes. So you can't give up yet—you have to fight. Just a

little longer. Use it—your pain and fear. Turn it into anger and fucking use it to save yourself!"

Nova's vision swam, but the scrape of Amanda's feet against the concrete floor told her all she needed to know. It was time to face the person who'd tried to hurt the people she loved.

Nova used her remaining strength to turn. She coughed, gripping the handle of the knife still inside her. She wiped her mouth with the other hand. It came away bloody.

I'm never going to get to see the people I love again. But she was the only one standing between Salem and Amanda.

Nova dug her feet in. "Salem, you get out of here, and you survive—whatever it takes."

"Nova... I can barely walk—"

"Then crawl." Nova peeked over her shoulder at the young woman who resembled more of a skeleton than human. "That's what we do—we survive no matter what it takes." Nova repeated the same speech she'd given Salem more than a decade ago when they were just two girls trapped in hell.

This time was different. Because this was where it would end.

"I'm going to kill you and her—it's only a matter of time—"

Nova put all her weight into a left hook. In the same instant she pulled the weapon from her belly and stabbed Amanda again with her right hand, striking hard and fast. Amanda used Nova's knife against her too, piercing Nova's shoulder before the metal clattered to the ground.

Her mouth opened as if she were going to say something and then she coughed, blood spraying over Nova's face, sticking to her skin. The tang of iron coated Nova's mouth— she tasted it on her tongue.

She fell forward onto Amanda, watching the life drain from her empty eyes.

"You don't get to hurt anyone ever again," Nova said as Amanda wheezed her last breath.

Nova rolled off Amanda, her back hitting the concrete as darkness encroached, hindering Nova's vision. Her head swam.

Salem crawled forward. "Nova—"

Nova coughed. "Go."

Salem shook her head. Greasy, matted hair shone under the one hanging bulb in the cell. "I can't leave you alone to—"

Die? Tears burned Nova's eyes, but she blinked them back. Agony throbbed in her stomach and shoulder. Pain was good —it meant she was alive. She pressed one hand into the wound on her abdomen and lifted the other to Salem's cheek as the woman bent over her. Cuts and red marks dripped blood from Nova's wrist—the cost of getting free. Jude would blame himself for this—she just knew it.

"Tell Jude that I forgive him. Tell him that I—I love him."

Salem's eyes widened.

"And my parents—my brothers." What would her last words be to everyone she cared about? "Tell them that it isn't their fault. And that Ricky can have all my weed." Nova forced a smile she didn't feel as her pain ebbed away and the room dimmed. Death was pulling her under. She shivered.

"Promise me you'll give Jude a chance. He's gonna need you as much as you're gonna need him."

Salem's lips moved but it sounded like she was underwater. Nova's eyes were so heavy. Each breath was a chore. Tears blurred her vision.

That darkness was all encompassing. Like a storm cloud, it swallowed Nova up. There was no white light—no tunnel. When her eyes closed for the final time, everything was black.

55

JUDE

Jude yanked open door after door of the production building, searching for Nova as his mind raced to think of all the places she could be—what that psycho could be doing to her. Was she dead? Was she terrified?

A heavy hand landed on Jude's shoulder. "King—"

Jude spun around. "Did you find her?"

Reaper's grim expression said it all. "She's not here."

"She has to be. She couldn't have disappeared into thin air."

"All their vans are accounted for."

"So she had another vehicle. Have Axel contact the hacker again. Ask him to hack into the traffic enforcement cameras, see what vehicle she left with so we can track it. The FBI—"

"Yo, we got something!" Cass called from the end of the hall. A few employees watched them intently from the glassed-in rooms on either side.

Jude pushed past Reaper and rushed the man. "What is it?"

"An emergency call just went out for a woman in distress

back at the apartment. They're sending ambulances and police."

Jude didn't stay to listen to the rest. He ran as fast as he could, shoved the front door open. It slammed against something—no, someone.

"Watch it, asshole!" A man walking a dog flipped him off.

Jude darted to his truck and jumped in. He cranked the key in the engine as Reaper slid in the passenger side without saying a word. The tires squealed as he cut off traffic and slammed his foot on the gas, ignoring the honking cars. He had the steering wheel in a vise grip.

"King—"

"Don't! Just don't even fucking say a word. We *left* her. Fucking left her in that building, and she was right under our fucking noses!"

The minutes ticked by like hours as he crossed town in only a fraction of the time he usually would. Jude had barely slipped the truck in park before he was out the door. Sirens blared in the distance, getting closer as he sprinted inside. An older woman with wide eyes held the door open, fear flashing in her blue eyes.

"Where is she?"

The woman pointed down the stairs.

Jude ran. Heart pounding. Ears ringing. He raced to the basement, his stomach in his throat. Terror at what he'd find gripped him with an iron fist.

His steps faltered at the artificial light bleeding into the dim space from the left of the stairway. *That wasn't there before. I walked right by her!*

Jude shoved the door open the rest of the way with a bang. He revealed a small dusty room with a table and single chair, along with a few bottles of water, a mini fridge, and a microwave. But the metal safe door that was half open was what drew his attention. The smell coming from it was putrid, laced with copper. *Blood.*

Jude ripped the door open and froze.

Salem! His sister looked up, meeting his frantic gaze, a shadow of the woman he remembered. Tears poured from her eyes as she held bloody hands to a wound on a far too still Nova.

He rushed to Salem's side as footsteps jogged behind him. Two more blood-soaked bodies lay motionless near the girls. *What the fuck happened here?* His focus homed in on Nova. Crimson red pooled around her on the filthy floor.

"No!" Anguish bled from him as he cradled her head in his hands, bowing to press his forehead to hers. "Don't leave me. Don't you dare fucking leave me, Freckles."

He pressed his hands to the wound and looked up at his sister and pulled her into his arms. "I'm so fucking sorry."

"She saved me—again." Salem stared at Nova, trembling, as if it took all her energy to remain upright.

"The ambulance is outside now. Let's get them help," Reaper said.

Salem eyed Jude's friend warily.

He still couldn't even process the fact that his sister was alive in front of him. "Go with Reaper. He'll keep you safe. I'll carry Nova out."

Jude slipped his shirt over his head. He ripped it with his teeth before wrapping it around her wound to keep some pressure, replacing his sister's hands. The grey cloth soaked quickly. But Nova still had a pulse, weak as it might be. He slid his hands gently under her. Nova's head and limbs hung limply as Jude ran out of the room and up the stairs.

"Police! Show your hands!" a man shouted from the stairwell.

"She's hurt! She needs medical attention now!" If these

assholes wanted to put a bullet in him to slow him down—they could. Nothing was stopping him from getting Nova help.

The officer kept the gun on Jude but nodded, eyeing Reaper's leather vest. "You're one of the Pirates MC?"

"He's with me," Reaper said.

The officer nodded and allowed them to pass. "EMTs are right behind me. Is the perp down there?"

Jude didn't stay to listen to Reaper's answer. He ran as fast as he could towards the ambulance. *If anyone is listening, whatever crystal goddess or moon powers that Nova believes in, please keep her alive. I'll do anything. Just don't take her from me.*

"Lay her here." The EMT opened the back of the rig.

"What can you tell me?" another asked.

"Female, twenty-eight. Stab wound to the lower lateral midline. Don't know blood type. Multiple injuries."

"Are you family?" the medic asked as the other hooked Nova up to the machines and examined her wound.

How to encompass all they were to each other? "I'm her boyfriend." It wasn't adequate but an efficient explanation.

"We need to go!" the EMT from inside the ambulance shouted.

Jude turned to his sister, torn. The woman he loved was dying and his missing sister was found—needing him.

A blaring noise screeched. Both EMTs moved into action while Jude stood there, helpless.

"She's flatlining."

One shouted commands while the other followed, working in tandem as Nova's limp body jolted under a shock.

The two doors shut, cutting him off—the last image of her hand hanging limply off the bed was burned into his mind.

"Nova!" He banged on the door as the vehicle drove away.

Reaper grabbed his shoulders to hold him back. Jude

swung his fist, but his friend dodged it, grabbing him in a bear hug and tackling him to the ground.

"They're sending another ambulance for your sister. Ride with her. You can't help Nova right now. They are doing their job to save her life."

A sob tore free, and Jude didn't give a fuck. Tears poured from his eyes as grief stronger than anything he'd ever known slammed into him, stealing his breath. It was more powerful than any explosion he'd ever witnessed. Shrapnel of what could have been, of the future he'd dreamed of with Nova, sliced through him, leaving jagged, bleeding wounds in his heart.

"Salem needs you to pull your shit together," Reaper growled.

Salem. His sister. She needed him. She was there—finally!

Jude took a deep breath, pulling all his pain, rage, and hopelessness inside and locking it down tight like the sailor he was trained to be. He nodded.

Reaper rolled off him, got to his feet, and offered Jude a hand. Jude took it and walked up to his sister.

She sat on the grass in front of the apartment, gaunt and filthy—a ghost of the young woman he'd last seen. She stared up at the sky, tears leaking from the corners of her eyes. How long had she been kept in that cement dungeon?

Jude crumbled to the ground in front of her to his knees. His palms skated up her crossed arms over cuts and bruises and dirty, torn clothing.

"I'm so sorry," Jude repeated to her.

Salem didn't say a word—she just nodded and stared ahead, wobbly even sitting as more police cars pulled in, sirens wailing.

A black SUV screeched to a halt before Agent Mallory and Agent Green exited. Jude wrapped his arm protectively around Salem's boney shoulders and wiped his eyes. The same police officer who had been first inside jogged past Jude to meet the agents. Another ambulance parked on the street. Everything was happening in a blur. Jude needed to get Salem to the hospital, and he needed to find Nova.

Agent Mallory walked up to him. "I have questions—"

Jude jumped to his feet, putting himself between the agents and his sister. He was going to do what he should have all along—protect her. "Well, you're gonna have to fucking wait. Salem needs medical attention, and I need to make sure the woman I love is going to survive."

She has to.

Jude spun around, picking Salem up in his arms. She was light—too light. He rushed past the agents, bringing Salem to the EMTs who'd just pulled a backboard out of an ambulance.

"Fine. We'll do this at the hospital, then," Mallory shouted after them.

Every inhale was like breathing in shards of glass. A mix of soul-deep agony and numbness coated his every cell.

Salem needs me.

Jude helped her into the waiting ambulance as the EMTs got to work. She lay there, eyes empty and dull with pure exhaustion. His sister was counting on him to be strong—she had no one else in this world. But he may never see the woman he loved alive again. The only way he could not fall apart was to shut it all off. To go so deep into himself that he didn't feel anything at all.

If only it had been him taken instead of Nova.

If only he'd been a better man.

56

JUDE

The next several hours were a blur. He didn't leave Salem's side, but he asked the nurse every hour for an update on Nova.

Reaper stood outside Salem's room like a silent guardian. He'd called the Emersons and let them know Nova had been found and what hospital they were at but Jude hadn't seen them yet. He was ashamed that he'd failed his promise to keep their daughter safe.

The FBI had come and gone, unsatisfied, with threats to return. Salem was being treated for malnourishment, dehydration, and superficial and infected wounds that would heal in time. It was the emotional and psychological scars he had a feeling she would carry with her forever. She hadn't said a word to anyone—not even the agents, much to Mallory's dismay.

Salem stared out the window by her bed, hooked up to wires and tubes that were slowly helping her recover.

Jude sat in the chair beside her bed. He reached for her hand and held it in his. She was so cold. His gaze dropped, catching on the dried blood still coating his skin. Nova's blood.

"She gave me a message for you." Salem's voice was a hoarse whisper.

Jude looked up at her. "Nova?"

His sister nodded. "She told me to tell you she forgives you and loves you. That I should give you a chance because we'd need each other to get through this."

Jude's heart clenched. Even facing death, his baby girl had been worried about him. *I don't fucking deserve her. But I swear on all that I am, if she survives, I'll do whatever it takes to be the man she needs.*

"Were you really looking for me?" Salem asked, her focus dropping to their joined hands.

"Of course. The moment I found out you were missing, I moved here to find you. I had Reaper and his club looking for you."

"Is that how you met Nova?" she asked.

"Yeah."

"And you love her?"

"I do."

She met his gaze. "She didn't deserve this."

"Neither did you."

Salem's green eyes darted to the bed once more as if she didn't believe him.

"Sal, I fucked up. Instead of being the brother you needed when you pushed, I gave up. I shouldn't have said what I did the last time we spoke. I should have tried to regain contact and make things right between us. This is my fault."

"Always trying to be the hero." She shook her head.

Her words pierced his heart like tiny barbed spears. "Sal—"

"Is Jude in there?" James's voice carried into the room.

"Yes," Reaper answered. "Wait—"

"Jude?" James entered, casting a sympathetic look to Salem. "I don't mean to interrupt."

Jude got to his feet as Nova's three brothers entered. "Is Nova okay? Have you heard anything? The nurses haven't said anything other than she's in surgery."

James looked like he'd aged twenty years since Jude had seen him the day before. The lines on his face were deeper and the dark bags under his eyes hadn't been there before. "She's out of surgery and in the ICU. Renita's with her now. Only one can go in at a time."

"Maybe you should talk out here?" Reaper suggested from the hallway.

Jude glanced at Salem.

She nervously bunched the blanket in her hands until her knuckles were white. "Go. She needs you."

"I'll stay with Salem," Reaper offered.

He wasn't the best choice for anyone needing a gentle approach, but Jude trusted the man with his life.

"I'll be right back," Jude promised Salem, pressing a kiss to her temple before filing out of the small hospital room behind the Emerson men.

"The docs said if she survives the night, there's hope for her." James's voice caught in his throat.

"Can I see her?"

James nodded. "I think she needs all the support she can get."

"I told you we should have chipped her," Nash grumbled.

Ricky snorted. "She would have chopped off your balls."

"It would have been worth it to find her before she got hurt," Nash said soberly.

A moment of silence passed. It seemed Jude and the Emerson men had more in common than he'd realized. They were all beating themselves up over not doing more to keep Nova safe.

"Is this your sister?" Roman asked.

Jude glanced through the open door to the bed where his sister lay catatonic once again. Reaper sat in the seat next to her, hands folded in his lap, staring at the blank wall across from him.

"Yeah."

"I'm sure she's got a long road ahead of her too. Renita wanted to check on her and you after she sees Nova. If you or your sister need anything, you let one of us know," James said.

"Thank you."

James shook his head. "It's me who needs to thank you and your sister. You brought my daughter back to me."

"You shouldn't thank me. I promised you I'd protect her and I failed. I'm so fucking sorry." Jude looked James in the eyes before meeting the gaze of his sons.

"From my understanding you were drugged too. There's no way you could have known." James placed a hand on Jude's shoulder. "You should probably get checked out as well because of the poison."

"You're not angry at me?" Jude asked.

"The only person responsible for this is Amanda. You didn't hurt my little girl. You did everything you could to save her."

Jude swallowed the lump of emotion in his throat. "Thank you, sir."

"You're family, Jude—whatever happens. Your sister included. Nova chose you. If Salem needs anything from a cheeseburger to a place to recover, we're here for her and you both."

Jude's knees threatened to give in. Here was a man who had every right to blame Jude, to take his anger out on him.

Yet James and his sons were extending a helping hand with understanding and compassion. Maybe Nova was right about the narrative he'd told himself. Perhaps he should take a page from her book and be brave enough to believe he deserved better. To trust he'd done everything he could.

But that guilt was a persistent motherfucker—sticky and heavy and so much easier to give in to than hope.

Nova's brown eyes flashed in his mind, drowning out the pain with his love for her.

"She's going to be alright—she has to be." Jude's words came out more as a plea.

"Damn right," Nash agreed.

"Fuck yeah," Ricky added.

"She's a fighter," Roman said.

"She's an Emerson. She won't give up," James said. "Now, go on and give her something to fight towards, son."

Jude took a breath and nodded before heading down the corridor, his heart in his throat.

Life would never be the same no matter what happened next. But he was going to do his best to reach the woman he loved and remind her she had everything to live for.

57

JUDE

J ude braced himself as much as he could before walking into Nova's room. But nothing could have prepared him for the stark contrast of the usually vivacious, smart-mouthed woman he'd fallen in love with to the ghost lying in the bed. Lines and tubes ran from machines and monitors to her skin. A thicker tube ran into her mouth, the swish of the machine breathing for her. She looked like a shadow of the woman he'd come to know over the last few weeks.

Jude's knees knocked, weak from the sight of her. He'd barely been able to keep his shit together while they'd taken her away. But seeing Nova so close to death was his undoing. His chest squeezed tight. His heart thudded a frantic beat. With everything inside him, Jude wanted to trade places with her. He stumbled forward to the plastic chair beside the bed. He sat before he fell over. Sliding one trembling hand beneath hers, he gasped. She was so cold. So pale. Bandages peeked out from her shoulder. A few stitches marred her cheek where she'd been sliced. Both wrists were covered in white gauze.

She'd been through hell—and she'd saved not only herself but Salem too.

"I'm so sorry, baby girl. I should have been there. Should have protected you." He shook his head. "I know if you could talk right now, you'd probably roll your eyes at me and say something smart just to get me going. You'd tell me how you can take care of yourself." Jude swallowed the lump of grief bubbling in his throat. If he started crying now, he might not be able to stop.

"I know you can—you did. You're so fucking strong and intelligent. It's not that I doubt your ability to take care of yourself. It's that I don't want you to have to. I want to be the one you run to. The one to keep you safe in my arms and never let you go. And I know the thought of the future scares you . . ." Jude leaned forward, gently smoothing his thumb over her hand. "So just focus on today. You promised me today, so you fight, Freckles. Because I'm gonna hold you to that."

And he did. Every day, Jude stayed by her side or with his sister as Nova remained unconscious. The doctors had no answers of when she would wake. Her vitals remained stable, but she didn't open her eyes as day, after day, after day passed.

Monday

Tuesday

Wednesday

Thursday

Friday

Saturday

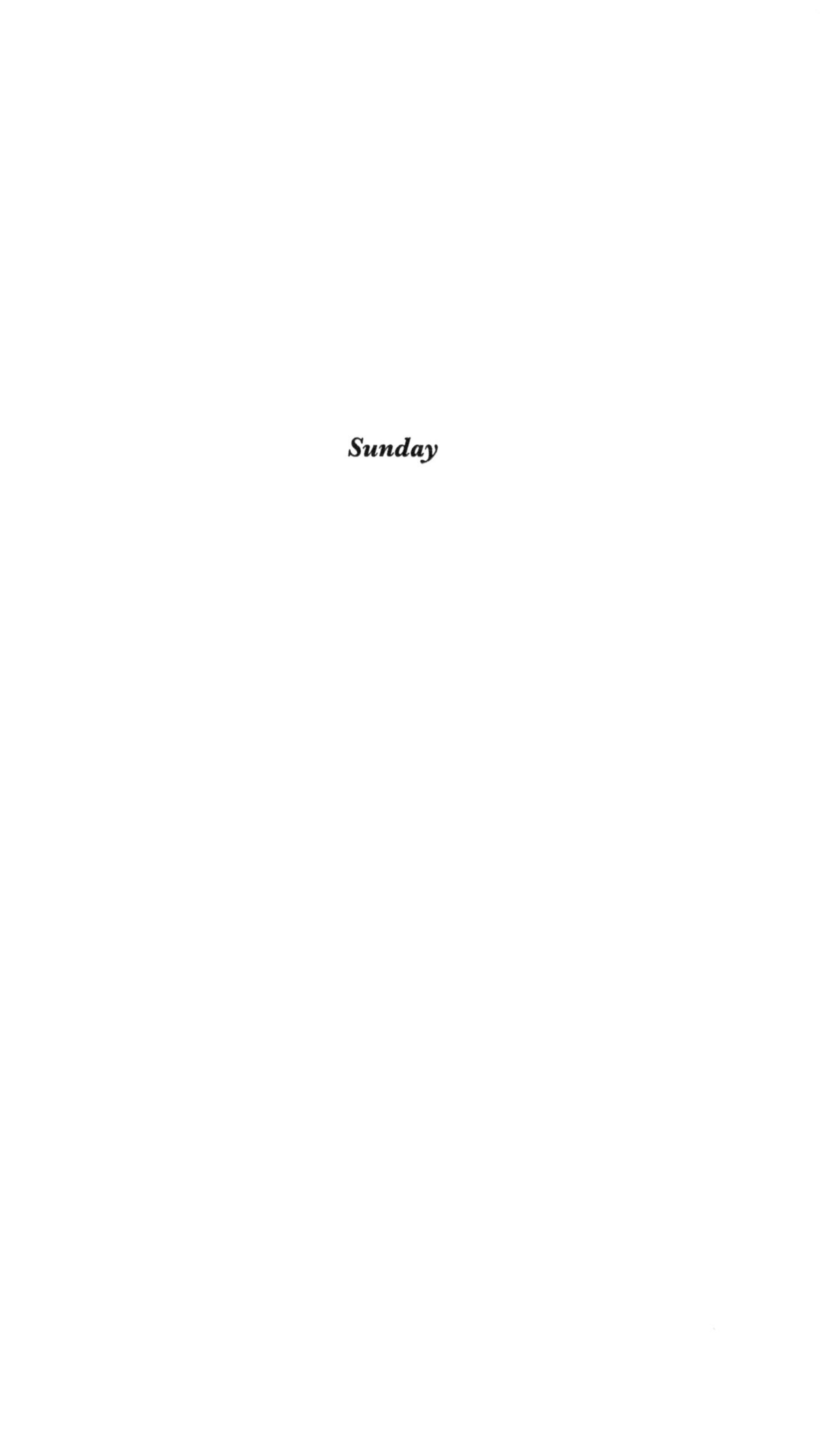

Sunday

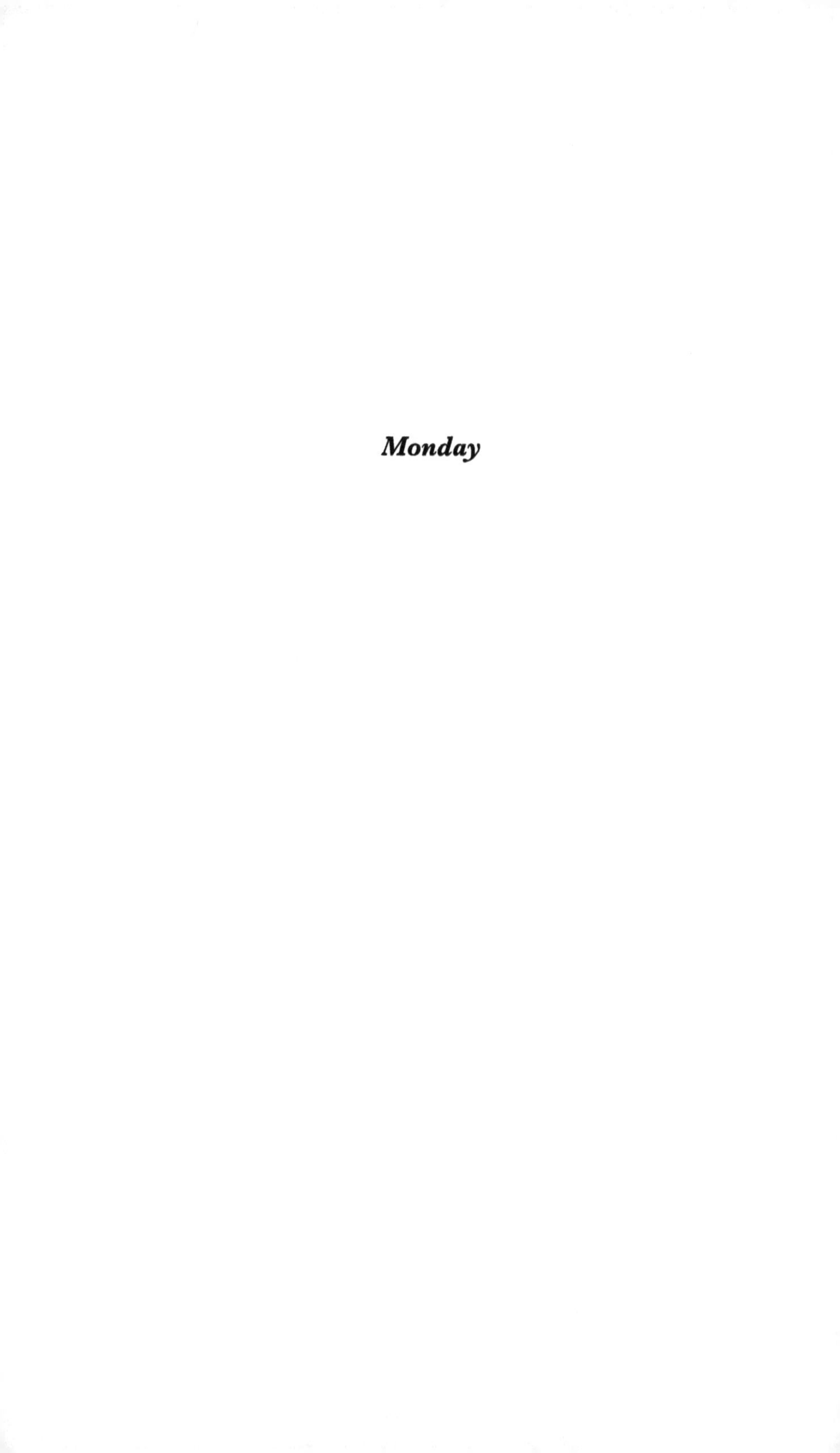

Monday

58

JUDE

Nova was never alone. Her family took turns sitting with her. Jude wanted to stay by her side the whole time but he had another person depending on him. Salem remained withdrawn, not speaking to anyone, but somehow Renita managed to get a few words out of her every once in a while. Reaper returned each evening to sit with Salem, watching over her while Jude went to be with Nova.

Jude felt completely powerless to help either woman. Nova's body slowly healed over the week, little by little. But those pretty brown eyes never opened. They'd removed the tube from her mouth a couple days ago and still, nothing.

Jude sat in the uncomfortable plastic chair at her side once more, a fresh bouquet in a vase balanced in his hands.

"Brought you flowers. I realized I don't know what your favorite ones are. So you're gonna have to deal with these—a wildflower mix because they made me think of you." He set them down next to the cards and flowers from everyone in the retirement community in Shattered Cove.

"I checked in with your Golden Girls. They plan on coming to visit once you're ready for guests. And Roger made me promise to keep him updated. He's worried about you—we all are."

Jude took her hand in his. She was still cool to the touch, but she'd regained some color. "If I thought bribes would work, I'd give you anything to get you to open your eyes." Jude cleared his throat. Leaning in, he swiped his thumb gently over the smattering of freckles in the shape of a shooting star on her cheek.

"I wish you would come back to me. I'll do whatever it takes to be the boyfriend you need—the Dom you deserve. So I need you to fight, little brat. You use that moxie and fight for your life. You come back to me. That's an order." He sniffed. "I love you, and I need you. We all do. But me most of all."

Jude pressed his forehead to her upper thigh, breathing her smell in mixed with the antiseptic scent of the hospital room. "I'm lost without you, baby."

Please, please wake up.

"Jude?" Nova's hoarse voice asked.

Jude shot up to sitting, barely believing his eyes. Was he dreaming?

Nova's eyes fluttered open, squinting and running around the room before landing on him.

"Nova?" Jude stood, leaning over her to get closer. He cupped the side of her face. Tears blurred his vision. "You're awake."

"I heard—you." Her voice scraped out. "Calling me —talking."

"I'm here." Jude grabbed the water by the bed and fed her the straw. She took a few small sips before he set it aside.

"Salem?" she asked.

"She's gonna be okay thanks to you. You saved her—saved both of you." Jude pressed a gentle kiss to her forehead. "I love you, Freckles."

Nova's eyelids drooped. "Tired."

He tried not to let the fact that she didn't say it back bother him. She was recovering from a near-fatal accident and on multiple drugs for pain. "Rest."

"Bossy."

Jude snorted, a smile turning up his mouth for the first time in what felt like eternity. It was nice to see she still had her fight.

"Stay?" she asked with closed eyes.

He took her hand in his once more. "I'm not going anywhere."

I never will.

The pit that had been in his stomach since things went sideways in Amanda's apartment disappeared, morphing into a warm, bubbly feeling—growing with each even inhale of Nova's chest.

She's gonna be okay.

He let out a long breath of relief and gratitude. And for the first time, hope burned so bright it swallowed up everything else, shedding light in the dark crevices inside him, burning away the guilt—the self-doubt. All that was left was a deep knowing that they would survive this—they had to. He needed them to spend the rest of their days together. And as soon as Nova was well enough, Jude would make sure she understood the depth of his feelings for her—of his loyalty and commitment.

And just maybe she'd give him the chance to prove it. He wouldn't even entertain the idea of a reality without Nova. She'd told Salem she forgave him, but she'd probably done it so he didn't feel guilty if she died—but what about now? She was alive. If she couldn't forgive him—if she didn't feel the same after all that had happened—*no. I won't go there.*

Failure was not an option.

59

NOVA

Nova sat up in the hospital bed and winced. Moving hurt like a bitch, but it was better than being dead.

"Do you need more pain meds?" Mom asked.

"I need a fucking blunt and to get the hell out of this place," Nova grumbled.

Her mother chuckled. "The nurse is getting your discharge paperwork. It's gonna take a little bit."

"I've already been here two weeks. That's plenty long enough. Salem already left." Nova's tone turned pouty.

Her mother's expression turned solemn. "Salem left against medical advice and is doing outpatient treatment. And you were unconscious for most of that time and then dealing with an infection."

Nova bit her tongue, wishing she could take the words back. "How is she?"

"How would you be if you were kidnapped and kept like an animal for two months without proper food or water, and having who knows what else done to you?"

Nova's shoulders sunk as she rested back on the bed. "I'm sorry."

Renita squeezed her hand. "I hate that you experienced it even for the hours you did."

"I never suspected Amanda. Makes me wonder if I'm just truly a bad judge of character." Nova's attention landed on the empty chair beside her mother. The one Jude hadn't sat in once since Salem had been discharged.

Now that he'd found her, would things be different? Was her loss the only thing that had kept them together? *How selfish can I be, thinking about myself when Salem's been through so much?* But if Salem needed her brother's help to get better, away from here . . .

"That psycho bitch fooled everyone," her mother said.

"Yeah." Nova nodded, not wanting to talk about it anymore.

"We put Salem up in your guest room so Jude and you could be close. We figured she'd be more comfortable there than in our house."

"Did she or Jude say how long they would stay?" Nova asked, picking a thread on the white blanket on her lap. He'd texted her and called every day, but it wasn't the same.

"She's got months of recovery ahead. She and Jude are having a rough time." Mom's gaze landed heavily on Nova's face. "Did something happen between you and Ju—"

Knock. Knock.

The door to her room opened and the face she'd wanted to see most popped through. Jude smiled but it didn't reach his tired, bloodshot eyes.

"Hey, do you mind if I have a few minutes with Nova?" he asked her mom.

"Not at all. I'm gonna go see what's holding those release

papers up." Her mom patted Nova's hand and slipped out the door.

Nova licked her chapped lips and shifted on the bed with another wince.

"Are you okay? Do you need more pain meds?" Jude stepped to her side, his brown eyes running over every inch of her.

"I'm fine. Just want to get out of this place."

He sat in the chair her mother had occupied. Jude's knees knocked against the bed. "I've missed you."

"Have you?" she asked, risking a peek over at him.

Jude's warm hand enveloped hers. "Of course I have. I wish I could be here with you every day, but Salem—things with my sister have been difficult to say the least."

A flutter of relief pulled some of the tension from her shoulders. "She's been through a lot."

Jude's chest rose and fell as he nodded, guilt marring his handsome features. Dark shadows underlined his eyes like deep bruises.

Nova squeezed his hand back. "It will take time and probably a lot of therapy, but Salem's a survivor." Nova spoke the words more as a manifestation than a fact. The Salem that was in that basement with her was not the same Salem she'd known all those years ago.

"Thanks for letting her stay at the house."

"Of course."

"Your family has really taken her in, and someone's always popping by to drop off food or check on her." Jude ran his hand up the back of his neck to his hair as if self-conscious.

"They tend to do that. Once you've been adopted into the fold, the Emersons will suffocate you with their over-caring," she teased, but the humor fell flat.

Nova turned to Jude, taking in the utter exhaustion

clouding his eyes. She didn't like the unsure place they were in. Anxiety curled in her gut. But she had to be sure. "You know, even if you weren't—if we weren't together—they'd still make sure Salem and you were taken care of."

Jude's brows drew together as if he were confused. "What does that have to do with anything?"

Nova turned her face away, tears burning her eyes. She had to know.

"Look at me, Freckles."

She sniffed and focused back on the man she'd fallen in love with. "You know when I was on the floor of that cell, bleeding out, thinking I was gonna die?"

His hand fisted around hers. "Fuck, Nov. It kills me you were put in that position. I should have—"

"Stop. Let me get this out." She took a deep breath. "It gave me some perspective, you know?"

Jude tensed. "About what?"

"Everything. My life up until that point. The choices I made. Us."

Jude's throat bobbed.

"All my life I've been trying to live up to some invisible standard. But I always fell short. In that moment, I realized it was all such a waste." Nova sniffed. "Because what really matters in the end are the experiences I've shared with the people I love. Everything else is just details. I've worried so long about expectations I either created for myself, setting myself up to fail, or society's rules to make you fit inside a box." Nova shook her head. "I don't want to waste another minute on any of that. I just want to be me, Nova Akua Emerson. The girl with two mothers and one amazing father. With three overprotective but lovable brothers and their families. The woman who turns all her ADHD traits her teachers said were negatives to see them as her strengths." Nova's chest warmed with confidence the more she spoke. "I'm the woman who opened up to love and gave every piece of myself to someone in a dynamic that forced me to be the most vulnerable. I chose the wrong partner before—someone who took advantage of that and broke my trust. I let him dim my self-confidence, but I won't do that again."

Jude's jaw pulsed. "He didn't deserve you."

"I learned from that painful experience. Just as I have this one. I'm not the same woman who walked into that apartment, Jude."

His brown eyes fell to their clasped hands as his shoulders sunk. "I'm so fucking sorry I didn't protect you."

"You didn't fail me."

"I did. I—"

"If she hadn't captured me, we never would have found Salem. She would have died in that hellhole, alone and terrified. Even if we'd figured out it was Amanda, she would have taken that secret to the grave just to be the spiteful bitch she was."

"Reaper could have gotten it out of her."

"You mean he would have . . ." Nova's attention darted to the door as she whispered, "Tortured it out of her? A woman?"

Jude's lips pressed shut. "If I would have known for sure she was the one behind all this, I can't say I wouldn't have myself."

Nova tipped her head, seeing Jude in a whole new light. Talking about hypotheticals was one thing but following through was another. And that look in Jude's dark eyes left no doubt which one he meant.

"She was a psychopath," he said, as if trying to make her understand.

"You don't need to explain yourself to me. I'm the one

who killed her." Nova swallowed. She'd actually taken a life. "Was it hard for you, when you killed for the first time?"

Jude's chest expanded as she took a deep breath before he sighed. "Yes and no."

She nodded. "I get that. I feel guilty that I don't feel guilty. Does that make sense?"

"Yeah, Freckles, it does."

"I knew she had to die. It was her or us. But the fact that I ended a life . . . that should make me feel worse, shouldn't it?" *Or do I have psychopathic tendencies too?*

Jude gently pinched her chin between his fingers and forced her to look at him as he leaned in. "As moral as we humans like to think ourselves, when it comes down to it—life is about survival. And sometimes others have to die for us to live. There isn't anything right or wrong about that—it just is."

"You know all the worst parts of me." Nova brushed her hand over his cheek, his scratchy perpetual five o'clock shadow comforting against her palm.

"I know all the bravest and best parts." He moved his fingers from her chin to wrap around her wrist and kissed her palm.

Fierce love rose within Nova like a tidal wave. But she wasn't done being brave yet. "I don't want children, Jude."

"What does that have to do with . . ." His gaze fell to her abdomen and then flicked back to her. "Are you pregnant?"

Nova shook her head. "Fuck no. But if we do this, you need to know. I never planned on being a mom. A fun aunt, absolutely. But I can barely keep my shit together. I can't be responsible for a little human—not full-time at least." She braced herself for whatever the outcome of this conversation would mean. "I know you have a lot going on with your sister right now. And I want to be there to help you both through it.

But you also need to know that I know what I deserve and I won't settle for less."

Jude nodded, hurt flashing in his expression as he dropped her wrist. "I see."

"No, you don't. Not yet." Nova shifted on the bed, biting back the pain as she clutched his shirt, not letting him go. "I deserve to be loved and treated like I'm the world to my partner, because I'm gonna give them the same back. I need someone who is protective and loving, but strong enough to take the lead and put me in my place when I need that push. Someone who won't let me scare them away when I get in my moods." She smiled. "Someone who knows what I need and moves heaven and earth to give it to me. Jude, I know what I deserve, and that's *you*."

Warm, trembling, calloused hands tightened on her wrists as he stared back. "You still want me?"

She nodded. "More than I've wanted anything in my life."

"Fuck, little brat, you scared the shit out of me. I thought you were breaking up with me."

"Nope. But we're not done yet."

"So I can't kiss you?" he asked, the corner of his mouth turning up.

Nova shook her head. "Not until you tell me what you need."

"You, baby. I just need you." He pressed his forehead to hers, inhaling like he was breathing her in.

"You have me—every piece, Daddy."

Jude's lips crashed with hers like they were two stars colliding. Everything else was stripped away, the room they were in, the sounds of feet shuffling outside in the hall, their pasts— nothing else existed but the feverish burn lighting Nova up from the inside out. She parted her lips, deepening the kiss and teasing him with her tongue. His soft, warm mouth melded with hers, stirring a longing stronger than she'd ever known.

This kiss was a beginning—it was everything.

"Anyone want to tell me how this all started?" Salem's voice cut through the dense fog like a knife.

Nova and Jude pulled apart at the same moment, turning to the woman standing in the doorway.

"Your appointment is done already?" Jude asked.

"Yup. You can tell your guard dog I can walk from one floor to the next by myself—I've been doing it for years." Salem pointed behind her with her thumb.

Jude visibly flinched from his sister's words. As much as Nova understood Salem's anger and need to lash out, Jude didn't deserve to be attacked and made to feel more guilty.

Before Nova could say anything, a dark shadow loomed over Salem.

"You got her from here, King?" Reaper's deep voice was cold as ice.

"Yeah, thanks, brother," Jude answered.

Salem sighed and peeked over at Nova. That icy exterior melted for one moment in time and then it was back, and she was as cold and stoic as her brother could be.

"Can you give us a few minutes alone?" Nova asked Jude, giving his hand another squeeze.

"Sure. I'll grab you some tea." He got up and walked by his sister.

"Gonna stand there or make yourself comfortable in the chair?" Nova asked as he left, closing the door behind him.

Salem took a few steps forward, her legs unstable, but she kept her chin high. Her long black hair covered half her face in shadow, highlighting her mossy-green eyes that seemed so much older than the twenty-seven years she'd been on this earth. She sat in the chair, crossing her arms over her chest.

"You doing okay?" Nova asked.

Salem rolled her eyes.

Nova laughed. "Yeah, I guess that's a stupid question."

"You and Jude, huh?"

"Does it bother you?" Nova asked.

"His life doesn't concern me."

Salem was putting up a brave front, trying to seem uncaring and unattached, but Nova understood it for what it was—Salem was just trying to protect herself.

"I was really mad at him when I found out who he was, not only because he'd lied to me, but because I remember being with you when you got that phone call about his deployment."

Salem shifted in her seat. "We don't need to talk about this."

"I think I'm the only one you have to talk about it with."

"Look, your family is being really nice, and I appreciate that. But I don't need your charity, and I just want to be left alone to get my body healthy and then I'm out of here."

"And going where?" Nova asked.

Salem's gaze dropped to the floor as she shrugged.

"I know what it's like to have nowhere to go and no one to rely on. It's the loneliest fucking existence. Why would you want to go back to that when you have an opportunity to be a part of a family?"

"They're not my family—"

"No, they're mine. And so are you."

"You haven't even seen me in—"

"Doesn't matter. Me and my mom—Renita—we came back for you, did you know that?" Nova asked.

Salem finally met her gaze.

"You had already been placed with Jude, so the state wouldn't give us any other information. I feel like I should have looked for you before now, just found you on social media or something. I'm sorry. I hope you'll give me the chance to make it up to you."

Salem leaned forward on her elbows, her shoulders sinking low as if she were ashamed. "You have nothing to make up to me for, Nov. You've saved me twice now."

Nova shook her head. "You saved yourself by surviving hell. I just provided the opportunity you needed to get away. And really, you saved me, too, by getting that help. I would have died without you. So, we're even."

The corner of Salem's lips flicked up for a second and then the ghost of a smile was gone. "I'll try to stay out of your and Jude's way while I'm here."

"You're never in the way, Salem. But I have to tell you, he did everything in his power to try and find you—to make things right."

Salem's lips pursed as she rubbed her hands over her arms. Haunted green eyes briefly met Nova's. "He was too late. My body might be alive—barely—but every other part died in that cell."

Nova reached for her friend. "Sal—"

Salem jerked back, eyes wide as she stared at Nova's hand in mid-air.

Nova pulled it back. "Sorry, I shouldn't have—"

Salem shook her head. "It's not your fault I'm broken. All you ever did was try to keep me together."

Nova opened her mouth to speak but Salem stood, walking out the door without another word.

Salem had a long road ahead of her, but Nova and Jude would be by her side—as much as she'd let them, anyway.

A small bubble of gratitude burst inside Nova. As painful as her experiences had been, she wouldn't know how to reach her friend without having known that hurt herself in some capacity.

And maybe what Amanda had meant to break them, in the end Nova and Salem could use to make them stronger.

"I've got those discharge papers. We're ready to go." Her mom walked into the room. "I see Salem came to visit. Glad to see you two got a chance to talk."

"Mom?"

"Yes?" Renita asked, grabbing Nova's bag.

"I love you."

Her mom dropped the bag and came over to Nova, then wrapped her in a hug. Nova didn't even mind that it pulled at her stitches.

"I love you too, Akua. And I always will."

60

JUDE

Four months later
New Year's Eve

Twinkling lights glimmered in the deep amber eyes staring back at Jude. His heart squeezed, expanding and full of something he'd never experienced—love. The trickle that had started when he'd first met Nova's gaze on that dark abandoned road had turned into a rushing river, carving out pieces of himself until it was as deep as the Grand Canyon—straight to his soul, branding it hers.

Nova's laugh was light and free as she spun on the dance floor and back into his arms. Her silky red dress clung to every delicious curve. The fabric looped around her neck and dipped low in the back all the way to her waist. Her nipples brushed against his chest. Jude inhaled her sweet amber scent, savoring the feel of her body moving against his as the upbeat music bled through the speakers.

He couldn't resist brushing his lips to her neck, kissing a

trail to the back of her ear and the small tattoo hidden behind it. She shivered in his arms, her tits hardening into points.

"Don't start something you have no intention of finishing." Nova smirked, pulling away enough to look at him as the song ended and another slow one started.

Jude glanced over her shoulder at the wedding guests milling about. It was like the rest of the world fell away when he had Nova in his arms. The barn was packed with Ricky and Everett's family and friends. They'd even invited Reaper and the rest of the Pirates MC to share in their special day.

"Who says I don't plan on following through?" he asked, sliding his hand up her bare back.

She snorted. "How about the fact that you haven't given me anything but vanilla sex since my hospital stay? Four months is a long time . . ." Nova nodded towards Casanova and Blade—the president of the Pirates—talking over beers in the corner in what appeared to be a heated conversation. "Maybe I'll see if Cass wants to have some fun."

The growl that ripped from his throat was instinctual as his fingers wrapped around her neck. "Don't even joke about that unless you want your ass so marked you won't sit for a week."

She smiled, a rebellious flicker in her gaze. "Promises, promises."

"You were stabbed. I'm trying to let you heal." His hand dropped to her waist, holding her just a little closer at the reminder of how close he'd come to losing her forever.

"It's been four months. The doc cleared me ages ago."

Jude ground his teeth together.

Her soft fingers smoothed over his cheek. "Jude?"

"What?"

"I'm more than healed. You won't hurt me—not in that way anyways."

He sighed, tipping his forehead to hers, breathing in her sugary exhale. "I almost lost you."

"Oh, baby." She hugged him, her head lying against his chest as they swayed to the soft melody. "It's gonna take something stronger than a psychopath with a knife to take me away from you."

Jude shook his head. "It's not funny."

"I know. But we need to get past this. Or else that bitch will come between us." Nova pulled back as the song ended.

"You're sure?"

"Absolutely."

He gripped the back of her neck and pulled her into a kiss. Her mouth parted, her teeth nipping at his bottom lip, stirring him on. Longing pulled at his every cell, urging him on to sneak away and give her exactly what they both craved.

Nova pulled back with a teasing smile. "I think I'll get a drink. Have you seen Sal?"

Jude scanned the crowd to the last place he'd seen his sister. She was still there, at a table in the back corner. Renita placed a full plate in front of her. Over the last few months, Salem had managed to gain some weight back, but despite everything, she remained withdrawn. She wouldn't talk to Jude except in short, snarky sentences. She stayed in her room at Nova's or walked the farm. Physically, she was recovering. Mentally and emotionally was another thing altogether.

Larry Washburn succumbed to his injuries and died. If he hadn't, Jude wasn't sure he could hold himself back from killing Larry himself after knowing what that monster had put those girls through.

"Reaper's watching over her." Nova nodded towards his friend in the dark corner, separate from everyone as he nursed a drink.

Reaper's gaze hadn't traveled far from Salem since they'd

pulled them out of that horrible place. Jude's chest tightened. "Yeah, a little too close."

"Leave him alone. He just wants to make sure his best friend's sister is safe. Would it be so bad for her to have someone looking out for her?"

"You don't know him—what he's done." Jude tried to forget what his friend was capable of, the blood on his hands.

"It can't be that bad if he's still your best friend."

Oh, if you only knew. "He's my only friend."

Nova rolled her eyes. "I'm not gonna argue semantics. Salem told me at Carrie's funeral that she feels safe when he's around. So don't ruin that or you'll be in even more hot water with her."

Pain stabbed Jude's heart. "I won't say anything as long as he keeps his distance."

"Speaking of distance, I went to grab a tea from the café the other day and guess who saw me and ran out the door as if his ass was on fire?" Nova asked.

"Who?"

Her brows scrunched together. "Chad."

"Huh. That's interesting." Jude tried to keep his comment casual, avoiding her eyes.

"Any idea why he bolted like I was Freddy Krueger?"

Jude shrugged. "I don't waste time trying to understand the mind of douchebags."

Nova slapped his chest playfully with a knowing look. "No more secrets."

Jude sighed. "Okay, I might have paid him a visit with Reaper."

Nova's gaze widened. "What did you do?"

"We took him for a ride and let him know exactly what happens to men who don't take no for an answer and continue to harass women. Taught him some manners and let him know what would happen if he ever bothered you again."

"Because you were jealous?" she asked.

Jude barked out a laugh. "Not at all, Freckles. I did it because he was bothering you and making you uncomfortable. Entitled little asshole needed to be reminded he wasn't top of the food chain." Jude gripped the side of her neck, his thumb brushing under her chin to tip her face up to him. "And because you're mine. No one fucks with you without consequences."

"I think I might have just come." Nova bit her lip.

Jude chuckled and pressed his mouth to hers in a chaste kiss—a teasing promise. The song ended and a more upbeat one began.

"You wanna get out of here?" she asked.

Jude tapped her nose with his finger. "Not yet. You can't run out of your brother's wedding this early."

She pouted, her bottom lip sticking out as she motioned to the other side of the room. "Fine. I guess I'm gonna go cool down and grab that drink."

Casanova took an empty seat at one of the stools at the bar.

Jude narrowed his eyes at her and wrapped his hand around her waist. "I'll come with you."

Nova laughed as they headed over. She stopped after two steps, her focus falling on her oldest brother dancing with his wife.

"I'm really glad Nash got his closure and his name cleared with the town's rumor mill."

"He seems happy." Jude admired the man from afar as Nash pulled Isabella close, nuzzling her neck. Isabella's smile lit up her whole face.

"Come on." Jude took her hand. "Let's get you that drink."

They walked up to the bar.

"What can I get you?" the bartender asked.

"Oh, I'll have a tequila shot, please." Nova smiled.

"No. Absolutely not." Ricky's voice cut in.

Nova crossed her arm over her chest. "And why not? I thought we were all here to celebrate you lucking out and somehow convincing this guy that marrying your dumb ass was a good idea."

"You two can't call a truce for one night?" Everett asked, wrapping his arm around his husband.

"Last New Year's Eve you got wasted on wine and were a bitch to my date with your mouth. I think tequila will only make your decisions worse." Ricky narrowed his eyes at his sister.

"Hey, now. I know she's your sister, but you call her a bitch, wedding or not, and I'm gonna have to take you outside and teach you some manners," Jude warned.

Ricky smirked at him, eyeing him up and down. "You're right. I just don't want anything to go sideways today."

"First off, it's really hot when you stick up for me." Nova reached down and gave Jude's ass a squeeze. "Second . . ." She turned to Ricky. "If I hadn't said what I did and scared her off—as tasteless as it was—you never would have gotten the balls to chase after Everett here. Isn't that why you're getting married today? It's the anniversary of when you actually gave in to your true feelings and kissed him?"

"She has a point." Everett shrugged.

Ricky sighed and tipped his head up. "Why do you have to be friends with my sister?"

"Because I'm lovable, fun, creative, and I got the good weed—should I go on?" Nova asked.

"I don't know why you were invited," Ricky grumbled.

"Because you love me too, big brother. Just admit it." Nova squeezed Ricky around the waist.

His scowl softened to a small smile before he kissed her cheek. "Yeah, I guess you're right."

"Now, I'm going to enjoy a shot—or two—and then take this guy home and fuck until the sun comes up. We won't be at brunch tomorrow, so don't come looking unless you wanna see a show," Nova quipped.

"Jesus Christ! Can you not tell me shit like that?" Ricky grimaced and linked hands with Everett. "Come on, babe. I need another dance."

"See you two later—or maybe not." Everett laughed as Ricky led him away.

"Why do you try to rile him up like that?" Jude asked, turning back to the bar.

"He makes it too easy. And it's entertaining."

Jude leaned closer, his fingers dug into her thigh hard enough to leave a bruise. "If you don't think I will hike you over my shoulder and carry you out of here to fuck this atti-tude right out of you, you'd be wrong, little brat."

He backed away to look at her face. Her black pupils were blown wide, Nova's lips parted as her chest rose and fell rapidly.

"Then maybe now isn't the time to tell you I haven't drunk a single drop of water today? It's been sweet tea and cham-pagne all afternoon." She smirked. "Oh, and I skipped break-fast and only had a granola bar for lunch."

Nova grabbed the tequila shot on the counter and downed it, eyes squeezing together before she sucked on the lime. Smacking her lips, she leaned forward, peering past Jude. "Hey, Cass, why the long face? This is supposed to be a cele-bration."

Cass? Jude stiffened at the casual nickname of the man to his right.

Casanova turned to her, his solemn face morphing to a smile. "Hey, Nova. Jude."

"We need another round of shots for all three of us, please?" Nova asked the bartender.

"I shouldn't have one. I've got somewhere to be in a little while," Casanova said.

"You don't look excited about those plans," Nova pointed out.

"It's not that. I just have a lot on my mind," he answered as the bartender placed the shots down.

"I'm sorry. I heard about the um . . . the fire." Nova cleared her throat. "How are the kids? The woman . . . she, uh, had children, right?"

Casanova nodded solemnly, a contrast to his usual happy and flirtatious self. Reaper had called and asked for Jude's help in the middle of the night two weeks prior and he'd answered. How could he not after all the Pirates had done for him, Nova, and Salem? Jude had had no idea he'd be stepping into a war zone in the next town over—Dark Cove.

"Yeah, they were placed with Patty's sister, Rebecca Cole. She's a therapist, so they should be in good hands."

Nova's eyes widened, recognizing the name. That was the same therapist Jude had reached out to initially, but he'd decided to go with another for his weekly sessions.

"It's good they had family. If they need anything, please let us know. We're more than happy to help," Nova offered.

Months ago, Jude would have scoffed. No one gave without expecting anything in return—at least that had been his experience until he'd met the Emersons.

"I will." Casanova nodded and stared at his half-empty beer.

Nova met Jude's gaze, worry flashing in her eyes. She had such a big heart, always wanting to help.

Those brown eyes widened and her mouth curled up like she had an idea.

"We were thinking of having a threesome. You want in?" Nova asked Casanova as casually as if she were offering him a glass of water.

"No we fucking weren't," Jude snapped.

She shrugged, her eyes full of devious mirth. "If you aren't up to it, you could always watch."

Red blanketed Jude's vision. His hands fisted at his sides and he ground his teeth, trying to keep his shit together because they were in a room full of people at a fucking wedding of all places.

Deep belly laughter rose from Casanova as the man stood and slapped Jude's shoulder. "Good luck with this one. I'm gonna head out. A round of dishing out punishment isn't a bad idea. Thanks for the inspiration, Nova."

Nova brightened, her mouth opening to speak.

"I would think very hard about the next words out of your mouth because it's not a matter of if, but *when* I punish you for this behavior." Jude's voice deepened with the threat as Casanova walked away.

"I was just going to say 'drive safe.' Geez." She rolled her eyes, but a smile curved her wicked mouth.

Jude sighed as she picked up a second shot. He took it from her hands and set it back on the bar.

"Hey—what do you think—"

Jude lifted her over his shoulder, his patience gone. This behavior would only escalate until she made a scene, and that was the last thing the happy couple on the dance floor wanted. Nova had made her point.

Jude passed a few gaping onlookers as she slapped his ass.

"Nothing to see here, folks. She's just had a little too much to drink."

He walked over to Salem first. "You okay to get home if we head out now?"

Salem flicked her gaze to Nova. "I'm staying with Mama E tonight. She's having a sleepover with Bailey, and I was invited."

"You don't have to stay away; I'll gag him so he's quiet," Nova teased, peeking around his hip.

Salem's face soured. "Eww. I don't need to know what fucking kinky shit you two get up to."

"I'll make sure she gets there safe." Reaper appeared by Salem's side, finally coming out of his dark corner.

"Yeah, wouldn't want me getting lost walking a hundred yards from the barn on the safest place in this whole goddamned town. Like I'm a fucking child," Salem grumbled.

"Thanks." Jude chose to ignore his sister's comment, nodding to his friend. He spun around and walked past the dance floor on his way to the exit.

"Oh thank God," Ricky said. "Get her out of here, and I'll pretend I don't know how you're keeping her away."

"Hey!" Nova swung her fist towards her brother but he dodged it.

"Goodnight!" He laughed.

"Congratulations!" Nova yelled back at them as Jude carried her into the frigid winter air. "It's freezing out here."

He smacked her ass before shifting her into a princess carry, tucking her against his chest. "Should have thought about that before you mouthed off, little brat."

Her bottom lip stuck out, but she snuggled closer. "The stars are pretty tonight."

He tipped his head up for the briefest moment, his feet crunching in the snow as he climbed the shoveled path up the hill towards their home. Jude turned to look at her. "Almost as beautiful as you."

"Psh. What a line. You're a softie, you know that?"

"You're gonna find out just how wrong that statement is as soon as we get through our front door."

She chuckled. "I like when you call it *ours*."

He hesitated, looking at her under the moonlight. "You're my home, Nova. Never felt that way about anywhere or anyone before. Probably never been anywhere long enough or felt safe enough. But as long as there's breath in my lungs, you're everything to me."

She blinked slowly, cupping the side of his face. "You mean it?"

He nodded, continuing up the path. "You own my heart and soul, Freckles."

"I love you too." She kissed him as the motion-activated porch lights flicked on.

Rather than heading up the steps, Jude walked over to his truck, opened the passenger-side door, and set her inside.

"What are you doing?" she asked as he slipped the buckle over her lap.

He shrugged off his jacket and laid it over her legs too. "I wanna show you something."

"Now? I thought we were gonna . . ."

He laughed. "Oh, I know what you thought. And you're not wrong. But waiting is part of your punishment." He closed the door and laughed.

When he got into the driver's seat, her arms were crossed over her chest and her bottom lip jutted out in a pout. "Where are we going?"

"Squid Ink."

"The tattoo shop? You gonna finally tattoo me? Cleo told me you've become a favorite of a few clients."

"You'll see."

"Gah! You're an evil man."

He slipped his hand under the silk of her dress and squeezed her thigh. "Just you wait, brat. Just you wait."

He smiled as he started the truck and blasted the heat. Nerves rattled around his bones. His hands were sweaty on the steering wheel as he pulled out of the driveway.

He'd never done this before, and he wasn't sure she'd even say yes. But he was gonna lay it all on the table, and if she wasn't ready—he'd wait. Jude couldn't waste another minute without letting this woman know he wanted to bind her to him in every way—permanently.

61

NOVA

Nova's breath puffed out in a cloud as she tugged the jacket over her shoulders with one hand and gripped Jude's warm hand with the other. He slid the key into the back door of the tattoo shop. After ushering her inside, he locked up behind them. The light flicked on. Nova blinked while her eyes adjusted, and she shivered.

"Cold?"

"Not too bad. It's warm in here."

"Come on." He led her through the back room to the hall.

"I've never been here at night."

"Cleo gave me a key yesterday."

A key? That meant—Nova walked behind Jude into a private area. A black leather tattoo chair took up the space in the center of the small room. Sketches of Jude's art hung around the walls along with a few Polaroids of his work on clients.

"She didn't just loan it to you? It's yours? You got your own space?" She turned to him excitedly.

His smile reached from those handsome full lips to his

mesmerizing eyes. "I do. She's still overseeing my work for a little while longer, but it's mine."

Nova wrapped her arms around him and squeezed. "I'm so proud of you."

He chuckled and patted her back. "Hop up on the chair."

Nova couldn't contain her glee. She clapped and wriggled into the leather seat. "Are you finally gonna tattoo me?"

"That was the plan before you mouthed off at the wedding." He turned his back to her, pulling out a desk drawer and dipping his hand inside.

Her stomach dipped. Of all the times to push his buttons. But how else could she get him to give her what she needed— what she craved? He'd been treating her like she was made of paper-thin porcelain since she'd left the hospital.

"You know I was just teasing."

"No, that was not teasing. That crossed a line." His tone left no room for argument. The room seemed to expand, making her feel infinitely smaller. Had she really gone too far?

Jude grabbed a container of black ink and squirted it into a small cup, lining up all his supplies for a tattoo. Hope welled inside her.

She cleared her throat. "I'm sure I can make it up to you."

"You think inviting another man to have sex with you is something to joke about?"

"I—"

"How would you feel if I'd done that with another woman?"

Something sour and violent lashed out like a whip, searing her chest.

Jude turned to her, pinching her chin between his fingers, forcing her to meet his gaze. "Answer me, little brat."

Nova swallowed the lump in her throat. It sunk to her stomach like a rock of shame. "I'd hate it."

If they'd discussed it beforehand, maybe . . . but the thought of sharing Jude with anyone else just didn't sit right. *Because he's mine.*

"I had something special planned for tonight, but now I have to dole out a severe punishment."

"You don't *have* to." It was more of a plea than a statement.

Jude exhaled, his head shaking slightly. "Then I wouldn't be a good Daddy, would I? Letting you get away with such defiance? No, there won't be any escaping this, little brat."

Not unless I use the safe word. He didn't need to say it. Jude wouldn't do anything more than she was willing to take.

"Yes, Daddy."

Satisfaction flickered in the hint of his smile. Her belly fluttered.

Jude grabbed a bottle of shaving cream and squirted some in his hand. "Now, hike that sexy dress up to your waist and spread your thighs like a good girl."

Nova shimmied, lifting the silk up over her bottom to her waist letting the jacket fall to the floor. The smooth material slicked against her skin like a live wire. As she parted her legs, her heart thundered in the mix of anxiety and the excitement of delicious anticipation.

He knelt down in front of her. The heat of his hand conflicted with the cool sensation of the shaving cream as he rubbed it on her thigh. Nova resisted the urge to squeeze her legs together. He took his time, no doubt trying to draw this out. But she'd gone too far tonight. And she would accept whatever punishment he deemed fit. *I deserve it.* In fact, if he didn't, she'd be very disappointed.

A flash of metal glinted as he pulled a straight razor out. Nova's breath stuttered.

"Hold still." He held her thigh in place with one hand and lined the metal blade at the edge of the shaving cream.

She sucked in a breath as the cold steel smoothed across her flesh, leaving smooth skin in its wake.

"You trust me, don't you?" Jude wiped the blade on a paper towel and swiped again.

There was something so intimate about having a partner shave you. The fact that he did it with a straight razor added a certain element of danger to it. The man exuded power and control. He might have been the one on his knees, but she was at his mercy. If he wanted to hurt her, he could, and she'd be powerless to stop him—a fact that made her pussy wet.

"With my life," Nova confessed.

He scraped the last of the cream off her leg with the razor and wiped her clean with a paper towel. "How about with this tattoo?"

"You have something in mind?" she asked.

"Yes, Freckles. I know exactly how I want to mark you." Jude stood.

She shivered. This time it had nothing to do with the cold. Heat swirled from her belly down to her pussy, spiraling into her limbs like an erotic fever, heating her from the inside out.

"I trust you. I know you'll make it beautiful."

Jude met her gaze. "Then get up."

Nova scooted off the seat. The silk of her red dress skimmed along the heated flesh of her thighs like a whisper of what was to come—a tease.

Jude tugged at the tie at his neck, pulled it off, and untangled the knot. "Turn around."

Nova spun on shaky legs.

"Hands behind your back."

She clasped her hands as close together as she could behind her. The smooth silk of the tie bound her wrists together comfortably. Warm fingers traced the back of her neck before he undid the clasp of the dress. Red silk slid down her body and pooled onto the floor, exposing everything except the flimsy excuse for a thong she'd picked out. Warm air met her exposed skin, pebbling her nipples.

"All night I wondered what you had underneath this dress." Jude's deft fingers trailed up her spine, over her shoulder, and around a breast as he circled her.

Nova leaned into his touch, seeking more—but the bastard pulled his hand away. A frustrated growl left her lips.

Jude chuckled. "Such a needy little slut, aren't you?"

"Please?"

"Please what?"

"I need you."

Jude collared her throat and tilted her head, pulling her higher. She stood on tiptoes as he nipped her earlobe. She shuttered her eyes and they fell to half-mast. Heady, glowing arousal mixed with the delicious high of subspace, expanding and pulsing within her. Those wicked teeth sunk into her neck, not breaking flesh, but oh so close.

She moaned.

"Fuck, you're perfect." Jude backed away, leaving her cold once more. "So needy. I bet your pussy is already soaking those flimsy panties."

Check for yourself. She had the mind to not say her thoughts out loud—maybe she *could* learn from her past mistakes.

Jude pulled a scrap of fabric from the pocket of his jacket, crumpled on the chair where she'd left it.

He held up the mask. "You can't look until it's done."

She blinked and nodded. Jude slid it over her eyes until everything went black.

The chair squeaked as if he'd sat in it. "Get on my lap, little one. Sit sideways."

Nova stepped blindly forward, bending her knees slightly to guide her without the use of her hands. The material of his dress pants was smooth against her cool skin. His warm hands gripped her waist, guiding her as she straddled him. He moved her legs to slide through the side of the chair, hanging over the armrest, while his other hand supported her back. His cock was already hard right beneath her, but not where she needed it.

Something cold sprayed over her leg where he'd shaved it. The antiseptic stung her nose.

"Look at you, at my mercy. Bound and blinded and loving every minute of it." Jude's voice lulled her into calm. "You have no idea what sick, twisted fantasies are playing through my head. All the things I want to do to you—and will."

His biting words only stirred the heat in her pussy. She clenched around air.

"Because there is nothing in this world more fucking beautiful than you at my mercy, a pathetic, writhing mess for me to play with."

She moaned, pressing her thighs together.

"To fuck." A gloved finger forced them apart before he traced the edge of her pussy lips, smoothing over the lace of her panties. Jude was so fucking close to her clit—this was pure torture.

"Mmmm. Daddy—"

"To abuse." Jude smacked her pussy—hard.

She gasped.

"And you're gonna let me like a good whore, aren't you?"

"Yes, Daddy. Anything you want."

"Good girl."

A buzz filled the room, seeming impossibly loud with her vision gone. She flinched. The sound moved closer.

A warm hand splayed over her thigh, bringing them

together once more. "Be still, and take the hurt like the pain slut you are. Earn my cum."

Another moan slipped through her lips, free and wild. Untamed, like the side of her that only ever came out with her Daddy. With the man who would protect her and love her as sadistically as she needed.

The needle bit into her skin. Shivers cascaded from the sharp vibration directly to her clit. She breathed out, riding the edge of pain blossoming on her thigh as she tipped her head back. Seconds blurred into minutes or maybe hours. She lost all track of time to the steady hum of the tattoo gun. To Jude's capable, strong hands, holding her thigh in place and wiping it every now and then. She'd never thought getting tattooed could be an edging experience, but holy fuck, this might just have been the hottest thing she'd ever done—besides that time in the woods. And he hadn't even fucked her yet.

"I'm sorry," she whispered.

The gun paused, lifting from her skin. He wiped her again. "For what?"

"For saying what I did to Cass—"

A growl rumbled from his chest. "Don't say his fucking name. Not here—not now."

Pain lanced her chest—and it wasn't the fun kind. She'd only meant to show remorse, but somehow she'd tainted the experience. Attempting to make it right, she slipped into humor. "Maybe you should tattoo your name on me while you're at it."

"Oh, I plan on it," he said before the clack of objects moving met her ears.

He shifted beside her, angling as if reaching behind her to his tray of supplies before the gun buzzed again. The needle felt different—bigger. She swallowed. She deserved to be punished, but his hand was gentle despite the violent prick of the needle sinking beneath her skin.

Everything inside her rebelled at being told what to do, against someone else's ownership. Yet his possessiveness turned her the fuck on. Because Jude never wanted to make her small, and despite his dirty talk, he never saw her as an object.

Time passed without any more words exchanged. She drifted in a floaty space, tethered only by his touch. The dull pain made her head floaty, better than any weed she'd smoked.

The buzz of the gun ended so abruptly, she flinched. The silence was somehow deafening.

Jude set his tool down with a *clack* and wiped her thigh more thoroughly this time. Something cool and soothing eased over the burn emanating from the sore flesh.

"Mmmm," she moaned.

"All done. You ready to see?" he asked.

"Yes."

Slap!

She gasped as a burning sting in the shape of his palm expanded on her exposed breast.

"Yes what?" he demanded, pinching her nipple.

"Yes, Daddy." Nova's toes curled, pleasure and pain melding together in perfect harmony.

Jude's palms cupped her breasts, massaging hard, adding another level of hurt. "Don't push me, little brat. I'm all out of patience for your disrespect."

"Yes, Daddy. I'm sorry."

Jude's hot breath heated her neck as his voice rumbled near her ear. "Not yet you aren't. But we'll get you there."

Nova's pussy clenched as a fresh wave of liquid arousal

dripped through the lace panties and down her thigh. Fuck, he was a pure fantasy come to life.

Jude pushed the blindfold up off her head. Nova blinked, her eyes adjusting to the brightness of the room before she looked down. A beautiful red rose with a crown of thorns adorned her thigh.

"It's stunning," she gasped before looking closer. "What are those dots and lines on the petal?"

"I chose a rose because it's delicate and beautiful like you." Jude's finger trailed over her cheek as he met her gaze.

"Delicate, huh?" She smirked.

One eyebrow rose as his mouth quirked. "It's also temperamental and protects itself with sharp thorns to stab people who wish to do the plant harm."

She laughed. "That sounds more like me."

"It's more than that, Freckles. It's who *we* are. I want every piece of you. The soft and the cutting. I want your sharp mouth to punish." He brushed his thumb over her bottom lip. "As well as your big, loving heart."

Just when she thought she couldn't possibly love this man more, a dam burst inside her, warm and glowing. Her chest expanded as she sucked in a breath, making room for more.

He gripped her neck, pulling her temple to his lips. "You taught me we can be both—to live in our duality. I can be loving and sadistic. Gentle and rough. You'll take my pain, and I'll give you pleasure."

"The most perfect dynamic." She smiled, tears of happiness blurring her vision.

Their story wasn't roses and butterflies. It was bruises and pain—raw realness. There was no hiding their worst parts because they'd uncovered each others' secrets one at a time, together. They'd seen each other at their best and also their worst—and they'd both chosen to stay. To commit to healing what they'd broken. To sink their nails into each other's flesh and hold on while everything tried to tear them apart—even themselves. But true love wasn't easy—it was messy and painful. To be so vulnerable with someone, and trust that they would protect those pieces, was brave.

"And these dots and dashes are morse code," he explained, releasing her throat to run his finger over a petal inked into her skin.

"What does it say?"

"It marks you as mine, and I won't apologize for it."

She sucked in a breath. He hadn't been joking?

"It says 'Daddy's little brat.' Because that's what you are. You're *mine*. Every piece of you."

The depth of love in his eyes was too much. She didn't deserve it, not after— Nova looked away.

Jude gripped her chin, forcing her to meet his gaze once more, holding Nova captive. "You push—and I'll push back until you feel safe enough to give in to me. Until you surrender and let me take care of you how we both need."

All Nova's life she'd dealt with people, doctors, teachers, and society telling her she was too much. Too loud. Too hyper. Too talkative. Too big. Forgetful. Lazy. Stupid. Deviant. Only her family and a few friends hadn't. But Nova had held back, made herself smaller to fit in and not be rejected. She'd taken to pushing others away before they could do the rejecting.

The people who matter won't care about that shit, baby. They'll love you for who you are. They'll see the wonderful, creative person you are because of how your brain works. Her mother's words repeated in her mind.

"Freckles? Do you hate it?" Jude asked, ripping her out of her head and back to the present. His expression carried a hint of vulnerability.

Nova shook her head. "No, I love it. I just . . ." Those

tears in her eyes threatened to spill over. "I'm just so happy I found you. That you want this with me." She sniffed. "This ownership thing? It goes both ways, right?"

Jude leaned back in the chair, unbuttoning his dress shirt one button at a time. His brown skin contrasted the white of the material as it parted. Colors peeked out that hadn't been there earlier that morning.

She gasped. "You got one too?" Nova eyed the raised skin over his heart—the rose that matched her own. "What does this one say?" She stared at the dots and dashes as he pulled his shirt the rest of the way off and dropped it to the floor.

"The tattoo says Nova's Daddy." He smirked. "It means that you own me too, Freckles. Heart and soul. Today and all the days to come."

"Wow, Jude. I—I don't know what to say."

"Are you mad? Scared? Regretting trusting me with something so permanent?" he asked.

Nova met his gaze and shook her head. "I probably should be fleeing for the hills. But I'm done running. I'm done believing I can't trust myself, or a man, for that matter. You were with me through it all—even when I didn't want you to be. You never gave up on me. You never sought to put me down or take advantage of me even when you had all the reasons in the world to. You never used me like that."

"And I would never."

"I know that now." She leaned forward and fused her lips with his, her hands straining the binds at her wrists.

Jude's palms slid up her breasts again, this time gentle and teasing. Nova moaned, opening her mouth. His teeth sunk into her bottom lip and tugged before he pulled back, leaving her wanting. Jude leaned over, inspecting the binds around her wrists. "Are these too tight?"

"No. Perfectly snug, and you left them lose enough so they aren't pulling on my shoulders."

"Good. You let me know if that changes." He cleared his throat, sitting a little straighter in the chair. "I have something else I want to ask you."

"What?" Her vision was hazy, her need for him overpowering. She'd do anything he wanted in that moment. Joy and love pulsed like physical things inside her. A powerful energy consumed her like a hurricane. Lust rippled through her every cell. She longed and hungered for the sweet agony only Jude could provide.

"Oh, Daddy. Please?"

"Please what, baby girl?"

"I need you so bad right now."

His smile was devilish with sadistic glee. It only turned her on more.

He dipped his finger between her thighs, coasting along the wet fabric between her bare pussy and his finger. "You're soaking my pants. Look how pathetic you are for my attention."

"I'll do anything. I just need you to touch me."

"Anything, huh?" Jude reached into the drawer beside the chair.

What would he pull out? Would it be nipple clamps? The razor again? How long would he torture her?

All her wonderings screeched to a halt at the sight of the glint of silver he pulled from the drawer. Nova gasped as shock and fear locked her in place.

And for once in her life, her mind went blank.

62

JUDE

Jude pulled the silver circular necklace from the drawer and held it up to Nova. Hopefully she wouldn't see the slight tremble in his hands.

Nova's mouth dropped open, her eyes widening.

Maybe this was a bad idea. Too soon.

"A collar?" Her voice was barely above a whisper.

Nerves skittered through him. "I know the last man that put one on you abused the privilege."

Most people in the BDSM community viewed a collar as having more importance than even a wedding ring. Jude wasn't saying he wanted to own her—but to fuse his life together with hers indefinitely. A promise to balance each other out, to share in the deepest intimacy with the most solid trust partners could have. To exchange their energy in a dynamic custom-built for the two of them.

"I know you're not interested in marriage. And I don't need that. But this . . . I've never done this with another person. I never felt I could handle the responsibility and the commitment. But with you . . ." Jude cupped the side of her face. "You make me want things I've been too afraid to ever hope for."

He dragged in a ragged breath. "We can wait if you're not ready—and if you never are, I'll understand. I just—"

"I'd be proud to wear your collar, Daddy."

Jude sucked in a breath, not sure he'd heard her right. "Say it again."

"I'm yours, and you're mine. I'd love a token to show the world that no one else knows me more than you, than my partner in life—my Daddy."

Jude pressed his mouth to hers, gripping the back of her neck. She moaned against him, the sound shooting straight to his cock. God, he wanted to be inside her, feeling her tight cunt squeezing around him as she came. But that would have to wait because his little brat needed her Daddy to show her he could handle her—all of her. Especially the pieces Nova didn't love herself.

Jude added pressure to his grip, guiding her off his lap onto her feet in front of the chair. He stood, breaking the kiss. God, he loved her like this, lips swollen, eyes bright and liquid with so much emotion. Tits hard, tiny bumps erupting over her skin as she shivered at his touch. She was so fucking responsive, and he would take full advantage of that quality for the rest of his life.

Jude walked behind her, unclasping the silver necklace he'd custom-ordered for her. There were only two keys. One he'd carry with him always, and one for her—only for emergencies.

He lifted the silver hoop to the front of her neck and secured it in the back.

She gasped. "It's cold."

He chuckled and twisted the key, locking it in place. Satisfaction lit him up like fireworks erupting inside. More happiness than he'd thought he'd ever be capable of containing poured out from his soul. But true joy wasn't meant to be contained—it was meant to be shared.

Jude grabbed the solid silver of the collar adorning her neck and tugged so it put pressure on the side of her neck, cutting off the blood supply as he bent forward to speak in her ear. "This right here is my ultimate commitment. Every time you feel the metal around your neck, you'll know Daddy's got you. No matter what. That's my promise today and every day."

Her eyes rolled back. A mix of pride and immense satisfaction surged through him. Her bliss was so arousing it was addictive. Jude released the metal and spun her around, supporting her unstable stance as he stared into her eyes. "This collar is the physical representation of my love—my protection, trust, and loyalty. I will always choose what is best for you, even if you don't agree or like it. I'll demand your submission and celebrate your independence. I'll support your dreams and help guide you as your Daddy into being the best woman you can be, Nova. It will be my greatest honor."

"I love you so much." She sniffed, tears dripping down her cheeks. Her makeup was smudging under her eyes.

She was beautiful like this, so open and trusting. He'd never take advantage of the faith she put in him.

"As much as I wanted to end this night with giving you so much pleasure you begged me to stop, I wouldn't want to fail my duties as your Daddy on the first night of this new phase in our dynamic." He smirked.

Nova's eyes flashed with a bit of fear, but deviant desire raged brighter in those amber eyes.

"We wouldn't want that, would we?" She smiled through her tears.

Jude swiped her cheeks, taking care of her with her bound

hands. "No, that wouldn't do. I take my job very seriously." He stepped aside, unhooking his belt.

The metal buckle jangled as he tugged it from around him. Her eyes widened. Jude folded it and then did so again until it was a controllable length, perfect for doling out his intended punishment. He sat back on the chair and lifted the armrests, freeing up the sides. Jude scanned Nova's face, checking for any sign she wasn't ready. Nervous excitement danced across her expression as she shifted on her feet.

He patted his thigh. "Now bend over my knee."

Nova walked to his side on wobbly legs and obeyed. Her weight settled over his thighs, pressing against his already hard cock. Her hands fisted in their binds behind her. Jude gripped them, checking the ties and her skin for any sign they were too tight. All seemed well. Jude clutched the wrist farthest from him, keeping her stable on his lap. Her feet only reached the ground because of the heels she still wore. But they would give her a little stability, and they looked hot as fuck on her, so he'd leave them for now. Her smooth, rounded ass clenched as if anticipating a spanking.

He gripped the luscious flesh and massaged it roughly. "You're gonna take your punishment like a good little brat, aren't you?"

"Yes, Daddy."

He tapped the leather over her ass lightly. Her body flinched nonetheless. Anticipation must have been eating her up. It was clear Nova knew she'd fucked up tonight. And it was obvious she felt bad about it. Now, it was his job to absolve her—to take away the guilt and show her that she was still loved and accepted. That she was safe.

Thwack. Thwack. Thwack!

Slowly, he tapped her ass with the leather as she wiggled.

Her ass bounced as he built up to a harder strike. She moaned, her hips lifting as if seeking more.

"Oh, are you enjoying this?"

"Yes, Daddy."

"I'll have to fix that. Dirty little slut likes pain." *Thwack!*

Nova gasped, her body arching—seemingly a primal instinct to flee the pain. It was pointless. Because she would take every stinging slap of his belt as punishment, earning her redemption.

"But this is a punishment." *Thwack! Thwack!* "I'm gonna tan your ass until it's so dark and hot and bruised you won't be able to sit for a fucking week. How would you like that? Huh?"

Jude lifted his hand a little higher, bringing the belt down hard onto the back of her thighs.

Thwack! Thwack! Thwack! Thwack! Thwack! Thwack!

"Ahhh!" Nova half stood on her tiptoes.

Jude yanked her back down on his lap, locking her in place, his elbow between her shoulder blades. His palm wrapped around Nova's bound wrist, holding her captive. His other hand was free to strike her at will with the brutal leather belt.

"Don't you fucking move. You're gonna take the pain you deserve for being such a pathetic slut who disrespected her Daddy."

"Yes, Daddy." Her voice came out a strangled sound somewhere between a gasp and a plea.

Thwack! Thwack! Thwack! Thwack! Thwack! Thwack! Thwack! Thwack! Thwack! Thwack!

"Owwww!"

Her whole body tensed, straight as a board. The flush of her skin darkened against the underside of her thighs and the bottom of her ass. Every sharp lash of the belt left a welt across her smooth flesh, getting darker with each strike. The jarring impact of the leather jiggled her ass. His mouth watered at the gorgeous sight. His cock strained against the zipper of his pants, biting into his flesh. But Jude was just getting started.

Whimpers fell from her lips as he continued his assault, taking every hit like the good girl she really was.

Thwack! Left cheek. *Thwack!* Right. *Thwack!* Left. *Thwack!* Left. *Thwack!* Left. *Thwack!* Right. *Thwack!* Right. *Thwack!* Right. *Thwack!* Right. *Thwack!* Left.

Jude alternated lighter taps, medium hits, and hard strikes so she would never know what to expect. Her ass clenched, trying to anticipate what was coming, but he loved to fuck with her head. Her body shifted, bucking and writhing on his lap. He pinned her down without relenting. Her whimpers and yelps grew with each punishing lash.

"Spread your pretty legs wide. Your slutty cunt needs to be punished for thinking of allowing another man inside her." Jude dropped the belt to the floor with a clank.

Nova shivered and opened her thighs. One leg slid towards the front of the chair, giving him free access to her pussy. She twitched as if anticipating another rough blow.

Jude bit back the praise at her obedience. This was a punishment, after all.

"Look at that cunt. So wet already." Jude pushed the lace aside and dipped his fingers inside her slick hole.

"Oh, Daddy, you feel so good."

"Shut up." He ripped his hands away, gripping the flimsy lace and yanking hard. "Hope you don't care about these panties." He ripped them off her and brought them to her face. "Open your mouth."

Her jaw dropped. He shoved the panties inside and pushed her chin to close it. "Now keep them in your mouth to stay quiet until I say otherwise. Take your punishment like a good girl. Unclench your hands if you need to say the safe word. Got it?"

"Yes, Daddy." She nodded and mumbled around a mouth full of fabric.

Jude didn't hesitate, give her time to adjust or warm up. He slapped her bare pussy with his hand.

Nova tensed, curling into herself as much as possible while folded and balanced on his lap. Her pussy gushed liquid arousal, perfuming the room with the scent of sex. Jude couldn't resist dipping his fingers through her lower lips, curling around her clit but not touching it directly, attempting to drive her mad. Whimpers slipped through the lace as he swirled his fingers. He pulled them out and brought them to his mouth, sucking her essence clean. Her taste lit up his tongue, musky and a little tart—just like the woman writhing on his lap.

Slap! Slap! Slap! Slap!

He punished her pussy. Nova's body went limp, every muscle relaxed. Jude checked her face, making sure she was still with him and just falling into subspace.

"You're almost there, baby. Doing so good, taking your punishment."

She blinked slowly.

Slap. Slap. Slap!

She screamed, the sound shooting straight to his cock. Fuck, he was so close just from the sight of her coming apart on his lap. Her cum splattered from her pussy as he lightly spanked it one more time. His hand was coated in her release. Jude spread it over her hot, reddened thighs. Over the welt blossoming on her flushed ass. He squeezed, massaging her scalding skin. She hissed. No doubt it burned and stung. He sunk two fingers into her cunt, fucking her with them and aiming for that spongy spot inside that would drive her wild, taking care to balance her pain with pleasure.

Her whimpers turned into moans muffled by the torn panties.

"Look at you, so fucking wet and needy. You don't think my cock can do the job alone?"

Nova shook her head, words muffled by the fabric.

"Guess I'll just have to show you how good I can use this cunt."

Jude lifted her as he stood. He untied her hands, gently massaging her wrists and inspecting them carefully as she stood on unsteady legs.

"Hands on that counter. Bend over and put that pretty heart-shaped ass in the air."

He didn't need the binds to keep her powerless and submissive; she went willingly.

Nova's hands planted on the stainless-steel counter. She arched her back and presented her ass to him. With her thighs dripping with her own cum, she was gorgeous. He gripped her swollen dark flesh and squeezed—she was so hot to the touch. She hissed. The tender skin on her ass must sting.

Jude unbuttoned his pants, tugged them down just enough for his cock to slip free. He was still partially dressed while she had nothing but heels on, pussy on display by his work station. The silver of her collar glinted in the overhead light of the room. Power was an intangible thing—it couldn't be taken unless it was truly given. And this woman right there had given him all of it. She trusted him to not abuse it, and he would never let her down.

Jude tugged on his cock, beads of pre-cum dripping from the tip as he groaned. Nova peeked over her shoulder, brown eyes heated as they dropped to his palm working himself over. A smile curved her lips.

"Now, spit out those panties. I want to hear you beg for forgiveness as I fuck you."

Nova's mouth opened, and the red lace fell onto the counter. "Don't be gentle."

I didn't plan on it. "You trying to tell me what to do, brat?"

Slap! Slap!

Her ass jiggled from the impact as she gasped and shook her head. "No, Daddy."

"Good. Because I'm gonna fuck this cunt until I bruise the inside of you just as much as I have the outside." He slapped her ass again, pushing his thumb into one of the darker spots where a bruise was already forming at the top of her thigh.

She screamed at the same time as his cock punched through her folds all the way to the hilt. He didn't give her time to adjust; there was nothing gentle about the way he possessed her body. Jude gripped the curly strands at the base of her neck, pulling as he drove his hips farther toward her. Nova screamed as he bottomed out.

He pulled out and did it again and again. The counter rocked slightly under the force as he fucked her harder and faster. His other palm slapped her ass over and over, alternating between that and reaching around to pinch her nipple.

"I'm gonna come—"

"Not yet. Naughty girls don't get to come. Not until you beg."

"Please! Please, Daddy—"

He thrust into her harder, her ass burning against him from all the attention he'd given it. After the belt, his hand wouldn't hurt her as much unless he increased the force behind it—so he did. She needed release and redemption, and that was just what he'd give her.

Slap! Slap! Slap! Slap!

"Ahhhhhhhh. Pleaseletmecome? Daddy, please!"

Slap! Slap! Slap! His handprint bloomed and darkened her tender, swollen skin. Her body was his canvas, and he left his mark with every stinging slap, every sharp lash of the belt. Each strike of his hand pulled something from him—energy exchanged. He gave everything he was. Her flesh rippled and jiggled under the impact, receiving everything he had to give. She took that energy like the good submissive she was.

"Pleeeeeease. I'll do anything."

Slap! Slap! Slap! Slap! Slap!

"Please! Forgive me. I'm sorry—I'm so sorry." Tears spilled out of her eyes, black mascara running down her beautiful light brown cheeks, intersecting with her freckles and dripping onto the table. Sobs wracked her body.

Jude released her hair and pulled out of her to spin her around. He picked her up, holding her close to his chest as he carried them over to the tattoo chair. She hissed as her ass clenched in his lap, no doubt sore from her punishment. She'd most likely feel this one for a few days, maybe longer. She settled on his lap despite how it must have hurt her. He smiled, his chest lighting with pride and gratitude at how well his little brat took the pain.

Jude rubbed gentle circles on her back. "Shhhh, it's okay, you're safe. I got you. Daddy's here."

She clung to him, crying harder. "I—I'm s-sorry, Daddy."

"I know, baby girl."

"I won't do it again. I hate that I hurt you." She kissed his bare chest above his fresh tattoo.

He squeezed her tighter, holding her head against his heart as he kissed her forehead. "I know."

She sniffed. "Am I forgiven?"

"You were forgiven before we even started this."

She cried harder. Minutes passed as her sobs died down to deep breaths. She totally relaxed into his arms, like she'd released so much pent-up energy. This was the calmest he'd ever witnessed her. Warm, glowing love expanded in his chest as he stared down at the woman in his arms. She'd gifted him her trust in his ability to care for her in a way not everyone would understand.

"Do you want to move to aftercare?" he asked.

She shook her head, wiping her face. "I want you. I need you inside of me."

Jude didn't say anything else. He pressed a kiss to her temple before he stood. Carefully, he set her on her feet, just long enough to lower his pants, socks, and shoes before he stepped out of them. He sat back in the chair, moving her to sit on his cock, legs on either side of him, bent at the knees. He gripped her waist and ever so slowly lowered her over him.

She moaned as the heat of her ass met his thighs. She bit her lip.

"You like that?"

She nodded.

"Not too sore?" he double-checked.

"It hurts so good. I can feel every ridge of your cock filling me, stretching me. I need to move."

"Then take what you need. Fuck Daddy's cock."

Nova arched, slowly riding him. She felt so good, so tight and hot clenching around him. It was his turn to be tortured. He gripped her hips, guiding her higher, slightly faster. Leaning forward, he sucked one nipple into his mouth, rolling his teeth and tongue over the sensitive hard point and swirling it around the barbell. He sucked around her areola, leaving love bites. Marking her with more bruises.

"Fuck, you feel so good—so perfect." She bounced on his lap, her breasts jiggling as she increased her speed.

He arched his hips to meet her on every thrust, driving hard and deep. His hand snaked around her throat, squeezing the sides of her delicate neck. "It will always feel like this because no one will ever fuck this cunt except me."

She lost it, screaming as she came. Her pussy clenched his cock like a vise. His balls drew up, pleasure tangling at the base of his spine and combusting.

White spots danced in his vision as her tits bounced from the force. Her expression twisted in pleasure. They came together as one. Two halves of the same whole, like yin and yang. Light and dark. Soul mates.

They sat in the chair, wrapped in each other's arms with heaving chests and slick bodies.

Jude turned to her. "Love doesn't seem like enough of a word to capture how I feel for you."

A tired smile curved her mouth as her eyes closed. "Same."

Jude and Nova would live happily ever after because every morning they'd promise today.

And wasn't that what love was? A promise you made every day. To stay. To give. To grow together. To learn. To experience. To listen to one another. To communicate even when it was uncomfortable. To protect. To stay through the difficult times life could bring. And to trust.

What story are you telling yourself to keep that love at a distance?

We all have them.

This is not the end. It's just the beginning . . .

A Bonus Scene and Nova's Battery Operated Boyfriends

Want to read the bonus Emerson Family dinner scene to see all the couples reunited in Renita's POV? Visit the website below to join our newsletter and get instant access to the bonus scene.

WWW.AMKUSI.COM/PTBONUS

To see Nova's battery operated boyfriends visit:

WWW.AMKUSI.COM/NOVATOYS

ACKNOWLEDGMENTS

This book is the longest we've written to date. We poured so much of ourselves into every page. Since we started the series, Nova's story was the one we looked forward to the most! But we couldn't have done it by ourselves.

Thank you to our beta readers. You take our raw, unedited stories and give us priceless feedback that we are truly grateful for.

We'd like to thank our sensitivity editor, Renita. You've been with us since the beginning when we didn't know what we were doing and saw potential. Thank you for your honest and blunt advice and always making sure we're putting the best product out there.

Writing a book can be a very anxious experience, and thanks to Lauren, our editor and writing coach, this process was much smoother than it would have been. You help keep us knowing if we're on the right track or not and smooth out the rough edges to make PROMISING TODAY what it is. Thank you!

Thank you so much Regina Wamba, for the striking and beautiful cover images you always provide.

And to our readers, reviewers, and ARC group, thank you doesn't seem like enough. Your support and reviews mean everything to us. We hope to keep putting out books you enjoy.

Thank you!

AUTHOR'S NOTE

Thank you for reading *Promising Today* and sticking with us through this series. It was exciting to dive a little deeper into some kinky fun with Nova and Jude. We hope you enjoyed the Emersons as much as we have. We're sure they'll make an appearance in future books in the Shattered Cove and Dark Cove world.

Wondering *what's next?* We've had a lot of interest from our readers in the Pirates Motorcycle Club and have decided to go a little darker in this next series. Jude and Nova are just a taste of some of the kinky fun ahead. So in the next series you'll get to explore Dark Cove and a sexy BDSM club with the Pirates MC.

First up is our playboy flirt Casanova and therapist Rebecca whom you met in **His True North.** There's a little reverse age gap, enemies to lovers, and some steamy masked fun at the BDSM club owned by the Pirates' president, Blade, and his wife, Piper. To read Blade and Piper's origin story, check out our book, **Veiled Truths.**

It's always bittersweet to end a series but exciting to start fresh on a new journey. Oh, the places we can go!

Thanks again for reading and supporting us,

Ash and Marcus

A. M. Kusi

THANK YOU

Thank you for reading *Promising Today*. We hope you are emotionally satisfied with Nova and Jude's love story. If you enjoyed this novel, please consider leaving a review on your favorite retailer and sharing it with your friends and family.

If you haven't read Nash and Isabella's story yet, check out ***Stepping Into Tomorrow*** (Book 1 in The Emerson Family of Shattered Cove Series).

If you haven't read Roman and Elise's story yet, check out ***Risking Forever*** (Book 2 in The Emerson Family of Shattered Cove Series).

If you haven't read Ricky and Everett's story yet, check out ***Wishing for Yesterday.***

Lastly, if you haven't read all the books in ***The Shattered Cove Series***, make sure you get your copy so you don't miss out any of the eight amazing romances.

Thank you again for reading *Promising Today!*

Cheers,

Ash and Marcus

JOIN OUR NEWSLETTER

The best way to get updates about new releases, sneak peeks, pre-orders, giveaways, and more is by joining our newsletter.

You'll also receive a FREE short novel that's not available on any retailer to read.

Visit the website below to join now.

WWW.AMKUSI.COM/NEWSLETTER

ABOUT A. M. KUSI

A. M. Kusi is the pen name of a wife-and-husband team, Ash and Marcus Kusi. We enjoy writing romance novels that are inspired by our experiences as an interracial/multicultural couple.

Our novels are about strong women and the sexy heroes they fall in love with, are emotionally satisfying, and always have a happy ending.

Discover more about us at:

WWW.AMKUSI.COM

To receive updates about new releases, preorders, give-aways, and more, visit the website below to join our newsletter today:

WWW.AMKUSI.COM/NEWSLETTER

After you join the newsletter, we will send you a FREE story to read.

To contact us, use this email address: amkusinovels@gmail.com.

Happy reading!

Ash and Marcus

tiktok.com/@amkusi.romanceauthor

instagram.com/amkusinovels

facebook.com/amkusi

pinterest.com/amkusinovels

ALSO BY A. M. KUSI

Stepping Into Tomorrow

(Book 1 in The Emerson Family of Shattered Cove)

Risking Forever

(Book 2 in The Emerson Family of Shattered Cove)

Wishing for Yesterday

(Book 3 in The Emerson Family of Shattered Cove)

A Fallen Star (eBook FREE on all retailers)

(Book 1 in The Shattered Cove Series)

Glass Secrets

(Book 2 in The Shattered Cove Series)

Defying Gravity

(Book 3 in The Shattered Cove Series)

The Lighthouse Inn

(Book 4 in The Shattered Cove series)

His True North

(Book 5 in The Shattered Cove series)

In The Grey

(Book 6 in The Shattered Cove series)

Brave Love

(Book 7 in The Shattered Cove series)

Hope Between Us

(Book 8 in The Shattered Cove series)

Beautiful Collision

(A Shattered Cove Novel)

One Holiday Kiss (eBook FREE on all retailers)

(A Shattered Cove Short Story)

Under My Skin (eBook FREE on all retailers)

(A Shattered Cove Short Story)

The Orchard Inn Series

(Our first complete steamy romance series.)

For a complete list of all our books, visit:

WWW.AMKUSI.COM/BOOKS